$33

You Can Run

YOU CAN RUN

REBECCA ZANETTI

THORNDIKE PRESS

A part of Gale, a Cengage Company

Copyright © 2022 by Rebecca Zanetti.
A Laurel Snow Romantic Thriller #1.
Thorndike Press, a part of Gale, a Cengage Company.

Thorndike Press® Large Print Romance.
The text of this Large Print edition is unabridged.
Other aspects of the book may vary from the original edition.
Set in 16 pt. Plantin.

LIBRARY OF CONGRESS CIP DATA ON FILE.
CATALOGUING IN PUBLICATION FOR THIS BOOK
IS AVAILABLE FROM THE LIBRARY OF CONGRESS.

ISBN-13: 978-1-4328-9777-2 (hardcover alk. paper).

Published in 2022 by arrangement with Zebra Books, an imprint of Kensington Publishing Corp.

Printed in Mexico
Print Number: 01   Print Year: 2022

This one is for the English Family
after our wonderful reunion
this last summer.
Also, for Uncle John, who is
missed so very much.

ACKNOWLEDGMENTS

After having writing seventy books, it's easy to run out of adjectives when thanking everyone who has worked so hard on this one, especially since I'm fortunate enough to have worked with many of the same people throughout my career. So please imagine all of the good adjectives to describe all of the people I'd like to thank:

Thank you to Tony Zanetti, Gabe Zanetti, and Karlina Zanetti — you're the best family in the world, and I love you all;

Thank you to my hardworking editor, Alicia Condon;

Thank you to the rest of the Kensington gang: Alexandra Nicolajsen, Steven Zacharius, Adam Zacharius, Ross Plotkin, Lynn Cully, Vida Engstrand, Jane Nutter, Lauren Vasallo, Lauren Jernigan, Kimberly Richardson, and Pam Joplin;

Thank you to my wonderful agent, Caitlin Blasdell, and to Liza Dawson and the entire

Dawson group, who work so very hard for me;

Thank you to my assistant and social media expert, Anissa Beatty, to Helen Hillman for her hard work, and to my fantastic street team, Rebecca's Rebels;

Thank you also to my constant support system: Gail and Jim English, Kathy and Herb Zanetti, Debbie and Travis Smith, Stephanie and Don West, and Jessica and Jonah Namson.

PROLOGUE

It was the best day of her life.

Tammy Jo Sullivan clutched the inside door of the ATV, her heart racing and her breath seizing. Being sixteen and able to date, finally, was totally sick. The best ever. She grinned and looked over at Hunter as he drove up the rocky trail of Snowblood Peak in the Northern Cascades.

He smiled back, his teeth a flash of white against his tanned face. His family had gone to Mexico for Thanksgiving break, and he said he'd spent most of the time in the pool now that football season was over and he could relax. She'd had to work at her mom's restaurant during the time off school, but that was okay.

Now she was on a date, in a four-wheeler, with Hunter freakin' Jackson. He was a senior and she a sophomore, and never in her life had she thought he'd like her. When he'd asked her out, to go RZR riding on

Saturday before the winter really hit, she'd nearly died on the spot. Now here she was, strapped into the passenger seat, watching the scraggly pine trees fly by on either side of them. She laughed out loud.

Sandy Jones turned around in the rig in front of them and waved. She was blurry through the back plastic window and her bright red hat flopped to the side.

Tammy Jo waved back at her friend, her smile so wide it made her cheeks hurt.

"Having fun?" Hunter twisted the wheel and turned them around another corner. The trail slid from mud to ice, and the tires spun. Mud and a sprinkling of snow covered the jagged rocks on his side of the trail, which led up into more dark, winter-stripped trees.

"Yeah," she said, holding on and not looking as the ground and trees dropped away on her side. "We're up high."

He brushed a little bit of mud out of his thick blond hair, mud he'd gotten while helping Tyson change a belt on his Polaris earlier. It was cool how good they were at fixing whatever went wrong. "You're safe. I know what I'm doing." As he spoke, the tires in front of them threw up mud with a trace of ice.

She swallowed. "Um, my dad said not to

go past the snow line since we've had such a rainy autumn. The ground won't be solid."

Hunter punched the gas pedal. "We're fine. Don't you want to see the top?"

For the first time, her stomach cramped. "My dad said —"

"The ground looks good to me. I'll keep a close watch on it." Hunter reached for the beer in the middle cup holder and drank the rest down. Although it was only nine in the morning, it was his fourth beer, but he seemed okay to drive. "Get me another, would you?" He tossed the can in the back.

The drop-off to her right made her head spin. "Um, when we stop. I don't want to take off the seatbelt right now." She closed her eyes until the dizziness passed.

"Sure." He reached over and placed his hand over hers.

Her eyelids shot open. Hunter was holding her hand. *Be cool.* She had to be cool. Even so, she turned her hand over and tangled her fingers with his. His were a lot bigger than hers, and his palm was warm. She bit her lip to keep from smiling again. Life could *not* get any better. Like, ever.

Several clumps of dirt and rock rained down from high above and skidded across the path. Hunter removed his hand from hers and used both on the steering wheel to drive.

The rig jumped, and Tammy Jo clasped the handle on the dash. "Um, the earth is loose. We should stop."

"We're fine." Hunter drove faster, his head down, as the vehicle bumped and jumped over the rocks.

The ground turned to pine needles and snow mixed with mud. Slushy with a side of freeze.

She craned her neck to look up the mountain. "There's a lot of snow higher up. It's not frozen, Hunter. Just the noise from the RZRs could cause problems. Vibrations and all of that."

He shrugged a wide shoulder. "I can handle it. Don't worry."

She stared over the side of the cliff, biting the inside of her cheek until it stung. Forlorn-looking spruce, pine, and alder trees peppered the embankment down at least three thousand feet to the bottom of a deep gulley.

She shivered.

The mountain roared.

She jerked her head. "What's —"

"Hold on!" Hunter yelled.

She gasped and swiveled as far as the harness would allow, to see snow and mud break loose from the craggy mountain face above them. "No, we —"

The avalanche poured down, right into them. The force struck the driver's side, nearly tipping them over.

"Shit!" Hunter yelled, furiously whipping the wheel to the right and turning the four-wheeler. The wall of mud and snow pushed them over the cliff, face first.

Tammy Jo slammed against her harness and pressed her hands on the dash, screaming. Terror ripped through her as they slid down the cliffside, close to a massive drop-off she hadn't seen from above. They were going to die.

"I need to hit a tree," Hunter gritted out, his hands and feet working wildly to keep the rig pointed down so it wouldn't roll over.

She couldn't breathe. The harness cut into her and her butt rose slightly off the seat, while her hair hung forward.

Hunter whipped the steering wheel, and they went into a skid, crashing into two pine trees on the passenger side. Tammy Jo careened against the door, and pain burst through her shoulder. She cried out.

"Hold on." Hunter grabbed her hand.

She blinked, tears falling down her face. Tree branches, snow, and mud smashed into the rig and went by toward the cliff, but the trees kept them in place.

"We'll be okay!" Hunter yelled, his body tense. "Just keep still. It'll pass."

She gasped out air, trying not to scream.

A branch thumped on the front window and she jumped. Then she looked closer. "Is that . . . ?" It looked like an arm attached to half a hand — with broken off nails.

More mud tumbled the flesh away.

Then a leg. Then another arm.

Finally, the roar of the avalanche died down.

A round object plunked onto the window and rolled to a stop. A skull with stringy blond hair coming out of the scalp stared right at them.

Hunter screamed, high and loud, his voice sounding just like a toddler on a carnival ride.

14

CHAPTER ONE

Laurel Snow swiped through the calendar on her phone while waiting for the flight to DC to board. The worn airport chairs at LAX were as uncomfortable as ever, and she tried to keep her posture straight to prevent the inevitable backache. Christmas music played through the speakers, and an oddly shaped tree took up a corner, its sad-looking branches decorated with what might've been strung popcorn. The upcoming week was already busy, and Laurel hoped there wouldn't be a new case. She stuck in her wireless earbuds to allow an upbeat rock playlist to pound through her ears as she rearranged a couple of meetings.

The phone dinged and she answered while continuing to organize the week. "Snow."

"Hi, Agent Snow. How did the symposium go?" asked her boss, George McCromby.

"As expected," she said, swiping a lunch meeting from Thursday to Friday. "I'm not a teacher, and half the time, the audience looked confused. A young woman in the front row had serious daddy issues, and a young man behind her was facing a nervous breakdown. Other than that, one guy in the last row exhibited narcissistic tendencies."

"For Pete's sake. We just wanted you to talk about the FBI and help with recruitment. You're a good face," George muttered.

Laurel tapped her phone when the Wi-Fi struggled. "My face has nothing to do with my job. I'm not skilled at recruitment or teaching."

George sighed. "How many people have you seen today who wore red shoes?"

Yeah, she should change the computer update meeting from Tuesday to Wednesday. "Six," she said absently. "Ten if you include maroon-colored shoes."

George laughed. "How many people in the last month have worn yellow hats around you?"

"Just eight," she said.

George warmed to the subject. "Right now, where you are in the airport and without looking, who's the biggest threat?"

If she changed one more meeting, she could fit in a manicure on Friday. "Guy waiting in the adjacent area for a plane to

Dallas. He's five nine, wiry, and has cauliflower ears. Moves with grace." Yes. She could fit in a manicure. "Another man to the north by the magazine rack in the bookstore is built like a logger and could throw a decent punch." Would there be time for a pedicure? Probably not.

"Why aren't you the biggest threat?" George asked.

She paused. "Because I'm currently performing parlor tricks for the deputy director of the FBI." She looked up to check her boarding time.

"I have a call on the other line. We'll talk about this when you get back." George clicked off.

Laurel didn't have anything else to say on the matter. Her phone buzzed and she glanced at the screen before answering the call. "Hi, Mom. Yes, I'm still returning home for Christmas." It had been three years, and her mother's patience had ended. "I promise. In two weeks, I'll be there."

"Laurel, I need you now," Deidre said, her voice pitched high.

Laurel froze. "What's wrong?"

"It's your uncle Carl. The sheriff wants to arrest him for murder." Panic lifted Deidre's voice even higher. "You're in the FBI. They're saying he's a serial killer. You have to come help."

Uncle Carl was odd but not a killer. "Serial killer? How many bodies have been found?"

"I don't know," Deidre cried out.

Okay. Her mother never became this flustered. "Is the Seattle FBI involved?" Laurel asked.

"I don't know. The local sheriff is the one who's harassing Carl. Please come help. Please." Her mother never asked for anything.

Laurel would have to change flights — and ask for a favor. "I'll text you my flight information, and I can rent a car at Sea-Tac." Murderers existed everywhere but Uncle Carl wasn't one of them.

"No. I'll make sure you're picked up. Just text me what time you land." Her mother didn't drive or like to be inside vehicles.

"Okay. I have to run." Laurel clicked off and dialed George's private number with her left hand while reaching in her bag for a printout of her schedule. Being ambidextrous came in handy sometimes. Though she didn't have many friends at the FBI, for some reason, George had become a mentor and was usually patient. Sometimes. Plus, she had just closed a serial killer case in Texas, and she had some juice, as George would say. For now. In her experience, juice dried up quickly.

The phone rang several times before George picked up. "I said we'd talk about it in DC."

"I need a favor," Laurel said. Her gaze caught on a younger man escorting an elderly woman through the terminal, both looking up at the flight information boards. "I don't have much information, but it appears there are at least a few suspicious deaths in Genesis Valley up in Washington State. I need to investigate the situation." There was something off about the guy with the older lady. He reached into the slouchy beige-colored purse slung over the woman's shoulder and drew out a billfold, which he slipped into his backpack.

"Wait a minute. I'll make a call and find out what's going on," George said.

"Thank you." Laurel stood and strode toward the couple, reaching them quickly. "Is everything okay?"

The woman squinted up at her, cataracts visible in her cloudy blue eyes. "Oh my. Yes, I think so. This kind young man is showing me to my plane."

"Is that right?" Laurel tilted her head.

The man had to be in his early twenties with sharp brown eyes and thick blond hair.

His smile showed too many teeth. "Yes. I'm Fred. Just helping Eleanor here out. She was a little lost."

Eleanor clutched a plane ticket in one gnarled hand. Her white hair was tightly curled and her face powdered. "I was visiting my sister in Burbank and got confused after security in the airport."

Irritation ticked down Laurel's neck. "Return her wallet to her."

Eleanor gasped. "What?"

Fred shoved Eleanor and turned to run.

Laurel grabbed him by the backpack, kicked him in the popliteal fossa, and dropped him to the floor on his butt, where he fell flat. She set the square heel of her boot on the lateral femoral cutaneous nerve in his upper thigh. "You know, Fred? There's a nerve right here that can make a person . . . bark like a dog." She pressed down.

Fred yelped.

An airport police officer ran up, his hand on his harnessed weapon.

Laurel pulled her ID out of her jacket pocket and flipped it open. "FBI. I think this guy has a few wallets that might not be his." She shook out the backpack. Several billfolds, bottles of pills, and necklaces bounced off the tile floor.

"Hey." Eleanor leaned down and fetched

her billfold and one container of pills. "You jerk." She swatted Fred with her purse.

He ducked and pushed the bag away. "Let me up, lady."

"Make him bark like a dog again," Eleanor burst out.

"Sure." Laurel pressed down on the nerve.

Fred groaned and pushed at her foot, pain wiping the color from his face. "Stop it."

The officer stuffed all of the contraband back in the bag and then pulled Fred to his feet once Laurel moved her boot. He quickly cuffed Fred. "Thanks for this. I've got it from here." They moved away.

Laurel reached for Eleanor's ticket. "Let's see where you're supposed to be." A quick glance at the ticket showed that the woman was going to Indiana. "Your flight is over here at gate twenty-one. Let me grab my belongings and I'll take you there." She retrieved her over-sized laptop bag and rolling carry-on before returning to slide her arm through Eleanor's. "The gate is just on the other side of those restaurants."

"Excuse me?" George barked through the earbuds. "Assistant Director of the FBI here with information for you."

"Please hold on another minute, sir," Laurel said, twisting through the throng while keeping Eleanor safe.

Eleanor looked up, leaning on Laurel. "How do you know my gate number? You didn't even look at the information board."

"I looked at it earlier," Laurel said, helping the elderly woman avoid three young boys dragging Disney-themed carry-ons.

Eleanor blinked. "You memorized all of the flight information with one look?"

"I'm still here," George groused.

Laurel took Eleanor up to the counter, where a handsome man in his thirties typed into the computer. "This is Eleanor, and this is her plane. She's going to sit right over here, and she needs extra time to board." Without waiting for a reply, she helped Eleanor to the nearest seat. "Here you go. You should be boarding in just a few minutes."

Eleanor patted her hand. "You're a good girl."

Laurel crouched down. "Do you have anybody meeting you at the airport?"

Eleanor nodded. "Yes. My son is meeting me right outside baggage claim. Don't you worry." She pressed both gnarled hands against Laurel's face. "You're a special one, aren't you?"

"Damn it, Snow," George bellowed through the earbuds.

Laurel winced. "I am happy to help."

Eleanor tightened her grip. "You have such lovely eyes. How lucky are you."

Lucky? Laurel had rarely felt lucky to have heterochromia. "You're very kind."

"You're beautiful. Such stunning colors and so distinct. I've never seen such a green light in anyone's eye, and your other eye is a beautiful dark shade of blue." Eleanor squinted and leaned in closer. "You have a little green flare in the blue eye, don't you?"

Laurel smiled and removed the woman's hands from her face, careful of the arthritic bumps on her knuckles. "Yes. I have a heterochromia in the middle of heterochromatic eyes. It's an adventure."

Eleanor laughed. "You're a pip, you are. God speed to you."

Laurel stood. "Have a nice trip, Eleanor." She turned to head back to her gate, her mind returning to her trip to Genesis Valley. She'd have to move all of her appointments in DC to the first week in January, so her brain automatically flipped dates. If she juggled a Monday meeting that week, she would have time for a pedicure. Maybe she could skip her Wednesday lunch with the forensic accountants to discuss the recently developed tactical reasoning software. The accountants rarely escaped the computer lab, and when they did, they always talked for too long. "Sorry about that, sir. What did you find out?"

George's sigh was long suffering. "Multiple body parts, including three skulls, were found this morning by kids four-wheeling on a mountain called . . ." Papers rustled. "Snowblood Peak."

Laurel switched directions, her heart rate kicking up. "Just this morning? It's a little early to be narrowing in on a suspect." She'd spent some time snowmobiling that mountain as a child with her uncles before leaving for college at the age of eleven. "Could be an old graveyard or something like that. Might not be a case."

"I know, and this is a local case and not federal, I think."

She paused. "Actually, it depends where the bodies were found. The valley below Snowblood Peak is half owned by the federal government and half by the state. It's beautiful country."

"Huh. Well, okay. We could have jurisdiction if you feel like fighting with the state and the locals." George didn't sound encouraging.

She never felt like fighting. "Don't we have an office in Seattle?"

"Yes, but it's in flux right now. We were in the midst of creating a special unit out of there called the Pacific Northwest Violent Crimes Unit, but there was a political shakeup, a shooting, and a bunch of transfers. The office is restructuring now, and currently in place I have two agents dealing with a drug cartel." Papers shuffled across the line.

"So I'm on my own with this case, if it turns out to be anything." Which was normal for her, actually. A flight from LAX to Seattle had been scheduled to depart out of gate thirteen, and a flight from LAX to Everett had been listed as gate seventeen. "Has my flight been changed?"

More papers rustled. "Jackie?" George bellowed. "Does Snow have a new flight?"

Laurel grimaced at the sudden pain in her ear.

George returned. "You've been switched to Flight 234, leaving in ten minutes. They're holding the door open for you, but we could only get you a middle seat."

At least the gate was close to her current location, and she'd be flying into Everett, which was a quicker drive to Genesis Valley than the drive from Sea-Tac. She loped into a jog, pulling her wheeled carry-on behind her. "I only have a weekend bag and my agency-issued Glock." She hadn't brought her personal weapon.

"I'm not expecting this to be anything. I'll give you forty-eight hours to see if it's a case we want or not, and don't forget, you called in a favor," George said.

Her temples ached. "Even so, you don't want me being the face of the FBI. I don't relate well to students or prospects." At least two people had actually left during her presentation.

"Get good with people," George countered.

She reached the gate and flashed her ID to the impatient-looking gate agent. The woman kept tapping her heel. "I'm boarding. If you get any more information on the skulls, please send it to my tablet so I'm not going in blind." Her stomach cramped with instinct as well as from her knowledge of statistical probabilities. Three different skulls found on the peak?

There was a murderer close to her hometown.

CHAPTER TWO

"Laurel? Laurel Snow?" a female voice asked.

Laurel had already clocked the woman and moved on. She paused as the wind pierced her thin jacket and the first spear of icy rain drilled her forehead outside the airport. "Yes?"

The woman hurried forward from a dented green Volkswagen Bug parked at the curb outside baggage claim in Everett. "I'm Kate Vuittron." She held out a manicured hand with scarlet-painted fingernails. "It's nice to meet you."

Laurel shook Kate's hand. The woman had to be in her early forties and was dressed entirely in red. Flowered red blouse, bright red skirt, and even red Mary Jane pumps with lighter red straps across the ankle. As if that wasn't enough, red streaks ran through her long blond hair.

"It's nice to meet you. You know my

mom?" Laurel asked.

Kate dodged a guy with three suitcases and then rolled her eyes. "Kind of? I applied for a job at the tea warehouse, but she doesn't have any openings. Deidre kept my info and called me this morning." She reached for the carry-on. "Let me take this. You sure pack light." She grasped the handle and moved efficiently to place it in the back seat of the Bug. "Hop in."

Laurel opened the door and slid inside, setting her laptop bag on the floor. Florida Georgia Line blared from the radio, and heat blasted her, taking the edge off the cold northern Washington weather.

"Sorry." Kate sat, shut her door, turned down the music, put her seatbelt on, and zipped away from the curb.

Laurel scrambled to secure her seatbelt. Horns blared behind them. She took a deep breath. "My mom hired you just to pick me up?"

"Yeah," Kate said, cutting off a bus as she switched lanes. "I think she felt sorry for me, but she shouldn't. I'm fine." Her tone of voice said otherwise.

Deidre had always had a soft spot for all wounded animals. Laurel eyed the woman. The manicure was good but home painted, the hair was a red spray on, and the jewelry was absent. Interesting.

"Thank you for picking me up. I have to make a quick phone call." Laurel took her phone from her purse and used official lines, going through the deputy director's tough assistant before reaching him. "Hello, sir. Did you dig anything up?"

"Yes." George loudly moved papers. "Let's see. This morning around eight, off Snow-blood Peak, at least three bodies were found by a bunch of kids who wrecked something called a UTV. Huh. Guess that's like a four-wheeler but with doors. Nice."

Rain with a hint of ice pinged against the windshield.

"Are the kids all right?" Laurel asked.

"Yeah. I talked to a doctor and they're upset, but physically all four are okay, with the worst injury being a dislocated shoulder. The hospital is keeping them for observation until tomorrow," George said.

That was a relief. Laurel swallowed. "Has the media become involved yet?"

"Not to my knowledge," George said. "You'll know more on the ground."

Laurel craned her neck to check out the nimbus clouds, their bellies dark and jagged while their tops grew even more swollen. "If it's raining near the city, it's snowing up on the peak. Has a team been sent up there

29

with spotlights?"

"Yes," George said. "I've confirmed that a state team from Seattle is up there now. They're trying to preserve everything they can, but the ground is wet and still a danger, so they have to proceed carefully. We don't have a federal team there, and even if you want jurisdiction, I'd prefer to work with the state on this."

"That makes the most sense." Laurel nodded. "If it gets cold enough, the frozen ground should assist us with recovery of the bodies that have been unearthed. Do you know if they have cadaver dogs up there yet?"

"Couldn't tell you," George returned. "I've given you everything I have. Oh, except I reached out to the Washington Fish and Wildlife offices, and they wanted to get into a pissing match over jurisdiction. In Washington State, they're fully commissioned cops, and the guy I talked to didn't give two shits I was the deputy director of the FBI. Just to let you know."

Laurel needed to examine the scene. "Who did you speak with?"

"Some guy at the local office." George's sigh was long suffering. "Hold on. I do have a contact in Washington State." A terrible rendition of Beethoven's Fifth crackled over the line for several moments before George returned. "Okay, here's the gist. The best hunter and tracker they have works remotely, and I'm sending you his information now. His name is Captain Huck Rivers and he's on a week of leave, but I'm sending you his home address. From the sound of it, this guy will be pulled in no matter what, so you might as well use him early if you're going to get involved. Good luck, Snow." He clicked off.

Laurel set her phone on her black pants leg. "I'd like to examine the scene before the storm obliterates more evidence." It was too bad she hadn't packed a sweater or thicker socks. "Do you have any ideas how I could reach Snowblood Peak?"

"Not really," Kate said. "I just moved to Genesis Valley a few weeks ago from Seattle, although I did grow up around here. I can't believe there are so many dead bodies."

Laurel pressed her hand against the door to brace herself. "Do you know a Fish and Wildlife officer named Huck Rivers?"

"Nope." Kate winced and cut across two lanes.

Laurel set her feet against the floor in a useless attempt to brace her body if Kate crashed the car. Her large bag opened up, and peach-colored yarn rolled across the

31

floor. She scrambled to shove it back into place.

Kate sped up. "You knit?"

"Yes. I'm part of a group that knits blankets and hats for NICU babies. When my hands are busy, my brain can work faster." She carefully set her smallest knitting needles back into place.

"Huh. That's an interesting hobby," Kate said. "Your mom said you were a genius who finished college in your teens."

Laurel stretched her fingers as they warmed. "I majored in several subjects at once, and my mom taught me to knit as a stress reliever when I was young. A few years ago, doing a project for school, I learned about the need for hats and so on for premature or ill babies, and the program morphed from there." She zipped the purse.

"Wait a minute. What morphed?" Kate glanced at her. "Did you just discover this group or create it?"

Laurel's cheeks heated. "I helped to create it, but I don't run it. Now I just knit." Pretty much. Well, she still handled some of the logistics, and her heart warmed every time she thought of those strong little souls fighting so hard to live. Her phone dinged and she held up the screen for Kate. "Here's Captain Rivers's address. Do you mind taking me to his place?" Hopefully Rivers wasn't up on the mountain already; she assumed he was still on leave.

"Yes. I promised your mom I'd take you wherever you wanted to go. She must've known you'd want to go up the mountain. Do you mind using your phone to navigate?"

"No problem." Laurel typed in the address and waited for the navigation program to take over.

Kate sped up the windshield wipers. "Did you grow up in Genesis Valley?"

"Until I was eleven years old, and then I went to college." Laurel shook out her fingers to warm them up.

Kate looked her way and then back out the front window. "You went to college when you were only eleven years old?"

Laurel nodded. "Yes." The surprised reaction wasn't a new one. "I was bored and needed a challenge." With her odd eyes and insatiable intellect, she'd been a different child. That was one of the nicest names she'd been called. She shrugged. It was all in the past.

"Sounds interesting," Kate said. "If you attended college so early, you must have a bunch of degrees in addition to starting nonprofit groups that knit for babies. What did you study?" The woman sounded honestly curious.

Laurel flattened her hands on her pants. "I've studied quite a few different disciplines and have degrees in data science, neuroscience, organizational behavior, bioinformatics and integrative genomics, game theory, and psychology with an emphasis on abnormal psychology."

"Sounds like you just want to figure people out," Kate murmured.

"I guess," Laurel agreed. "Or maybe I just want to figure myself out."

Kate reached over to turn up the heat. "Have you?"

"I do not believe so," Laurel said thoughtfully. "The older I get, the less I seem to know. Do you ever feel that way?"

Kate's mouth turned down. "I have three daughters, and I definitely feel that way. Trust me." The woman didn't wear a wedding ring, but it wasn't Laurel's place to ask.

Laurel searched for the most logical conclusion and finally had to ask a question. "Why are you wearing so many different shades of red?"

Kate turned down the heat. "I wondered if you were going to ask."

"I didn't want to insult you by asking in

case you have a compulsion," Laurel admitted.

Kate finally cracked a smile. "The high school is having a Christmas fundraiser called Red and Green tonight to make money for the sports teams, and I'm trying really hard to help my girls get used to their new school, so I signed up to help. I chose red." She cut Laurel a look. "My job is to just drop you off, because I have to attend this fundraiser for my kids. If I can somehow make friends with a couple of the moms, then maybe I can help the girls. They're having a rough time of it with the move."

That made sense. "I appreciate the ride, especially since it looks like we're headed into the mountains," Laurel said.

"Are you sure you just want me to drop you off at some man's home in what looks like the middle of nowhere?" Kate asked.

"Yes." Laurel took a deep breath. "Captain Rivers's week off just ended. Let's find him, and he can take me to the crime scene."

Lisa Scotford awoke shivering in the cold, her bare butt freezing on the cold metal floor. A flickering lantern illuminated the interior of her prison. A blanket lay in the corner and she crawled to it, wrapping the scratchy wool around her nude body and huddling down. Her head hurt. She blinked away the fog and pain to focus on the situation.

Where was she?

One minute, she was leaving her apartment outside of Genesis Valley and getting into her car, and the next . . . nothing. Something hard had hit her head and then blackness. Gingerly, she reached to the back of her head and winced at the lump there. When she pulled her hand back, blood coated her fingers.

Nausea attacked her, and she shifted to the side, heaving up the leftover spaghetti she'd eaten for lunch at her apartment.

The wind howled outside, and ice clattered against the metal.

She looked down inside the blanket. Whoever had kidnapped her had taken her clothes. Her stomach lurched again, and she dry heaved. How long had she been unconscious? She had taken the upcoming week off work, saying she was headed out of town, when she'd planned to meditate and figure out her life with some alone time. Nobody even knew she was missing.

Terror made her feel lightheaded. Her skin prickled.

Despite unsteady legs, she stood, keeping the blanket around her. The harsh material smelled like a mix of different perfumes, and something had dried down the side of it. Could be blood. She pushed her mind away from the thought. She had to get out of there. Her throat hurt from the cold, and the floor freeze-burned her feet, but she tiptoed quietly across it to the metal double doors. Was she in some sort of cargo hold? Like the ones she saw in harbor ports on television shows?

Four metal hooks had been attached to the walls near the floor, and she didn't want to think about why. Blood and other frozen liquids dotted the area between the hooks, but the smell of bleach covered whatever they'd been.

Trembling, she reached out and tried to turn the lever to open the door. Nothing. She tried harder, but the thing didn't move. It had to be locked from the outside.

She looked up at the metal roof and then along all the walls, searching for a weak spot. Nothing. Then she pressed her ear against the metal, listening for any sign of whoever had kidnapped her. Her legs shook. There was only one reason for him to take her clothes. She had to figure out a way to get free.

Merely the wind whistled outside, the sound forlorn. "Hello?" she croaked. When there was no answer, she cleared her throat and started to scream. She yelled for as long as she could, until her voice gave out.

Nobody came to help.

CHAPTER THREE

Captain Rivers lived outside of Genesis Valley up a winding road blanketed by pine and cedar trees shivering in the bitter storm. A screeching wind hurled snow and freezing rain across the unpaved driveway to a log cabin placed at the bend of a swollen river. The cabin logs had darkened with age but were as solid looking as the craggy rock cliff on the opposite side of the river.

Kate rolled the car to a stop in front of a two-car garage. A massive wooden shop with four metal garage doors lay to the north, surrounded by bare trees. Her phone rang and she glanced at the screen. "They're almost set up for the dinner."

Laurel scouted the location and noted a figure moving inside the house. So the captain was home. Good. She opened her door and tugged her carry-on luggage from the back seat before slinging the large laptop bag over her shoulder. "Thank you for the ride."

Kate sat back. "Are you sure you just want me to leave you?"

"Yes." Rivers was a captain with Fish and Wildlife and wouldn't shove a woman back into an oncoming storm, even if she was FBI. Probably. "Have a good time at your fundraiser."

"I'll do my best," Kate said. "Good luck to you, too."

"Great. Thanks." A dog barked from inside, the sound more cheerful than angry. She stepped out of the car, and her feet instantly chilled in the thin black flats that had been perfect in Los Angeles. Swallowing, she gathered her light suit jacket tighter around her torso and ducked her head against the wind to hustle up the porch to the solid wooden door. At least she'd chosen to wear black slacks today with her light cream-colored blouse and jacket. She knocked just as Kate's taillights disappeared down the long drive.

The dog barked louder inside.

A male voice rumbled an order and the dog subsided.

The door opened to reveal a man.

Laurel almost took a step back. Six foot four, black hair, brown eyes, solid shoulders.

Large boned hands, wide chest, rugged jaw. His shaggy hair curled beneath his ears, looking both uncared for and surprisingly appealing. The brown eyes had flecks of gold around the irises, and they held a world of experience. Some good and a lot bad. He had to be in his early thirties, but if she believed in her mother's teachings, he'd be an old soul. "Captain Rivers?"

He didn't open the door but instead scrutinized her from head to toe. "Who's asking?" His voice was both unwelcoming and such a low timbre it was soothing. Interesting.

"I'm Laurel Snow, and I need your help." Every instinct she had told her not to flash her badge.

He immediately opened the door. "You're not dressed for the weather." His expression remained difficult to read. "You look like a Fed."

Nobody had ever said that to her. "I do?"

"Black pants, wrong shoes for the local terrain, carefully clipped and beige-colored fingernails." He cocked his head to the side. "Except the hair. You don't have the hair of a Fed."

She also didn't have an answer for that, which was unusual for her. "What do I have the hair of?" When was the last time she'd

41

ended a sentence with a preposition? Possibly in grade school.

"Not a Fed," he said. "It's too long and it probably cost you a fortune to get that color."

This was the oddest conversation she'd had in ten years. Maybe twenty. "I don't pay for color. Or a cut, usually." She hadn't had time for such indulgences in far too long. Maybe she should get a haircut from a professional hairdresser instead of an elderly neighbor who had arthritis and cloudy vision.

"You're telling me that's your natural hair color?" He leaned in closer, bringing the scent of pine with him.

She frowned. "I'm not telling you anything. It's just hair." For Pete's sake. "It's brown."

"We both know that's not brown. It's auburn, and that combination of brown and red is unreal. Mostly." He looked down at the dog sitting patiently at his side. "Right, Aeneas?"

Laurel tilted her head to study the canine. His markings were unique: a white hourglass shape across his face, surrounded by black fur. The white fur continued down his chest and covered each paw. "Aeneas? As in Homer's *Iliad*?"

42

"More like Virgil's *Aeneid*," Huck returned.

A chilly wind blasted her, and she rubbed her arms. "He's beautiful."

Huck opened the door wider and gestured her inside. "Where the hell is your coat?"

"In Washington DC." She stepped inside a sparsely furnished cabin that was messy but fairly clean.

"Why?" He stood much taller than she, even in his sock-covered feet. His left sock had a hole in the toe. Two duffel bags, a folded tent, and muddy boots had been dropped by the other side of the door.

"This was an unexpected detour." She looked at the gear. "Are you going somewhere?"

Captain Rivers shut the door. "What can I do for you, Laurel Snow?" He crossed his arms while his dog remained patiently at his side, both of them looking like predators in a calm mood.

She faced him directly. Appealing to his need to protect would be her best move. "I am with the FBI and need a guide up Snowblood Peak. It has been years since I headed that way, and I could use help."

"Why?"

She paused. "What do you mean, why? They've found at least three dead bodies,

43

and there are no doubt more. I'd like to observe the scene before the weather wipes out the evidence. Will you at least let me borrow an ATV?" What kind of Fish and Wildlife captain didn't want to investigate the scene of a murder himself?

"What are you talking about?" His jaw hardened.

"This morning bodies were found." She looked at the gear by the door and then at the dog. "Oh, I understand. You were training out in the wilderness." That also explained why he and the dog looked so rough. "That's why you don't know anything about the dead bodies, right, Captain Rivers?"

"Huck. My dad was Captain Rivers." He scrubbed a hand through his hair, ruffling the heavy waves even more. "You're right. I've been unplugged for three days up in the mountains training with Aeneas. No service. Just got back thirty minutes ago and was going to grab something to eat. What's this about dead bodies?"

Laurel condensed the report for him, and he was shoving his feet in the muddy boots and grabbing the heavy-looking flannel coat off the packs before she'd finished.

"Let me know where you're staying in town, and I'll call you after I've reviewed the scene." He moved toward the front door.

"No." She crossed her arms.

He paused. "Excuse me?" Apparently the captain wasn't accustomed to people disregarding his orders.

"I'm here to do a job, and it's important for me to view the scene." Although she was going to freeze. Hopefully his UTV contained a heater. "Either we go together, or I find a UTV myself and drive up there. I believe it would be much more efficient if we worked this in tandem." In fact, she could use his knowledge of the area. Though she'd grown up in Genesis Valley, she had left at age eleven, so it wasn't as if she truly knew her way around.

"I don't have time to babysit you on the mountain," he said, his voice a low growl that most people probably heeded.

Laurel had dealt with a few of the darkest criminal minds there were. One cranky mountain man couldn't deter her. "I don't require a babysitter. I do, however, require an authorized Fish and Wildlife officer to escort me out into the wilderness and provide background information. Are you, or are you not, that officer?"

Instead of answering, he strode to a hall closet and quickly unlocked a safe cemented into the wall above the top shelf. Without turning, he withdrew a badge on a chain and a black gun that looked like a Smith & Wesson M&P 2.0. She made another mental note about him. Washington's Fish and Wildlife officers were fully commissioned police officers. He strapped a tactical holster to his left thigh and around his waist, tucking the gun safely against his leg. "Lady? I don't need you with me."

"It's agent, not lady, and I don't care what you need." She kept her temper at bay because it would serve no purpose to become angry.

His low sigh was long suffering. "Fine. You can come with me, because I'll just be called out to rescue your ass if you go alone."

Her temper started to stir, apparently not caring that it would accomplish nothing to smack him on the nose. "As much as I appreciate your belief that not only do I need a knight in slightly muddy armor, but that you could also possibly be that rescuer, I promise I require only your knowledge and not any of your *no doubt* impressive mountain-man skills." Her voice was just calm enough to sound slightly haughty, and she was fine with that fact. So much for using his protective nature to get her way.

His grin was quick and a surprise, making

him look much more approachable. Almost human. Then it disappeared completely. "You're cute when you get your panties in a bunch."

He did not just say "panties" to her. Was he trying to tick her off enough that she'd leave in a huff? Since he waited for a response, that had obviously been his plan of attack. So she smiled. "I'm not wearing any, Captain." Then she met his gaze, and it was his turn to be thrown off stride.

His eyes slowly darkened from light topaz to the deep stout color of a good beer. "Fair enough." With that very minor concession, he turned back to the closet and tossed her a dark blue parka. "Why aren't you dressed for the weather?"

"I was in LA," she said, slipping her arms into the thick material and zipping it up. The coat engulfed her, reaching to her knees.

He grabbed gloves and a knit hat for her, before looking down at her feet. "I don't have snow boots your size." Shaking his head, he reached into the rear of the closet on the floor and dragged out well-worn, women's leather hiking boots. "These aren't for snow, but they're better than what you're wearing." He pushed them her way.

"Thanks. Whose boots?" She slipped out

of her flats and inserted her feet in the scratched boots, even though she was just wearing thin socks. The boots were slightly too small, so she didn't ask to borrow heavier socks. They wouldn't fit.

"Old girlfriend's," he said. "Broke up a while ago."

Apparently the ex didn't need her boots. Laurel might not be a PR person, but even she knew how to extend an olive branch so the remainder of the evening would go more smoothly. She did need his assistance, after all. "I appreciate your assistance."

He pulled leather gloves on his hands. "I'm not a helpful guy, so please remember that in the future and don't end up abandoned on my doorstep again. For now, I'm going to check out the crime scene, and you might as well come along. But walk where I tell you to walk and don't cause me any more problems than you already have."

Well. All right then.

CHAPTER FOUR

After unloading his personal UTV from the truck they'd driven as far as they could up the mountain, Huck waited until she'd buckled in to the leather seat and then made sure the heat was on high enough to warm the woman next to him. Laurel Snow. She looked like an actress pretending to be an FBI agent on a television show. The stunning colors in her hair had caught his attention immediately, with the reddish brown nearly glowing in the storm. Then he'd caught sight of her incredible eyes. One was a light translucent green and one was a midnight blue with a star of green in the upper-right part of the iris.

The fact that she didn't wear colored contacts to hide the difference revealed both confidence and acceptance of life's challenges. Plus, she'd known the origin of Aeneas's name, which showed she at least had education if not brains. Something told him that she also had brains.

"Would you turn down the heat?" She studied the storm outside with an intensity he could feel inside the small cab.

Huck flipped the dial, and the blast of heat weakened.

Laurel leveled that intriguing gaze on him. "Thank you." She settled back in the seat. "Do you mind answering some questions?"

He did mind, so he grunted and kept an eye on the trail. His left leg ached, letting him know the storm was getting even stronger.

"Why Snowblood Peak?" she asked. "Could it be the name? If this is a serial killer and not some weird graveyard, then could the dumping of the bodies there be as simple as the name of the mountain?"

He slowed down to drive over several chunks of rapidly freezing mud. The UTV bounced and he kept it squarely on the trail.

"Captain Rivers? What do you think?" she asked.

He didn't think anything yet. "Over a cliff is a good place to hide bodies."

She nodded. "That's what I figured. I only snowmobiled the mountain once with my uncles, but I studied a map en route to your home."

A map? He barely kept from shaking his

head. The answers she wanted weren't going to be found in any map. "What unit are you with, Agent Snow?" he asked. Maybe his boss could call hers and get her out of his way.

"Laurel," she said, staring out the front window as the snow pelted them. "I'm not with a unit. I hold a supervisory position as a specialist, sent to assist in certain cases such as this one appears to be."

She seemed awfully young to have reached such a high rank. "Such as violent crimes and possible serial murders?" He kept his hands relaxed on the steering wheel. His headlights were strong and illuminated the snow-covered trail; it was a good thing he'd switched out the tires for tracks last week.

She cleared her throat. "Yes. Violent crimes and possible serial murders." Now she sounded stiff but not defensive, just matter-of-fact. "It's my understanding that the Seattle FBI office is heavily involved in another case right now, so if this is an FBI matter, I'm on my own."

He didn't know exactly what kind of case this was yet, but it wasn't an FBI matter. "We've got this," he muttered.

"Such decisions are beyond my pay grade, but if it's a serial murder, I'll keep the case," she said, looking over at Aeneas in the back seat. "I take it he's a search and rescue dog?"

Aeneas's ears flicked and he turned his head to look at her.

"He's a Karelian Bear Dog," Huck said, turning the wheel to navigate the UTV around a sharp rock to head farther up the mountain. Visibility was less than he liked. He tried to banish the thought that dead bodies had been found in his backyard.

"Really? I haven't heard of that breed." The woman sounded surprised.

Several chunks of solid ice rained down from above and Huck swerved to keep from getting nailed. "It's a specialty breed that chases bears. We have a program in Washington to deal with problem bears and citizens, and Aeneas is one of the best. He's also secondarily trained in search and rescue as well as detecting and locating poached wildlife and human remains."

Apparently bored with the discussion, Aeneas put his head back on his paws, waiting for his chance to get to work.

Huck turned another corner, and the world lit up. "Looks like they managed to get every spotlight they had access to up here." The cliffside was bright through the falling snow, and figures dressed in yellow hazmat suits worked diligently, gathering objects off the ground. Three tents had been set up to protect evidence from the weather. He parked his UTV behind two department UTVs and three snowmobiles. "Your boots won't give you much traction on this ice and snow, so be careful, City Girl," he said.

She released her harness and opened her door. "City girl? I grew up in Genesis Valley, Captain Rivers. I'm a country girl all the way." She stepped gingerly onto the frozen ground and shut her door, pulling on the borrowed gloves.

Country girl? He didn't think so. He jumped out and opened the rear door to secure Aeneas's search and rescue collar and activate its beacon. When the dog wore that particular collar, he knew it was time to work. The bluish collar he wore when chasing bears away from civilians was a lighter weight. "Down," Huck ordered, and the dog jumped gracefully onto the icy trail.

Crossing around the front of the rig, Huck waited for Agent Snow to finish placing the hat on her head. Snow blitzed them, covering her cap within seconds. That spectacular hair flowed over her shoulders and down her back, catching flakes and making them sparkle before melting. He'd never seen hair that color in real life. "This way," he murmured. She was a distraction, that was for sure.

She reached him, surprising him again with her small stature. The woman had to be five foot two, if that. Yet she stood straight and seemed taller, thanks to her quiet presence. Blinking against the snow, she leaned over and peered down the embankment, where the techs struggled against the weather. "Let's go to that tent." She pointed one glove-covered hand toward the nearest tent, which was still at least twenty yards down the rapidly disappearing trail.

"All right. You're gonna have to hang on to my arm, Agent," he said, holding out his arm as if he'd invited her to dance. He didn't want to make nice with the woman, but he wasn't going to let her get hurt, either. "Those boots won't give you much traction, and you'll tumble down."

She hesitated only a second before gripping his arm with her gloved hand. "If I fall, don't let me take you down with me."

The idea tickled him, and a chuckle emerged before he could stop it. Even when she stiffened next to him, he couldn't banish his smile, even though amusement felt unnatural on his face. The woman was half his size and wearing crappy boots in the beginning of a winter storm. She couldn't get him down the mountain if she tried. "I'll keep that in mind." She also hadn't read him correctly if she thought he'd let any woman fall down a cliff.

"Good." She moved forward, toward the closest thing to a trail leading down to the nearest tent.

Cadaver dogs wove through the storm, while several teams smoothed snow and mud around in different areas. "Let me go first, and you put your hands on my shoulders," he said. It'd be easier if he could just carry her down to the tent, but no FBI agent would want to arrive on scene like that, save one with a broken leg.

"Okay," she breathed, her nose turning pink.

He turned, braced his feet, and waited until her hands curled over his shoulders before stepping over the edge onto the roughly cut path. His boot slipped and he regained his balance, waiting to make sure she was okay behind him.

"You're too tall." Her hands slid down his back to press against his waist. "I'll keep my balance this way."

He ducked his head against the stinging wind. Maybe he could leave her with whoever was in charge of the scene. If they needed his skills, they'd ask. Aeneas scouted ahead, his red beacon showing his location.

Huck kept his balance and noted the clean

turns of the makeshift trail. They soon reached the nearest tent, and Huck opened the flap wider for Laurel to walk inside, where she wiped snow off her face.

Upon seeing Huck, Captain Monty Buckley looked like he'd swallowed charcoal. "Hi." Buckley slid their way from the opposite side of the tent, his white eyebrows lifting. "I didn't call you in. Why are you here?"

Huck took in the captain of the regional office. Monty was in his late fifties and strong as the mountain around them. Solid and quick. His white hair was thick above his weathered face, and he wore a Fish and Wildlife jacket with a rip down the side. "The FBI showed up on my doorstep."

Monty frowned and then looked at Laurel. "Well, hello."

Huck moved an inch farther away from the woman.

She held out her blue glove, her puzzled gaze going from one man to the other. "FBI Special Agent Laurel Snow."

Monty accepted the handshake. "Fish and Wildlife Captain Monty Buckley."

Laurel released his hand and stepped to the side, getting her first view of a table under the tent. "Oh."

Monty nodded. "We've found remains

from at least eight bodies and probably more."

Huck's gut rolled. "Shit." He turned and looked up the hill. "What's the theory?"

Monty scratched ice off his head. "The theory is that the bodies were all tossed over the cliff from the main trail rather than coming from above said trail, where the first muddy avalanche started. When the snow pushed the kids and their UTVs over the side, they actually rolled over and disturbed the bodies, which were unearthed and tumbled with them. We have a lot of retrieval to do, so I probably would've called you in eventually."

Huck didn't argue, but nobody called him in unless they were desperate, and it was still too early for that.

A dog barked twice from the darkness below. "Sounds like we found another body," Monty muttered.

Laurel looked up the hill. "If the kids hadn't caused the slide earlier, what are the chances of the bodies ever being discovered?"

Monty shook his head. "Off the trail, it's nearly a cliff, and the land drops even farther yards away. People ride and hike that trail, but over the cliff, it's almost impassable, and sometimes the snow remains all year."

Laurel looked at the various bones on the table. "So it's possible the bodies never would've been found." She sounded as if she was talking to herself. "He didn't want them to be found." She stepped around Monty and moved toward the folding table.

Huck fought the urge to stop her. There was no need to protect an FBI agent from the gruesome sight, so why were his instincts kicking in?

She leaned over to see better. "These are all in different stages of decomposition." Then she straightened and looked over her shoulder. "We need to get these packaged and sent to the ME's office as we find them rather than waiting until we have more."

"We're already on that." Monty pointed toward the open flap of the other tent, which revealed a couple of techs carefully bagging up body parts.

Huck didn't want to look at the two skulls, complete with tufts of stringy hair.

Laurel leaned closer to the remains. "What are these bite marks?"

Huck blew out a breath and moved unwillingly toward her, where he pointed at the deep cuts. "Those are coyote and those are owl. The smaller ones could be anything.

58

We aren't going to find all of the pieces, Agent. You need to know that."

She looked up, and those intriguing dual-colored eyes shone bright. "We'll find more than we want. We always do."

A chill skittered down his spine.

CHAPTER FIVE

The gelid wind hurled ice against the front windshield as if possessed by a hunger to infiltrate the warm truck cab.

Laurel huddled in the heavy coat, her hands splayed on her legs as engine heat bombarded the interior of the truck. She kept silent while Huck fought to keep the vehicle on the road and the dog snored in his crate in the back seat. She turned to double check the UTV strapped to the truck bed. Snow and ice already covered the metal.

Huck took a turn, somehow seeing even when she couldn't.

"Thank you for driving me," Laurel said, mindful of manners.

Huck grunted.

All right, so she might not have given him a chance to refuse, considering she'd climbed back into his truck when the storm became too harsh for anybody to stay on the mountain. It was morning but still dark. "If you don't mind my asking, what's the problem between you and Buckley?" Even though Huck was supposed to be on vacation, and his arrival had surprised Buckley, there was something more at play — a sense of distrust. Laurel had watched the interaction between Huck and the rest of the officers, and frankly, there hadn't been much as Huck worked the scene with his dog and found two more bodies. She needed to know what kind of dynamic she was dealing with here.

Huck didn't answer. The truck slid toward a tree and he swore, pressing the brake and then the gas pedal in a smooth motion that kept them on the road.

She shivered. "Huck?"

"There's no problem between Buckley and me." Huck's voice didn't invite more discussion.

Fine. She'd figure that out later. "Where are we going?" She couldn't see a thing.

"My place. It's close."

"Agreed." The recovered remains were on the way to the ME's office, but she wanted to get back to work. "How long is this storm predicted to last?"

"Through the day," Huck said, ducking his head to peer into the snow. "That's why

Aeneas and I headed home earlier than I'd planned. Good thing, too." He jerked the wheel to the right and the vehicle bounced over a clump of ice.

"We'll need to go back out as soon as possible," she said. How many bodies were being buried by snow and ice right now? She couldn't think about that. "I want to believe that we found all the bodies, that they're from a graveyard, and it's a coincidence that at least one of them was obviously murdered by strangulation. But those don't exist, right?"

"Coincidences?" he asked. "Dunno."

She flexed her toes inside the boots to make sure they still functioned. "A coincidence is merely a forced structure created by our minds as we search for causal reality. People add separate facts together in an attempt to find reason where there is none."

He rolled to a stop in front of a massive metal shop, cut the engine, and opened the truck door. "You don't believe in evil?"

She'd seen too much to discount the idea. "If evil exists, it's because we choose to allow it. I don't believe it's a force of its own." She opened her door and hopped out. The moment her boots touched the icy ground, she realized her error. Her feet flew out from under her, and she gasped, trying to find purchase.

Gravity prevailed.

Her right ankle twisted, and she fell, landing with her leg beneath her. Pain flared up to her knee.

Huck was instantly at her side, crouched down. He brushed wet hair off her face. "Did you hit your head?" This close, he smelled like pine and male.

"No," she said, gingerly moving her weight. "I may have twisted my ankle."

He grunted, and without waiting for permission, lifted her off the ground. His body was solid and warm against her. "Aeneas, come."

The dog scouted right outside the door, no doubt taking care of business. He barked twice as if in agreement.

As they walked toward the cabin door, the world was a sheet of white with a keening wind. The cold blasted them, and she lost her breath. Huck ducked his large body over her and hustled through the freezing storm and up the stairs of his porch.

"I'm fine," Laurel protested, her ears heating.

Huck held her securely, snow coating the shadow along his jaw. "Right."

She didn't have a choice. At least she'd

slipped here and not in front of the techs and emergency personnel. Only Huck and Aeneas had witnessed her debilitating fall.

He kicked open his door and walked inside to put her on the sofa.

Laurel struggled out of the parka and stretched out her leg. "I think it's okay." Her ankle had twisted when she'd gone down, and now her entire foot felt numb.

Aeneas ran into the kitchen and slurped water noisily.

Huck shed his jacket and hat before crouching near the sofa. His hair was messier than before but still looked good on him. "Hold on a sec." His hands were sure as he untied the boot and gently pulled it off. He then slid the lightweight sock off and carefully probed her ankle. "Does this hurt?" The man really did have a protector complex, although awareness dawned in his eyes, and he retreated immediately.

The feeling of his warm hand on her skin was the opposite of painful. "No." Her voice came out a little breathless. What in the world was wrong with her? She must be sleep deprived. Yes, he was appealing, but she had a job to do.

His gaze rose to her face, his expression appraising and then withdrawing. "Swollen. Not broken. I'll get ice and Advil." He stood and moved toward the kitchen.

She gently turned her foot, which protested with a twinge of pain. Advil would take care of the problem.

Huck returned with pain killers, a glass of water, and a bag of frozen peas to place on the ankle. He handed them over silently and then moved to start a wood fire in the fireplace across from the leather sofa. Soon the crackle of logs and heat filled the room. He tossed a blanket at her. "I'll get your carry-on and laptop bag from the truck."

Silence descended when he jogged outside and then returned, placing both by the sofa.

"Thanks," she said, her temples aching.

He gracefully moved back to the kitchen.

Her stomach growled. "I can help cook something."

He grunted.

So. They were back to the grunting and silence. "You're not big on communication, are you?" she asked, her eyelids growing heavy as she looked over her shoulder at the kitchen.

"No." He removed food from the fridge and started a skillet. "You a vegetarian or vegan or anything?"

"No." She rested her cheek on the back of the sofa and watched him.

He cooked quickly and efficiently, and

soon the log home filled with the scent of scrambled eggs and maple bacon. "Do you need to call anybody to tell them you're safe and waiting the storm out here?" He asked the question as he brought her a plate laden with delicious-smelling food.

She shook her head and accepted breakfast, her mouth already watering.

"Why not?" He moved back to the kitchen and returned with a mug of steaming hot coffee. "No sugar or cream. Sorry."

She took the warm drink and sipped delicately. Delicious. "Thanks. I texted my mom while you were cooking."

He sat in the adjacent leather chair with his plate and dug in.

They ate in silence for a while, and Laurel surreptitiously studied her surroundings. The home had that bachelor feeling. A flatscreen sat above the fireplace mantel, and older pictures of people had been placed carefully on the wall by the door. "Is this your family home? I mean, did you grow up here?" She turned to the one picture on the table near the sofa.

Huck's grunt held a tone of affirmation.

She took the picture, which showed a sizable man with Huck's bone structure next to a petite pregnant woman, the two of them standing beneath a snowy tree. She wore a gray crocheted cap over her blond hair and fluffy pink mittens on her hands. A gray dog sat between them. "Your parents?"

"Yes." He set his empty plate on the sofa table and kicked back with his coffee.

"Are they still —"

"No." He took a deep drink. "My dad died ten years ago from prostate cancer when I was in the marines and far from home. Didn't even tell me he was sick." He rolled his neck. "Hell. Probably didn't even know or go to the doctor. Dad was stubborn."

That was difficult to imagine. Laurel hid her smile. "What about your mom? She was beautiful, by the way."

Huck shrugged. "Don't know. She didn't want a kid but agreed to have me when they discovered she was pregnant. She gave birth and was gone the next week." He sounded like he didn't much care.

Laurel lost her smile. "I'm sorry."

"Nothing for you to be sorry about." He tipped his head back and finished his coffee, his expression blank.

For some reason, she wanted to ease him. "What about the dog in the picture? He's a cutie."

"Never met him. The old guy died about a month before I was born." Huck set his empty mug next to his plate. "My dad loved dogs. Huckleberry was his companion for fifteen years before I came along. We've always had dogs."

"Huckleberry?" she asked, surprise tickling through her.

His expression was one of exasperation, not amusement. "Yes. I was named after the family dog. Dad loved that dog and figured he'd at least like me, so he named me Huck. Just Huck. No berry on the end of the name. Huck Delta Rivers."

Her chin dropped. "Delta? Did he know you'd be a soldier?"

"No. My mother's name was Delta, and he figured I should have something of hers." Again, Huck sounded almost bored. Apparently a coping mechanism. "I always meant to change my middle name but didn't get around to it."

That was a landmine she didn't have the energy to tiptoe through. "Oh."

He was quiet for a few moments as if fighting an internal battle. Finally, he spoke. "What about you? Big family?"

Ah, so he'd decided on manners. Laurel yawned. "No. Just my mom and me, basically. But I do have two uncles and an aunt who also live on the family farm, which includes several hundred acres, so the houses are far apart, anyway." It had been too long since she'd been home.

Huck studied her with those world-weary eyes. "No dad?"

"No dad," she confirmed. They seemed to have the lack of a parent in common. "After my mother's parents died when she was sixteen, she went a little wild and headed to Seattle to live wherever she could. I believe she partied and tried several street drugs. When she became pregnant, she returned home and gave birth to me at seventeen." It was illogical to miss something one had never had. "She doesn't know who my father was, and I've accepted that." But sometimes, she still wondered. Was the heterochromia of her irises genetic? It was possible. Her red hair color, caused by a recessive gene, came from both of her parents.

Huck grunted and turned to look at the billowing storm outside. "I'll take you to your mom's when the weather subsides."

Her mind organized facts while she reached for the needles and yarn from her laptop bag to keep her hands busy. She had to turn the conversation to the bodies they'd found, because he was withdrawing so much he might just leave her to work the case alone. "I noticed cameras in the parking area at the bottom of Snowblood Peak. How long do you keep recordings?" The needles clacked together.

"Six weeks," Huck said, eyeing the small booties. "Fish and Wildlife have the cameras in case a hiker goes missing and to catch poachers. I'm sure the local office will collect the data and provide a list of license plates."

That was good. "I seem to lack a team right now, so I appreciate any help you can provide," she said, masking a yawn.

"I'm not part of any team," he said.

"Why not?" she asked. The sofa was too comfortable to ignore.

He kicked back and shut his eyes. Manners . . . done.

She fought sleep and kept knitting. "The last body we found before the storm forced us out was probably . . . what? Deceased for two weeks?" The victim had been intact enough to reveal bruises still marring the flesh at her neck. "If Fish and Wildlife has pictures and videos going further back, we might have the killer on tape."

"Snowblood Peak is easily accessible from that area," Huck murmured, his eyelids still closed. "But it's possible the killer parked elsewhere and rode through, so don't get your hopes up."

"I never do," she said, yawning again.

"Hope isn't what catches killers."

Huck stretched his neck. "The dumping ground is partly on state land, which abuts federal land. You should leave the case to the state and return to DC."

Should her feelings be hurt that he didn't want her around? They weren't. She tried not to yawn again. "You don't think the two agencies should work the case together?"

"Don't know and don't care." With that, he stood, gathered the dishes, and took them to the kitchen. "The storm is letting up — probably temporarily. I'll drive you home."

The man seemed even more solitary than was she. Interesting.

CHAPTER SIX

"Thanks for the ride," Laurel said as Huck pulled into her mother's driveway, morning light glittering across the snowy yard.

"You're welcome."

She turned to study the cute old farmhouse that was located down a long private driveway with mature trees on both sides. Christmas lights sparkled from every corner, and even a couple of the outside trees were all lit up. "I'll need the list of license plates as well as the results of any attempts to locate the owners of the vehicles."

"Call Fish and Wildlife," Huck said.

She frowned. "Isn't that you?"

"No." He stared out at the drifting snow. "Besides, it'd be better if the FBI took a back seat on this."

"So you indicated." She stepped out of the vehicle and put weight on her injured ankle. It held her easily with only a twinge of pain. So she pulled her overnight bag from the back seat along with her laptop bag. "The bodies are on both federal and state land, you and your officers know the area, and I have access to federal databases as well as profiling knowledge. The logical result is that we work this case together."

He scrutinized her, his topaz-colored eyes dark in the dimming light of dusk. "Call Fish and Wildlife, Agent. This isn't my case."

So they were back to "agent" again. "I believe this is your case," she murmured. "However, I don't want to pull rank. It's not my style."

One of his dark eyebrows rose. The one over his left eye. "You don't have any rank to pull. You're in my territory." He didn't seem to be speaking about the issue of state versus federal land.

She had no patience for jurisdictional battles. There was a killer out there dumping bodies down long cliffs. That was all that truly mattered. "So long as you don't urinate all over the place, your declaration of territorial rights doesn't concern me."

His instant grin contrasted with his grumpy message. "I'll try to keep it in my pants, Laurel."

She had no reply to the humorous innuendo, especially since it was the first time he'd used her first name. The way the consonants rolled around on his tongue and out of his firm mouth uncurled something heated in her belly. "Thanks for the ride." She shut the door and strode along her mother's shoveled rock path to the weathered, red front door. Genuine barn planks made up the outside of the entire home, and a myriad of wind chimes in different shapes and tones hung from the eaves above the front porch. The porch swing and furniture had obviously been stored for the winter, leaving a set of mysterious-looking gnomes scattered to guard the perimeter.

Christmas lights had been strung along every eave and around the windowsills and twinkled merrily.

She used her key to unlock the door. Her mom kept the door locked at all times. "Mom?" She stepped inside and warmth instantly surrounded her.

"Laurel?" Her mom hustled through the kitchen alcove, wiping her hands on a towel. "Oh my. I was getting so worried." She hurried to Laurel and surrounded her with a strong hug. "Where were you? You said you were staying with a colleague to ride out the storm, but that was a man in that truck. Who was he?" Panic edged her voice and she hugged harder, engulfing her daughter.

Laurel sucked in air and hugged her mom

back. "Just a colleague — nobody for you to worry about. I can take care of myself."

Her mom released her. "Let me look at you." Her stunning green eyes were tinged with worry. "You look tired." She brushed a soft hand over Laurel's forehead. "So tired. You poor thing. Traveling always did take it out of you. Come right in here and have some tea. I've created a new blend with dried huckleberries, peppermint, and vanilla that provides balance and immunity." She slipped her arm through Laurel's and tugged her through the comfortable great room to the sprawling country-style kitchen. She pushed Laurel onto a thick wooden chair by the round table.

Laurel breathed deep and let her muscles finally relax. "How are you?"

"I'm well. The season has been quiet, and the tea orders are abundant." Her mom handed over a plate of sugar cookies and then took down two heavy mugs from the cupboard and poured from a kettle already bubbling on the industrial ceramic stove. "I've been following my cards and have expanded the offerings this month."

Laurel sighed. "I sent you the market data, which indicated that you should offer more spiced teas for the holidays."

"I read the market data and then read my

75

cards for backup." Deidre let the tea cool. "I also checked other sources."

Laurel hid a groan. Was her mother paying money to spiritual gurus again? Most were darn con artists. She looked her mother over, feeling like the adult in the room.

Deidre looked fantastic. At five-ten, with short blond hair and a yoga instructor's body, Deidre Snow had always been a gentle soul who exuded a quiet hint of nature. Even working on her teas, she wore white yoga pants with a pink-colored tank top beneath a bright green sweater. A silver necklace with a round, pink, quartz stone hung to her solar plexus, and matching earrings dangled from her small ears.

"Here you go." She set the mugs on the table and took the adjoining seat. "I'm calling this blend 'Winter Health' since the huckleberries have so many healing properties."

Laurel breathed in the delicious aroma and then cupped the mug, taking a sip. Warmth and just the right amount of sweetness slid down to her stomach. "I love it. The huckleberries add a richness to the vanilla's mellowness."

Her mom blew on her mug. "I know. I'm working on a new blend now with huckleberries and cacao, but I don't have it right yet. I need some other spice as well." She took a deep drink. "I can't thank you enough for creating this business model for me so I can just work on my teas. The winter line is already doing well, and I only need a couple new blends for the spring line. Besides the cacao, I think I want a new citrus combination."

Laurel took a cookie and bit into it. If love had a taste, it was in her mother's cookies. "Are you going to add pastries or food to the offerings?" It had been a question for at least a decade.

"I don't think so. I've had my horoscope read by three experts, and it's probably a bad idea right now," her mom said. Laurel had helped her start the tea business nearly ten years before, calling it Pure Heart Tea, and the ensuing subscription service had given her much-needed financial independence. "We're offering a winter-themed design for the apothecary jars, with new ribbon and labels. Sales have increased again."

"That's wonderful." Laurel reached out for her mother's hand. "I'm so proud of you."

"The tea was all me and the business all you." Her mom blushed. "It's still sweet of you to say. I'm proud of you. My brilliant,

77

hard-working daughter. When was the last time you slept?"

"I caught a couple of hours this morning on Huck Rivers's sofa." Laurel took another sip.

Deidre paused with her mug almost to her mouth. "Huck Rivers?"

"Yes. Do you know him?" Laurel asked.

Deidre slowly shook her head. "Nobody knows him. He lives outside of town and is called in when a person goes missing, usually. I hear that he's not nice to anybody."

Laurel could see that. "The man is laconic at best and cantankerous at worst." Although he did have broad shoulders, intriguing eyes, and a charming grin. "I'm fairly certain he doesn't like me."

"He doesn't like anybody." Her mom huddled over her tea. "Thank you for coming home when I called, Laurel. I'm sorry to ask for your help again, to depend on you."

"I'm dependable," Laurel quipped, just to elicit a smile from her mom. She reached into her carry-all bag and drew out her knitting needles, automatically starting to create a tiny hat with the peach-colored yarn. "Now tell me what's going on with Uncle Carl. I didn't get any hint that the Fish and Wildlife officers even had a suspect list yet.

Why does the local sheriff think he's a suspect? And where is he right now?" If Carl had been detained, Laurel was going into town.

Deidre's hands fluttered. "I don't know. Carl called me from the sheriff's office yesterday, just before I called you, and said he'd been asked a bunch of questions about dead bodies. I think the sheriff has it out for Carl. Just because his main job is digging graves at the cemetery, people think he's bad." She kept her gaze on her cup. "It's the scar across his face. That wasn't his fault," she whispered.

"I know." Laurel patted Deidre's hand. Her uncle had been in a snowmobile accident years ago and had sustained damage to the skin and nerves in his face. "Where is he now?"

Deidre swallowed. "He headed up into the mountains for some peace, he said. The sheriff won't like that."

"Agreed," Laurel said, banishing emotion. She needed to think.

Deidre shook her head. "Do you think we have a serial killer in Genesis Valley?"

"It's too early to say," Laurel said, glancing at her mom's hair. "All I know is that the deceased women were all blond, so that's something for you to keep in mind.

Please be even more careful than normal." Her experience told her it was a serial killer, or killers working together. She made a mental note to check on local security systems now that she was back in town. "I need to make a phone call."

"Sure." Deidre returned to the kitchen and opened the refrigerator to bring out a basket of fresh-looking eggs.

Laurel quickly dialed a number.

"Deputy Director McCromby's Office," Jackie said.

"Sorry you're working on a Sunday, Jackie," Laurel said. "Could I please speak to the deputy director? I'll be quick." She'd learned early that promising brevity gained the desired results.

"Hold, please," Jackie said, and Tchaikovsky's *Serenade to Strings* wafted through the line.

The music cut off. "Snow? How bad is it?" George asked.

"At least ten dead females, all with common characteristics," Laurel answered. "We're dealing with a serial, and I want the case. It looks like Fish and Wildlife is taking the lead, so we need to either pull rank or insist on a task force that includes the FBI. The bodies were found on federal land — it's ours." She had to protect her uncle.

80

George groaned. "The Seattle field office is underwater right now. I can't spare a team."

"What can you do with Fish and Wildlife?" she asked.

George was silent for a moment. "Fish and Wildlife in Washington are state officers, fully commissioned. They're qualified to handle this, but I can get you on the team. Let me make a call." He clicked off, and Schubert's *Symphony Number Eight* played quietly.

The sizzle of eggs filled the peaceful kitchen.

The music ended and George returned. "I just talked to the governor, and she's going to take care of the situation and have Fish and Wildlife request your assistance as a consultant. If that doesn't work out, I told her we'd take jurisdiction from them, and since she's running for office on a public safety platform next year, she wants the case."

Laurel bit her lip. "Thank you. What do I have for a support team here?" Fish and Wildlife wasn't going to like the situation; she required her own base.

"You have your terrifying brain and country-girl good looks," George retorted.

Laurel rolled her eyes. "I need a temporary

office with at least a small support staff."

"I'll have Jackie send you a budget, but you're on your own with staff. That's the best I can do right now." George ended the call, obviously not interested in arguing about it.

Laurel set her phone down. "Mom? How well do you know Kate Vuittron?"

"Not well," Deidre said, dishing up the eggs. "She applied for a job with Pure Heart Tea, but I can't justify taking on another employee. Her husband, the rat bastard, left her for his dental hygienist, who's in her early twenties. I saw those two galivanting around town like Christmas arrived early."

Laurel paused. "That's terrible. When did it happen?"

"Oh, early in the spring, I think. He and the chickie moved here, and Kate did the same so the girls could be closer to their father, but she needs a job." Deidre clucked her tongue. "Can you hire her?"

"Yes," Laurel said, making a quick decision. "I need her phone number."

"I have it somewhere." Deidre motioned toward a pile of papers, sticky notes, and napkins in the corner. She brought over the plates of eggs, her brow furrowed. "This situation has set my instincts on fire. We need to do a reading and possibly an immersion with the moon's energy. I have a feeling — a strong one. Life is coming for you, Laurel Mary Snow."

The statement ought to sound exciting, or at least amusing. Instead, a clump of ice descended into Laurel's stomach.

CHAPTER SEVEN

Monday morning arrived, and Laurel had a plan at least.

"I'll rent a car later today," she said as Kate narrowly missed hitting a snowplow. "You shouldn't have to drive me around." Plus, Laurel wanted to live to see her thirtieth year, and she had nine months to go.

"I appreciate the job." Kate honked at a light blue Buick and then zipped around the elderly lady driving it. "Now that my oldest can drive, it helps with all the car-pooling. In Seattle, the girls played every sport you can think of when they weren't participating in all of the other school activities. Hopefully they'll join activities here." Her voice dropped, and she drove around two trucks that were probably going the speed limit.

Laurel pressed both feet against the floor in an instinctive move, even though the brakes were nowhere near her. "I'm sure they will," she croaked.

Kate gripped the steering wheel. "I hope so. How was your first real night home?"

"Good, thanks," Laurel said. "My mom made veggie lasagna, read my cards, and sent me to bed. I slept better than I have in months." Perhaps longer than that.

Kate flicked a glance her way. "You believe in tarot cards?"

"No." Laurel gripped the door handle. "My mom believes, and I enjoy her readings. It's a useful tool for figuring out what's going on in your own mind, I think."

"What did the cards say?" Kate finally slowed down for a school bus. So that was her limit. School buses. Good to know.

Laurel tried to swallow over the lump in her throat and made a mental note to run Kate's driving record when the woman wasn't present. "The cards, according to my mother, show both a sharp change in my life as well as a strong male influence on the romantic side." Her shoulders slowly relaxed down to where they should be. "I think my mom wants a man in my life, although she never seems to like or trust the ones I date."

Kate pumped the brakes. "Sounds like a good mom."

"She is," Laurel said softly as Kate sedately followed the school bus. "Tell me about the office space."

Kate shook her head. "Oh, it was tough to find — took me all day yesterday. First, I called a realtor and was told no way." She glanced sympathetically at Laurel. "Genesis Valley doesn't have many open rental spaces right now. Or ever, they tell me." She rolled her neck. "It seems most of the rental spaces in town are owned by the church, and they're full."

Laurel thought back through the few times she'd actually been in town over the years. "The community church?"

"Yes. I think the town was founded by the church way back when, and it's a good group. There just aren't that many buildings, you know?"

"I understand." Laurel watched the snowy trees outside. The storm had finally ebbed and was now just dropping slow flakes of snow.

"So, I phoned around, trying to call in favors, but I didn't have luck there, either." Kate sighed. Today she wore jeans and a light red sweater, and the streaks had been washed out of her blond hair. "Then I remembered a conversation I overheard at the grocery store last week. Guess what?"

Laurel eyed her. Was she supposed to respond? "What?" she asked.

"The GSA owns several properties in Tempest County and two in Genesis Valley." Kate thumped the steering wheel. "Ha. How do you like that?"

Laurel smiled. "That's brilliant." The U.S. General Services Administration, an agency of the federal government, owned and leased out property all over the country. "I take it the GSA leases out their properties in this territory, and there was an available space?"

"Luckily, yes," Kate said. "I made several phone calls, and believe it or not, I found somebody on a Sunday. The lease form is being emailed to me for you to sign. In the meantime, we can move in and get organized." Several miles outside of town, she pulled into a wide parking lot in front of a stately, two-story brick building. "This isn't how I imagined a big time FBI office, but I did what I could."

Laurel frowned. "Staggers Ice Creamery leases from the federal government? I had no idea." She remembered eating chocolate fudge delight with sprinkles with her mom when she came home during school breaks. Then her gaze caught on the sign above the farthest doorway. "Oh."

Kate winced. "Yep. Turns out Fish and Wildlife needed a bigger venue and started renting from the GSA last year."

"Actually, having the agency close is advantageous." Laurel unbuckled her seatbelt. "I take it we're on the left of the ice creamery?"

"Uh, no." Kate wiped hair away from her forehead. "Fish and Wildlife has the two stories to the right, and Margie's beauty school takes up the two stories to the left. Her sign blew away in the storm last night. We, um, are on the second floor of the ice cream parlor in the middle of the building. Well, after we clean out the space."

Laurel studied the building. "We won't have the usual security measures, but since we'll most likely be here only for one case, I suppose that's okay. Wait. Where's our entrance to the second story?"

Kate opened her door and hopped out of the vehicle. Snow landed gently on her sweater and melted. "We share the doorway with Fish and Wildlife."

Laurel stepped out of the car, her feet cozy in the old pair of winter boots she'd found in the back of her childhood closet. The long green skirt and heavy sweater she'd borrowed from her mother were out of her comfort zone, not to mention too big. Her blue wool coat was in the back seat and she dragged it out, her oversized laptop bag fitting nicely over her shoulder. "Thank you for finding this location," she said, shutting her door.

"You're welcome." Kate stomped through the ice to the door beneath the Fish and Wildlife sign. "We don't need a sign, do we?"

"Definitely not." Laurel followed her inside a small vestibule with three doors. One was a glass door to the right that showed a reception area and Fish and Wildlife posters on the wall, while two plain wooden doors were closed straight ahead. They must both lead to the units on the upper floor. A large black plastic mat covered the entire floor. She kicked snow off her boots and then indicated the door to the left. "I take it this is us?"

"Yep." Kate wiped off her boots and opened the door, which revealed a wooden stairway leading up. Dingy, ripped wallpaper featuring cancan dancers wearing red or blue feathers covered the walls. "We might want to paint if we're here for any length of time."

Slush mixed with dust on the steps.

When they reached the top, Kate opened another door to a wide reception area holding a glass pastry display case in front of a wood paneled wall. An open doorway split the room evenly, leading to a long hallway. "Huh. The whole place smells like waffle cones."

Laurel inhaled. Waffle cones and sugar. "Now that's ambiance."

Kate skirted the display case and walked through the open door. "It looks like the hub is back here."

Laurel quickened her pace and craned her neck to see better. What would the offices be like? She strode through the door to find a well-structured space. "Somebody must've used this for offices before." On the left of the hallway were restrooms, what appeared to be a storage room, and possibly a small conference room; on the right were a kitchen area and larger conference room; and three offices were located against the rear wall. The only windows in the place were in the reception area and the three offices, and yet skylights from above let plenty of light in.

The storage room held cement blocks, abandoned doors, a folding chair, pieces of floor trim, and what looked like cans of pink paint.

"That looks like a good office," Kate said, indicating the farthest office space, which sat in the northeast corner across from the biggest conference room.

Laurel nodded. "As soon as I get the budget from DC, we can equip the place. For now . . ." She moved to pick up a cinder block from the storage room. "Let's move these into my office."

Kate frowned. "Why?"

Laurel took in the abandoned doors leaning against the far wall. One was a dingy green that appeared fairly smooth. "I need a desk." A killer was out there, hunting blondes, and the only thing that mattered was that he be stopped.

Now.

Huck accepted the change from the grocery cashier and shoved it in his pocket. The kid appeared to be around sixteen with purple streaks through her dark hair and a nose ring that looked infected. "Thanks."

The cashier grinned and looked at the items in his cart. "Dog food, beer, toilet paper, and Advil. Dude, you might as well just wear a T-shirt that says 'bachelor.' " She looked at his dirty jacket and then reached beneath the counter for a flyer. "We're supposed to give these to everyone. The Genesis Community Church is hosting a Christmas soup kitchen every Thursday night through

December, in case you're hungry."

He took the flyer. Did he look homeless? He stared down at his faded jeans, worn boots, and old coat. Whiskers covered his jaw. Yeah, he needed a haircut. "Thanks." Turning, he hefted the dog food over a shoulder and grasped the two plastic bags with his other hand. His bum leg hurt like a bitch, but he made it outside and back into the gently falling snow without limping. "Kid thought I was homeless," he said to Aeneas after dumping everything in the truck.

The dog blinked.

Huck started the truck just as his phone buzzed. "What?" he answered.

"Aren't you cheerful as usual?" Frank Melinoli was the department director in charge of the Washington Fish and Wildlife Agency.

Huck already knew what was coming. "No."

"Too bad," Frank shot back. "We have a serial killer on your mountain, and I've let you stew alone in the woods for too long. It's been two years since I transferred you, Huck. If you need counseling, I'll pay for it myself. You don't have to go through official channels."

"I'm fine," Huck growled, his leg aching. "I'm aware we have a killer, Frank. I saw the bodies." The small blonde with the bruised neck would haunt his dreams, but she'd have to stand in line to do it.

Frank sighed. "I don't have time to argue with you, considering I just spent an hour being ordered around by the governor. So here it is. We're taking the lead on the investigation, and you're the captain in that region, so you're now lead and will liaise, or however they say it, with the FBI agent there. Got it?"

An image of Laurel's dual-colored eyes shot through Huck's head, and his mood turned even darker than the clouds piling across the sky. "Monty Buckley is the captain in charge here. I'm just a search and rescue guy with a title and no office."

"Buckley has prostate cancer and can't take this on," Frank said bluntly.

Huck dropped his head. "I didn't know."

"Nobody knows," Frank said. "Keep it that way. I just spoke with him, and he's assigning you an office to use until you find this killer."

"I don't need an office," Huck muttered.

"Too bad. Monty is sending all of the information his folks have compiled to the FBI agent, and you're expected to reach out to her today. See him first." Frank hung up.

Huck slammed his phone on the seat.

Aeneas barked and then settled down.

"Just great." Huck drove out of the parking lot onto Main Street and then followed the road several miles, turning onto Jagged Rock Road and driving twenty more miles before sliding into the parking lot fronting the headquarters of Fish and Wildlife. Huh. The sign on the building, right in the middle, said STAGGERS ICE CREAMERY. A smaller sign to the left noted that a beauty school had opened there. Fish and Wildlife had a small sign above a wider door to the far right.

He parked and jumped out, opening Aeneas's door. If he was stuck with an office, they were stuck with his dog. He strode inside a vestibule with wooden flooring covered by a large black rubber mat. Two closed wooden doors were straight ahead, while a glass door to the right led into Fish and Wildlife. He shoved the glass door open and nodded at the officer behind the reception desk. "Hi, Ena. Is Monty around?" He'd met her two years ago, at their former office, when he'd had to fill out paperwork, but he hadn't seen her since.

She was tall with broad shoulders, black hair, and a genuine smile. "He's waiting for you. I'm glad you've come off the mountain."

"It's temporary." Huck strode through a door to the left and walked along a series of shoulder height file cabinets that separated the hallway from the bullpen. Several officers worked at desks arranged in formations of four. He walked to the end of the file cabinets and straight into Monty's office. It was decorated with pictures of fish and one of Monty's wife from years ago, before she'd passed away. "Here I am. I don't need an office."

Monty looked up from a pile of papers, his white hair poking in different directions. "The welcome celebration will have to wait, and you have an office whether or not you want one." His jaw was hard and lines fanned out from his eyes. "If nothing else, the dog might want somewhere to sleep." He stood and walked past Huck to the bullpen, then continued down a hallway to an empty office at the very end, beyond what appeared to be a vacant office. "Most people don't want to be this far from the action, but I figured it was perfect for you. Plus, the conference room is across the hall, so you won't have to go far if you want to throw a party."

Smart aleck. Huck walked inside the office, which took up the northeast corner of the first floor. He looked up at the ceiling.

"Who's above me?"

"Nobody at the moment. The second floor above us is vacant, although it looks like the FBI just rented the second floor above the ice cream shop," Monty said.

There was a wide window, a utilitarian desk already stacked with case files, two guest chairs, and a new dog bed in the corner. His throat closed. Monty had bought Aeneas a bed?

Monty slapped him on the shoulder. "Thanks for coming in on this."

Like he'd had a choice. Huck hadn't made an effort to get acquainted with any of the team, and he didn't mind the distrust shining in Monty's eyes. But the guy had bought Aeneas a bed, and apparently he was fighting cancer. "Glad to help."

Monty snorted and turned back toward the bullpen.

CHAPTER EIGHT

For no logical reason, Laurel smoothed down her hair before striding into the reception area of the Fish and Wildlife offices. A youngish woman with long black hair who was wearing a beige-colored uniform with a shiny badge on her chest sat behind the reception desk. "Hi. Can I help you?"

"Yes. I'm Laurel Snow, and I'd like to see Captain Rivers," Laurel said, her file folder and notes in her left hand.

"I figured. I'm Officer Ilemoto. You can call me Ena." Wildlife posters covered the wall behind her. She pointed through an open doorway to the right. "You can go on back. Hang a right at the end of the file-cabinet created hallway, go to the very end, and you'll find Huck's office. Far northeast corner."

Laurel kept the surprise out of her expression. "Thank you." She walked past the file cabinets, turned right, and kept moving beyond the cubicles, ignoring the curious looks from the officers. After passing a couple of offices, she reached the final one, a corner setup like hers. "Captain Rivers?" She waited in his open doorway, noting he had the same view from his wide windows as she, although his windows comprised two walls instead of her one.

He sat behind a monstrous wooden desk strewn high with file folders and papers. Aeneas snoozed in a plush blue dog bed in the corner. The walls lacked decor. "Huck. Remember?"

Considering she had an eidetic memory, yes. "Huck. I thought —"

His hair was already ruffled, and today he wore a black Henley with a rip near the right wrist. He filled the material out so the tee stretched tightly over his broad chest. "The ME already called and yelled at me about interagency cooperation and how valuable his time is these days. I'm driving." He flicked a glance at his wristwatch. "He doesn't want to see us until two this afternoon. I'll swing up to your office and get you then." He turned back to setting up his computer.

She cleared her throat and waited until he looked up at her again. "I've been perusing the notes sent to me earlier this morning, and there's a witness I'd like to talk to. She's a professor up at Northern Washington Technical Institute, and since the school is located near the ME's office, I thought we could drop by and interview her."

Huck twisted to better face her, and in the light from the window, his eyes were a lighter brown with golden flecks. "We're compiling our lists and doing background checks before reaching out in person. Isn't that protocol, even for the FBI?"

"Yes," Laurel said, ignoring the subtle dig. "Except Dr. Caine's SUV was parked in that lot seven times during the last six weeks. We'll end up speaking with her anyway, so I thought we could hit two birds with one trip. You know?" She could go alone but had wanted to try to coordinate agency efforts.

Huck moved a pile of papers to the side of his keyboard. He tapped a pen on the desk. "I thought most serial killers were male?"

She nodded. "Definitely. But this woman might be a good witness, since she has parked in the lot so many times. Perhaps she utilizes one of the jogging trails. From the investigation so far, her vehicle shows up on the record more than any other. I can interview her alone but didn't want to appear to go around you."

Huck stretched his neck. "Monty?" he bellowed.

"What?" Monty popped up behind Laurel, and she slipped inside the office and to the side.

"Why haven't we gotten a hold of Dr. Caine from Tech?" Huck asked in a lower voice.

Monty shrugged. "We've left several voice messages, but she hasn't called back. We just started calling yesterday. The woman is probably busy."

Huck scrubbed a hand through his unkempt hair. "I guess it wouldn't hurt to track her down, since we'll be in the vicinity." He pushed back from his desk and reached in the drawer for his gun, slipping it into his thigh holster. "We can talk to her, grab lunch, and then go see the ME. I'd rather eat before we meet with him."

Monty's face cleared. "Great. Glad you're on it."

Laurel wished once again for her own clothes. Her mom's flowery skirt was out of place for the job. "Have you had any luck with missing persons yet?" It'd be nice to identify some of the victims.

"No," Huck said.

"I have a colleague in DC digging into VI-

CAP's database for similar crimes," Laurel said, moving toward the door. "I haven't rented a vehicle yet, or I'd offer to drive."

Huck walked around his desk and whistled for the dog.

Monty cleared his throat as the dog jumped to his feet. "You can leave the dog here, if you want."

Huck shook his head. "He sticks with me."

Another man with trust issues. Not a surprise. "We shouldn't be inside too many places for too long," Laurel said. She'd never had time for a pet and hadn't researched the bonds they could form with humans, but there was something intriguing and appealing about the black and white beauty with his adorable nose. Although, he'd kept his distance from her. How could she learn to relate to a dog? There had to be a manual on the subject.

"He can come with us," Huck said, snatching keys off the edge of his desk. "If I have to leave him in the truck, he has his own battery-operated heater in the back seat as well as water, although he won't need it." He gestured Laurel out of the office and pressed a large-boned hand to the back of her waist. "Thanks for offering, Monty. I appreciate it."

There was more warmth and respect

between the two men than had been evident at the crime scene. Had something happened?

Laurel preceded him through the office, feeling the curious gazes again. When they reached the freezing cold outside, she moved toward his truck. "What was that about? You don't trust your colleagues with your dog?"

Huck opened the passenger side door for her. "Aeneas is a working dog, and he needs a set routine." He waited until she'd climbed up and settled herself in the seat. "I like rules. Everyone in my life sticks to them, and I don't like anything that disrupts our schedule." With that, he shut the door.

She blinked. Was that statement aimed at her?

Northern Washington Technical Institute exemplified the aesthetic of modern architecture surrounded by wild nature. Glass and steel buildings angled elegantly over the campus, and Huck wove expertly through the streets to a structure that held classrooms on the first floor and faculty offices on the second.

Laurel scrolled through her phone. "According to the school's website, Dr. Caine just finished a class and should be holding office hours right now."

"Good." Huck parked in a visitor slot and turned off the engine. "What does she teach, anyway?"

"A surprising variety of classes," Laurel mused, reading through the faculty descriptions. "She has degrees in computation and neural systems, social and decision neuroscience, game theory, biochemistry, and . . ." Well, that was fascinating. "Philosophy with a practical ethics emphasis."

Huck looked at her as more snow fell on the front window. "Sounds smart. How old is she?"

"This doesn't say," Laurel murmured. "Based on the number of her degrees, I'd say she's been at this for at least a few decades. I'm curious to meet her. The philosophy degree is incongruous with the science and mathematics focus." She opened her door and stepped carefully down to the icy ground.

Huck let Aeneas out, crossed around the truck to the glass and steel door of the building and opened it for Laurel. "If you say so."

Laurel walked inside and instantly warmed. Spotting a curved stairway, she wiped her boots on the rubber mat and walked across the stained concrete floor to ascend the hanging steel steps. The railing was steel with a glass partition extending to the cement steps beneath it. "I believe her office is to the right in the corner." She'd memorized the layout of the building after one look at the schematics. She turned right and walked beyond several closed office doors to the last one, which held a silver-rimmed bulletin board tacked with impeccably aligned flyers and schedules. She knocked.

"Come in," a female voice called.

Laurel opened the door wide. "Dr. Caine?"

"Yes?" The woman didn't look up from the papers on her desk.

"I'm FBI Special Agent Laurel Snow, and this is Washington Fish and Wildlife Captain Huck Rivers. We'd like a moment of your time." Without waiting for an invitation, Laurel stepped inside and walked across the hard concrete floor to one of the two guest chairs opposite the desk.

When Dr. Caine looked up, she was much younger than Laurel had expected. Surprise flashed across her face. "FBI?" Her pink mouth gaped open, and she stared at Laurel.

"Yes." Laurel forced a smile and gestured to the chair. "May we?"

"Yes." Dr. Caine caught herself and then

104

smiled, her gaze direct. Openly curious. She spoke with a barely noticeable British accent. "Please. Have a seat." Her hair was platinum blond, thick and wavy, while her eyes were a dark blue. Her skin was smooth and unlined, showing her to be possibly in her late twenties or early thirties.

Laurel stared back. "I'm sorry. I expected someone older from your biography."

Dr. Caine laughed, the sound controlled. "Child prodigy, I'm afraid. I entered college young." Her gaze flickered to Huck and ran over his length as he took a seat while Aeneas did the same at his feet. But she turned back to continue studying Laurel. "You appear young for a special agent."

Laurel kept the smile in place. "Yes. Seems as if we have that in common."

"Don't we, though?" Dr. Caine said, sitting back in her leather chair. "What can I help you with today?"

Huck settled his bulk more comfortably in his chair. "Fish and Wildlife officers have been calling you since yesterday."

Dr. Caine glanced over at her blinking phone. "Ah. I've been busy and haven't had time to check my messages. Is there something going on?"

"Yes," Laurel said. "We've had an incident on Snowblood Peak, and your Escalade has been parked at the trailhead numerous times in the last six weeks. We were hoping you might've seen or heard something that could help us."

Dr. Caine set her pink-tipped nails on her desk. "I don't understand. What kind of incident?"

"Why do you go to Snowblood Peak so often?" Huck interjected quietly.

She turned toward him. "I like to jog on the trails. Running along uneven terrain is good for the cardiovascular as well as muscular systems, Captain." Her voice lowered, becoming throaty. Sexy. Was she flirting with Huck?

Laurel tilted her head. "There are many good running trails right here around the college campus. Why don't you use those?"

"Who says I don't?" Dr. Caine continued her appraisal of Huck as she spoke. "I like to keep in good shape, and I look for different trails because I get bored easily, as I'm sure you do, too, Agent Snow." Her focus returned to Laurel. "Laurel Snow. It's an interesting moniker, no? Whimsical and cold at the same time. I wonder. What's your middle name?"

Laurel smiled. "Dr. Caine —"

"Abigail. Please." Abigail reached for a gold-plated pen. "While jogging that area, I did see one gentleman more than once. He actually said hi to me one time, and we walked together for a while, but it was chilly and a scarf covered most of his face. What was his name? Darn it, he told it to me. I'll remember. I promise."

"Was he in a UTV?" Huck asked.

Abigail twirled the pen in her fingers. "No. He was walking the trail up Snowblood Creek. I remember him because he moved fast but wasn't jogging. It was odd."

"Could you describe him?" Laurel asked.

Abigail scrunched her face. "I don't know. He was tall, I think. I didn't give him much thought, but I will now, if it helps. I meditate every evening, and I'll try to focus on remembering him. Right now, he's just a blur, you know?"

Not really, but not everyone had Laurel's memory skills; even a very intelligent person might not. "We'd appreciate any help you could provide." She surreptitiously studied the office. The glass desk was feminine and the furnishings modern with chrome filing cabinets along one wall. The opposite wall held a wide window flanked by several diplomas. An oil painting behind the professor perfectly captured the local Calico Mountains with dark thunder clouds above. The scene evoked a feeling of awe and possible doom. "What a lovely painting."

"Thank you," Abigail said. "My mother painted a series depicting the mountains around Genesis Valley."

"She is very talented," Laurel murmured. "Do you paint?" There was something about the professor that intrigued her. Was it because they were both prodigies?

Abigail shook her head. "I'm afraid not. I've found that those who paint camouflage too many secrets within the strokes. How about you, Special Agent Snow? Where do you bury your secrets?"

108

CHAPTER NINE

Huck kept an eye on the storm outside, which threatened to start up again, even as his instincts thrummed alive beneath his skin. The professor was an interesting woman, and she knew it. Definite ego there, but with her intelligence and beauty, she'd probably earned it.

"I don't much care for secrets and usually miss subtext," Laurel said, tearing her gaze from the painting.

Huck thought it was stunning with those dark purple streaks that suggested a wild storm. "Besides the odd, tall man you saw, can you think of anybody else you've noticed around Snowblood Peak in the last couple of months?" he asked. What kind of genius professor used words like odd and tall? Shouldn't she have a better recollection? Or maybe she was just brilliant with math and science and not people. He could under-stand that. Half the time he'd rather be in the woods than around other people. Make that most of the time.

Sometimes he wished his job dealt only with animals. Unfortunately, people usually ended up being the worst kind of beasts.

The professor smiled at him. She looked professional and feminine in a light pink suit with a shimmery white blouse beneath the jacket. "There have been many ATV riders out there getting in their last muddy rides before snow and ice block the trails. Now will you tell me what's going on? It might help me to remember if I understood the situation correctly."

Laurel nodded. "We've found a series of bodies up on the peak. Well, on the cliffs below the peak to be exact. The last victim appears to have been dumped a couple of weeks ago, Dr. Caine."

Dr. Caine's blue eyes widened. "Bodies?"

"Young blondes," Laurel added.

Abigail set down her pen. "That's horrible. Truly terrible."

"Agreed," Laurel said quietly. "That's why we could use any assistance you might provide."

"Please, call me Abigail. I insist." Abigail tilted her head to the side. "Is that what you do, Laurel? Chase serial killers all over the country?"

Huck glanced at the agent next to him. She hadn't invited the professor to use her first name, now had she? He had the oddest sense that he was watching a chess match between two experts. This was weird.

Laurel appeared relaxed in the light beige, leather guest chair. "That's exactly what I do."

"Isn't that interesting?" Abigail touched her lip with her tongue. "A child prodigy, one with obvious rare intelligence, but instead of attempting to solve the mysteries of the universe, you delve deep into the criminal mind. You play with evil."

"I don't play at all," Laurel said smoothly. "One might question your interest in philosophy as well, but we don't have time for theoretical pursuits right now."

Huck frowned at the interchange. Was there some woman thing going on that he couldn't grasp?

Laurel smiled. "Before we go, do you have anything else to add?"

"I do." Abigail settled her elbows on the desk and cradled her hands, watching Laurel. "A colleague of mine is conducting a research trial on people with heterochromatic eyes. While six in a thousand may have different-colored eyes, most aren't discernible. It's rare to find such an obvious differentiation of color, and to have a partial heterochromia within a complete heterochromia? You're the most unusual of humans."

"My mother always did say I was a unicorn," Laurel said. "Thank you for the offer, but I don't have time to participate in a study."

Abigail shrugged. "Also, are you cognizant of the fact that only one to two percent of the population has genuinely red hair?"

"The red highlights in my hair are from a bottle. It's good to know my hairdresser does a decent job," Laurel returned.

Abigail's smile was more catlike than sweet. "For a federal agent, you're not a very accomplished liar." She crossed her legs. "Your tendency to nictate gives you away."

"Blinking?" Laurel retorted.

"Indeed. This has been a particularly riveting interlude, Agent, quite outside the quotidian. What are your thoughts, Captain Rivers?" She brushed her white-blond hair off her shoulders.

Huck kept his neutral expression in place. "I wonder if professors use such large words to prove that they're smart or that their audience is dumb." What the hell did quotidian mean?

Abigail paused and focused entirely on

him as if actually seeing him for the first time. "Aren't those one and the same?"

"No," he said shortly, glancing at his watch. If they didn't get a move on, he'd miss lunch, and he was already becoming irritated at the time wasted on this interview. "Now. I have a series of dead young blondes on my mountain, and I'd really like to catch the bastard who put them there. Do you, or do you not, have anything to add to my case?" He glanced at Laurel. "Our case, I meant."

To her credit, she didn't roll her eyes.

"Well, I haven't seen anybody murder and then toss a woman off a cliff." Abigail tucked a strand of hair behind her ear, revealing light pink diamonds at her lobes. "I can't think of anything to help you right now, but if you'll leave your cards, I'll be in touch. Often after I've meditated, I can recall events more clearly."

Huck stood and tugged a business card out of his back pocket. "Here you go." He had to get out of there.

Laurel stood and reached for a card from her phone case. "Use the cell phone number at the bottom because I'm not in DC right now, and we don't have office phones set up in Genesis Valley as of yet. I hope you can recall something helpful."

Abigail took the cards and tapped them against her palm. "I hope so as well."

Huck waited for Laurel to exit the office and followed her, walking briskly down the stairs and outside where he could breathe again. He sucked in freezing cold air and forced his body to simmer down.

"Are you all right?" Laurel asked as snow dotted her stunning hair.

"Yeah. Sometimes I feel claustrophobic and need to just get outside. I didn't like her office." Why, he didn't know. "What is wrong with that woman?"

Laurel smiled, looking like a blazing fire in the midst of a pale world. "Well, based on our brief meeting with her, I'd hazard a guess that she has narcissistic personality disorder." She shoved her hands in her coat. "Or she's just a total bitch."

Huck burst out laughing.

Laurel chuckled and headed for the passenger side of his truck.

The hair at the base of his neck itched, and he looked up to the second-floor windows. Dr. Abigail Caine lifted a hand in good-bye.

His gut clenched.

Tempest County's ME's office was located adjacent to the hospital, and no doubt there was a corridor tunnel between the two. They had to leave Aeneas in the truck, but Huck had made sure the heater was on in the back seat, and the dog was already napping.

Laurel let Huck take the lead once they were inside and followed him through a labyrinth of offices and labs to an elevator that took them to the basement level. She rubbed her arms.

"Cold?" Huck asked as the elevator opened.

"I'm not ready for winter, and these aren't my clothes," she admitted. DC had enjoyed an unusually warm autumn, Los Angeles had been downright warm, and now she had to acclimate herself to rapidly freezing temperatures.

"Those clothes don't look like you." Huck held the door open for her. The man seemed to be a gentleman, even though he kept his distance and didn't talk much. The moment she'd made him laugh earlier had been a treat for her. He had an excellent laugh. Deep and rumbly with genuine humor in it. Her Uncle Blake had a similar laugh, but it wasn't quite as deep. "You don't know what clothes do or do not look like me," she said, emerging into a quiet area with a set of blandly upholstered chairs against a wall.

"Good point." Huck lifted his head, looking around. "Dr. Ortega?" he called out.

One of the two swinging metal doors opened, and a man in his early sixties emerged with a file folder in one hand. He wore a white lab coat over jeans, a green shirt, and striped, blue tie. His black hair was liberally sprinkled with gray, and his goatee had given up the fight and turned completely gray. "Who are you?"

"This is FBI Special Agent Laurel Snow, and I'm Huck Rivers from Fish and Wildlife," Huck said. "The office should've called ahead."

"I'm Dr. Ortega." The doctor was about five foot ten with brown eyes and a swimmer's body. He didn't offer to shake hands. "I'm understaffed and dealing with seven overdoses from a new drug on the streets of Seattle. You must have some pull to get your case thrown to the front of the line." His frown was dark.

"Tortured, mutilated, and strangled young women should go to the front of the line," Laurel said, a snap in her voice.

Ortega straightened. "Fine. Come on in."

The chemical smell of antiseptic burned Laurel's nostrils, but she followed him into a stark conference room with too-bright white walls. The doctor took a seat and opened his folder while Laurel and Huck sat.

"This is just a preliminary report. So far, we have the body parts of eleven different women," Dr. Ortega said, reaching for glasses from his pocket and perching them on his nose. "I called everyone in, and we worked throughout the night. Identifications are just now coming in."

Huck's phone buzzed and he glanced down. "The weather has let up enough that the state techs are heading back up the mountain. The state is coordinating with the FBI and taking the lead on the search and recovery efforts."

Laurel nodded. It made sense that the locals would take the lead since they were familiar with the territory. "Could you determine cause of death, Dr. Ortega?"

"Yes. For three of the bodies, I determined cause of death to be strangulation," Dr. Ortega said. "My assistant is making copies of all the prelim autopsies for you both. The bodies range in approximate age from nineteen to thirtyish so far. All Caucasian, blond from what we could tell, with unhealed fractures throughout the bodies."

Laurel blew out air. "The freshest corpse?"

"Death was approximately one week ago. Woman, aged twenty, named Gretel Shar-

117

ter, a runaway out of Missouri four years ago," Dr. Ortega said, sliding a missing person's report across the table. "We sent her prints in and just received this about five minutes ago."

"What was she doing in Genesis Valley?" Huck murmured, looking at the smiling young blonde.

Ortega shrugged, his gaze somber. "That's your job. I can tell you that her prints were matched quickly because she was picked up in Seattle for prostitution last year. Other than that, my information is limited to the state of the body."

Laurel looked away from the picture. "What injuries did you observe?"

Ortega slipped off his glasses, folded them, and tucked them neatly back in his pocket. "There were three bodies still intact enough to run kits. They were positive for sexual assault, and ligation marks were found on the wrists and ankles. Bruises dated back to most likely a week."

Laurel pushed the paper back to Ortega's file folder. "Based on the three bodies you could study, what was the approximate timeframe between kills?"

Ortega shook his head. "Based only on the three freshest corpses, and keep in mind there could be more, I'd say about a month." He scratched his chin. "I've sent prints and DNA to the FBI and the techs are running them now. Well, the prints. The DNA may take a little while, as you know."

"Did you get DNA from the rape kits?" Laurel asked.

"No. We did find spermicide as well as traces of condoms," Ortega said. "We swabbed the bodies and sent samples to the FBI, as instructed by my boss. The FBI is already pulling rank."

"We do have the best labs." Laurel didn't care about rank. She had to find this guy. A desperate need to hunt him down flamed through her. "The bodies were all naked and left in the elements for at least a week. DNA is a long shot."

"It is," Ortega agreed. "We scraped teeth and beneath fingernails as well. Hopefully we'll see results."

It was doubtful. This guy seemed meticulous. She turned to Huck. "How difficult would it be for one person to take a body up the trail and dump it over the side?"

Huck's eyes had darkened the more they talked and were now the color of burned tree bark. "It'd be easy in a UTV or Side by Side. You could zip the body into a large pack, put it in the back seat or even strap it to the bed. It'd look like food or camping

119

gear. Then you ride up the trail, wait until you're alone, unzip the bag and throw the body."

She tapped her lip. "The killer wouldn't need to be incredibly strong in that case." She turned to the ME. "Were there any fibers found on the bodies?"

"Yes. Rough and wool, like from a blanket. A common winter blanket. We've sent the fibers to the FBI lab," Ortega said.

Well, it wasn't a big clue, but at least it was something. "Thank you," Laurel said.

Ortega closed his file folder. "I'll make your copies for you. We might as well get organized before more bodies come in." He quietly stood and left the room.

Huck's phone buzzed and he looked down to read the screen. "They found another one."

CHAPTER TEN

The workday had long finished when they returned to Genesis Valley, so Laurel asked Huck to drop her off again at her mother's home. There were two other trucks and an older SUV already parked in the driveway. Family dinner? After seeing the remains of young women while meeting with Dr. Ortega, she wasn't in the mood. "I'll get my own car sometime tomorrow," she said, opening the passenger side door to jump out.

"No problem," Huck said, sounding as weary as she felt.

She paused. "Are you going back up the mountain?"

"Not tonight. Another storm is coming in, and we've halted the search. Maybe tomorrow."

Laurel fought her desires versus good manners. Good manners won. "It looks like my mom may be having a family dinner.

Would you like to join us?" It was the least she could do, considering he'd driven her around all day.

"No." He softened the refusal with a slight smile. "I've had enough of people today and want to go home with my dog. Thank you for the invite."

Her disappointment that he'd refused was a surprise. "All right. I'll see you tomorrow." She shut the door and half bent to counter the wind on the way to the porch. He was already pulling out of the drive when she opened the front door to the bustle of a good-sized gathering and the smell of home-cooked chicken casserole. The good kind with potato chips on top.

"There's my girl." Uncle Blake rushed in from the kitchen and swept her up, hugging her with his strong farmer's arms. "You got even shorter. How is that possible?" He plunked her down on her feet, sending a jolt through her spine.

She slapped his chest, knowing he'd say those very words. "I'm taller than ever. Let me look at you. Mom says that Aunt Betty has you on a cleansing diet." Her mother was always thorough in her weekly emails.

Blake sighed. "It's true. I spend most of my time in the bathroom, but tonight I get to splurge and have real food." In his late fifties, Blake Snow looked like the farmer he'd been for decades. Brown hair tinged with gray, green eyes like his siblings, and a logger's chest, wide as a barrel. He still had a slight belly, but the cleanse was definitely working. Like Deidre, he was tall, looming over Laurel at six foot six. And a half. That half had always given him an edge over his brother, and he was quick to add it when talking about height. "I heard you're home for a good while."

"Hopefully not," Laurel said. "Wait. I mean I like being home, but I want to find this killer soon and then relax for the holidays." Instinct as well as experience whispered that the killer wasn't going to be found easily.

Blake slung a heavy arm around Laurel's shoulders. "If anybody can find this douche-bag, it's my girl."

"Laurel!" Aunt Betty bustled out of the kitchen, her brown hair down around her shoulders, chunky turquoise jewelry at her neck and ears. Her dark brown eyes spar-kled, and she looked curvy in a tiered, forest-green gauze maxi skirt beneath a flowered blouse and long gray cardigan. "Did you shrink?" At just under six feet tall, her aunt grinned.

"Don't encourage Blake," Laurel chided,

letting her aunt swallow her in a lavender-scented hug. "I think I might be growing."

"Right." Her aunt leaned back to study her. "You look tired. Come in and have some tea."

It was fortunate that most of life's ailments could be solved with a good cup of tea, at least according to her family. She let her aunt pull her into the kitchen, where the mixture of aromas made her stomach growl.

Her mom looked up from tossing a salad. "Did Huck Rivers drop you off again?"

Laurel allowed her aunt to push her onto a chair at the round table already set for four. "Yes."

Aunt Betty frowned. "Huck Rivers?"

Laurel fought the urge to groan. "We're working a case together, although he doesn't like FBI agents. He has tolerated me so far because the working relationship is mutually beneficial, but he has strongly suggested I return to DC and let his department handle the case."

Betty poured two cups of tea and handed one over, taking a seat. "He's an enigma. In town, the guy is curt to the point of being rude, but the second anybody goes lost, he's the first to climb the mountain or dive into the river."

Laurel watched steam rise from her mug. "He's on the dive team, too?"

"Yes." Betty nodded. "I believe he has some demons, and that's being kind. I'm sorry you have to work with him."

"Agreed," Blake said, leaning over Deidre to snatch a piece of chicken. "Rivers also has a nasty temper when it blows. I saw him nearly take a man's head off last year. Of course, the man had shot a deer out of season, but even so. Huck is better off in the wilds doing his job."

Betty leaned forward, her eyes alight with the thrill of gossip. "He's always up on the mountain by himself. I don't like you being alone with him."

Laurel took a sip of her tea, and citrus exploded down her throat. Warm and delicious. "I have a gun, Aunt Betty."

Deidre brought the plates to the table. "Knock it off, you two. I've never met him, but I heard that Huck was a sniper in the military."

Blake smoothed back his thick hair with one hand. "Yeah, and sometimes that type of strategic mindset needs to find another outlet. For now, he doesn't need to drive you any longer, Laurel. We brought your aunt's Volkswagen Tiguan for you to drive. It's a 2010 model, but they last forever, and it's in much better shape than the truck your mom keeps in the garage but never drives."

Laurel paused. "You didn't have to do that." Although it would be nice to have a car she trusted, and Blake was an excellent mechanic.

"I'm not using it," Betty said. "We just use it around the farm, and the snow tires are new. We insist."

Laurel smiled. "Thank you. That solves a lot of problems for me."

"Including having to be around Huck Rivers," Blake said grimly.

The back door opened, and Uncle Carl walked inside, then carefully toed off his snow boots in the alcove.

"Carl," Deidre said, smiling and moving toward him. "You remembered family dinner."

He shuffled his feet. "I found time." Then he looked up and smiled at Laurel. "Welcome home." He clasped his hands together as he hovered in the doorway. "I didn't kill those women."

"I know." Laurel gestured to one of the free chairs. This uncle wasn't a hugger. "Come sit. We're just getting ready to eat."

Carl made his way around the table to take one of the six chairs. "Thank you for the invitation," he said, remembering his manners.

"You're always welcome," Deidre replied, bringing over another place setting. The table fit six easily. "You know that, and I'm glad to see you away from the Dairy Dumplin' for a night. You can't eat their burgers every day, Carl. You're getting older and should watch your cholesterol."

"I like the Dairy Dumplin'. They've got salads, too." Carl brushed his grayish black hair away from his hard-boned face. Like his siblings, he was tall at six foot six and had green eyes. He spent most of his time alone but made an effort with family. He'd been briefly married, and as far as Laurel knew, he'd never really dated anybody after the marriage had ended. A snowmobile accident had left him with a long scar that cut across the right side of his mouth and up to his hairline, the skin on either side puckered and his lips misshapen. "It smells good in here," he said.

Everyone sat, and Deidre started dishing the casserole. "How is your case going, Laurel?"

Laurel pushed the image of dead blondes out of her mind. "It's slow right now."

Blake dug into the chicken the second his plate landed in front of him.

Betty shook her head and forced salad onto his plate, narrowly avoiding his already moving fork. "The entire town is abuzz about the murders." While Deidre stayed remote with her teas and home-centered business, Betty kept a finger on the pulse in town at all times. "The town sheriff was at Schmitt's Deli this morning saying that the killer has to be a local who knows the area."

Carl groaned. "I didn't kill anybody. Even if the murderer is a local, it ain't me."

Laurel paused with her fork almost to her mouth. "The local sheriff? We haven't even seen a sheriff. Who is it these days?" She hadn't paid attention the last couple of times she'd been home.

Betty took a bite of mashed potatoes. "Sheriff Upton York. He moved here about five years ago from South Carolina and ran for sheriff. From the sound of it the other day, he's front and center with the investigation."

Laurel frowned. "I haven't even met the guy."

"He's a blowhard," Carl said after chewing thoroughly.

Laurel swung her head to her uncle. She'd planned to wait until after dinner to speak with him, but this was an opening. "Why did the sheriff call you in for questioning?"

Carl shrugged a thick shoulder. He'd dressed in a good red flannel shirt and Carhart jeans for the family dinner. "I got a couple of tickets last year."

"Four tickets," Deidre corrected. "For parking in a new unloading zone in front of the post office."

"It wasn't an unloading zone last year. They can't just change it," Carl muttered.

Diedre looked at her older brother. "Yes, they can. Didn't the sheriff also bug you while you were fishing up the river last summer?"

Laurel picked onions out of her salad and dug into the watercress. "North of town?" Iceberg River flowed through the mountains behind Huck's cabin. "At the base of Snowblood Peak?"

"Yeah. There's good rainbow trout there," Carl said, taking a drink of the white wine in front of him. "The sheriff accused me of littering, which I did not do. I would not litter."

Laurel ate more chicken, her brain jumping into her investigation. "Have you ever seen anything suspicious around that area? The river parking area also serves the UTV trail up to the peak as well as all of the walking trails around the base of the mountains."

"No," Carl said. "I usually go at dawn and

don't see many other people. When I fish, I like to be alone."

"You always like to be alone," Blake said to his older brother, sounding accepting of that fact. "Not that I blame you. How is your job going, anyway?"

Carl finished off his glass of wine. "It was a busy summer at the cemetery. I dug a lot of graves." Carl had worked at digging graves most of his life. "Not sure if I'll dig any for the bodies Laurel found."

She hadn't actually found them, but she didn't argue. It was nice to have Carl speaking with the family. Sometimes he disappeared for months, and he'd held such habits as long as she could remember.

Carl rubbed a finger across the wide scar on his temple.

"Are your headaches worse?" Deidre asked, finishing her salad. "I have more of that medicinal tea for you. It relaxes the muscles and can help you sleep. Make sure you take one of the pouches before you go."

Carl didn't answer but instead finished his meal. "Thank you." He stood and walked to the doorway.

"We have dessert, Carl," Betty said, pushing more salad onto Blake's plate.

"Don't like sweets." Carl stepped into his boots, his dark gaze meeting Laurel's.

130

"Thank you for coming home but be careful. Snowblood Peak is a dangerous place. Always has been." He turned and opened the door, walking out into the billowing snow. The door shut quietly behind him.

Blake smiled at his sister. "He never changes, right?"

Deidre sipped her wine. "It was nice of him to show up tonight, though. I thought that he might just disappear again after the sheriff yanked him into the station."

Laurel stared at the closed door. For her entire life, she'd just accepted her uncle as eccentric, and it wasn't like she'd been home a lot to interact with him. "Was he so introverted before the snowmobile crash?"

"He was always a little peculiar," Blake said, finally giving in and eating his salad. "But he got worse after his head injury. Even though he's the oldest, it feels like Deidre and I have always taken care of him, in a way."

Deidre dished more casserole onto Laurel's plate. "He's harmless, though."

Laurel couldn't tear her gaze from the door. With her uncle's size, he was anything but harmless. She shook the thought off and returned to the family dinner. The nagging concern wouldn't leave her, though. Maybe this local case was getting to her in a way other cases had not. Now she was seeing suspects in the unlikeliest of places.

Should she run a background check on her own uncle?

CHAPTER ELEVEN

The storm continued to batter the world as Laurel drove into the parking lot of her new office to begin her morning. Her heart instantly sank. Multiple news vehicles were stationed around the lot, and a group of people had gathered near her doorway. She smoothed her hair away from her face and stepped out of the Volkswagen, grabbing her laptop bag as she exited. Unfortunately, she'd had no choice but to borrow another outfit from her mother, this one a long pink skirt with a peasant blouse. At least her coat covered most of her clothing.

She pushed her way through reporters to the doorway, stopping short at seeing two men standing to the side, both with microphones held near their faces. One wore a Genesis Valley sheriff's uniform and the other a Washington State Fish and Wildlife uniform.

Oh, crap.

"It looks like the FBI has deigned to make an appearance," the sheriff drawled, his eyes beady.

The reporters turned to her, and the nearest one, a woman in her early forties, shoved a microphone in Laurel's face. "You're with the FBI? What is your response to the sheriff's claims?"

Laurel fought the urge to run through the doorway. "Considering I haven't met the sheriff during the three days the FBI has been working this case, I have no idea what his claims might be." She leveled a look at the sheriff. "I've been up on the mountain, interviewing witnesses, and at the ME's office, sheriff. Where have you been?"

The man appeared to be in his late thirties with a severely receding hair line, dark eyebrows, and a thick brown mustache. He was about five foot ten and built like a wrestler. "I've been doing my job. This is a local matter, and we'd appreciate it if the federal government let us do our jobs."

Cameras rapidly snapped pictures.

The sheriff puffed out his chest. "Go back to the big city, Agent."

The Fish and Wildlife officer just glared and didn't say anything. Apparently he hadn't received the memo about their working together.

"Who are you?" Laurel asked the older man.

The guy's chin lowered. He had to be in his midsixties with a bald head, beady brown eyes, and a beer gut. "I'm Deputy Chief Mert Wright, and I agree with the sheriff."

Well, then. Laurel forced a smile. "So much for interagency cooperation, gentlemen." It looked like she might be on her own, but she had caught more serial killers than those two combined, so she wasn't going to stop now. "If you don't mind, I need to get back to work." Now she focused on the cameras catching her every movement. "There's a killer out there, and the last thing we have time for is a pissing match over territory. When you boys grow up, give me a call." With that, she opened her door and walked inside.

Once the door shut behind her, she smacked the heel of her palm against her head. That was not good. Not at all. "Kate?" she called out, climbing the stairs and reaching the reception area, then crossing through the doorway to the hall.

Kate emerged from one of the offices with her hands full of file folders. "Did you see the disaster outside?" Today she wore dark jeans and a sweater.

Laurel sighed. "I saw the group of people and just turned the situation into a disaster. I'm not good with PR or people." She walked beyond the restrooms to the offices. The entire floor smelled like waffle cones and dust.

Kate sneezed. "As soon as we get our budget approved, we'll hire someone to clean. We sneezed all day yesterday."

"Great job. Thank you." Laurel started toward her office, but paused by the open doorway to the left, to a room she'd figured would serve as a small conference room. Three blond, teenaged girls were inside, pushing different laptops together. "Hello?"

Kate hustled up. "These are my girls, Vida, Val, and Viv, ages twelve, fourteen, and sixteen in order. They're helping to contact the FBI through those old laptops, but I'm hoping we'll get much better computers soon."

Viv, the oldest girl, had straight blond hair with wispy bangs and was the shortest of the three. "I think this room was a computer room, because it has no windows or skylights, so it's perfect for a computer center. I hope it's okay that we took it over." She grinned. "We copied your door desk idea." The kids had set up three doors on blocks, creating an efficient work area.

Val had long, straight hair without bangs. "I've never worked for the FBI before."

Vida, the youngest, was the tallest and had curly blond hair to her shoulders. "We're not really working for you, but we'll help where we can."

Laurel took in the setup. "I appreciate it."

"At the very least," Kate said, "I have an email account with the FBI now, so I can try to request furnishings."

"Fantastic," Laurel said, then turned back to the sweet teens. "Keep up the good work." She would go through the records sent from Fish and Wildlife again. "In fact, would you three like to be detectives for the day?"

"Yes," all three said instantly.

Who knew? They might be able to dig up useful information. "How about you conduct research on the Internet and all social media channels for Dr. Abigail Caine, Carl Snow, and Captain Huck Rivers?" From a professional perspective there wasn't a reason for her to request background information on any of the three, but she liked to know who she was dealing with, and she was curious to learn what was out there about Uncle Carl. She needed a computer guru, but the kids would have to do for now. Hopefully Fish and Wildlife would share any additional information they found in the video surveillance.

The girls squealed and all moved to their laptops, which ranged from a dented pink to a bright red.

"You need chairs," Laurel murmured.

"We have chairs in the car," Kate said. "Viv? Go get them, would you? They're lawn chairs, but they should do."

Laurel was working with teenagers, dented laptops, and lawn chairs. Who knew? With social media, perhaps the girls would find what she needed. "Kate? Do you have a computer?"

Kate nodded. "Yes. It's in my bag by the ice cream display case. It's old and slow, but it works. Who would you like me to spy on?"

Laurel bit her lip. "How about you do a search for missing persons fitting the general descriptions of the victims and also one for the sex offender registry in the western part of the state? We'll also need to arrange an hourly rate for your daughters, since they're working. They deserve to be paid, and I think I have a small budget to use. Thanks." Her phone rang and she lifted it to her ear while turning and walking toward her office. "Agent Snow."

"I heard the news got a hold of the case

and you've already pissed off the local sheriff," George said. "I like being the assistant director of the FBI, Snow. Don't screw things up."

"I won't." Her hands itched to knit something. It had been too long already. "While I have you, sir, could you tell me everything you know about Captain Huck Rivers? It's odd that he doesn't seem to be more actively involved with the regional Fish and Wildlife office."

"Already looked him up," George said, sounding smug. "Figured you'd ask, so I called a buddy of mine who's on the commission that oversees the Washington State Fish and Wildlife Agency." Ice clinked in a glass over the line. "Apparently, Rivers was part of a crew that dealt with the killings in Broad River near the Washington and Oregon border a couple of years ago."

Laurel filed through her memories. "I recall something about that case, but I was consulting in Germany at the time. Remember, you arranged for me to assist with the Dark Alley Killer in Berlin?"

"Yes, that's right. Anyway, in Huck's case, they had a serial killer working the line between the two states. The guy took boys aged between six and eight, and a state congressman had a son kidnapped along with another boy." More ice rattled in a glass as George drank what was probably one of his usual diet sodas. "Rivers tracked the guy to the water and saved one kid but was too late for the other. He lost it and nearly beat the killer to death — guy also happened to be a local preacher. The killer used God as part of his ritual, which is just sick and was one of the reasons Huck Rivers lost it."

Laurel could understand. "Was he diagnosed?"

"Yeah. PTSD, but the congressman called in favors and got Rivers assigned back at home with the deal that he works remotely and only during search and rescue type scenarios. It was supposed to be temporary for a couple of years, but my contact didn't know what was supposed to happen when those two years were over," George said. "Oh, before I forget, I'm pulling an agent from Portland to help you out. Quick FYI, though. They weren't sorry to lose him. Oh. I have to go." He clicked off.

Laurel rubbed her eye and her phone dinged again. "Agent Snow," she answered.

"Agent Snow. Hello," began Dr. Abigail Caine, her British accent almost unnoticeable over the phone. "That was quite a press conference I witnessed on the Internet a

140

few minutes ago. Most people might think you lost your temper for a moment there."

Laurel flipped the light switch in her office. "But not you?"

"No." Abigail chuckled. "I know better. Everything you do is deliberate, and you meant to bring the public's attention to the serial killer case, challenge those doltish-looking men to work with you, and show that you won't be cowed. You accomplished quite a bit with one little statement, didn't you?"

"You're giving me too much credit," Laurel said, shrugging out of her coat. "What can I do for you, Dr. Caine?"

Caine cleared her throat. "Abigail. I really must insist, Laurel."

Laurel sat on her folding chair and draped her coat over the back of it. She required furniture sooner rather than later. "Did your nightly meditation assist your memory?"

"Yes," Abigail said. "I feel it would benefit your case if we met and talked it through. I'm actually in town for a meeting and can be at your office in about thirty minutes. Are you free?"

Curiosity mingled with warning inside Laurel. Encouraging Abigail might be a mistake, but the woman could have pertinent information. "That would be fine. I take it you learned the location of the office from the press conference?" Maybe she could get enough furniture in the next few minutes to make the conference room useful.

"Yes. In fact, I've spent some time at the ice cream shop beneath your offices. They offer delectable pastries and lattes. Shall I grab us something to drink?" Abigail asked.

"No, thank you," Laurel said automatically. A latte sounded delicious, actually. "My assistant already brought in cappuccinos today. I'll see you when you get here." She clicked off the phone and walked down the hallway. "Kate? I'll need one more chair in my office for a meeting I'm having in a short time." She glanced at her watch. "For now, I'm running down to grab coffees. What would you all like?" She looked inside at the kids.

"Hello?" a male voice bellowed before a man strode through the doorway. He looked like an old-time detective or cop with his brown trench coat, thinning gray hair, and round belly. He had to be in his midfifties, and his hazel gaze ran over Laurel. "You must be the girl in charge. Nice press conference earlier."

Kate sputtered. "Who are you?"

"I'm FBI Agent Walter Smudgeon from

Portland. DC transferred me here to assist with the Snowblood Peak murders." He looked around. "Unfortunately."

Laurel took in the newcomer. "Call me girl again, and you're fired." Did she have the power to fire anybody? Maybe.

He blanched. "Sorry. I meant no offense." His gaze was earnest.

"You're forgiven," Laurel said instantly. Whatever had gone wrong in Portland had no bearing here, as long as he did his job. Although she did need more background on the man.

Kate visibly relaxed. "Tell you what. I'll run downstairs for coffees while you show Walter to whatever office you want him to have during this case." She snapped her fingers at her girls. "You all get vanilla steamers with no caffeine. Laurel?"

"Caramel latte, two shots, almond milk," Laurel said, studying her new agent. The guy was sweating after merely navigating the stairs.

Walter drew out his wallet and handed Kate forty dollars. "Coffee is on me."

Nice. Good olive branch. Kate obviously thought so as well, because she accepted the cash without arguing. "What's your poison?"

Walter hitched up his belt. "A quad-latte

143

with whipped cream."

Kate managed not to wince. "I'll be right back." She turned and clip-clopped across the worn wooden floor in high-heeled brown boots.

Laurel motioned for Walter to follow her to the closest office, which was down several feet on the other side of the hallway from the computer closet in the northeast corner, leaving an empty office between them. "You can have this space." The room was good sized with windows looking at the snowy mountains outside. "We're supposed to have furniture soon." Hopefully. If she had to put in a call to DC to make it happen, she would later that afternoon.

Walter looked at the view. "Works for me." He turned to face her. "Where are we on the Snowblood Peak case?"

"We'll have a briefing this afternoon after I meet with a witness, and I'll provide a profile," Laurel said. She'd studied the case file after dinner the night before, and she was ready with the profile. Two more of the deceased women had been identified, and they'd all been young, living high-risk life-styles. Seattle seemed to be the guy's hunting ground.

"I'm looking forward to it," Walter said.

Laurel looked around at the vacant space.

"For now, you could create a case board in what's going to be the main conference room, just down the hall to the right office. All you have to do is run to the store first and buy whiteboards as well as tape, magnets, and markers."

"No problem," Walter said, drawing off his trench coat to reveal a dingy, white dress shirt, stained light blue tie, and beige-colored dress pants that were stretched at the seams. He wore a brown leather shoulder holster that housed his weapon, and his badge had been secured to his belt. "I guess I'll get to work."

CHAPTER TWELVE

Laurel tried to get comfortable on the folding chair as she sipped her latte and read through the case file one more time, itching to pick up her knitting.

Viv, the oldest teenager, knocked on her open door and walked inside with a dark blue file folder in one hand, her smoothie in the other, and her laptop tucked under her arm. "I borrowed file folders from the Fish and Wildlife lady. Oh. Nice chair," she chortled.

Laurel looked at the bright pink chair across from her desk that Kate had borrowed from the ice creamery downstairs. The wooden legs of the chair had been painted a comforting yellow. "Thanks. I like to keep it professional looking in here."

"Funny." Viv seated herself, then shoved the file folder across Laurel's desk. She wore jeans, a yellow sweater, and dangly blue earrings. "This was so much fun. Is it hard to get a real job with the FBI?"

"No. But you should keep your options open and study a lot of subjects before deciding," Laurel said. "You're smart and capable and can do anything." How many times had her mother said those words to her through the years? Even when she was the youngest by far in class and her mom was working two jobs to pay rent wherever they were, Deidre built her up. Thank goodness her scholarships had paid for her tuition.

Viv blushed. "That's so cool of you to say." She leaned in. "I think I might want to chase serial killers. Why do you do it?"

Laurel blinked. It was rare to hear the question put so bluntly. "Sometimes I don't know," she admitted. "I feel like anybody who *can* stop monsters . . . should stop monsters." The simple explanation allowed her to avoid delving into her own psyche.

Viv swallowed. "I get it. Is it true that most serial killers are men?"

"Yes, although there have been a few female serial killers," Laurel said. "Aileen Wuornos is the one you hear the most about, although Amelia Dyer quite possibly murdered hundreds of children and was hanged in the late eighteen hundreds."

Viv looked out the window. "Even so, it

makes sense that most of the killers are men. Men suck."

Laurel pursed her lips. Was this about a bad breakup? If so, Laurel wasn't the person with whom to discuss it. "I actually haven't figured men out. As a gender, I mean."

"They're baboons." Viv turned back and grinned. "Have you ever been married?"

"No. You?"

Viv rolled her eyes. "Funny. My dad is a dick. Do you like yours?"

Laurel shrugged. "I never met him and have no idea who he is or who he was. My mother didn't remember."

"Huh. That kind of sucks." Viv shook herself out of her funk and pushed the file folder closer. "I loved investigating people on the Internet and didn't even feel like I was doing anything wrong, since I was helping you out. That guy Huck Rivers is seriously hot."

Laurel hid a grin. "If you like that type. What did you find?"

Viv opened her laptop to show a vlog by a pretty woman of about twenty-five. "This is Rachel Raprenzi, and she's a reporter with ULCT, an Internet news organization, in northern Oregon. I went back through several of her reports. Seems she was engaged to Huck Rivers for three months

148

before the Broad River killer case started. From what I can tell, and I'm just guessing, Rachel reported a lot of things she wasn't supposed to know, and then after the case was solved, she gave several interviews about Huck and how he was dealing with the situation after saving the congressman's kid but not the other boy. Then that was it. No more reports about Huck at all."

Laurel sipped her drink. "Sounds like Captain Rivers didn't like being talked about." Who did? She looked closer. Rachel Raprenzi had blue eyes, long blond hair, and twin dimples. Was that his type? Not that it mattered. "Good job, Viv."

"Thanks." The girl's eyes gleamed. "Here's one of the photos I found of him — shaven."

Laurel looked at his hard-cut jaw. "I think I like the scruff on him."

"Me too." Viv laughed. "Also, Dr. Abigail Caine is fascinating. I can't wait to meet her."

"Really?" Laurel flipped open the file folder. "What about her caught your attention?"

Viv took a long sip through her straw. "Her bio says she grew up in the western United States, but I couldn't find any record of her."

Laurel straightened. "She has a British accent." Had the woman faked an accent for some reason? It was possible with a narcissistic personality disorder. Perhaps the professor had been playing games with Laurel.

"Sure," Viv said. "Dr. Caine studied at Oxford, and I found some old pictures on a college website where she looked really young. But I couldn't find much before that. All of that is hard to access, while her professional life is much easier to get."

"What else did you dig up?" Laurel asked, curious.

"Well, she studied at different universities, taught at Harvard for a bit, and then took the job with Northern Washington Tech," Viv said. "She's on tenure track, whatever that means." Her eyes lit up. "I love being a spy. Guess what else?"

Was Laurel supposed to answer? "Um, what?"

"Dr. Caine is loaded. Like richer than rich." Viv took a deep drink of the smoothie before continuing. "I found an article from a pot magazine online. When marijuana was legalized in Washington State, she bought into a state-sanctioned marijuana growing operation only thirty miles from here. She doesn't need to work ever again."

"She requires a challenge for her mind,"

Laurel mused. "Does she own the operation herself?"

"No." Viv leaned forward and patted the top of the file folder. "I printed out the state documents for you but haven't had time to really go through them. It looks like she helped to create an LLC called Deep Green Grower's Company that's taxed as an S corporation with two other people, John Govern and Robert Caine."

Laurel looked down at the paper. "Robert Caine? Is he Abigail's husband or a different relative?"

"Dunno." Viv bounced on her seat. "I can't believe how easy it was to find out stuff about her."

Laurel nodded. "It's easy and dangerous, these days. You did a great job, though." Maybe Laurel could get one of the techs in DC to do a deeper dive on Dr. Abigail Caine. "Her degree in biochemistry would allow her to create her own strains of cannabis." However, there was no professional reason for the philosophy degree. Abigail was a beguiling mystery, to be sure. "I'll find out how she's related to Robert Caine." She needed to send an email with all of her requests later that day. Sometimes it took a while with the FBI.

"Maybe they were married before or

something." Viv sucked the remainder of her drink. "I couldn't find anything on him or the other guy. I've never heard of John Govern." She looked around. "You need a garbage can."

"I need a lot of things."

Viv set her empty cup on her leg.

Kate poked her head in the door. "Dr. Abigail Caine is here to see you."

Laurel closed the file folder. "Bring her in, please."

Time to play chess again.

For her trek to Genesis Valley, Abigail Caine had worn dark blue jeans, a ruffled white shirt, and a light pink suit jacket. Her earrings were Chanel, her necklace Van Cleef, and her handbag a Birkin in orange. She looked at the chair and then smiled. "You need furniture."

Laurel noted the Prada boots on Abigail's feet. The ensemble worked for the woman, even appeared understated. That took talent. "I'm sure furniture will be here soon. For now, please take a gummy-bear colored seat."

Abigail sat and crossed her legs, setting the Birkin on the floor. "I have the perfect painting to put behind your desk. The colors would be beautiful in the natural light coming over that mountain." She wiped a piece of lint off her jeans. "The blues and greens would also look lovely behind your dual-colored eyes. What do you think?"

Laurel placed her hand on the closed blue file folder. "That's very kind of you, but I am unable to accept gifts from . . . witnesses."

Abigail's grin was quick. "I like the way you play, Laurel. We both know I'm not the killer, but I appreciate the slight hint that you're looking at me." She smoothed white-blond hair over her shoulder. "It's nice to be noticed."

Laurel casually pulled a yellow legal pad from beneath the file folder. "Did you remember anything more about the man you saw near Snowblood Peak?" She reached for a pen tucked near her laptop.

"Yes." Abigail tapped her fingers on her thigh. "Did you conduct a background search on me?"

The woman needed to be the center of attention, now, didn't she? "Of course," Laurel said. "Tell me about the man."

"He was very tall with thick dark hair going gray," Abigail said. "What did you find in my past?"

Laurel couldn't quite get a read on the woman. "I discovered that you're the partial

153

owner of a cannabis farm."

Abigail's laugh was a low chuckle. "Yes, I am. It's very lucrative, as I'm sure you can imagine." She tilted her head. "The other two owners are my brother, Robert, and our friend John. We're quite the trio."

Laurel tapped her fingernails on her file folder. "Please tell me about those two."

Abigail lifted a delicate shoulder. "No. They have a right to their privacy. Even though cannabis is legal in Washington and we're licensed, not everyone agrees with our choices." She leaned forward, her eyes sparkling. "Although we are making a lot of money."

"I'm sure." Laurel stayed in place. "Back to the case. Tell me about the man you saw near the Snowblood Peak trails."

"He was tall with gray hair — probably around fifty-five or so," Abigail said.

"What else?" Laurel asked.

Abigail hummed. "Let's see. Both times I saw him, he wore a large, green flannel jacket and carried a walking stick. While he didn't seem to require assistance walking, perhaps he kept the stick to hit something. Or somebody." Her eyelashes fluttered. "Could I have been in danger that entire time?"

It was doubtful Abigail Caine had ever

been in danger. Laurel shook her head. "I don't know. The killer I'm hunting certainly likes to harm blondes."

Abigail leaned forward. "He's still out there. Perhaps I should dye my hair? What have you told your mother to do with her blond hair?"

Laurel kept her expression neutral. "Apparently you conducted research of your own."

"Of course," Abigail said. "As one prodigy to another, I admit you're fascinating. Since you no doubt were going to run my background, I felt it only fair to run yours. You'll be proud to know that your mother's teas are amongst my favorites. She puts love in every apothecary jar, doesn't she?"

"So I've read," Laurel said evenly. She needed to get that security system installed at her mom's home, and she definitely had to do a deeper dive on Dr. Caine's background. For now, she made a show of glancing at her watch. "Is there anything else you remember?"

Abigail's eyes narrowed. In the morning light from the wide window, they somehow looked a darker blue than before. "My memory is actually quite good, and I was wondering, shouldn't Captain Huck Rivers be here right now? That charade of a press

155

conference earlier notwithstanding, it appeared the other day that you two were working the case together. In fact, I'd have to say you seemed in tune with each other."

"I believe our agencies have gone their separate ways," Laurel said dryly.

"Oh," Abigail breathed, her expression softening. "In that case, would you mind terribly if I asked him out? He's so handsome and breviloquent. That's an irresistible combination for me — I don't know why. But I'd never do anything to breach this mutual admiration and curiosity you and I have developed."

What kind of game was the woman playing? "Feel free to reach out to the captain," Laurel said. "When you do, make sure you let him know how his breviloquence intrigues you. Guys love that kind of thing."

Abigail chuckled. "That's kind of you, but I believe you're as drawn to him as am I. What is it about dangerous men that appeals so to intelligent women?"

"You think Huck is dangerous?" Laurel asked.

Abigail's cheek creased in a smile. "I think he's deadly and so do you. It's all over him. Have you asked yourself why that sense of impending danger is so attractive to you? Don't you wonder? What is it?"

Laurel exhaled slowly. If she denied Huck's attractiveness, she'd be lying and would have "blinked" again. "I don't ponder silly questions. Why do you?"

Abigail rubbed her hands together. "Do you ever feel like all of the pieces have finally started to drop into place?"

"My pieces are already where they should be." Laurel set the pen down on the paper and stood. "It was kind of you to come in to provide more information, Dr. Caine. The FBI appreciates it."

Abigail also stood. In her boots, the woman was about five foot nine, so she was probably five six in her bare feet. "You're very welcome." Her chin rose.

Anticipation licked through Laurel.

"Before I forget, the man in the wilderness took pains to conceal his face. He did give me his first name though," Abigail said. "The man called himself Carl." She leaned in, her eyes gleaming. "I hope that helps."

CHAPTER THIRTEEN

Laurel couldn't eat the delicious-smelling lunch Kate ordered from Teranzoina's pizzeria. Carl? Was Abigail telling the truth or had her background research on Laurel led to Uncle Carl? There had been no mention of a scar, but if Carl had concealed his face, Abigail might not have seen it. "I don't trust a word out of that woman's mouth," Laurel muttered, although she'd have to hunt down Uncle Carl later that day and ask him some uncomfortable questions.

She stalked into the conference room to find that Walter had neatly set up a board with pictures of the identified deceased women, a place for suspects — which pretty much was limited to Carl right now — and unknowns. "Good job."

"Thanks." Walter leaned against the wall with pizza sauce on the corner of his mouth. Snow covered the skylight above him. "I turned in the receipts for the supplies to Kate."

Laurel moved to the other board to memorize an aerial map of Snowblood Peak, the river, and the surrounding land. "This is fantastic." She leaned in to study the topography. "The only way up the peak is this one trail." She cocked her head, murmuring to herself. "He would've wanted to visit the site afterward. If that wasn't possible, where would he go?"

Walter stepped up to her side, smelling of pepperoni. "What do you mean?"

She looked at the area. "This killer is organized and ritualistic, and most likely returned to the place where he disposed of the bodies. If he couldn't get there because of our investigation, is there a place he could visit to view the peak?" It was doubtful, because the cliff fell off steeply to a valley that had no ingress or egress. In the spring, when Fish and Wildlife searched again, they'd have to use helicopters to go in.

Walter pointed to an area about a mile from the parking lot. "That's the only spot. There's a nice picnic area, and if you go to the other side of the river, you can see the peak in the distance. But you can't see the cliff or the valley, so he wouldn't be able to see the bodies."

"Nobody could see the bodies," Laurel murmured. She looked outside, where the snow had finally stopped falling. "How long a break do we have with the weather? I need to see that picnic area."

Walter drew out his phone and scrolled through an app. "It's supposed to start snowing again tonight. For at least the next week." He cleared his throat. "Um, I wanted to thank you for giving me a chance here."

It was as good an opening as she would find. "What happened in Portland?" Not that she had evidence that anything specific had happened.

He sighed. "I got divorced a year ago. She left me. High and dry and in pain." His gaze didn't meet Laurel's. "I took to the bottle, and it got ugly. I didn't do my job." He wiped a hand across his forehead. "I was drunk most of the time and my colleagues covered for me, but I still screwed up. There wasn't any specific incident, and I'm working hard to be better."

It was all anybody could ask of him. "Works for me." She looked out the window. "Are you up to hiking a mile in the snow?" The guy was part of her unit now, and she was too smart to head into the wilderness alone.

"Sure." Walter licked the sauce off his lips.

160

"I have heavy snow gear in my rig. What about you? Those boots won't do it."

"They're surprisingly warm, and I have a heavier coat and gloves in my SUV," she said. "I need to run an errand now. How about I meet you in the parking area, say, around two this afternoon?"

Walter nodded. "No problem. Since you and I are the only investigators on the team, do you want to give me the profile of the killer while we hike?"

"Yes." Since it appeared the state and local authorities weren't going to work with her, Walter was the only person to share information with right now. Hopefully she could get the others to change their stance, because they'd have a better chance of finding this guy if they worked together. "I'll meet you at the area. Thanks, Walter." She grabbed her laptop bag and coat, then walked through the office to the reception area, where Kate sat on a bar stool behind the glass counter. "Any chance we have furniture coming?"

"I'm working on it." Kate swiveled on the bar stool. "I went through the GSA and so far haven't had any luck. But I'll keep trying."

"Thank you."

"No problem. I tried for a requisition to

get somebody to take down that silly wall-paper and repaint the area, but since we're only here temporarily, my request was denied. Sorry about that," she said, glaring at the faded wallpaper covered by half-naked women.

Laurel had stopped noticing the walls. "Well, you tried. I'm going to run a couple of errands and then meet Walter at the base parking area of Snowblood Peak. There's a chance we won't return today. Your kids did a good job."

"Thanks." Kate looked at Laurel's blouse. "You need a heavier jacket."

"I have one in the SUV as well as a pair of my mom's jeans." The jeans were '70's style with wildflowers embroidered down both legs, so she hadn't wanted to wear them to work. Also, she'd need to tuck the bottoms into her boots. Laurel smiled and went down the steps, then forced herself to walk into the offices of Fish and Wildlife. A young man with freckles and light blond hair sat behind the reception desk. "Hi. Could I see Captain Rivers for a moment?" she asked.

The man winced. "Um, let me check." He lifted a nearby phone and pressed a button. "Captain? The FBI agent who moved in above the ice cream shop is here to see you."

He listened and then hung up. "Huck says you can go on back."

Laurel hadn't showed her badge, so rumor of her business in town had obviously spread. She steeled her shoulders and walked around the file cabinets, noting several curious gazes as she passed by the cubicles to the hallway and then down to Huck's office. She didn't much care if she ran into the sheriff or the deputy chief on her way.

Huck sat behind his desk with a stack of manila folders in front of him, while Aeneas snored on a plush dog bed in the corner. Huck looked up when she entered. "Did you have to piss off not only my boss but the local sheriff?"

Aeneas lifted an eye, stretched to his feet, and lumbered over to nudge her hand with his nose.

She scratched behind his ears. "They started it."

Huck lowered his chin. "Laurel."

The way he said her name held a low rumble of warning. One that heated her abdomen in a way that was anything but professional. She frowned. What was happening? Sure, he was attractive, but this was business. Was Abigail correct that his aura of sheer danger drew her? Or had Abigail just planted the idea in Laurel's head?

"Laurel?" Huck asked. "You still with me?"

She jerked. "Yes. Just thinking through the case. Is there any way we could work together?"

Huck's eyebrow rose. "After your stunt earlier? No." While he didn't seem angry, he did appear dismissive.

"Very well." She straightened to her full height. "I'll provide you with a copy of the profile once I type it up, just so you have a basis from which to work. Have a nice rest of your day." With that, she turned and strode back through the office, feeling somehow bereft. She'd enjoyed working with him for a day.

Would he accept Abigail's invitation for a date?

Laurel frowned. She didn't care. She rolled her shoulders to banish the sudden itch between them.

Jagged ice encroached on the silent headstones in Genesis Valley Cemetery, the sharp points of icicles straining toward the frozen ground and the dead buried beneath. A slice of weakened sun attempted to pierce the bloated clouds but was quickly snuffed out. Laurel stepped out of her SUV, and the wind rattled the naked branches of the surrounding trees, pricking the exposed skin on her face.

She ducked her head and hustled toward the storage unit concealed beyond the shivering trees at the far corner of the graveyard. "Uncle Carl?" She knocked on the heavy wooden door.

It swung open. "What are you doing here?" Carl gestured her inside. Today he wore a blue flannel shirt, gray pants, and rubber snow boots.

She stepped inside the building that stored unmarked gravestones, shovels, and other burial equipment. "I called the main office and they said you were taking inventory out here." The wind shook the walls, and she stepped closer to the ancient wood-burning stove that heated the building.

"Yes. It's inventory time." He reached for a metal clipboard sitting on a stool.

She cleared her throat and flipped through her phone for the picture of Abigail's driver's license that Walter had acquired and texted to her at her request. He was doing a good job, so far. "Do you recognize this woman?"

Carl leaned closer and his shirt slid to the side, revealing scratches at the base of his neck. "She's pretty. Maybe I recognize her?

I don't know. Should I? Dunno from where, though."

Laurel swallowed. The walls closed in, even as they sheltered her from the brutal wind. She shook off the illogical feeling of unease and concentrated on the moment. "This woman remembers seeing you hiking beneath Snowblood Creek. Have you ever used a walking stick?"

"No, but I guess I might've used my fishing rod tube as a crutch a few times after I rolled my ankle." Carl pushed hair away from his face. "Why?"

Heat flushed down Laurel's back and she moved away from the blazing stove. "She mentioned seeing you several times, and I thought you might be a witness in my case. Do you remember seeing or hearing anything suspicious while you were out fishing or hiking?"

"No." He rubbed his graying whiskers. "I doubt I saw that pretty blond woman out by the river. I would've remembered. She looks like the weather lady on Channel 2. That's where I remember her from." He moved to the first stack of unmarked gravestones. "I'd like to get back to work before the next storm hits. This morning, I didn't even get the chance to plow my drive before coming to town." Uncle Carl lived on the

166

family farmland a few miles from Laurel's mom in an old cabin surrounded by trees.

"Of course. Uncle Carl? What happened to your neck?" Laurel asked.

He paused in the midst of counting the markers and touched his clavicle. "I was trimming the trees on the south side of the cemetery and got scratched. It's normal, and I put antiseptic on it, so don't tell your mom. She worries." He reached into his pocket and drew out a couple of candies. "Oh. These are good." He tossed one toward Laurel.

She caught it and glanced down at the wrapped purple drop. "Grape?"

"Huckleberry," Carl said, unwrapping his and popping it in his mouth. "The Genesis Valley Church makes and sells them locally, with half of the proceeds going to the elementary school. Things actually taste like real huckleberries, not just purple sugar."

Laurel tucked the candy in her purse. "Thank you. Do you have anything else that might help me in my investigation?"

He shook his head, his gaze not meeting hers. But he rarely made eye contact, not even on Christmas. "No. Have you been listening to the sheriff? Am I a suspect?"

She stepped back, her chest aching. "Why would you be a suspect?"

He did meet her gaze finally, and his eyes were so similar to her mother's that her stomach cramped. "Because you're questioning me. I might not be the smartest guy around, but I can tell when you're in cop mode."

She shook her head, her breath quickening. The last person she'd want to hurt was her shy uncle. "No. I'm just following up on a witness's statement and wondered if you were another witness. Anybody familiar with Snowblood Peak and the surrounding trails might have information they don't realize we need. If you were a suspect, I wouldn't be talking to you alone." That might not be the truth.

"Oh." He smiled. "Okay." The wind clattered ice against the outside of the storage unit. "You should get going, Laurel. Another storm is coming."

She shivered, too far from the fireplace to feel its heat. "All right. Call me if you think of anything else, okay?"

"I will." Carl turned and pushed his hair away from his face. "I'd never kill anybody. Just thought I should tell you."

"I know." She opened the door and strode back into the punishing weather. It was entirely possible that Abigail had been taunting her. If so, she'd done a good job.

CHAPTER FOURTEEN

Laurel slid the SUV to a stop in the vacant parking area at the base of Snowblood Peak. In front of the vehicle, a low rolling fog wound through the trees with ghostlike tendrils, and she shivered. She opened the door and secured her coat, zipping it up and then pulling a hat onto her head and gloves onto her hands. She'd tucked a flashlight in her pocket and her gun at her waist. The solid feeling of the weapon gave her a sense of control in the desolate area.

The wildly flowered jeans were warm on her legs but uncomfortable stuffed into her boots because they were too long.

She surveyed the area. The lot had been plowed that morning, but solid ice had hardened over the asphalt. Silence, complete and full, surrounded her as if the wilderness held its breath; even the wind had given up the battle for now. Snow and ice hung motionlessly from the surrounding trees.

Alone. She was entirely alone, the sole breathing human for miles.

A tingling at the base of her neck brought her to a standstill. Slowly, she scanned the entire area around her, but only saw watchful trees, sharp rocks, and frozen brush. Against all logic, adrenaline surged into her bloodstream, urging her body to flee.

She centered herself and kept her hand loose in case she needed to reach for her weapon. She looked up at Snowblood Peak. Its jagged edges rose high, puncturing the bellies of the turgid clouds. Even from this distance, she could see icicles hanging precariously from the rock face, waiting to drop and slice through an unsuspecting animal.

Her shiver this time wasn't caused by the chilly weather.

She squared her stance and stared at the peak, mute witness to the atrocities carried out on the trail. If only the rocks could talk.

A rumble sounded from the road, and a dinged-up blue truck stopped next to her SUV. Walter jumped out, slapping a hat over his wide head. "Sorry I'm late. Had some trouble getting the engine to start." He zipped up a heavy-looking green parka and drew the hood over his hat. "You ready?" He tucked gloves over his beefy hands.

Relief slowed her heartbeat, and she gave herself a second to regain control. "It's good to see you. I was letting my imagination run away with me out here by myself."

Walter wiped at a yellow stain on his coat and tucked a flashlight into his pocket. "You don't seem like the imaginative type. More like a Mr. Spock than a Captain Kirk."

Laurel pulled her gloves farther up her wrists. "Thank you?"

"Wasn't an insult. Just an observation." Walter clapped his gloves together and looked down the trail. "Although, I get it. Standing here with just the two of us, I can feel those souls wandering beneath that peak. Like they're stuck in that valley until we figure out what happened."

"You believe in ghosts?" Laurel asked, truly curious.

"No, but I believe in souls, good and evil." Walter peered up at the darkening clouds, his eyes more brown than green in the already dimming light. "We'd better get a move on. The storm is coming."

"Yes." She shook off her unease, turned, and led the way through an opening in the short metal fence enclosing the parking area, then followed a trail thick with snow. She sank in up to her knees, so she kicked her way between the trees just waiting to dump their load on her head.

"Want me to take the lead?" Walter asked, already huffing behind her as they followed the trail down toward the picnic area by the river. At least one of his knees popped every few yards, and he was mouth breathing, which indicated that his body was under duress.

She shook her head and slowed her pace so his breathing could level out. "Not yet. I'm fine for now." If the man had a heart attack, she wouldn't be able to carry him back up the trail. Was there a polite way to recommend he try to breathe out of his nose, so his body received the message that he wasn't being attacked? "Let me know if you need a break."

"I don't," he said shortly, but a cough ruined his curt response. His cough was wet, indicating that his lungs were having problems with either the exertion or the cold air.

Perhaps bringing Walter had been a bad idea, although she'd had to follow protocol. Backup was a must in this type of situation, especially since she wasn't knowledgeable of the area. She'd much rather be with Captain Rivers, as he no doubt knew the area better than anybody else. She would not wonder if he had accepted a first date with Abigail Caine. It was none of Laurel's business. She shrugged off regret and kept descending, holding onto an ice-encrusted wooden railing as she maneuvered down some steps to another trail below. Snow clung to her gloves. Sound finally penetrated the heavy silence as she edged closer to the water.

The river crackled along its craggy banks, scraping ice across the protruding rocks. She took a break, bending over to catch her breath. With the frigid air and thick snow, it was difficult to continue, and she was in better physical shape than was Walter. She swallowed, and the freezing air burned her throat. Why hadn't she thought to bring a lip balm? Her lips were already cracking.

Walter lumbered up next to her, panting louder than any animal. He coughed and the sound was wetter than before. He turned his head and spit into the snow. Hopefully it was just phlegm and not blood.

She looked up and over, seeking any hint of red in the snow. Nope. No red. Good. "Are you okay? This is tougher than I expected." She'd hoped the snow would've melted a little. Her borrowed jeans were soaked, and even though she'd donned long underwear beneath them, her skin was cold and wet. Very uncomfortable. The boots weren't waterproof, and her toes hurt. Actually, that was good. The second she couldn't feel them, she was in trouble. "Walter?"

"I'm fine." His cheeks were a damask color and sweat dripped down the side of his face. He'd paled beneath his eyes until dark circles stood out. His jowls shook around his jaw and his Adam's apple moved rapidly.

She fought the inclination to measure his pulse. "If you want to guard this area, I'll continue to the bridge we saw on the map."

"I'm guarding you," he retorted, his skin gray beneath the ruddiness.

She stood upright and stretched her neck. "I'm a good shot, Walter. I don't need guarding, but I always take backup. You're struggling, and if something goes wrong, I won't be able to carry you up this trail before you freeze to death." While she didn't like being unkind, she'd like it less if he stroked out and died.

Snow began to fall. "Crap," Walter muttered. "I'm going with you. Let's do this now. If the next storm is as bad as it looked on the Weather Channel, this is going to be our only chance for a while."

Well, he was an adult, and she wasn't going to pull rank yet. She turned and found purchase with her boots before continuing along the trail by the icy cold river. If she stayed to the left of the trail, closer to the water, the snow wasn't as deep. Her way became easier as the trees thickened, providing shelter above them. After another half hour of walking, they reached a whimsically arched bridge that spanned a narrow stretch of the river.

"There you go. We just cross that and we'll be at the picnic area. The place should have a name, don't you think? Instead it's just listed as a picnic spot on the maps." Walter grabbed his belly and coughed several times. "I'm fine. Guess I should start working out more."

Laurel looked at her watch. She couldn't let him rest any longer. "It's after three. Let's record the area and get out of here before we lose more daylight." She turned and grabbed the wooden railing of the bridge to haul herself up and through the snow. The flashlight in her pocket felt leaden, but she trudged onward, reaching the center of the bridge and then descending. Her boots slipped several times, but she kept her balance by utilizing the thick railings and watching her foot placement carefully.

Finally, she reached the other side and waited for Walter. He rejoined her with a pained wheeze. Snow clung to his hat and parka, which bulged in the middle. He pointed. "That way, back up the river. The picnic spot is just a few hundred yards from here, and the outhouses are yards beyond that in the trees against the rocks and away from the river."

"I see picnic tables." Out of nowhere, the wind kicked into an angry gale, nearly tossing her backward. She spit out snow and then lowered her head, fighting both the wind and the thick snow to travel the short distance. Her ankle ached from being twisted the other night, her thighs protested, her toes tingled with pain, but she trudged onward. A picnic table came into view, buried to the seats. She turned to stare across the river and up to the north, spotting one side of Snowblood Peak. "There it is."

Walter shoved through snow, his breathing labored. "Yeah." He looked up. "See how the peak is visible but the other side, where the bodies were thrown, is not? There's no way the guy could come here and see anything."

"He could see the peak," she murmured, shivering in the cold. "Imagine it. He's here, surrounded by cheerful picnickers and people rafting the river, and only he knows about those bodies. They're just barely hidden, but he's in control. Oh, he came here, Walter." It was unfortunate there weren't any Fish and Wildlife cameras anywhere near them. She backed against the picnic table. How many times had the killer sat right there?

The snow began to fall faster, and the wind blew icy flakes sideways. "How do you think like a psychopath so easily?" Walter asked.

"I don't know," she said, stepping on the buried seat to plant her butt on the picnic table. That was a question she'd never wanted to delve into too deeply, and now certainly wasn't the right time to even think about it. There was no question genius and madness almost overlapped on the clock of life, and her ability to dig into the criminal mind lived in the half-minute between those two. She let herself feel the moment and do her job without questioning herself. "Yeah. He sat right here and watched the peak. The face watched right back," she whispered.

Walter took out his cell phone and started snapping pictures. "I'll record the area for our case board," he said, apparently ignoring her statement.

"Thank you." She closed her eyes and let the cold batter her, imagining a summer

day with the killer on the tabletop and tour-
ists all around, having no idea who or what
he was. He'd love that. Get off on it. Maybe
look for his next victim? Or were all of his
victims high-risk young women taken off
the streets of Seattle? Hopefully the techs in
DC would be on it. She'd sent several
emails before leaving the office.

"I'm done with the pictures, and we need
to go. This storm is coming in hard and fast.
I can barely see. Do you have what you
needed?" Walter asked.

"Yes." She had a better feel for this guy
than she had before. "Thank you for coming out here." The wind blew her hat off,
and she caught it, shoving it back into place.
"Let's get out —" A flash of color near the
river caught her eye. "What is that?"

Walter squinted through the now-swirling
snow. "I don't see anything."

"Look at the area closer to the bridge."
She jumped off the table, kicked snow out
of her way, and created a trail down to the
river's edge at the side of the bridge. Her
heart thumped and she tried to run faster
but nearly fell on her face and had to slow
down. Her ears rang and her heart dropped
to her aching feet. "Oh, no," she whispered.

A naked female body, gray and frozen in

death, lay on the icy rocks, feet in the water and blond hair tangled in the snow.

CHAPTER FIFTEEN

"Holy shit." Walter struggled by Laurel's side. "Is that a body?" He grabbed her arm and stumbled along.

Laurel reached the body and crouched down, careful to restrain herself from disturbing the surrounding area. Her injured ankle protested with a spasm, and she rode out the pain. Sorrow attacked her on the heels of dizzying anger. She breathed deeply to keep herself under control. "She's young. Maybe nineteen or twenty." The woman had blond hair and ligature marks on her wrists and ankles as well as bruising on her neck and body. Her eyelids were closed and her skin a pale gray from being frozen. "She was placed here between the last storm and this one, so maybe in the last twelve hours?"

Walter turned his head and coughed, the sound rattling. He heaved several times but didn't throw up. "Sorry. Need to stop drinking."

Laurel looked at the bridge and across the river. "He didn't hide her this time. Since we found his dumping ground off Snow-blood Peak, is he showing off for us?"

"How could he be? There's no way he'd know we were coming here," Walter whispered, looking around at the rapidly darkening day. He set his hand on his weapon, which was visible beneath his coat. "I didn't tell anybody about our plans. Did you?" His voice rose slightly.

"No," Laurel said. "But it makes sense that searchers would canvass the surrounding areas while the storm abated." She stared at the dead female and fought the human urge to cover the body with her coat. Nobody should be laid to rest like that. Even though the woman had passed on, it was a travesty to leave her cold and alone.

"Then why?" Walter snapped.

Laurel shook her head, careful to keep snow from landing on the body. "I think he's playing a game with us. If we find this body and witness his handiwork, then he wins. If we miss the body, then he leaves us another one. Either way, he wins."

Walter scratched his forehead. "So he didn't really care if we found her?"

Laurel shook her head. "The victims don't mean anything to him after they're dead."

Yes, she was getting a clear picture of this guy. "He'll keep leaving victims for us now that he's engaged. We interrupted his game, and now he's going to force us to play."

"That's nuts," Walter snarled. "Look what he did to her. There's bruising on her inner thighs."

"I know," Laurel said quietly, trying to banish her feelings so she could think more clearly. "We have to get the body out of this weather."

Walter reached into his jacket and drew out a radio. "No cell service out here, but I came prepared." He looked over at the bridge. "We didn't see her when we crossed, but I was watching my feet to make sure I didn't slip. How about you?"

"Same," Laurel said. She stared beyond the picnic area at the solid rock face leading up to another set of peaks. "Is there a way to reach this area besides following the trails we just used?"

Walter shrugged. "I don't know."

If not, how close had they come to seeing the killer? There hadn't been tracks, so they'd missed him by at least an hour if not more. That feeling of being watched that she'd had in the parking area — was there a place he might have hidden? She couldn't think of where, but that instinctual warning had been intense.

Walter frowned and looked around. "I know from the maps that we're on state land right now. This side of the river and mountains all belong to the state rather than the federal government."

Laurel leaned over and scanned the ice-burned flesh. "He had you for a while, didn't he?" she whispered. Shallow cuts accompanied the bruising across the woman's ribs and down her hips. "She wasn't just tossed here. See how her feet are set between those two rocks so the body doesn't get pulled into the river?"

Walter leaned closer. "Yeah, and her head is settled in an indentation as if he kicked a small hole for it."

Laurel pointed to the woman's hands, which lay palms down with the fingers perfectly extended. Snow began to pile up between the fingers and cover the nails, which were painted a dark red with no chips. "It looks like he painted her nails before he placed her by the river." She craned her neck to see the feet in the water. "Same with her toes." They were a bright and unblemished red. "There wasn't any mention of nail polish in the autopsies of the other victims, and the one body I saw didn't have painted nails."

Walter paled as the wind blew the bottom of his parka tight against his body. "So this is a new thing?"

Laurel forced herself to drop into the mind of the killer. "Is he making her pretty for us? Or is he just messing with us? I don't know." She leaned closer. "Is that eye shadow?" It was difficult to tell if the woman wore makeup because of the gray tinge to her skin. "I think so. Her eyelashes are very dark as well, and that's probably mascara." Not one smudge showed beneath the victim's eyes. Had the killer polished her nails and made up her face after bringing her out to the picnic area? "He likes to take risks."

"Why would a man do up her face like this?" Walter scouted the darkened trees beyond the outhouses. "Keep an eye out. He might be watching us."

"It's possible but doubtful. He wants to play for a while, but getting caught now wouldn't work for him. Shooting us might, though." She scouted the entire area. "He's not here, Walter. We have to protect the remains as best we can from the elements. Just in case he made a mistake this time."

"This guy doesn't make mistakes," Walter muttered, his hand waving the radio.

As she blinked snow out of her eyes, her

neck chilled and her skin prickled. The murder was under state jurisdiction for the time being, which actually was fine with her. "Call in Fish and Wildlife, and then let's try to find something to protect the body."

Walter made the call on the radio, which crackled ominously. Then he tucked it away. "We could use one of our coats to shield her, but then we'd risk hypothermia. It's not worth taking that chance, Agent Snow."

"Agreed." She moved to the other side of the victim and put herself between the wind and the body, taking out her cell phone to capture the macabre scene before snow concealed everything. "This will have to do."

Walter crossed to her side and dropped noisily to his haunches to help block the wind. He breathed out of his mouth again. "They shouldn't be too long. We left a trail, right?" His grim smile didn't convey humor.

The snow had already covered their trail, but their location would be easily found. Laurel finished taking her pictures, fighting both the snow and piercing wind. The light continued to die, and the temperature dropped as the wind and snow picked up speed and strength. They took turns trying to protect the body and then moving around to keep their limbs from freezing. Finally, lights and the sound of movement came from the other side of the river.

"It's about time," Walter groused, standing and groaning as he stretched his back.

Laurel shivered and put her gloved hands in her pockets.

Aeneas barked and bounded through the snow to them. Snow covered his nose as well as a green jacket that protected his body from the elements.

"Hi, boy," she said, her teeth chattering.

Using bright flashlights, three officers followed the dog, all wearing heavy Fish and Wildlife coats, ski pants, and wonderfully thick-looking boots. Laurel recognized Huck, Monty, and Ena. Huck and Ena carried a stretcher between them. Laurel waved and her freezing arm protested.

Huck set the stretcher to the side and reached her first. He dragged a silver blanket from a pack strapped to his back. "You're too cold." He settled the material over her shoulders as Ena did the same for Walter. Even in the storm, he smelled like pine and mint.

Laurel caught herself before she could move into Huck's heated body to warm up. The guy was not inviting, and there was a heater calling her name from her SUV.

Monty flashed his light over the dead woman. "She's frozen solid. Let's lift." He gingerly stepped into the clear river and grasped her ankles as Huck reached for her shoulders. They easily lifted her and set her on the stretcher.

Huck finished securing the body with straps. "I want to put a blanket over her." His face was a hard mask.

"I know," Laurel said, stepping closer to his solid form. "I do as well, but if there's any evidence on her, we don't want to contaminate it if possible. She can't feel the cold any longer, Huck."

"Small comfort." He stopped staring at the woman's icy face. "Let's get out of here. We're all going to be okay." His face still held fury, but his voice was deep and re-assuring, even heard through the screaming wind. "We cut in a decent trail on the way here, although the snow is starting to pile again. Aeneas will lead, then Ena, then Walter, and then Laurel. Monty and I will bring up the rear with the body on the litter. Go. Now."

Nobody argued. Apparently Huck took point out in the wilderness rather than Monty.

The wind battered Laurel's freezing face and the snow bombarded her, but she tugged out her flashlight to light her path as she followed Walter. Even though he was gasping for air, he maintained a decent speed. After a while, Laurel moved on autopilot. One foot in front of the other. When her ankle protested, she tried to put more weight on the other foot. Walter stumbled and she reached out to help him, but he caught his balance first.

The cold became freezing and then nothing. Not a good sign. She had no choice but to keep moving forward. When the numbness became unbearable, she flicked through *The Iliad* in her head as a tribute to Aeneas.

Finally, blue and red swirling lights flashed through the snowy trees.

Laurel kept moving.

They rounded a bend to find an ambulance and paramedics waiting. Huck and Monty hefted the body into the back of the ambulance, strain on their faces.

Huck looked at Laurel. "You both need to get checked out."

"No," Walter said, his steps sluggish. "I'm going home and taking a long shower with a bourbon in my hand." He wiped off his windshield and opened his door, looking over his shoulder. "Do you need a ride, Agent Snow?"

"No," she said, her throat hurting. "Thank you, though. After this, you should call me Laurel, don't you think?"

"Sure." He started his truck, waited a moment, and then slowly drove out of the lot. Could he even feel his hands? His gloves had been high quality, so maybe he was feeling better than she did right now.

"You're not driving," Huck said, crossing his arms.

Her hands weren't working, so it was difficult to argue with him.

The paramedics shut the ambulance door.

"I don't need medical care, but I shouldn't drive," Laurel said.

Huck nodded to the paramedics. "She's okay. Take the body to the ME's office." He tossed keys to Ena. "You okay to drive?"

"I'm fine," the woman said.

"Great. We're up late, so let's get some sleep tomorrow. Pick me up around ten in the morning. By then, the ME should have a preliminary report for us. Thanks." Huck took Laurel's arm and escorted her to her SUV. "Keys?"

Laurel tried to dig them out of her pocket.

Huck took over, easily extracting them before opening the passenger side door and helping her in. "Hold tight for a sec." After shutting the door, he wiped the snow off the front window, then took off his coat and tossed it across the back seat for Aeneas to sprawl on. Finally, he slid inside, started the

189

engine, and turned on the defroster. "Tell me now. How bad are your toes and fingers?"

They were warming up already now that she was out of the storm. "They tingle and hurt, but I have full feeling," she said, holding back a gasp at the pain.

"Good." Huck reversed out of the lot and swung around to drive down the road. "You need warm food and possibly compresses, and my place is closer than your mother's. Let's go there and check you out. After I feed you, I'll take you home. Deal?"

She didn't want her mom to see her in pain, and dinner sounded like a good idea. Her stomach rumbled. She'd only had that latte earlier in the day, and her body required fuel to repair itself. "That's a good idea." Her teeth started to chatter.

CHAPTER SIXTEEN

Huck settled Aeneas down as the microwave went to work on the pot pies he'd purchased the day before. The hot food filled the kitchen with a delicious aroma. "Are your boots off?" he called to the great room, where he already had a fire going.

"Yes." Laurel's hair was a curly mass down her back, and in the firelight, the natural red highlights in the brown caught the glow of the flames.

He hadn't liked seeing her lips so blue and her body so small in the angry storm. He poured two glasses of warm bourbon and crossed to the sofa, where she sat wiggling her toes in front of the fire. "Drink this."

She looked up, her blue and green eyes bright in her pale face. "You're a little bossy, Captain."

"I'm a lot bossy, and I told you to call me Huck." He sat on his coffee table and reached for her foot, drawing off the sock.

191

Her toes were a healthy shade of pink. He secured them in one hand, struck by how cold they still were. With the fire crackling behind him and the storm raging outside, a sense of intimacy wound through the room. He ignored it. He'd do this for any colleague. "Wriggle them."

Amusement tilted her lips, but she did as he'd ordered while simultaneously sipping her drink.

He lightly pinched each one. "Do you feel this?"

"I do and I do not like it. Stop pinching me." She tipped back her head and drank the entire glass. "Oh, that's warm. So warm and nice."

He secured her other foot and checked out the toes. "You're doing all right. No permanent damage and I don't see frostbite. Your boots worked better than I expected." He then took her hands. They were small and in proportion with the rest of her, but her fingers were long and her nails short. "Do you feel this?" He pressed against each of her fingers, noting how fragile her bones were.

"Yes." She wiggled both hands.

The skin appeared healthy and unburned.

He released her and sat back to study her face. "Your skin is burned, and your lips

192

chapped. I'll get you some lotion that will help." He handed his drink to her.

She accepted it, swirling the amber liquid in the crystal glass. "I know it was your job, but thank you for coming out to get us and the body."

He should find the lotion for her. Hurry away from her. There was something undeniably delicate about this brilliant woman, and she drew him in a way that would be a disaster for them both. Yet he set a knuckle beneath her chin and lifted it anyway. Those dual-colored eyes knocked him back as usual. "I'd come and get you even if it wasn't my job."

Surprise lit her eyes.

He was such a jackass. "I'll get you the lotion." Releasing her chin, he began to stand, noting that her shoulders were still shivering. "Keep this blanket on you." He tucked the heavy material across her lap. "Food will also help." The last thing he needed was to get involved with an FBI agent, especially one who tried so hard to hide her soft underbelly. While he might not be a genius like Laurel, he'd always been able to read people, and he sensed that this woman's brain was constantly fighting her heart. He wasn't the guy to ease her struggle when he had so many of his own.

She settled back on the worn cushions and drank his bourbon.

He moved to the kitchen and took the pot pies out of the microwave before heading into the lone bathroom for lotion. Where had he put that crap? Finally finding the tube at the back of the cupboard beneath the sink, he returned to find Laurel with her head resting against the sofa and her eyes closed, breathing softly. "Laurel?"

The woman didn't stir.

He sighed and dug her cell phone out of the pocket of her coat, which she'd left hanging by the door. Interesting. She didn't have it password protected. Must be a personal phone and not her FBI-issued one. He scrolled through and pressed DIAL for "mom."

"Hi, Honey. What's up?" came a woman's voice.

He cleared his throat. "Um, hi. This is Fish and Wildlife Captain Huck Rivers. Laurel is fine, but she got a little cold out investigating today, and she's sleeping on my sofa." This was a new one on him. He'd never checked in with anyone's mother before. "I, ah, can wake her and bring her home. Or just bring her asleep, actually." Her body had shut down to heal and warm itself, and it'd be easier not to awaken her.

"Or I can let her sleep here, but I wanted to let you know where she is and get direction from you."

Laurel's mom was silent for several moments. "I know where you are. If you hurt my girl, I'll come for you."

Okay. That was weird. Wasn't the woman some sort of Zen-tea guru? "Got it," he said. He grimaced.

"You're lucky that Laurel texted me when she arrived at your house an hour ago. She wasn't sure when she'd make it home," Deidre said.

Of course. Huck shook his head. His father had never worried much about him, so he'd never had to check in with anybody. It made sense that Laurel had already texted. "In that case, I'll let her sleep. Thank you."

"Have her call me first thing in the morning. If I don't hear from her by eight, I'm calling the sheriff." The woman hung up.

Huck stared at the phone in his hand. Right. He laid it on the sofa table next to Laurel and nearly jumped out of his socks when his phone buzzed from his back pocket. What the hell was wrong with him? He lifted it to his ear and dropped into the chair by the fireplace, watching the sleeping woman. "Rivers."

"Hi, Captain. Is there any reason you didn't call me with the information that another body was found?" Deputy Chief Mert Wright snapped.

Huck immediately stood, snatched his now-empty glass off the sofa table, and stalked back into his kitchen. "The body is at the ME's office, and I don't have any other information at this time." He poured himself a generous refill and then returned to his seat, a headache starting to thrum at the base of his skull. The last person he wanted to deal with was the moron who'd held a news conference side by side with the dumbass sheriff. "I planned to call you tomorrow."

"When we're in the middle of a serial killer investigation, I expect to be kept up to date by the minute," Wright said.

Huck tipped back a deep drink of bourbon and almost moaned when the heat hit his gut. "Like I said, when I have information, I'll share it." He watched the firelight play through the flames that highlighted Laurel's hair. Auburn was the only way he could describe it. Brown, red, even hints of blond . . . and it was natural. Regardless of what she'd said to Dr. Caine. "The vic was female, young, bruised, and blond." There. Now his boss was up to date. At least he'd headed back to Seattle after creating a shit-storm with his press conference in town.

The sound of shuffling papers came over the line. "The media got a hold of the story, and I just finished speaking with the governor. She wants an interagency task force set up, and for some reason, she wants you to head it."

That was because the governor wasn't a moron, unlike the deputy chief. "Fine," Huck said, his fingers itching to run through Laurel's hair. He had to get her out of his place as soon as possible the next day. She was a temptation he neither needed nor wanted. Well, one he didn't need, anyway. "Is that all?"

"No." Wright sighed. "The governor insists that the FBI be included, especially that short, young agent with the pretty face and weird eyes. Apparently her track record for catching serial killers is remarkable enough to impress our governor as well as the AG. We've already coordinated with DC, and she's on your team. Whether you like it or not." Now he sounded smug.

Huck hated smug. "Wouldn't think of having a task force without her. She seems bright and hard working." He tipped back his glass and drank the contents in one swallow, unable to look away from the fragile form on his sofa. Small and easily breakable weren't his thing. Never had been. So why couldn't he stop looking at her delicate bone structure and the gentle slope of her slightly parted lips?

Wright sputtered. "What? You hate working with anybody — even your own team. Don't tell me you're falling for this chick."

"Not my type," Huck said honestly. Laurel was nowhere near his type, and he knew it. "I don't think you're supposed to call an FBI special agent a chick. This one carries a gun and doesn't seem afraid of anything or anyone. Just FYI."

"While this one may be brilliant, rumor has it she doesn't work closely with others. An FYI for you," Wright returned.

Huck stretched his back and set the glass on the mantel. "Then we have that in common. We're dealing with a serial killer who all of a sudden wants to play games." Laurel had filled him in on the way to his cabin. "I'd think that having a profiler, one known to have impressive skills, would be a good thing for all of us. We need to catch this guy before he kills another woman."

"Agreed," Wright said. "We'll keep the county police informed, but right now, the task force consists of you and Monty from Fish and Wildlife, Sheriff York from the local community, and the very impressive chick with the freaky eyes and red hair from the FBI."

Huck swallowed his irritation. "Her hair isn't red, and her eyes aren't freaky. They're heterochromatic." He'd looked it up the other day for no reason other than curiosity. Yeah. That was it. He finally tore his gaze away from her sleeping form. "You're not on the task force?" He didn't hide the grin in his voice.

"No. The governor thought I'd be more helpful elsewhere," Wright said, *almost* concealing his annoyance over that fact.

Yeah. The governor definitely had a brain. "Very well. I'll be in touch when I have news."

Wright cleared his throat. "You've been much more accommodating about this than either I or the governor expected." Now the guy sounded regretful. Had he looked forward to an argument? "I don't need to remind you that fraternizing with an FBI agent, especially considering your issues, would be a public relations nightmare. The governor hates PR problems, as you know."

"Then why are you reminding me?" Huck drawled, stretching to his feet. "I am happy to work with the other agencies, and I doubt I'll be in close contact with the FBI agent.

But thanks for having my back. Got to go." He clicked off the call.

Laurel mumbled something in her sleep, stretched, and rolled off the sofa.

He dodged forward and caught her before she could hit the wooden floor. "Laurel?"

She breathed easily and didn't stir.

He grinned. When she slept, she was out. He shook his head and strode with her to the bedroom. Her clothes were still wet, and now his T-shirt was damp.

Aeneas barked from the other room, no doubt wanting to be let out one more time before going to sleep.

Huck placed Laurel dead center in the middle of the bed so if she rolled over, she wouldn't fall. "I'll be back in a little while," he whispered, turning and exiting the room after throwing a blanket over her. If her clothing was still wet when he returned, he'd have to do something about it, and he didn't want to think about that.

Right now, he needed to let his dog out, lock the SUV, and secure his homestead for the night. His job never ended. He slipped on his boots, whistled for the dog, grabbed his coat, and headed out into the storm.

His muscles already ached from the cold. Hopefully he could be quick about it this time.

CHAPTER SEVENTEEN

Snow fell from the rooftop, hitting the ground with a thud, and Laurel jerked awake. Warmth surrounded her along with peaceful quiet. She took inventory. Soft sheets, heavy blankets, a heated body behind her. Her eyelids shot open. Heated body? Wait a minute. She gingerly turned around to see Huck Rivers on his back, the covers pushed to his waist, his eyes closed and his breathing even. One sinewy arm was up and curved beneath his head. Man, he had big hands.

She experienced a full body roll at the sight.

Sleep had calmed the normally harsh lines of his rugged face, although the dark whiskers covering his sharp jawline gave him a wild look. His chest was muscled with a nice amount of hair that led south. His form was a solid presence in the bed, and he took up more than his share of space. Although, it was his bed, so perhaps it was all his share.

His eyelids opened and his gaze focused instantly on her. "Morning." The low rumble of his voice caught her in inappropriate places.

She took stock of her clothing. An overlarge shirt covered her, but her legs and feet were bare and extremely toasty. No bra, no long underwear, but her panties were in place.

"Your clothes were wet. I didn't look." His grin held the hint of a rogue. "Much."

She blinked. "You could've left me on the sofa."

"I could have, but you fell off once and wouldn't stop shivering. Putting you to bed was the safest way to protect you from yourself." He stretched and a lot of natural muscle flexed. "Body heat and warm blankets are the best way to fix shivering, and you slept peacefully all night. Well, mostly. Did you know that you talk in your sleep?"

She settled back down, resting her face on her hand as she looked at him. "Yes. Not all the time, though."

"Who's Lucas?"

She closed her eyes. "I talked about Lucas? Seriously?"

"If he's a rat-bastard jackass, then yes, you talked about Lucas." Huck pushed a way-

202

ward curl off her forehead and then drew back his hand quickly. He shook his head.

She sighed. "Lucas is my ex, and he's most certainly a jackass." Why the heck had she talked about him? "For a profiler, I really don't read men very well. Or anybody close to me, I guess." She'd always wanted to be good with people but was better with cold facts. Her gaze raked Huck's very impressive chest. "Your sternum is perfectly symmetrical." She stretched out her free hand. "May I?"

His eyes darkened. "Sure."

Wonder, a new feeling, filtered through her when she placed her palm over his chest. The muscles felt just as strong and solid as they looked. Her body awakened. "I'm not looking for a romance," she whispered.

"Neither am I." He remained still, watching her in a way she wasn't sure anybody had before. With hunger and warning in his amber-colored eyes.

"I like you and we're here. Want to take advantage of the moment?" she asked.

He flattened his broad hand over hers on his chest, swallowing even her wrist. "Do I want to? Yes. Am I going to? No." He tightened his hold and lifted her hand, gently placing it back on the bedcovers before rolling toward her and revealing even more corded muscle in his bicep and tricep areas. "We should get going."

Curiosity took over. "You don't find me attractive?" Had she misread his expression? That was rare for her.

"You're beautiful," he murmured. "I think you know that."

She shook her head, catching her hair on the pillow. "Not true. Some people find me pretty, while others think I'm weird looking. My eyes throw people off. Do they throw you off?"

"I like them," he said, his gaze running over her face. "The colors are spectacular, and I like that you don't hide the difference by using contacts."

She swallowed. "Oh. Are you seeing somebody?" If so, she really should get out of his bed.

"No."

She paused. What in the world? He was a puzzle missing a piece. An equation lacking a differential. "Oh. You don't like me." That wasn't new for her, either. Most people didn't understand her, and frankly, she often didn't understand herself. She really should get to work.

"I like you fine." He tugged on a piece of her hair, his gaze fixed on it. "Here's the deal, Laurel. I'm not a quick, take-the-edge-off or take-advantage kind of guy. When I'm in a woman, I'm *in* that woman."

Her mouth went dry. Desire filtered through her in a combination of estrogen, progesterone, and testosterone, quickening her breath and tightening her nipples. "I'm not that small, Huck. Sure, we have definite size differentials, but I promise you, all of our parts were made to work together." Her mother would think it sweet he'd been worried about her.

He barked out a laugh. "I was speaking metaphorically, not physically, Agent."

She wasn't following him. How fascinating. She opened her mouth but couldn't think of a thing to say.

He released her hair. "Distance isn't an attribute in my relationships, and if I sleep with a woman, that's what it is. A relationship. I give as much as I take, and I expect as much as I give." His gaze softened. "I don't want that right now, if ever again. I can't be responsible for somebody else and would rather be alone, anyway."

"Okay."

"Plus, I think I'd have a hard time dating you."

Should that hurt her feelings? Oddly enough, it did. "Why?"

He shrugged.

She lowered her chin and studied him. Finally went with her brain instead of her rioting body. "Oh. I see."

One of his dark eyebrows rose. In the bed, in the morning light, it was an arrogant movement. But it worked for him. "You do?"

"Yes." His job, his past, his childhood without a mother. "I understand." He couldn't sit by and watch a woman he was dating put herself in danger without stepping in front of her. He was a protector — a modern-day warrior. It was impressive that he recognized those traits in himself, and even more impressive that he hadn't just jumped on her invitation for one morning. She pushed the covers off her legs. "I have to get to work. Thank you for letting me stay the night." Faltering for only a moment, she headed toward the bathroom, which had an entrance off his bedroom as well as the living room.

His gaze heated her butt as she walked away.

Light snow drifted through the heavy mist as a warning of another oncoming winter storm. Laurel parked in front of her mom's garage and jumped out of the SUV, dressed in her clothing from the day before, including the horrible, flowered jeans. She'd refused coffee or breakfast at Huck's, needing to get home and into the shower. She jumped over the snow to the front porch, eyeing the red Escalade parked to the side of the house. Her mother had a visitor?

The door opened and Dr. Abigail Caine walked out wearing a form-fitting black sweater, tight white skirt, and black leather boots. A high-end leather jacket completed the look perfectly. "I really hope you'll think about it," she said, a file folder in her hands.

Deidre followed, pulling a gray cardigan tighter around her tall form. "I appreciate your interest, but my partners and I aren't ready to branch out at this time." Her face was pinched, and her gaze darted around.

Abigail spotted Laurel, and her gaze traveled to Laurel's dirty boots, smudged jeans, and windblown hair. "Someone had a wild night."

Laurel moved closer to the women, her gaze direct and her focus absolute. She felt an instinctive urge to protect her mother, and her intellect fought to catch up. "What are you doing here?" She edged to the side, closer to her mom.

Abigail's smile widened. "Business. Tell me. Were you with our Captain Rivers?"

Laurel looked up at her mom. "What is going on?" Her weapon was at the back of her waist, and right now, there was no need to pull it. Even so, she wanted to. What had Abigail been doing in her mother's house? In her mother's *home*? This was taking the game too far. Much too far. "Mom?"

Her mom frowned and looked from Laurel to Abigail. "Do you two know each other?"

"Not really," Abigail said smoothly. "We did meet the other day, however. I'm possibly a witness in the Snowblood Peak murders." Her eyes danced and she leaned closer to Deidre. "Can you believe that? It's insane. Agent Snow interviewed me the other day. I might've seen the murderer." She lowered her chin. "Did you find the man I told you about? Carl?"

"Carl?" Deidre asked, her eyes widening. "What does Carl have to do with this?"

Abigail's red lips twitched just enough to be noticeable. "Wait a minute. Do you know a Carl?"

Laurel didn't believe in getting angry. Emotion interfered with intellectual processes. However, sometimes the body took charge. "Mom? Give me a second with the professor, would you?" She gestured toward the Escalade, barely preventing herself from taking Abigail by the arm.

"Um, sure?" Her mom turned back inside and gently shut the door.

Abigail looked over her shoulder. "So. That's trust. Interesting."

"Get off the porch before I take you off the porch," Laurel snarled.

Abigail's chuckle was a mellow trill. "Oh, Laurel. You must do something about that temper." She strode across the porch and down into the mist, a bright beacon of danger in the haze. "Apparently one night with the captain didn't burn off enough tension. Tell me. Is he as good with his hands as he appears he'd be?"

Laurel followed her, the chill of the wind scraping her skin. "I'm not a game player, Dr. Caine. What are you doing here?"

At the vehicle, Abigail turned to face Laurel. "Everything isn't about you, Laurel." For the first time, a flash of anger crossed the woman's patrician features. "This was just business, and frankly, it's none of yours. Get over yourself, as my students would say."

"Bullshit." Laurel looked up the four or so inches to Abigail's face, which was turning pink from the cold. "If you want to play smart girl chess with me, then fine. But leave my family out of your narcissistic exploits. You've read me wrong if you think

I'll allow anybody to use them as pawns."

Abigail stepped closer to Laurel, right into her personal space, her expression lighting. "What is it like? That passion? Your need to protect and defend that comes from nowhere near your impressive brain?" She leaned down, curiosity glowing behind too-blue eyes. "Tell me. I want to know. The love for family — it doesn't come naturally to you. How do you have it at all?"

It was a good question, and one Laurel wasn't going to explore with this woman. She banished all emotion as she responded. "What is your fascination with this serial killer case?"

"Oh, Laurel. You know I couldn't care less about any serial killer case. This is all about you." Abigail flicked snow off Laurel's shoulder with a pink-tipped nail. "Do you believe in the Moirai?"

Laurel snorted. "The goddesses of fate? No. Neither do you, Dr. Caine."

Abigail straightened. "No. I don't suppose I do. However, I was becoming bored and fatigued with life, and all of a sudden, there you were." Her gaze traveled over Laurel's hair. "A crimson beacon in a gray world. An object of fascination, a mystery for me to solve. Don't you want to be solved?"

Laurel made sure to meet the woman's

gaze directly. "There are many diagnoses I could make with you. Sometimes the simplest explanation is the best."

"Meaning?" Abigail inhaled and licked her bottom lip.

Laurel brushed a snowflake off her aching skin. "Lady, you're batshit crazy. Stay away from me." She turned and walked up the snowy steps and across the porch.

"I wouldn't turn your back on me, were I you," Abigail called out.

Laurel opened the front door and walked inside, shutting it without looking back. Taking a deep breath, she leaned against it, willing her heart rate to slow down to heart attack range.

Her mother stood near the mantel. "What the heck was that all about?"

"If I knew, I'd tell you. What was she doing here?" Laurel asked.

Deidre leaned over and flicked on a Santa lamp. "She's part owner in the Deep Green Grower's company, and they're interested in partnering with Pure Heart Tea to create and sell a CBD oil–based tea. It's a good business opportunity." Her hands shook. "I told her we weren't looking to expand, and she became a little demanding. I didn't like it."

"I'm glad you declined her offer." Laurel

211

raised a hand before her mom could argue. "There are tons of good growers out there, and if you want to find one to work with, I support you. Don't go into business with Dr. Caine. Trust me."

"Oh, I do. I don't want anything to do with such a bossy woman." Deidre looked her daughter over. "Are you okay? Did that Huck Rivers try anything?" A muscle ticked in her jaw.

"Actually, I tried something, and he said no," Laurel mused.

Deidre stepped back. "Oh. Well." Her hands fluttered until she clasped them tightly together. "I'm sure you haven't eaten. How about I make you chocolate chip pancakes while you shower?"

"Thanks, Mom." Laurel might not understand love any better than Abigail, but she felt it, and she'd do anything to protect her mother.

Anything.

CHAPTER EIGHTEEN

"Thanks, Monty," Huck said, surveying the Fish and Wildlife conference room. Matching green file folders had been placed at each seat at the table, and photos had been taped neatly to a case board at the head of the table.

Monty shrugged. "I couldn't sleep and came in early. I've never been part of a task force before. That body yesterday . . ."

Huck nodded. They'd both seen their fair share of bodies, but nothing like the blonde left naked in the snow. Huck hadn't realized the extent of the torture inflicted upon her until he'd read the ME's report when he'd arrived at work. Dr. Ortega must've worked all night. The clinical descriptions had made the coffee curdle in his stomach. "Hey. I know you want to keep things private, but if you need a break, let me know."

"I'm fine," Monty said grimly. Yet his attitude toward Huck had softened slightly.

Laurel Snow walked into the office. "My boss in DC told me to report to a task force this morning. It's a good idea. I'm pleased we're on the same track." She met his gaze directly, without any embarrassment over their time in bed earlier. "What can I do?"

Huck gestured to the chair to his left, away from the door. "Have a seat and look through the file. Are you ready to give a profile today?"

"I am." She kept tugging at the light yellow sweater she wore over a pink corduroy skirt that emphasized her small waist. Though he'd always liked taller, curvier women, she appealed to him in a way others hadn't. "Did we receive the ME's report?"

"Yes," Huck said as Genesis Valley Sheriff York arrived, strutting to the end of the table. Huck might've caught a slight eye roll from Laurel.

Huck leaned over to flip open his file folder. "In front of you is the entire case file, including copies of the preliminary autopsy reports, information on known victims, photographs, and witness statements. Dr. Ortega spent the night performing an autopsy on the newest body, and we have an identification. Her information is listed on the third page. Her name was Lisa

Scotford, age twenty. She lived outside of Genesis Valley."

Laurel looked up. "Was there a missing person's report filed on Ms. Scotford?"

"No. Somebody should go speak with her family after this meeting. The notification was conducted earlier today, and they had no idea she was missing," Monty said.

Sheriff York straightened up in his chair. "I live in the same area as the family, so I made the notification, and the parents were devastated. Lisa lived alone in an apartment near Lola Creek and was last seen three days ago. It wasn't unusual for her to do her own thing for a few days, so the family wasn't worried."

Laurel looked up. "Lola Creek? By the Genesis Community Church?"

The sheriff straightened. "Yes. The family are all members, as am I, and the funeral will take place there once the body is released." He hitched his pants up over his belly. "The family is heartbroken, but I still got them to answer a few questions. Lisa wasn't dating anybody and hasn't for a long time, since high school. She dated a Bob Jerome all through high school, and he's currently attending Notre Dame. I verified his location on the way in today. Lisa was thinking about attending the college but

215

hadn't applied as of yet."

Laurel's thoughtful look was sexy. She probably didn't know that. "Where did Ms. Scotford work?"

The sheriff's mouth opened and then shut. "The family didn't say."

"How about her closest friends? We should talk to them," Laurel said.

The sheriff's face turned a mottled red. "Like I said, I got everything there was to get out of the family. They should be left alone."

Laurel's face cleared as if she'd just noticed the sheriff was getting pissed. Even so, she didn't backtrack but instead just looked curiously at him. Her factual mind must cause her to miss subtext and irritate people. How often did she get caught off guard?

Huck had the erratic urge to step closer to her and block the sheriff's view as much as possible.

Laurel placed her hand over her file folder. "We'll need to talk to the parents again and get a list of her friends as well as a better feel for her routine and habits." She looked up at Huck. "Has her apartment been searched?"

"Of course," the sheriff snapped. "The local yokels know how to process a scene,

Agent. For your information, there was no sign of a struggle at her apartment, so she obviously wasn't taken from there."

"Did she drive a vehicle?" Laurel asked, her mind apparently working through the case.

The sheriff's mouth snapped shut.

Huck held up a hand to stop the interchange. Laurel was doing her job, and the sheriff was being an ass. "Let's get the rest of the information out on the table."

As the sheriff leaned forward, a blue vein stood out on his forehead. "I'm telling you to leave the family alone. They offered all the help they could."

Deciding not to listen to the blowhard, Huck continued the meeting. "The ME's report indicated sexual assault, torture, and denial of food and water. Ms. Scotford's laptop and phone were found in her apartment and have been secured." He nodded to Laurel. "Special Agent Snow is prepared with the profile." He pulled out his chair and sat.

Laurel stood. "We're looking for a white male, aged twenty-five to forty, familiar with this area. He lives in the area, in fact." She didn't look at the board or her papers but instead concentrated on the group assembled around the table. "He's organized and plans well, showing he's intelligent and in control. Obviously, his victim type is young and blond, but he's changed his MO now that we know about him. He's getting bolder."

"You say that because he kidnapped a lower-risk victim?" Monty asked.

"Yes," Laurel said. "He's no longer taking prostitutes from Seattle." She pointed to the file folders. "The eight victims that have so far been identified have been runaways or prostitutes, last known locations Seattle, surrounding towns, or Portland. With Ms. Scotford, he also used a new dumping site — one we could find — for the first time that we know about." She rolled her neck. "Finally, he painted the nails of the last victim and made up her face. As if making her pretty for the authorities."

"He wanted to make her presentable?" Monty asked. "Why would a man do that?"

"He's playing with us," Laurel returned. "He's showing us what he can do. That he's in charge and can do whatever he wants, basically."

The sheriff stirred in his chair. "We don't need a profiler to tell us that. Do you have any relevant information?"

Huck slowly turned his head to pierce the man with a look.

Laurel ignored the question and continued, unperturbed. "The suspect is comfortable in the outdoors, but he has a regular job and is most likely in charge of his business. His neighbors like him, his friends believe they know him, and he's good at pretending to be one of the guys, but he isn't. He mimics human behavior but doesn't feel the way most people do."

"Right," the sheriff drawled. "We all watch television, Agent Snow. This guy is a sociopath who can't love or feel anything."

Laurel faced York directly. "Wrong. He's a psychopath who feels quite a bit, especially when kidnapping, raping, and killing. It's a misconception that sociopaths and psychopaths can't feel love, Sheriff. They can and they do. It's just in a different manner than you do." She smiled. "Hopefully."

Huck sat back, no longer feeling the need to throw his pencil at York's face. Laurel could take care of herself. The "hopefully" was a nice touch. It took him a second to realize that she wasn't being sarcastic. Had she missed the sheriff's sarcasm?

"Since this is a small-town case, I think I should take the lead," York said.

Laurel shook her head. "Actually, since we're dealing with dumping grounds in the wilderness and most likely a remote storage area for keeping and torturing victims, it makes sense that Fish and Wildlife take lead on this."

Huck's upper lip curved. Laurel wasn't arguing with the asshat for show; she really believed what she said. He'd never met such a logical person before. "Agreed." He stood. "Thanks for the profile."

She took her seat. "One more thing. This guy is in the system. He's good at what he's doing and has been breaking laws for years. I'd do a deep dive on juvenile crimes, including peering into windows, torturing animals, maybe even attempted rape. He'll have a criminal file already."

Huck nodded. "We'll dig into criminal files for Genesis Valley and Tempest County as a whole." What the hell. He might as well really piss off Sheriff York. "Okay. Monty, use whoever you need in the office to identify the remaining victims and then perform background dives on all of them. Let's see if they crossed paths at any time. We need to find out how this guy found them." He tapped his fingers on the case file. "Also, have a team come at this from the killer's background. Let's do a deep dive on sexual predators in the area and then search for crimes similar to these world-wide."

Huck looked around. "Also, I'll ask Ena to obtain a warrant to dump Lisa Scotford's phone and her computer. Sheriff York, I need you to work the town for any witnesses or leads."

Laurel watched Huck, her gaze curious.

He focused on her. "You and I will investigate Lisa Scotford since she's a new direction for this killer. I'd like to interview her family, trace her steps in the last week, and see where we end up. Sound good?"

Laurel stood, her case file tucked beneath one arm. "I'll report to my team upstairs and meet you in your lobby in ten minutes." She walked out of the room, right past the sheriff as if she'd already forgotten his existence.

Huck hid a grin. She just got more likable every day. He gathered his paperwork and strode out of the conference room. Hopefully there was a thermos in his office he could fill with coffee and drink all day. He walked through his office door and stopped short at seeing Dr. Abigail Caine sitting in his guest chair, with the papers that had been stacked there now neatly piled on the floor.

She smiled red-tinted lips. "Hello there, Captain Rivers."

■ ■ ■

Yana huddled in the cold container after a long night of screaming for help. How had she gotten here? She'd been asleep, and something had woken her. Before she could turn over in the bed, her head had all but exploded, and she'd passed out. The lump at the base of her skull hurt and still bled. Who had hit her?

She'd awakened in this metal container, freezing to death, without any clothes. There was only a crappy lantern and a scratchy wool blanket that smelled like body sweat, old perfume, and blood. She'd been captured late Tuesday night. Had the kidnapper been watching her, or had he just gotten lucky? She always took Wednesdays and Thursdays off work because she earned better commissions at the car dealership by working long weekends, so nobody even knew she was missing yet.

Where was she?

What time was it? It had to be early morning or even afternoon on Wednesday. Her throat hurt from screaming for so long, but there was nobody around to hear her except the wind and the storm. Her nails bled from scraping against the lever to open the door.

It was locked, and there was no way out.

When was he coming back?

He'd left her without clothing, just like all of the dead women they'd found tossed over Snowblood Peak. Then they'd found that other victim by the river, dead and naked after being strangled. She'd read the early breaking reports with fascination, just like everyone else.

She let the tears fall. She'd use the lantern against him if he came back. What if he didn't? What if her kidnapper got in some car accident and died? Nobody would ever find her. Her stomach growled, already hungry. How long could a body go without water?

A prayer came to her mind, one she'd learned at her church. The Genesis Community Church congregation would come looking for her the second she was discovered missing.

She sank to the floor and wrapped the coarse blanket tightly against her prickling flesh. Her hair was blond, she was twenty-five, and she fit the description of all the other victims she'd read about in the paper. She'd broken up with Davey a month ago, and she didn't have plans for the next couple of nights, so there would be nobody to even miss her until she failed to show up

223

for work on Friday morning.

Had the kidnapper known her schedule, or did he just not care?

If he didn't return, she'd die alone here. Worse yet, what if he did come back?

CHAPTER NINETEEN

"Hi." Huck paused for a second in his doorway.

Dr. Abigail Caine sat in his guest chair, her long legs crossed beneath a short red skirt. Black leather boots with red bottoms hugged her shapely legs, while her black sweater hugged every other part of her. A whiff of French perfume, the fancy kind that smelled like spiced roses, wafted around her. "I do hope I'm not bothering you."

He glanced at Aeneas in the corner, sleeping on his bed. Usually the dog pestered guests for love, but apparently not this guest. "Not at all." Tossing the file folders on an already tipping pile, he walked around and sat in his chair to keep the desk between them. He hated having a desk. When this case was over, he wanted his former deal back. The one that kept him away from any sort of a team. "What can I do for you, Dr. Caine?"

"Abigail," she purred, leaning toward him. A shiny diamond necklace in the shape of a spike hung between her generous breasts, which were outlined nicely beneath her thin black sweater. "I insist." She was tall and blond and definitely his type, but his instincts put him on edge with her.

What was it about this woman that set him off? Was it the way she looked at him — as if he were a steak hanging in a butcher's counter? He'd normally like that kind of thing, but not from her. What was it? He glanced at his watch. "I just have a minute. What's going on?"

She pushed her platinum blond hair over her shoulder. "I didn't know whether to contact you or not, but I couldn't let this rest. I saw a man several times in the vicinity of Snowblood Peak, mainly near the river and hiking trails. His name was Carl, and I told Agent Snow about him, but she didn't seem inclined to follow up on the lead. Then I discovered that she has an uncle named Carl, and when I googled him, it was the same man. I found his picture as one of the minority owners of the Pure Heart Tea Company, and his face is horribly scarred. He tried to hide it when I was with him, but when I saw his picture online, all of those memories came flooding back. You can't miss him." Her eyes widened dramatically. "I know Laurel Snow is a good FBI agent, but when family is involved, all rules are banished. Don't you agree?"

He leaned back in his chair. "No. For me, the rules are never banished." Hopefully she'd read everything into that statement that he intended. "Tell me about this Carl. What did you see him do?"

"Oh, nothing." She uncrossed and then recrossed her legs the other way, her thigh muscles flexing. "I just saw him several times on the trail. He was using some sort of crutch to get through the weeds."

Huck tilted his head. "Carl was injured?"

"Oh, no." She shook her head. "Perhaps that's why I remember it so clearly. He was moving quickly and seemed to be in good shape. It was as if . . ." She looked over at Aeneas as though thinking and trying to remember. "As if he was pretending to use the crutch." Her hands fluttered and she clasped them in her lap. "It's silly. Perhaps I shouldn't have come."

If the woman was telling the truth, it was information Huck needed. "Tell me everything you remember."

Abigail tapped one nail against her full bottom lip. "Well, Carl smiled at me, and one time he watched me walk by, just stand-

227

ing there against a pine tree. It was a little creepy. . . . I can't explain it. The way his eyes just followed me. You know, we're just animals, like all the rest out there in the woods looking for prey every night. Our instincts, once heeded, often lead to inevitable results." She shivered. "I just thought you should know about him."

"I appreciate it." Why hadn't Laurel said anything last night? There had been plenty of time to chat in the SUV on the way to his place, although she had been freezing and trying to warm up. "Did Carl ever say anything to you?"

"No," Abigail whispered. "That was weird, too. The way he stared at me but didn't say anything." Her hands trembled and she glanced down at them. "Look at me. Now I'm psyching myself out, as my students would say." For the first time, she looked vulnerable and not in full control. "Have you ever just had a feeling about somebody?"

"Yes, and that instinct has saved my life before," he said. "Those feelings or instincts are what keep us alive. How many times did you see Carl?"

"Oh." She breathed out. "I don't know. It had to be four times? Yes, I think that's right."

He gentled his voice as he would with any trembling animal. "You're doing great. Just stick with me for a minute. The first time you saw Carl. When was it?"

She swallowed. "Um, the first time I saw him was probably a year and a half ago in the summertime. On that occasion, I just noticed him on a UTV, leaving the parking area. He nodded at me as he drove by, and if I'd never seen him again, I probably wouldn't even have remembered the incident."

Huck sat straighter, the hair on his arms prickling. "Tell me about the UTV. Did it have a back seat or a bed area?"

She winced. "I don't remember. It was just a UTV. I didn't really look it over. Just saw him and his intense eyes. They're green, and they made an impression on me — as did his horribly scarred face. So much so that I might've blocked out that scar until I saw it again. It's just so terrible. His face was partially concealed before, but still, there was a scar. Can you believe I blocked it out?"

"Keep that image in your head if you would. For the next few days. If you get a better picture of what he was driving, that'd be great. Do you remember what he was wearing?" Just how good was her memory

229

of that day?

Her eyelids wrinkled. "I don't. Sorry."

That tracked since she didn't remember much about the UTV. "How long until you saw him again?"

She bit her bottom lip, drawing out the movement of her white teeth as she apparently tried to remember. "It was that autumn because the leaves were changing, and I remember thinking it was one of the last times I'd be able to run before rain and snow made it too uncomfortable." She ruffled her hair, which pressed her bra against the loose weave of the black sweater. It was a paler gray color.

Did she want him to notice the bra was gray? He studied her face. She was looking at the dog, frowning and trying to remember. He winced. Noticing the gray bra was on him. He had to get his head back into the investigation. "Was Carl in a UTV when you saw him the second time?"

"No. He was in an ATV with four tires and no back seat or bed or anything. Just him on the four-wheeler. I remember because he smiled that time like we were old friends. Then he winked."

Huck dug a pencil out from a stack and started taking notes. "He winked at you?"

"Yes, and it was disturbing." She shook

230

her head, sending the blond tendrils over her shoulder. "I know this sounds silly, but when he winked, the entire movement lacked levity. Creepy isn't a word I like because it isn't concrete enough, but that fits. It was just . . . haunting." She sighed and the British accent emerged more heavily. "After he drove by, I changed my mind about jogging and got back into my car and drove home."

Huck made a quick notation. "Give me a sec." He reached for his phone and dialed Monty.

"Hey," Monty said by way of answer.

"When you're finished with the other work I assigned you, would you conduct a background check on Carl . . ."

"Snow," Abigail said. "When I googled him, his last name was Snow."

So the guy was Laurel's uncle on her mother's side. "Snow. Carl Snow. Thanks." Huck ended the call before Monty could question him. "Tell me about the third time, Abigail."

She smiled, looking younger now that she'd shared her fear. "I like the way you say my name."

He pursed his lips. All right. He didn't want her to like the way he said her name. "The third time?"

231

She rolled her eyes and visibly relaxed in the worn guest chair. "The third time was this spring, and that's the time he was using a crutch. He stopped under a tree and watched me. It was after I'd already run the trails, so I just kept going back to my SUV." She lost the come-hither smile and looked frightened again. "My heart was beating so fast after I saw him that I can remember the relief when I locked my doors inside the vehicle."

Even though she was a flirt and possibly a narcissist as Laurel had said, she was still a witness who appeared frightened. "There was one more time after that?" He kept his voice level and calming.

She nodded. "Yes. Early September, I was feeling . . . restless. I don't know. Bored. I don't do well bored. Do you, Captain?"

Her penchant for quickly switching from business to personal made him uneasy. He was accustomed to being in control, and this woman threw him off balance — and not in a good way. "No. Are you still feeling bored?" he asked.

The left side of her mouth lifted slightly, and she leveled those blue eyes on him. Curiosity and tension flowed from her. "Oh, no. Not at all. Isn't life full of surprises?"

If she was talking about him, she was way

off the mark. "I don't like surprises," he warned her.

"Normally, I don't either," she said, leaning toward him as if sharing a confidence. "In fact, it's very difficult to surprise me. I suppose that's why the situation is all the more special. Right?"

He frowned. "What situation?"

She lifted one delicate shoulder. "Finding myself in the middle of a serial killer investigation, of course." Her tongue teased the corner of her lips. "Although, you're intriguing as well, Captain Huck Delta Rivers."

So she'd looked him up online. Was that supposed to be flattering? It wasn't. "The fourth time you saw Carl was during autumn," he reminded her. "What happened that time?"

"That time, he was back in the UTV and drove right by me without looking." She gingerly touched the diamond spike necklace. "I was mollified and then, of course, started to doubt my earlier fears. Had I overreacted?"

"That's a normal reaction," Huck said. "Do you remember if the UTV had a back seat or a trunk?"

She looked down. "I really don't. I'm sorry, and I'll keep trying to remember." She smiled and then looked up at him.

"Maybe you could help me?"

"You can call me at the office any time." Huck stood and reached for his jacket. "I have to get going." Then he paused. "Do you know the Scotfords?" he asked.

She pursed her brightly painted red lips. "Scotford? No. That name doesn't ring a bell. I'm sorry."

Huck shrugged into his jacket and strapped on his belt with the thigh holster. "Thank you for coming in today."

She drew her wool coat off the back of the chair and moved in front of him, handing it over. "Would you like to meet for a drink tonight?"

While he appreciated directness in a woman, this one set his teeth on edge. He gently helped her into her coat, his movements both efficient and quick. "I appreciate the offer, but I can't make it."

"All right. Another time, then." She smiled at the dog. "Bye, puppy," she purred.

Aeneas looked up and then away. Wow. He really didn't like the woman.

Huck trusted his dog. He gently grasped Abigail's arm to lead her from his office and through the bullpen. "Aeneas, come."

Monty emerged from his office, his gaze squarely on Abigail Caine's long legs. He blinked several times.

Huck cut him a look and escorted the woman around the file cabinets to the reception area, almost running Laurel over.

Laurel's eyes widened.

Abigail smiled. "Well. Isn't this interesting?"

CHAPTER TWENTY

In the parking lot, Laurel settled into Huck's truck and secured her seatbelt as he did the same. Snow drifted lazily down to coat the windshield, and he flicked the wipers into action. Aeneas settled in the back seat and sneezed.

Abigail sat in her red Escalade, flipping through her phone. She turned and smiled through the icy window, lowering her chin as she did so.

Laurel watched her, trying to dig into the woman's head. Abigail had been so pleased to see Laurel that she'd purred slightly, and she'd also run her hand over Huck's arm when she'd said good-bye.

What had they spoken about?

Huck backed his truck out of the parking area. "Tell me about Uncle Carl."

Laurel tore her gaze away from Abigail's.

Interesting. "Dr. Caine met with you this morning to tell you about my uncle?" What game was the professor playing now?

"Yeah. She also asked me out." Huck turned onto the river road at the end of town.

The conclusion of that conversation was none of Laurel's business. She should not ask. She should keep her own council. "Did you accept her invitation?" Curiosity was often an illogical master. Her face heated.

"I said no." Huck glanced her way and then focused back on the icy road. "She's odd. Aeneas really doesn't like her. Somehow she ticked him off. Also, I can't explain it, but when I'm around her, it's like being back in the desert with a scope aimed at my chest. The woman makes my nape itch."

Laurel relaxed into her seat and chose not to explore why she felt relieved. "You have good instincts."

"They've saved my life more than once." He slowed down to drive around a chunk of ice that no doubt had fallen off a logging truck. "Although, I see the appeal. She's gorgeous and mysterious, and definitely knows how to flirt." Now he sounded thoughtful.

Laurel fought an extremely rare urge to punch him. She did not hit people. "I wouldn't think you'd like tattletales." She winced. Had she just descended into pettiness? Yes. Darn it. Was she jealous?

"I wouldn't think you'd hide material information about this case," he returned easily.

She ducked her head. "You're right. I should have informed you about Abigail's claim that she met my uncle. But she gave me his name after having had time to research my life, and I believe she's playing some sort of game with me. I'm a challenge to her."

Huck kept an even speed, and the river flowed by outside, lined by trees heavily laden with snow. "Because you're both smart? Both child prodigies?"

Laurel shook her head, irritation clogging her throat for a moment. "Perhaps? She's easily bored, narcissistic, and most likely sadistic. For some reason, she's latched on to me, waging a battle I can't understand." There was a puzzle piece missing in this situation. Laurel shifted uneasily. She always found the answer, but this time, it was eluding her. "I don't understand her motivation." Was boredom enough? It might be for a sadistic narcissist.

"What's her end game?" Huck asked.

Laurel turned as much as the seatbelt would allow to look at him. He was in uniform today, badge clipped to his belt, gun strapped to his thigh. He'd shaved that morning, but a shadow was already appearing on his masculine jaw. "I don't know. Right now, the goal seems to be you."

"Wonderful," he muttered.

Laurel could not agree more. "I feel like she wants to beat me at some game only she understands." Laurel watched Huck's broad, capable hands on the steering wheel. "That would mean solving the case, but she doesn't seem to care about the case really. This feels . . . personal." So the personal aspect had to be Huck. "She did meet with my mother about a business opportunity." Laurel flopped back in her seat and groaned.

Huck chuckled. "You're not used to having trouble figuring things out, are you?"

"No," she said shortly.

"My gut tells me it isn't her, but is there a chance she's the killer? That she's murdering other blondes?" he asked.

Laurel watched as a hawk landed on a high up branch and sent snow pounding down. "I don't believe so. She doesn't fit the profile."

"What if your profile is wrong?"

She chewed her lip. "I can't answer that."

"That's a subject we'll have to revisit, then." The road wound away from the river and farmhouses began to dot the area. "Let's switch topics. Why didn't you tell me about Carl?"

"Because Dr. Caine didn't mention the scars across my uncle's face when she first told me about the man she saw. The scars are prominent, and there's no way she could've missed them," Laurel said. "Which begs the question, why is that woman messing with my head?"

"I don't know, but she's definitely focused on you." He shook his head. "I'm with you on the scars, and I believe she lied. Even so, just for the moment, forget that you know Carl and profile him for me." Huck drove between apple groves and slowed down to allow a rafter of wild turkeys to finish waddling across the road.

The request was a fair one. "All right. I did talk with him, and he denies ever seeing or speaking with Dr. Caine." Laurel took a deep breath and tried to remove the emotion she felt regarding her family. "Carl Snow is an introvert who's uncomfortable around most people. He's sixty-one years old and works as a grave digger at the cemetery."

"Grave digger?" Huck asked.

Defensiveness rose in Laurel; she recognized it and squelched it. "It's a solitary and necessary job. Carl lives alone in an old cabin on the family acreage. Mom and Uncle Blake also live on the family farm, which encompasses miles. Carl was married in his twenties, but his wife left him." Laurel searched her memory. "Her name was Nami Loscrom, and she wanted the big city, and a much more exciting life than he could offer. That's all I remember hearing about her."

Huck turned down another snowy road, this one leading back to the river. "Have you seen a picture?"

"Yes," Laurel said. It was easy for her to call the image from her memory. "Nami was short with black hair and pretty green eyes. She was not blond."

Huck glanced her way and then back to the road. "Has Carl ever been in trouble with the law?"

"Not that I'm aware," Laurel said. "To profile him, he's a loner. But he can and does interact with family, and he's a minority owner in my mom's company."

"Does he participate?" Huck asked.

"No. She made him an owner to supplement his income, I think." Laurel rubbed a hand down her face.

"What is the deal with the tea company?" Huck asked. "Does your mom grow her own tea?"

"She grows a couple of varieties but imports most of them. Then she performs rituals involving the moon, certain stones, and so on, before packaging the tea in jars or smaller pouches. She started by selling them at farmer's markets and then branched out online, now including a subscription service that has become quite lucrative," Laurel said evenly.

Huck's eyebrows rose. "Do you believe in all of that? The moon and stones and such?"

"No, but a lot of people do," Laurel said.

"Did *you* enlarge the business with the Internet and subscription service?" he asked.

"We both did," Laurel said. She might've done most of the heavy lifting, but her mom did all the work preparing the teas.

"Does your other uncle work with the tea?" Huck asked.

"No. Blake and Betty grow pumpkins, Christmas trees, and squash. They also have a large apple orchard as well as several acres dedicated to cattle. Blake is a farmer," she said, her heart warming. "They're good people."

"I'm sure," Huck murmured. "Tell me more about Carl."

She kept herself from sighing, knowing

this was business. "Carl doesn't have pets and is methodical and organized at his home. His furnishings are sparse but well maintained." She shook her head. "I don't see him as a psychopath, but I'm family, so too close to make that determination." The last fact was difficult to admit, but it was the truth. She cleared her throat. "Carl sustained a facial and head injury when he was in his early twenties, and that changed him, according to my mom."

"Can't a head injury lead to psychosis?" Huck asked, driving through a wooden archway toward a small town center.

"Yes," Laurel admitted. She looked around at what appeared to be a town square. "Does this suburb of Genesis Valley have a name?"

"No. It's unincorporated county land," Huck said.

Laurel turned to him. "If this is county land, why did the Genesis Valley sheriff conduct the notification to Lisa Scotford's family? This is out of his jurisdiction."

Huck's eyebrows rose. "The different authorities help each other out in this neck of the woods, so it's not unheard of for him to come here in an official capacity. Plus, he did say he lived in the area and knew the family from church."

Laurel studied the small businesses around the center of the area, including a diner, small convenience store, fish and tackle store, a coffee place, and several others. "This is quaint."

Huck grunted in response, driving out of the main area and several miles down a just-plowed road. He took another turn into a residential section and drove more miles, finally parking in front of a three-story wooden apartment building surrounded by other apartment complexes. A creek ran behind the buildings, small enough to already be frozen over. "Lisa's apartment was on the second floor. Let's check it out."

Laurel pulled on the borrowed mittens from her mother, and her fingers instantly warmed from the perfect knit. She jumped out of the truck, looking around at the various Christmas decorations on each balcony. Everything from shiny lights to plastic Santas to sparkling presents and poinsettias. "What's the demographic here?"

Huck led the way toward the nearest outside stairwell. "Younger couples and kids attending Genesis Community College, mostly. If you keep heading east on that road, you'll end up at the college. Swing west, and you'll arrive back in Genesis Valley."

She connected the dots in her head. "Was Lisa a student?" She hadn't seen that in the case file.

"No. I've put in a request for her tax information. Right now, I don't know where she worked, if she did." Huck pulled open a heavy-looking metal door and revealed a hallway lined with light blue carpet. "Her apartment is number fourteen."

Laurel stepped inside first and walked down the wide hallway to Lisa's door, which had been sealed by the county police.

Huck drew a pocket knife out of his jacket and cut the seal. Then he opened the door, and for the first time, walked in front of Laurel rather than waiting for her to enter.

She paused. The man was usually a perfect gentleman, even in business situations. Oh. He thought there might be a threat inside, and to be safe, he'd entered first. Despite the sealed door, he had morphed into protector mode. Perhaps that was his natural domain. The notion intrigued her . . . and quickened her breath. Apparently her body found his protectiveness sexy, which meant her mind did as well.

Huck cleared the small apartment quickly, his hand resting on his weapon. "There's still fingerprinting dust on some of the table-tops."

Laurel walked inside and paused, taking in the entire room to get a feel for the victim. She'd liked bright colors. The sofa was an older denim one, probably a hand-me-down or garage sale find. Fluorescent-pink and electric-yellow pillows brightened the blue material. A dingy, brown recliner next to the sofa had been spruced up with a neon-yellow blanket in a classic stockinette stitch design.

To the left lay a small kitchen with hot-pink baking canisters on the counter. The table had been painted a deep blue, as had the four chairs. A treadmill stood near the balcony, which held several outdoor Santa figurines, one with a surfboard over his shoulder.

The woman had been young and lively.

Laurel exhaled and kept her brain engaged by checking out the tiny, spotlessly clean bathroom before going into the bedroom. The room was more monochromatic and peaceful than the other areas, with a light pink bedspread, white pillowcases, and a painted white bookshelf over by the window. Many of the shelves displayed pictures and figurines, but one held a series of books — mostly fantasy and young adult paranormal books.

Her jewelry box held mostly silver and

moonstones. A quick check of the bedside table revealed lip gloss, an open box of condoms, and a half-full bottle of KY Jelly.

"Got it," Huck called from the other room.

Laurel moved out of the too-quiet bedroom. It was as if the room knew Lisa wasn't returning. She shook off her unease. "What did you find?"

Huck stood by an open drawer in the kitchen and held up an envelope. "I found a recent paycheck. Lisa worked for the Genesis Community Church."

"How far back do the paycheck envelopes go?" She moved closer.

"There are only two." He unfolded the paper. "This stub only shows the current year, and it looks like she worked there all year. We'll have to get IRS information to see if she worked there before. It's weird the sheriff didn't mention that she worked at the church."

The sheriff didn't seem to be a good investigator, based on her few interactions with the man. Laurel settled her jacket more securely around her shoulders. "He seems lazy to me. Besides, the family didn't know everything about Lisa, since they said she wasn't dating anybody. I found condoms and lube in her bedside table."

Huck's eyebrows lifted. "She was young and probably didn't want her folks to know that she was sexually active. We'll know more when we get her phone and computer dump." He looked around. "It's weird, right? I don't know anybody who leaves home without their phone. Especially a twenty-year-old."

"I agree. It's possible she forgot the phone, but I think that's odd as well. It's more likely that the killer took her from here, and she didn't even have time to struggle."

Huck took an evidence envelope from his front pocket and slid the paystubs into it. "Let's hit the church."

CHAPTER TWENTY-ONE

After leaving Lisa Scotford's apartment, Huck drove away from the creek to the river road and then followed it farther into the wilderness. Finally, a snow-covered field opened up in the distance. He turned left onto a paved, tree-lined road and drove toward the river. "There's the church."

Laurel leaned toward her window for a better look. The Genesis Community Church appeared to be a typical country church. Freshly painted, the wooden structure had a steeple, stained glass windows, and several wings. "That is a large building," she murmured.

Huck parked the truck up front, past the few vehicles already covered with snow in the sprawling, paved parking lot. "I believe much of the surrounding land, including the individual farms and businesses, are actually owned by the church."

"That makes the church very powerful in

this area," Laurel murmured, studying the innocuous-looking building.

Huck grunted.

Laurel had spent enough time with him to recognize the sound as his grunt of agreement. She grinned at the thought and unbuckled her belt before stepping out into the falling snow. "What do you know about the pastor?"

"Nothing," Huck admitted, jumping out, motioning Aeneas out, and shutting his door before continuing. "Both he and the church are very present in the community, but I am not. They have a website, and they claim their congregation is full of love and light, and that the church is a good place for people looking for a simpler, safer, and more Godly life." He waited at the front of the truck.

Laurel walked carefully over the ice to reach his side. "From what I've heard, the church does a lot of good in the surrounding areas."

Huck grunted. His boot steps thunked on the worn wooden steps to the church's narthex, where he stopped and pulled open the left door. "Yeah, whatever."

Oh yeah. The preacher involved in Huck's last case had turned out to be a murderer. Man, she hoped he didn't have a blind spot when it came to church leaders, because she needed him on this.

She stepped inside a serene vestibule with a table holding pamphlets, a bulletin board with different announcements, and unlabeled twin doors on either side of her. Silence hung peacefully, as it only did in churches. She strode down the nave, between the deeply polished pews, and looked at both the north and south transepts. At the wall end of each, tall stained-glass windows with no discernible figures sparkled despite the meager light outside. Vibrant blue, red, purple, and yellow sections colored the glass. "Those are beautiful," she whispered.

Huck looked around.

She then turned forward to see a high pulpit to the left, a lectern to the right, and an area most likely for the choir behind that. The chancel led to the altar, and behind it, another lovely stained-glass window was visible. This one was translucent enough to show the river and a high mountain peak outside.

"That's Orphan Peak," Huck said quietly. "We rescued three campers off the other side last winter. The thing is a beast to climb."

"Still part of the Cascades?" Laurel asked.

"Yep." Huck turned. "Let's find somebody." He strode back down the nave and paused at the two closed doorways. "What do you think? Left or right?"

The door to his right opened and a man walked through. "Oh. Hello." He instantly smiled and hurried to deposit stapled information sheets on the table. "How can I help you?" He appeared to be in his midthirties, with deep-brown skin, short, curly brown hair, light brown eyes behind wire-rimmed glasses, and a hard-cut jaw shaven smooth.

"We're looking for the pastor," Huck said, standing eye to eye with the man. They both had to be about six foot four, but Huck was much broader.

"I'm Pastor John. What can I do for you, officer?" The pastor pushed his glasses up his nose and then looked over at Laurel. His head cocked and he blinked several times. "Oh. Hello. And you are?" He moved toward her, taking her hand in both of his. Behind the glasses, his eyes intensified. A burst of color ran over his high cheekbones.

She calmly extracted her hand.

Huck grunted. "This is FBI Special Agent Snow. We're here on business, Pastor."

The pastor visibly shook himself and retreated a step. "Of course. My apologies.

252

You're just very . . . striking, Agent Snow."
He didn't look away from her face and even
ducked his head to stare better into her
eyes. "Did you know that some Native
American cultures believe those fortunate
souls with different-colored eyes can look
into heaven and earth at the same time?"

She wanted to step away from him. "Yes.
Such eyes were referred to as 'ghost eyes.'
Do you believe in legends, Pastor?"

He smiled. "I'm not sure about legends,
but I believe in gifted and talented people.
As well as beautiful women." He gestured
toward the open doorway. "It's a quiet day
here at the church, but we do have a lun-
cheon in about an hour for newly married
couples. Come on back to my office, where
we can get comfortable."

Huck's grunt this time was anything but
cheerful. "Can the dog stay here in the
entryway?"

"Sure," the pastor said.

Huck motioned with his hand, and Aeneas padded near the door and lay down,
nose on paws.

"Good boy." Huck waited for Laurel to
follow the pastor and then stuck close to
her back down a long hallway with several
offices and meeting rooms on each side.

"The other side of the main church has

several classrooms as well as two gathering rooms for wedding receptions and such," Pastor John said, leading them into a spacious office with a wide window looking over the glacial river and mountains beyond. "Please. Have a seat." His plush seats were covered in a thick, flowered material.

Laurel sat as Huck did the same. "Pastor John —"

"John," the pastor said. "You're not members of the congregation, so please just call me John. We're pretty informal here." He sat behind what appeared to be a hand-carved cedar desk polished to perfection. The dents and dings in the wood suggested it had been in place for decades.

"Pastor John, do you know Lisa Scotford?" Huck asked, retaining the use of the man's title.

Pastor John's smile disappeared, and sorrow slid across his face. "I heard about her death and am stunned. Lisa worked here at the church for the last two years, assisting our scheduler and accountant, as well as coordinating the teenage outreach program." He swallowed rapidly, his eyes glistening. "She was an incredibly sweet person. I just can't believe somebody killed her."

"When was the last time you saw Lisa?"

Laurel asked.

"Last Friday." Pastor John's hand trembled as he lifted a pen off his desk to place it in a square-shaped pen holder decorated with paper mâché elephants and shaky, first-name signatures. The clearest one was by a kid named Bert. "Lisa had this week off, and I thought she was going shopping in Seattle with friends, but I don't know that for sure."

"Do you have a list of her friends?" Huck asked.

Pastor John reached for a stack of papers and tapped them into order. "I know some of her friends in the church and can write you a list, but she also had a life outside of the community. She was twenty and trying to find herself." He dropped his head. "That will never happen now. At least she's with God."

Laurel stretched her ankle. It was still giving her a twinge once in a while. "Do you know who Lisa was dating?"

John looked up and met Laurel's gaze. "Dating? No. I didn't think she was dating anybody." He sat perfectly still.

Huck's chin lifted and his gaze narrowed. "We found condoms and lube in her bedside table. Fresh ones. She was definitely dating somebody."

Pastor John shook his head and used his knuckles to wipe the side of his mouth. "That surprises me. I honestly had no idea she would have sexual relations outside of marriage. We believe in the sanctity of marriage here." He frowned. "There were two men she seemed to be friends with. Ryan Kennedy and Larry North. But they seemed more pals than anything else."

"What about her family? Tell us about them," Laurel said.

Pastor John straightened his keyboard. "They're a good family. Mark works construction, Annie works part-time at the Corner Diner, and Lisa was their only child." He rubbed his chest. "It's heartbreaking. Truly heartbreaking."

"We are sorry for your loss," Huck said. "How long have you been the pastor here?"

Pastor John smiled. "I was hired as the assistant pastor four years ago after getting my master's in theology from Milton University in Chicago. I couldn't wait to get to the country where I could really get to know my parishioners."

Laurel studied the office. There were papers and files across the desk, three file cabinets against one wall, and the two chairs. The free wall held diplomas, a myriad of pictures showing groups of people building houses, and two large photographs. One was of Pastor John. She looked at the other photograph.

"That's Pastor Zeke," Pastor John said. "This is his office and his church. He needed a break and told me he was going on a walkabout, but I expected him to return by now. Although he did hint he might not come back." His voice softened at the end and trailed off.

Laurel cocked her head. "You have a missing pastor, and nobody has filed a report?"

"No." The pastor shook his head. "More than a year ago, during Pastor Zeke's last sermon, he told the entire congregation that he was embarking on a spiritual journey God had called him to undertake. He said he might not return for a long time." Pastor John tapped his chest. "I have to believe that the good Lord is watching out for my friend."

Laurel stood and moved closer to the picture, which had a small gold name tag at the bottom. Pastor Zeke appeared to be in his sixties with a bald head, sharp features, and tinted spectacles. In the picture, he stood near the biggest pine tree out in front of the church, looking both solid and reassuring. He was short but appeared to have presence. Laurel moved a foot to the left.

"This is a nice photograph of you." In the picture, Pastor John sat on the steps of the front porch of the church, smiling into the camera. She glanced at the gold name tag. "Pastor John Govern?" Awareness had her turning around. Wait a minute. John was such a common name, she hadn't even considered the possibility.

Pastor John chuckled. "I know. With a name like that, I had to be a pastor, right?"

Huck straightened, and his shoulders looked too broad for the chair. "John Govern? As in Abigail Caine, Robert Caine, and John Govern, owners of the Deep Green Growers Company?" Huck lost the agreeable look and went full-on investigator.

Laurel factored this newest information into the equation. "You own a marijuana growing and developing company?"

The pastor sighed. "Yes, I do. Well, I'm one-third owner." He shrugged. "Cannabis is legal in Washington, and we believe in working on the land. I have no ethical dilemma about owning the company and making money. I do a lot of good with my income, and I'm not going to apologize for it."

"Do your parishioners know about your other endeavors?" Laurel asked.

Red bloomed into his face. "No, and I'd

258

appreciate it if you didn't advertise the fact."

Perhaps the pastor did feel an ethical dilemma after all. But not enough to stay out of the growing business. Laurel turned around. "Tell us about Abigail Caine."

Pastor John's eyes blazed. "She's brilliant and an excellent business partner. We dated briefly, but our fundamental views were too different for us to continue. Although I pray nightly that she will let God into her heart."

They'd dated? Interesting. "She doesn't believe in a higher being?" Laurel asked.

Pastor John shook his head. "No."

Huck kept his focus on the pastor. "She believes in you, Pastor. Enough that she didn't inform us that you were the third partner in the pot farm."

Laurel played off Huck's statement. "Your voice rose a little when you spoke of her. Did her denial of God anger you?" Was the pastor angry at blondes in general? She ran through what little she knew about the man. Yes, they definitely needed more information about him.

Pastor John frowned. "No, it saddened me. Horribly. As I said, I hope she finds God. I believe it will happen."

"Humph," Huck said, crossing his arms.

Laurel gave him a look and partially turned. Her elbow caught on a picture and she moved to center it on the wall.

Then she leaned in. Several older photographs showed a younger Pastor Zeke with what appeared to be groups of students. Laurel ducked her head. "Wait a minute." She looked closer and then snatched the picture off the wall, taking it to the pastor and pointing at a pretty girl wearing a thick coat and knit hat. "Her face — she looks familiar."

Huck leaned over. "Shit."

Pastor John blinked. "Oh. Yes. That's Abigail Caine. I thought you knew."

"Knew what? That she was a member of the church?" Huck asked, his voice pitched low.

"No," Pastor John said. "That Abigail Caine is Pastor Zeke Caine's daughter."

CHAPTER TWENTY-TWO

Laurel dropped back into her chair. "Pastor Zeke Caine?" Abigail was becoming more intriguing by the second.

"Yes," Pastor John said. "I'm sorry. I thought you knew all of this already."

"Obviously not." A chill swept along Laurel's arms. "What about Robert Caine? Your other partner in the growing operation?"

"Robert is also a wonderful business partner." Pastor John clasped his hands together on his desk. "Robert and Abigail are night and day — half-siblings. Pastor Zeke isn't Robert's biological father. His mother was married before she met Pastor Zeke, and I believe Robert was already four or so years old at the time of her second marriage."

"So Pastor Zeke Caine adopted Robert?" Laurel asked.

Pastor John nodded. "Yes. Robert and his

family are members of the congregation. Robert has a leadership role, and his wife, Jasmine, is in charge of scheduling the married women's bible studies. They're a kind couple, but I don't believe Robert is close to Abigail. As I said, she's still finding her way." He sat up. "That reminds me. Lisa Scotford and Jasmine Caine were friends, I believe. They worked closely together here at the church."

It looked like Laurel's afternoon would entail interviewing both Robert and Jasmine. Her mind spun.

Huck looked at Pastor John. "Were Abigail and her father close?"

"No. Absolutely not," Pastor John said. "I think she was very angry that he lost her to the state after her mother died. At least, that's the impression I've gotten from her. She's very tight lipped about the situation."

"Could you expand on that issue?" Laurel asked. "Tell me more about Abigail and her feelings."

Pastor John clasped his hands together, a veil dropping over his expression. "I'm sorry. There's nothing else to add on the subject, and I probably broke the confidence of a friend by mentioning it. Abigail deserves better."

Laurel swallowed. "Perhaps Pastor Zeke

Caine's disappearance isn't such a mystery after all."

Huck stood. "The dog has been alone long enough. Thanks for your time, Pastor." He turned and strode out of the room.

Pastor John's dark eyebrows rose. "Is it me or any church?"

Laurel moved to follow Huck. "Thank you for your time, and I'm sure we'll be in touch." She quickened her pace but didn't catch up to Huck until he and the dog were already in the truck, so she hopped into the passenger side.

"That guy's hiding something," Huck said, starting the engine and driving rapidly down the plowed road. "I'm hungry."

"Me, too," Laurel said, her mind spinning. Dr. Abigail Caine's father was the Genesis Community Church pastor, who was now missing. Although her ex-boyfriend, the new pastor, didn't seem too worried about it. Laurel tried to organize her thoughts as Huck drove quietly back to the quaint square where the area's businesses were grouped together.

They ate lunch at the Corner Diner. Aeneas sat beneath the table, and nobody seemed to mind. Laurel dug into her Cobb salad. "Remaining unincorporated probably saves this area funds when it comes to public services."

Huck sat across from her in the comfortable burgundy-colored booth, thoughtfully eating the fat fries he'd ordered with his burger. "I suppose so." He leaned back so the waitress could refill his water cup. The woman was in her late forties and had focused all of her attention on him while they were ordering. She was full bodied, and her breasts almost brushed his arm. Huck didn't seem to notice.

Laurel did. She shook her head after the waitress had sashayed away. "Do you have this effect on all women?"

He paused in the middle of pouring more ketchup on the paper in his basket. "Huh?"

"Nothing." Laurel sipped her diet soda. Her mother would not be happy with the chemical intake, but sometimes a woman needed a vice. "What did you think of the pastor?"

Huck tilted his head. "I'm not sure. The fact that he keeps his pot business a secret from his congregation seems disingenuous to me. However, his private life isn't their business. He doesn't seem too worried about Pastor Caine, although he did seem quietly concerned about Dr. Abigail Caine."

"That just shows he has a brain," Laurel said thoughtfully. She ate more of the lettuce. The dressing had a hint of spice to it, and the entire bowl was delicious.

The waitress returned, this time with a pitcher of diet soda to top off Laurel's glass.

Huck gave her a smile, and the woman twittered. "If you don't mind me asking, did you know Lisa Scotford?" he asked.

The waitress sobered and her thickly made-up eyes watered. "Yes. She was a sweetheart and often spent time here doing paperwork in a booth. She liked apple pie." She sniffed. "It's so sad." Her gaze landed on the weapon strapped to Huck's thigh. "Do you have any idea who hurt her?"

"We're working on it," Laurel assured her. "Was Lisa ever here with anybody? We know she had a boyfriend, but we don't know who it was yet." Unless there were several men in Lisa's life, but that seemed unlikely.

The waitress withdrew the pitcher. "You should talk to the pastor at the church. He's the one who runs the community."

That was an interesting turn of phrase. "What do you mean, he runs the community?" Laurel asked, reaching for her glass.

"Nothing. I didn't mean anything." The woman took another step back.

Huck leaned toward her. He glanced at her name tag. "It's okay, Delores. We're the good guys. We don't want to cause any problems with the church or community. We just want to find the person who raped and strangled Lisa before leaving her body naked in the freezing snow."

Delores paled, which made her bright blue eyeshadow glow on her face. "Wh . . . what I meant was that the church owns most of the businesses in town, including this one, and we don't want bad press. It's a wonderful church, and we give so much back to others. We're just a small-town community that takes care of its own so we have a safe place to live." She shuffled her feet. "At least, I thought it was until Lisa got kidnapped."

Laurel kept eating and motioned subtly for Huck to keep questioning the woman. She was too charmed by him to run away.

Huck reached out and patted Delores's arm. "I'm so sorry about that, and I will find the person who hurt her. I promise."

Delores swayed toward him. "I'm sure you will, and I'm so thankful."

"It would help if you told me anything else you knew about Lisa," Huck said. "Who did she date?"

Delores shrugged. "I only saw her with other young people from the church. I never noticed her kissing or snuggling in a booth with anybody. I'm sorry. Although she and Jasmine Caine ate and worked in the booth here many times, so if anybody knows who Lisa dated, it'd be Jasmine."

A second waitress sidled up, obviously having overheard the conversation. She was in her early thirties with curly black hair, smooth brown skin, and sparkling dark eyes. "Do you have any idea who killed all of those women?" she asked.

Laurel read the woman's name tag. "Hi, Jaida. We're following up on several leads."

Huck smiled, all charm. "If you have any information that would help us with the case, we'd really appreciate it."

The women gave basic information that didn't help much, but Laurel thanked them anyway. Then they moved off to work the rest of the quaint restaurant.

Laurel finished her salad. "Do you think that you disliked Pastor John so much because of the killer in your last big case? The preacher?"

"No." Huck's phone buzzed, and he lifted it from his back pocket to read the screen. His expression shifted to cop mode.

Laurel set down her fork. "What is it?"

He looked up, his gaze a deep brown. "Ena got the warrant an hour ago, and our tech dug into Lisa's cell phone and computer, which weren't even locked. There are hundreds of texts and emails, some quite sexually graphic, between Lisa and good ole Pastor John Govern."

Laurel tossed her napkin on her plate. "I did not get a hit on that from him. At all. Did you?" The pastor was good at keeping secrets.

"I did not," Huck said, pushing his water glass to the side. "Let's head back to the church and have a nice discussion with him before going out to interview Robert and Jasmine Caine. Lunch is on me."

Laurel stood. "Thanks. I wonder what else is Pastor John Govern hiding."

The pastor was nowhere to be found when they returned to the church after their very late lunch. Huck and Laurel debated the necessity of putting out a BOLO on Pastor John Govern as Huck drove through another residential area to farmland, where he found the long, fence-lined driveway belonging to Robert and Jasmine Caine. "I think we should bring him in officially," Huck reiterated.

Laurel watched the snowy fields fly by outside as winter darkness slowly pressed in. "It's one strategy, especially since he no doubt knew we'd discover he'd been dating

Lisa. But this man is entrenched in the community, and he doesn't mind stepping out of the proverbial pastor box. He owns part of a marijuana growing farm, for goodness sake."

Huck couldn't argue with that. "True. Plus, Lisa was of the age to consent, so he didn't break any laws. Although he clearly broke church doctrine, with the sex and all before marriage."

"Your voice deepens when you get sarcastic," Laurel mused quietly.

Huck glanced her way. In the gray day, her hair was like a beacon of fire. He didn't blame the pastor for his initial reaction to her beauty. He found it even more alluring that the woman had no clue as to her appeal. "All right, we won't put out the BOLO unless we fail to locate him after tomorrow morning. Then, it's BOLO city."

"Agreed," Laurel said, sounding distracted.

Huck followed the driveway around another bend. The snow-filled fields were vacant, but several red barns dotted the landscape in the distance. A sign loomed to the right, indicating this was the correct way to the Caine Stables and Riding Academy. "It looks like Robert Caine has diversified his portfolio."

Laurel turned to face him, and her dual-colored eyes glimmered in the drizzly day. "Have you noticed we keep coming back to Abigail Caine?"

"Yes. Hopefully her half-brother will be able to shed some light on the woman. I don't like enigmas."

"Neither do I," Laurel murmured.

Huck pulled around a circular driveway in front of a white clapboard farmhouse, complete with deck currently in full Christmas mode. Green and red lights hung from every eave, a series of fake poinsettias covered the entire porch, and a lit-up cross made the snow sparkle around an outside tree covered with bright blue lights from top to bottom. "They're certainly in the spirit."

"Humph." Laurel opened the truck door and jumped down.

Huck followed suit and waited for her at the front of the truck while Aeneas made good use of bushes by the garage. Her boots were the same ones that lacked traction, so Huck kept near in case she started to slip. "You want lead on this?"

She shrugged. "We've been playing off each other well so far. Let's just see where the interviews take us."

He liked that about her. No pulling rank

270

or one-upmanship. She just wanted answers. Did she even have an ego? Everyone did, right?

The door opened before Huck could knock, and the man standing inside jumped. "Oh. Sorry. You took me by surprise." He smiled at Huck and then turned to Laurel. The smile disappeared and his mouth gaped open. Both of his blue eyes widened, and he stepped back. He was about six feet tall and looked like a country guy with a red flannel jacket, jeans, boots, and a cowboy hat. His face was angular with a short beard and mustache. "What the hell?"

Huck's instincts flared and he moved forward, partially putting his body between Laurel and the threat. "Excuse me?"

The guy shook his head, looking shocked. "What is going on? Who are you?"

"Honey?" a woman called from inside the home. "Who's at the door?"

Huck lowered his chin and made sure his hands were free in case he needed to take this guy down. "I'm Captain Rivers from Fish and Wildlife, and this is Special Agent Laurel Snow from the FBI. We just want to ask you a few questions." What the hell was wrong with the guy?

The man swallowed and shook his head like a dog with a face full of snow. "I'm

271

sorry. I, uh, I'm sorry. I saw the gun at your waist, Agent Snow. FBI? On my doorstep?"

It was an extreme reaction to seeing a Fed, but the man did grow pot. Perhaps he'd done so illegally in the past and hadn't gotten rid of his fear.

A woman slipped up to his side and smiled. "Hi. What's going on?"

The guy stepped aside. "I'm being weird." He smiled. "I'm Robert Caine, and this is my wife, Jasmine. Please come inside." He opened the door wider and gestured them inside, smiling at the dog. "He's adorable and more than welcome inside."

Laurel gave Huck a puzzled look but followed them inside a house all but puking Christmas decor. Huge, decorated tree in the corner, villages on antique furniture, and several cross-themed pillows on the sofa and matching chairs. The mantel was alive with pictures of family gatherings in holiday frames, and a low fire crackled merrily in the fireplace. Even the music, coming softly from what looked like the kitchen, crooned holiday songs.

Jasmine gestured them to the sofa. "I might've gone a little bit overboard with the decorations this year."

"Might have?" her husband asked, laughing. "Yeah. Might have." He tossed his hat onto a peg, walked around a sofa table covered with snow globes, and took one of the chairs.

Huck moved to sit nearest him with Laurel on his other side on the sofa. "Sorry to just drop by like this. I didn't figure we'd find you at home."

Aeneas sat by a tall figurine of Santa and tilted his head, one ear cocked, as he studied the red and white ceramic face.

Robert nodded. "I came home for an early supper and was just leaving when I almost ran you over on the porch. Sorry again about that." His gaze flicked to Laurel's gun. "You just caught me off guard. We're legal growers, you know."

Yeah, Huck had figured the panic was drug related. "We know," he said.

Jasmine hovered near the sofa. "Can I get anybody coffee or tea? I also have some fresh scones."

Laurel smiled up at her. "That's kind of you, but we just ate. Please, have a seat. If you don't mind answering a few questions, we'll get out of your hair."

Jasmine took the other chair. She was short and curvy with long brown hair and brown eyes. Her peaches and cream complexion made her look like the girl next door. She wore jeans and a white sweater, and her socks had elves on them. "What kind of questions?"

Laurel turned more toward her. "We understand you were friends with Lisa Scotford."

Tears instantly sprang into Jasmine's eyes. "Did you catch that man Carl who killed her?"

CHAPTER TWENTY-THREE

Laurel's stomach clenched. "Carl? What do you know about a suspect named Carl?"

Jasmine clutched her hands together. "Nothing, but Abigail called and left a message yesterday about the situation. She told us all about Carl and that he's the prime suspect, and to be careful and stay away from him, just in case. I mean, the man digs graves for a living."

Laurel sat back. Abigail had surely known that the Caines would be interviewed. "Do you have any independent knowledge, besides what Abigail told you, that a man named Carl had anything to do with Lisa's death?"

Jasmine shook her head. "No. Is it not him?" She turned tearful eyes to her husband. "What if they never find out who hurt her?"

"They will," Robert said. "Don't worry, honey."

Huck cleared his throat. "Were you and Lisa close?"

Jasmine's lips trembled, and a tear fell onto her smooth cheek. "We were good friends. I volunteer at the church quite a bit, and she works, I mean *worked*, there. We organized many of the events together. I'm only a few years older than Lisa, but she was so mature, I felt like we were as close as sisters." She wiped her eyes.

Robert rubbed his chin. "Do you have any idea who killed her?" he asked Huck. "Who would do something like that?" He frowned, his brows dark slashes on his handsome face.

"We're working on it," Huck said. "For now, do you know who Lisa was dating?"

Robert's eyebrows lifted. "Dating? I don't think she was dating anybody."

Jasmine's cheeks turned a lovely shade of pink.

Robert looked at her. "Sweetheart? You're blushing like that Santa over there."

She winced. "Lisa did have a boyfriend, but it was a secret. I promised not to tell anybody."

Robert's upper lip lifted in a surprised-looking grin. "Even me?"

Jasmine fidgeted in her chair. "Yeah, even you. I'm sorry." She looked at Laurel. "Lisa was dating Pastor John. They'd been seeing each other for at least six months."

Robert's chin dropped to his chest. "Seriously? Pastor John and Lisa? Just dating or . . ."

Jasmine blushed even more. "More than dating. They were intimate." She sighed. "Lisa loved him, and I think he loved her. I don't know why they didn't make it official. She was hoping that he was going to propose at Christmas." More tears gathered in Jasmine's eyes. "Now that will never happen. I guess I'm glad she found happiness and love before she died."

Robert's mouth opened and then closed. "Wow. I had no idea."

Jasmine grimaced. "They were good at keeping secrets, but Lisa had to confide in somebody. I so hoped they would get married." She looked at the window, at the sparkling lights outside.

Laurel kept her voice calm. "Is there something else, Jasmine?"

Jasmine squirmed and her face lost the blush. "I shouldn't say anything, I know, but . . ."

"What is it?" Huck asked, his tone firm.

She jolted. "Lisa was late," she whispered. "I mean, with her monthly . . ."

"Lisa was pregnant?" Huck guessed.

"I don't know. But she was late, and I know she was going to take a test if she didn't get her period by the weekend," Jasmine whispered.

Laurel shared a look with Huck. "Did she tell Pastor John that she might be pregnant?" Laurel asked.

"I don't think so," Jasmine said, her voice catching.

The autopsy on Lisa's body was more important than ever. What if she'd been killed by somebody other than the serial killer? What if somebody, somebody like the pastor, had committed a copycat murder? She looked at Huck.

"On it," he said, reaching for his phone and sending off a quick text. "We don't have the final report yet — I'll have Dr. Ortega take a closer look." He slipped his phone back in place and looked at Robert. "Did you know Lisa very well?"

"Just through my wife," Robert said. "She seemed like a happy young woman. Always smiling and cheerful." He shrugged. "I've met her family at the church, and they're nice people, always willing to jump in and move chairs or bring coffee or whatever. They were involved with Pastor John's outreach into nearby cities. It's a good family."

Huck turned his head. "Outreach?"

Robert picked at a string on his jeans. "Yeah. The church has always given as much as possible to the area around Genesis Valley, and Pastor John has tried to offer help and the gospel to the nearest cities. We have a couple groups who take food to the homeless and try to share the word of God."

"Does he administer to prostitutes?" Laurel asked.

"Oh, he administers to everybody who needs it," Jasmine said, her eyes wide. "I like that the church is getting bigger and involving more people. I feel the church, with God on our side, should do as much as possible, you know?"

Huck's gaze narrowed with pure suspicion, and Laurel couldn't blame him.

Pastor John had spent time in Seattle and Tacoma. Was there a way to connect him to one of the prostitutes? One of the missing women? Laurel focused on Robert. "Is there anything else either of you can tell us about Lisa?"

They both shook their heads.

Laurel cleared her throat. "Do you mind if we discuss your father?"

Robert's eyes darkened and he leaned toward her. "Not at all. Please tell me somebody is finally going to take his disappearance seriously. I've called the locals, the state police, the feds, and even the news media. My father would never have stayed away from the church for this long. He loves our church."

"What do you think happened to him?" Laurel asked.

"I don't know." Robert shifted his weight on the damask-covered chair.

She read his expression and body language: he appeared open and eager to discuss the matter. "I have to ask you some difficult questions, and I'd like you to understand that my goal is to find your father. All right?"

"Sure," Robert said. "What kind of difficult questions?"

"Tell me about your relationship with Zeke Caine. How old were you when he adopted you?"

Robert reached for a cookie on a snowman-shaped platter on the sofa table. "My biological father died from leukemia, and my mother traveled for a while with me, finally stopping here in town and finding her place with the church when I must've been around four years old." He scratched his beard. "To be honest, I don't remember any of it."

"Pastor Caine adopted you at that time?"

Huck asked.

Robert nodded. "Right around that time. I started calling him father after they were married, so it must've been the same time. He's a good father, and I miss him." The man spoke about the pastor in the present tense.

"When was your sister born?" Laurel asked.

"Half-sister," Robert snarled. "We don't share full blood, let me tell you."

Laurel leaned back. No love lost there. "I thought you said Abigail called earlier. It sounds like you're in touch."

Jasmine shook her hair and the strands fell softly around her shoulders. "Oh, no. She left a message. We don't speak to her if possible." She shivered. "There's just something so . . . not right about her."

Robert squirmed as if fighting himself. "Listen. I don't have any proof, and I'm sure it's a sacrilege to even say anything, but I'd ask her about our father's disappearance. I mean, he disappears two years after she returns to the area and starts teaching? It could be a coincidence, but . . ."

Jasmine clutched her hands. "Oh, Robby. Abigail isn't the nicest of people, but she wouldn't have hurt her own father. Come on." The music shifted from *Silent Night* to

281

Rudolph, the Red-Nosed Reindeer.

"I know. You're right," Robert said, his tone gentle.

Jasmine lifted the cookie plate and held it in front of Laurel. "Please take one. It's a new recipe."

Laurel chose a bell-shaped cookie with thick yellow frosting. "Thank you."

"For you, Captain?" Jasmine half stood to extend the platter.

He lifted a hand. "Thank you, but I'm allergic to nuts, and I can see a couple in there. I appreciate the offer, though."

Laurel frowned. That was news. She bit into the cookie and nearly moaned, finishing it quickly. "That is the best cookie I've ever had."

Jasmine grinned and blushed prettily. "Thank you. It's the frosting, to be honest. I've worked for years on it."

"You should taste her strawberry pie. I've seen adults nearly come to blows at the church picnic for the last piece." Robert winked at his wife.

Laurel kept herself from taking another cookie. One was enough. "Do you mind telling us about Abigail?"

Robert's amusement faded. "Sure. She came along when I was five years old, and within a few years, was smarter than anybody in the room. But she didn't use that gift from God to do good. Instead, she was always getting in trouble and trying not to get caught. Being bored is the absolute worst thing for Abigail, and everyone around her, because she'll make you pay for it." He shook his head.

"Was she ever treated by a professional or diagnosed by a psychologist?" Laurel asked as gently as she could.

Robert barked out a laugh. "No. Of course not. Most people couldn't see the evil in her, and she usually managed to blame me for her mischief. Then Mom died, Dad got distant, and some good wind of fate, in the figure of the local authorities, took Abby away." He looked down at his hands. "It was one of the best days of my life."

"Oh, Robby." Jasmine stood and walked over to plunk herself on his lap. She kissed his forehead.

Laurel watched them. What would it be like to have somebody like that, a partner in life? She'd never come close in a romantic relationship. "How did your mother die?"

"River rafting," Robert said quietly. "It was a family trip, and she fell out of the boat and hit her head on a rock. She didn't drown, but a brain hemorrhage got her anyway. I was in my teens and Abigail was around twelve." He leaned his head on his wife's neck.

Huck eyed the cookies as if he wanted to risk the allergic reaction. "Why did the authorities take Abigail out of the house?"

Robert settled an arm around Jasmine's waist, holding her securely on his lap. "Nothing bad was going on. Abby tested off the chart on the state tests at school, and a couple of the teachers wanted her sent to gifted programs. Our father dropped into a depression after Mom died, and he wasn't taking as good care of Abby as he should. He would've come out of it, but they went after him, and he didn't fight the authorities. He just let her go."

Jasmine rubbed his shoulders. "I'm sure your dad regretted that time."

"He really did," Robert said. "I know he tried to contact Abby through the years, but until she came back home, she never answered his calls or letters."

"What happened when she returned home?" Laurel asked, her instincts awakening.

"She called him, and they got together for lunch. Then she called me, and we met up. I had hoped she'd changed, but I could tell right away that she was back to her old games. She spoke unkindly about Jasmine, and we'd just gotten married," Robert said.

Jasmine rolled her eyes. "I still think we could've worked that out. Sometimes a sibling doesn't like a new family member."

"You don't know her," Robert insisted. "She's like a poison that works slowly. You end up dead before you even realize you were infected. Trust me."

Huck shifted his weight. "Do you really think Abigail would harm her own father?"

"Yes," Robert said instantly. He looked at his wife. "I'm sorry to say that, and I'll pray to the Lord that I'm wrong."

Jasmine moved uneasily. "If that's true, and I hope it isn't, are you in danger from her? I mean, if she hurt your father and you're a witness, will she come after you?"

"No," Robert said. "She's not afraid that I'm a witness against her. If she comes after me, it'll be because she's bored and feels betrayed. To Abby, everyone is here for her amusement, and if you let her down, she thinks you did it on purpose. She has to make you pay. So she wouldn't come for me, sweetheart. She'd rip out my heart by coming for you."

Icy fingers crept along Laurel's spine. That was a good description of a person with a sadistic, narcissistic personality disorder.

Jasmine turned to look at Huck. "If you

question Abigail, could you say you didn't talk to us?"

"She'll know they talked to us," Robert said wearily. "She probably knew they'd talk to us before *they* knew they would. She's that smart."

Huck smiled. "We'll inform her that we didn't learn anything from you and we're quite irritated about it."

Jasmine visibly relaxed against her husband. "Thank you. I appreciate it."

Laurel stood and Huck did the same.

Robert set Jasmine in the chair as he stood and escorted them to the door and outside to the lavishly decorated porch. Aeneas ran ahead to the truck, his tail wagging. "If you're dealing with Abby, watch your backs. Or even your front. It doesn't matter which direction she comes from. She'll hit you before you even know she's there, and she'll do it laughing."

"Thanks." Huck shook hands with the man.

Laurel did the same. "We'll be okay, Robert."

He released her. "Only if she wants you to be okay, Agent Snow. If she doesn't, if she has you in her sights, you're as good as in pain right now — you just don't know it yet." With that, he turned back inside and shut the door.

The sound of the door lock engaging scratched through the cold, quiet night.

CHAPTER TWENTY-FOUR

It was after ten at night when Huck pulled into their shared parking lot, and Laurel's stomach was growling, her late lunch long forgotten. After finishing the interview with the Caines, they'd returned to the church to wait for Pastor John. When he didn't return, they spent time speaking with Lisa Scotford's neighbors and then community members who'd worked with her but didn't learn any new information.

Laurel looked up at the darkened windows of her office. They should get some holiday lights or something. Then she slipped out of his truck, which he'd parked next to her SUV, turning toward him before shutting the door. "I'll see you tomorrow. What time do you want to start?"

He sat in his seat and looked at his watch. "It's after ten now. Aeneas and I are headed home to relax. How about we meet around seven tomorrow morning? That'll give us time to go through today's daily reports from Monty before creating a battle plan. What do you think?"

"Seven is perfect." That would give her time to work out first. She needed to burn energy and loosen her clenched muscles. "I think we should interview the Scotfords, track down Pastor John, and then speak with Dr. Caine again. She keeps interfering with the investigation, and I'd like her take on her father's disappearance." It wouldn't be the first or the last time that Laurel worked more than one case at a time. In fact, it was rare she was working just one case.

"Great," Huck said grimly. "Can't wait. The pastor had better not be in the wind." He looked up at the darkened sky. "Drive carefully. There are drifts across the road, and it's pure ice beneath."

She had eyes to see the danger for herself but was beginning to appreciate his protective nature. If she had any real friends, she'd find somebody to set him up with. But the people she knew were more like acquaintances. Opening the SUV door, she sat inside and started the engine. Did she regret her lack of friends? She'd been a decade younger than anybody in college and graduate school, and then she'd focused solely on her career. Had she missed an important part of life? Maybe it was too late to form the skills to make friendships like she saw on television. She shut the door.

Huck appeared at her front window with an industrial-sized scraper and made quick work of the front and side windows. Wow. He moved fast. She hadn't seen him jump out of his truck.

A whirlwind spread through her abdomen. She rolled her window down. "I meant to buy a scraper today in town but forgot, so I planned to let the defroster take care of that. Thank you."

He opened the back door and tossed the scraper on the floor. "You'd still be here in twenty minutes if you waited for the window to defrost." The door shut quietly.

She smiled. "That was kind of you." Did she even know how to flirt? All of a sudden, she truly wanted to know how to flirt. To catch his attention, although that would be a mistake. They were much too different in personality type, and the fable of opposites attracting never ended well. "Thank you."

Without answering, he turned and jogged up the sidewalk, disappearing inside the door to the building, which was now wrapped like a Christmas present. Somebody had been busy earlier. She rolled up her window.

Laurel resisted the impulse to follow him and offer to buy him dinner. "You're losing it," she muttered, pulling out of the parking lot. "Now you're talking to yourself. You know, madness and genius are flip sides of the same coin."

Enough of that. The ground metaphorically shifted beneath her when she thought about Huck Rivers. When was the last time she'd had her hormonal levels calculated? She was pushing thirty, so perhaps the biological clock legend had some truth to it. Her mother most likely had a tea for that.

The windshield wipers rhythmically scraped falling snow off the window, and the heat poured through the vents, making her drowsy. She blinked several times to keep awake. The night was dark, the trees silent, and the world wintery.

She drove for several miles outside of town toward her mother's house, rethinking the events of the day. Had Pastor John known of Lisa's possible pregnancy? A burst of wind tossed ice and snow across the window and she slowed down, turning up the speed of the wipers. Then she continued around a curve, careful of the ice.

A sharp *crack* blew open the back window. Ice flew inside and she ducked, instinctively slowing down.

Another crack echoed, and a projectile glanced off the top of the vehicle. That was a shotgun! She hit the gas pedal and looked frantically around, trying to find the threat.

Fast and ominous, a tall truck roared out from between two trees, fishtailing on the road behind her. Even from a distance, she could see the darker shade of chains secured to the overlarge tires. The driver partially leaned out, pointing a handgun at her car, the snow falling and lightening his black sweatshirt.

She swerved around another curve just as bullets pinged along the right rear side of the SUV.

Gasping, she fumbled for the phone in her laptop bag and pressed the button. "Dial 9-1-1," she yelled, speeding up but swerving across the ice. She overcorrected and managed to bounce off the opposite snowbank and into the middle of the road.

"9-1-1, what is your emergency?" a calm female voice asked.

"This is FBI Special Agent Laurel Snow, and I'm on Birch Tree Road being pursued. Shots fired and agent under duress," she yelled.

The truck burst forward in a rush of speed and smashed into the rear of her SUV.

She fell forward and the vehicle spun in a wild circle. The phone clattered onto the floor. She regained control and punched the gas, driving down the middle of the deserted road, her ears ringing. There was no way she could outrun the truck. She caught sight of another curve up ahead and pressed the gas pedal even harder, wincing as the SUV jumped and then started to slide.

She hit the curve and let gravity take over, spinning the vehicle into the trees. The passenger side hit with the crunch of metal on bark. Her seatbelt jerked her back, stealing her breath, just as the airbag blew into her face. Pain flared along her forehead and dust flew up her nose.

Silence reigned.

Gasping, crying, she yanked her weapon out of her waistband and jumped out of the vehicle, falling in the snow. Panting, she managed to slog through the freezing drifts to the nearest tree just as the truck skidded to a stop.

She dropped to her knees, aimed, and fired.

Huck went ice cold when the call came over the radio. He dialed into the office. "Play me the 9-1-1 call," he ordered, spinning the truck around in his driveway and listening.

He'd turned off Birch Tree Road to get to his place, and Laurel should've continued on it to reach her mother's house on the other side of the forested land. The operator played the tape for him, and his gut hurt.

He pressed the pedal and careened down his road before turning onto Birch, fishtailing until he regained control. Two other officers and an ambulance were also on the way to the scene, if there was a scene, but he was several precious minutes ahead of them all.

Why had he let her go home alone? He should've at least driven her.

Then he shook his head. He hadn't been on a date with her. Not in a million years would he have driven Monty, or another colleague, home. Damn it. He slammed his fist on the steering wheel, and Aeneas looked up from his bed in the back seat. "You might need to work tonight, buddy," he said. What if Laurel had been shot? Or run off the road? Or, God forbid, taken?

He went even faster, much too fast for the icy conditions. In fact, he had to use all of his strength to keep control of the vehicle.

Aeneas barked from the back seat.

"I've got it," Huck said tersely. He slid around another curve and nearly passed the half-buried SUV off to the side of the road in the trees. Instead, he stopped and jumped out of the truck, pulling his weapon free of its holster. "Laurel?" he bellowed, opening the back door and letting Aeneas have his head. "Find her, boy. Search." Then he edged around the back of the truck. He could only see one vehicle, and her call had mentioned a truck following her, so where was that truck? "Laurel?"

Aeneas barked and bounded through the snow toward the SUV. He reached the front door and barked three times before sitting. The front door opened, and Laurel staggered out, covered in snow, her gun in her hand. Blood covered the right side of her face.

The relief that shook Huck nearly dropped him to the ground. Seeing her alert with Aeneas guarding her, Huck immediately scouted the entire area, gun out, looking for the threat.

"I think they drove off," Laurel said, sounding dazed.

Huck waded through the deep drifts to reach her, the snow reaching his thighs. "Are you hurt?" He reached out and secured her weapon since her hand was shaking.

"No." The woman looked dazed.

Ah, fuck it. He lifted her against his chest and powered through the snowbank to his still-running truck, where he set her in the passenger-side seat. "Look at me."

She faced him, her legs out. "I'm seeing clearly and have acceptable cognitive function. However, I might be sliding into shock."

He reached across her and turned the heat up to full blast. "Let me see." He turned on the extra cab lights and scrutinized her face. "Where is the blood coming from?"

"What blood?" She gingerly reached up and touched her eyebrow. "Oh. I see."

Sirens wailed down the road, followed by swirling red and blue lights. The sheriff pulled to a stop first, with an ambulance and paramedic van right behind him. Monty arrived next in a Fish and Wildlife rig, followed by Special Agent Smudgeon in a battered blue truck.

Laurel looked over her shoulder. "Oh, crap."

Huck's chest lightened as the paramedics struggled through the snow. "She has a cut on her face somewhere, but I don't see any other injuries." He stepped back so they could get closer, not liking it. At all. So he opened the back door and motioned Aeneas in. The dog happily jumped inside and lay down out of the snowstorm.

Monty hustled toward him, slipping on

the ice. "Is she okay?"

Huck nodded. "Yeah. Call for a tow to get the SUV out of the trees, would you? We want the state lab to take a look at it for bullets as well as paint from an obvious impact." The entire rear of the blue SUV was scraped with white paint. Irritation clawed through him again. Laurel could've been killed.

She leaned to the side as the paramedic gently wiped off her face. "I returned fire, and I think I hit a tire, but I'm not sure. I definitely hit the truck."

"Did you see the driver?" Huck asked.

"No. The driver was only a figure behind the dark window, and he or she kept the interior lights off. The truck was an older Chevy, no plates, big tires, and many dents. Probably rusty, but it was hard to discern in the dark." Laurel winced as the paramedic finished removing the blood.

Huck leaned closer. "Does she need stitches?"

"I don't think so," the male paramedic said, reaching for his bag. "I'm Bert. What's your name, gorgeous?"

"Laurel," she said, snowflakes falling on her boots.

The paramedic was around sixty and built like a truck. His hands looked gentle, and his motions were quick. "The cut is right above the eyebrow, and a butterfly should do it." He quickly bandaged the injury and then shone a light into Laurel's dual-colored eyes. "Let's check you for a concussion." He ran her through a series of tests and then silently packed up. "You're good to be transported to the hospital for more tests. All right?"

She shook her head. "No. I'm good."

The paramedic frowned. "Your chest and ribs are going to be sore from the seatbelt, and your head might hurt from the airbag as well as the impact. You were smart to wait for backup in your vehicle instead of walking in the storm, so let's be smart now and go to the hospital."

"No." Laurel put snap into her voice. "I'm fine."

Agent Smudgeon hesitated at the end of Huck's truck. "Laurel? I sent the information you gave Huck to our database and will write a report when I get in tomorrow. If you don't want to go to the hospital, can I take you home?"

"I've got her," Huck said, before Laurel could answer.

The sheriff came closer. "You can't give any sort of description of the shooter?"

Laurel's left cheekbone was starting to

swell, and she held an icepack supplied by Bert against it. "I didn't see the shooter. Only the truck."

The sheriff sighed. "Should we insist that the girl goes to the hospital?"

Laurel cut him a glare. "The girl is fine. Why don't you go find whoever was driving that truck?" With that, she swung her legs inside Huck's rig and shut the door.

Huck looked down at the blowhard. "You heard her." He moved past the man toward the wreck. Laurel would want her phone and laptop bag. "Get to work, Sheriff," he called over his shoulder. "Now."

CHAPTER TWENTY-FIVE

Laurel adjusted her position in the passenger side of Huck's truck. Her head ached, and her ribs protested, but otherwise, she felt surprisingly healthy. Fortunate to be alive and relatively unharmed. Adrenaline still buzzed through her blood, and she needed an outlet for it.

Huck drove through the storm while Aeneas snored in the back seat. "You did good," he grunted.

She looked over at him. "Excuse me?"

He slowed down as snow blew across the road. "The speed you must have used to crash the car, jump out, and shoot? That's impressive. You're a fine agent, and not only because of your profiling skills."

Well, if that didn't instantly refocus her adrenaline, nothing ever would. "Thank you for coming so quickly," she murmured. She'd never forget the sight of him jumping out of his running truck and scouting the area, his body hard and tough, his gun out and ready. Sure, he would've done the same for anybody in trouble, but there had been an edge to his voice when he'd called her name. An edge just for her. So she took the chance. "I don't want to go home alone."

His jaw tightened, but he didn't respond.

Curiosity, along with unease, kept her quiet. If he didn't say anything, then they could forget she had said it. Of course, they were both so tense, a night together would be beneficial. And the guy was hot. Seriously.

She was awkward when it came to dating, or when it came to this, and that was usually all right with her. Not this time. This time, she wanted to be smooth and charming. That wasn't happening.

Then he turned down the lane to his house.

Her breath caught. Then she quickly texted her mother that she was in a minor wreck and not to worry in case the news picked it up, plus that she was staying with a friend for the night.

He parked outside the first garage door of the sprawling shop building. "Stay in your seat." Jumping out, he released the dog and then crossed around to open her door, leaning in to stare in her eyes. "Tell me the truth. Are you hurt? Dizzy? Foggy at all?" If the man got any sweeter, she might have to reconsider her analysis of opposites not being good for each other.

"No. My brain is fine." She yelped when he plucked her out of her seat and turned, striding for the front door of his cabin. Then she laughed.

The dog wisely finished his business and ran in behind them, hustling into the kitchen to eat.

Huck set her on the back of the sofa and unbuckled his belt and thigh holster, placing them on a table near the door. He turned back to her, his gaze glittering.

Then they were on each other. He tangled his fingers in her hair and kissed her, his mouth cold from outside and his tongue hot enough to burn. His kiss was rough and demanding, contrasting with the firm hand holding her in place.

Heat and need shot through her body, landing between her legs. She shoved her hands up beneath his shirt and coat, scratching along his ripped abs.

He tore his mouth away and unzipped his coat, his gaze dark and hungry. The coat dropped to the floor, and he grasped her zipper, then tossed her coat on top of his. "If you're hurt, let me know. Anything.

Promise?"

She nodded. This kind of need couldn't be healthy. She'd read about wild desire in books, but never in her life had she *wanted* like this. Mere hormones and the earlier adrenaline rush didn't fully explain the feelings coursing through her.

He slowly drew his shirt over his head and revealed that chest she'd wanted to play with before. Hard and muscled.

She reached for the zipper of his cargo pants.

"Not yet." He grasped the bottom of her sweater and drew the soft material over her head before dropping to his knees. Even on his knees, his head remained level with her ribcage, although she was perched on the back of the sofa. The difference in their sizes, so obvious in the moment, spiraled her desire even higher.

He bent his head and gently traced his fingers over her ribcage. "You're bruised here." Then he leaned in and kissed the spot where his fingers had touched.

Her abdominal muscles contracted, and her thighs widened. "I don't hurt," she gasped.

He reached behind her and unhooked her plain pink bra, drawing the straps down her arms and revealing her breasts. He cupped them both and then ran his knuckles across her clavicle. "Bruised here, too," he murmured, leaning in and licking along her collarbone.

Nerves fired inside her, shooting electrical currents through her body. She shoved both hands into his thick dark hair and held on. While she'd expected fast and wild, he was giving her controlled and attentive. Even though she'd claimed to be unharmed, he was double-checking before proceeding. He was also driving her insane. "Huck." She pulled on his hair to force his head up. Then she leaned down and took his mouth.

He planted both hands on her thighs and tilted his head, taking over the kiss as naturally as breathing. Without warning, he stood and lifted her, his hands firm on the back of her legs. Then he moved toward the bedroom, still kissing her, still in control.

She trembled, her nails digging into his shoulders, returning his kiss. The man reminded her of the storm outside, wild and free, natural and beautiful. Unfathomable and dangerous.

He set her on the bed and crouched, unlacing her boots and sliding them off. "Any pain in your ankles?" He slipped down her socks and caressed her feet, ankles, and up her legs.

"No," she breathed. The only pain was the one getting stronger and more insistent . . . for him.

He levered himself up and reached for her skirt, drawing the thick material and her panties down her legs in one smooth motion. "You're beautiful, Laurel." He leaned over and kissed her right hipbone, surprising her. "So small." His hands caressed her flanks, carefully avoiding the bruises across the front of her ribcage. "So fragile."

She clasped his arms and tried to pull him up. "I'm not fragile."

He cocked his head like a predator spotting prey. "Is that a fact? Let's see how well you shatter." With a wicked grin, he nipped her abdomen and then moved farther down, unerringly finding her with his mouth.

She arched off the bed, fire lancing through her.

He planted one large hand over her abdomen and pressed her down to the bed. "You have enough bruises, darlin.' Hold still." Then his mouth went at her, lips and tongue, and he held her in place. His teeth sank into her inner thigh with a bit too much force, and then he focused all his attention on her sex.

She climbed fast and hard, breaking with a cry so quickly her mind didn't have time to catch up with her body. The waves were wide and hard, and she rode them, holding her breath. Finally, she breathed out in relief.

When he lifted his head, satisfaction in his smile, she could only gape. Sometimes it took her forever to reach orgasm. "Wow."

His laugh slid along her skin like it belonged just there. He stood and unbuckled his belt, kicking his boots off before shoving his cargo pants and boxer-briefs to the floor.

Her mouth watered. Captain Huck Rivers was in proportion with the rest of his spectacular body. She studied two bullet scars near his right hip and a healed knife wound in his right thigh, only a half-inch from his femoral artery. He'd been very lucky to have survived.

She sat up and reached for him.

"You get to take it easy this time." His voice was teasing but his hands firm as he settled her back down. "Are you sure you're up to this?"

"Yes, and so are you," she said, scooting up the bed, smiling at her own joke.

His answering grin was a reward. She was rarely funny.

He grasped her hips and helped her, lifting her up and then settling her down with her hair splayed across the pillow. "Your hair is beyond description." Rising over her, he reached into the bedside table for a condom, which he ripped open with his teeth.

She took it and leaned down to roll it over his impressive length. "Nothing is beyond description." Except perhaps the breathless way she was feeling right now.

He settled over her, pushing inside, so slowly she held her breath. He took his time, letting her body accommodate itself to him. His intensity, the way he looked at her, made her want to shy away, but he wouldn't let her. Huck Rivers took intimacy to a new level, one she didn't know how to navigate. "Huck?" she whispered.

"I'm here with you." With one final twist of his hips, he shoved all the way inside her.

She gasped and stilled, her body stretching around his, her nerves firing along his length. He was more than with her. He was all around her. She lifted her thighs and slid them against his hips.

"There you go," he said, smoothing her hair away from her face. Then he buried his face next to her ear, inhaling. "Strawberries and something else. Something just you and this spectacular color." He lifted himself up, fully embedded inside her, and captured her gaze. "You're a perfect mix of colors. Green and blue, red and copper. Such a contrast

— it's beautiful."

Nobody had said that to her before, and in Huck's voice there was a sincerity and hint of vulnerability that touched her.

"Huck," she murmured, tracing his hard jawline up to his hair and digging in with both hands.

He flashed her that wicked smile again. Balancing himself with one hand, he pulled out of her, then pushed back in.

She gasped and exhaled as endorphins flooded her body. "Let's see what you've got, Captain," she whispered, releasing his hair and scoring his flanks until she could reach around and sink her nails into his butt. The man had a very fine butt.

His jaw clamped and he powered inside her, not holding back.

She responded instinctively, letting her body take over for her mind. Endorphins and hormones no longer mattered. Only that feeling, that driving, desperate, tingling feeling that promised ecstasy. That guaranteed unbelievable pleasure.

Only that and the man giving it to her existed.

She shoved her hips up to meet his thrusts, digging her nails into his flesh, holding on with all she had.

He changed his angle and slammed into

308

her even harder, triggering a climax that had her gasping for breath. She shut her eyes and saw sparks as hot waves shuddered through her.

He dropped his face to her hair, burrowing, his body jerking deep inside her with his own climax. He turned his head and licked the shell of her ear before kissing the vulnerable area behind it on her neck.

She gasped and tried to calm her breathing.

He shifted up on one elbow, lazy satisfaction in his light brown eyes. "You okay?"

She tried to stop panting. "Just that the word 'wow' is overused in today's society. It should be sacred."

His chuckle stirred something more than the physical in her, and warning began to clang in her head. Then he withdrew and stood, going into the bathroom to take care of the condom. When he returned, he slid them both beneath the covers and spooned his overly large body around her.

"I, um, don't require cuddling," she said, her face heating.

He nipped her earlobe. "I have to admit, I wasn't sure we'd fit with the size difference. Thought I might have to hang you upside down by the ankles or something."

She laughed before she could stop herself

and then slowly let her body relax against his heated front. "Upside down, huh? I don't think so."

"Hmmm," he rumbled, pulling her closer. "Go to sleep, Agent Laurel Snow. I need my beauty rest."

This intimacy with him was too alluring. Too appealing. His playful after-sex side was no doubt reserved for only a special few. Her eyelids grew heavy.

Then his phone buzzed.

He reached down to the floor to shake out his pants and retrieve his phone. "Rivers," he barked. His body stiffened behind her. "When? How many? Okay. Get a full team, and I'll meet you at the base in twenty. I have my pack here." He clicked off.

She turned around to face him. "What happened?"

"Lost snowmobilers on Titan Cliffs. They were supposed to be back hours ago, but nobody called it in." He stood.

She sat up, holding the covers to her chest. "You could drop me off on the way."

He was already turning to grab clothing, distancing himself in more ways than one. "No. Your house is in the opposite direction. Just get some sleep. I'll take you home later."

She kept the covers in place. It wasn't as

if she'd wanted anything more than one night. Even so, she waited until he'd loped into the kitchen before dropping the covers and fetching her clothing.

Her right inner thigh still ached from his bite.

CHAPTER TWENTY-SIX

Laurel spent the morning knitting and working through the puzzle of the case in Huck's quiet kitchen. She finished her coffee just as he strode through the doorway and hung his snow-filled coat on the hook in the alcove. "Hi." Aeneas ran for the kitchen and jumped on his bowl of food, shaking snow off as he landed.

"Hi." Huck's eyes were bloodshot and his movements slow. "Sorry it took so long to make it back."

"No problem." She poured another cup of coffee and walked barefoot across the kitchen to hand it to him. "I assume search and rescue is part of your job."

He accepted the coffee and drank half of it down. "Thanks."

Should she feel awkward? She did. Yes, she felt awkward. Interesting. Long ago, she'd banished that feeling from her repertoire. People didn't understand her, and that was all right. So why now? "Um, did you find the lost snowmobilers?"

"We did, and they're all going to be fine. Two are at the hospital being treated, one for frostbite and the other for a broken leg. Three others are fine but hungry and tired." He rolled his shoulders and then kicked off his boots, holding his coffee with one strong hand. "They got caught in a spill and were smart enough to dig in and stay warm. We had to carry one guy out on a litter, and that's why I'm so late." He glanced at her face, his expression inscrutable. "That's quite a bruise. How's the rest of you?"

"Slightly sore but nothing bad," she said. A purple lump had risen beneath her right eye, and with the bandage above her eyebrow, she looked as if she'd taken a bat to the face. The bruises across her ribs and down her side were uniformly purple, as was the strap mark across her upper chest. "I did borrow some ibuprofen."

"Good." He looked at the clock hanging next to the mantel. "I'll take a quick shower and then run you to work. Monty texted earlier and requested a task force meeting sometime early next week. We might need to use your office. Apparently Fish and Wildlife is having trainings in their conference room all week."

313

"Your office," she reminded him. "You're with Fish and Wildlife."

He shook his head. "I work for F&W, but I'm not part of the office. My desk there is temporary."

A horn honked outside. She winced. "I wasn't sure when you'd get here, so I called Kate to pick me up." Then she looked down. "I was able to wash and dry my skirt, but my sweater was a mess, so I borrowed this shirt. Is that okay?" The shirt was long and gray, and tucked into her skirt, looked fashionably too big.

"Uh, yeah." He drank the rest of the coffee and turned to look out the window. The distance between them widened enough that even a woman unable to read subtext caught the tension.

She slipped into her boots. "Thank you." Maybe contemplation later would explain why this felt so uncomfortable. "I'll see you at work."

His smile was both tired and relieved. "Yeah."

She hurried to the door, securing her laptop in her bag with her gun and phone in it. "All right. See you then." She opened the door.

"Laurel?"

She partially turned around. "Yes?"

"This was a one-off." He set the cup on the table by the door, his expression unreadable. "Just thought I'd make that clear."

She couldn't help the surprised chuckle that burbled up. "I'm not interested in you, Huck. Believe me. We're clear." She tripped but made it out the door, shutting it and running through the snow to Kate's bug. "Thanks for picking me up," she breathed once inside and buckled up. Then she frowned. "You need a winter car."

Kate pulled out of the wide driveway. "I know. Funds are tight." She glanced at Laurel's face. "That's quite the bruise."

"Car accident. Well, not an accident. Whoever shot at me is still out there, so we all need to be careful until I find the guy." She liked that Kate didn't ask questions about Huck.

"So, you and the quiet mountain man?" Kate asked. So much for not asking.

"No," Laurel said.

Kate slowed down when the car started to slide. "Oh."

Laurel shifted on the cold leather seat. She'd never trusted people, and she'd missed out on the teenaged skill of girl talk. Perhaps it was time to change that. "We had sex."

Kate coughed. "Oh. Um, was it good?"

315

"Beyond good. It was phenomenal." Laurel sighed. "I'm not looking for a romance, but it still hurt this morning when he said it was a one-off."

Kate jolted and turned her head, her eyes wide. "He said that? Actually said that it was a one-off?"

Laurel nodded.

"What a . . . dick," Kate exclaimed.

Laurel laughed. That statement alone made her feel better about the entire situation. "I thought so. It was rude, right?"

"Rude and dickish. Honest, but he could've been nicer about it." Kate turned down the long driveway to Laurel's mother's house. "I have to tell you, preparing my three girls for the real world and how rotten people can be is a full-time job. Of course, their father already taught them that lesson."

Laurel winced. "Does he see them often?"

"When he can take time away from his bimbo," Kate said, shaking her head. "The state makes him pay child support, or he wouldn't even do that." She slowed near the front porch. "Laurel? Is there any chance this job will be permanent? I saw the benefits package for an FBI full-time employee last night while looking through the contract for my temporary position."

316

Laurel's heart ached for the woman. "I don't think so. Well, maybe? My boss mentioned that the FBI was looking to create a unit out of Seattle to deal with violent crimes. If that actually happens, I'll definitely recommend you to whoever creates it."

"That person won't be you?"

"No," Laurel said. "I'm better as a consultant."

Kate parked the car. "Not a team player, huh?"

Laurel opened her door. "I wouldn't know how to be one." She smiled and caught sight of one of Uncle Blake's farm trucks near the garage. How sweet. He had brought her another vehicle to drive after she'd crashed the SUV? She definitely owed him. "Thanks again, and I'll see you at the office in about an hour."

The skies opened up and pelted hail at her. What else could go wrong this morning?

Deidre Snow huddled in the corner of her kitchen, her butt on the chilly wood floor and her head against a cupboard. One she'd lovingly painted a cheerful yellow color years ago. Kitchens should be cheerful.

Life should be cheerful.

The storm railed outside, and ice slashed against her windows. Trying to get in. Just like her imaginary boogeyman. She could swear somebody had been watching her house the last couple of nights. Oh, she hadn't seen anybody, but the nagging worry hung over her head. Was she imagining things again?

She clutched the keys to her truck in her hand, as she'd done all night, but she couldn't bring herself to go to the garage and get inside it. All. Night. Her baby was in danger with a mountain man who didn't like people, and she didn't have the guts to go rescue her.

The sob that came from her chest was an embarrassment.

She was an embarrassment.

Oh, the town saw her as an eccentric but successful businesswoman who wore flowery dresses and dangly jewelry, but it was a facade. She didn't know a thing about business. Laurel had set up the tea operation, and she'd only been a teenager at the time. All Deidre did was what Laurel had taught her. The business had nothing to do with her true gifts.

She believed she could reach beyond the veil. Her rituals with the moon and the teas, especially the ones she imported before creating her subscription jars, mattered. They infused healing properties into the teas.

They had to matter. Otherwise, what good was she?

She didn't have the energy to go to her knitting room and work. Sometimes it was the only way to soothe the demons raging within her.

At least she'd taught her daughter to knit. She pulled her knees to her chest and rocked back and forth, soothing the panic coursing through her. The heated, breathless, desperate panic that still caught her by the throat after the nightmare. The one in which she was a teenager, back in a new Chrysler, fighting for her life. Losing her innocence.

The front door opened, and she fought a scream.

"Mom?" Laurel rushed toward her, dropping to her knees. "Mom?" She smoothed back Deidre's blond hair from her sweaty brow. "Hey, there." Her voice calmed and her eyes, the dual-colored eyes that sometimes reminded Deidre of the worst night of her life, softened. "Panic attack?"

Deidre gulped. How wrong was this? Her daughter was soothing her. "Yes. I'm sorry." She couldn't help the tears that pricked the back of her eyes.

Laurel gently helped her off the floor and into a comfortable chair at the table. "Let me get you some tea. That will help." She turned back and started a kettle. "There are keys in your hand. Were you coming to get me?"

Deidre dropped the keys on the table. "I wanted to get you. Leaving you alone like that. I'm so sorry."

As the kettle heated, Laurel turned around to face her, today wearing a shirt too large for her small body. A man's shirt. "Mom. I'm a trained FBI agent."

Deidre looked at the lumpy bruise on her daughter's face. "One who's in danger. In your text, you didn't tell me you were injured in the wreck last night. I figured you blew a tire or something."

"I'm fine," Laurel said. "I can handle danger. They kind of train you for it, actually." She smiled, her gaze searching.

Sometimes, when her daughter looked at her like that, Deidre wanted to run. To hide. "I'm sorry you had to stay with that man all night."

A blush colored Laurel's high cheekbones. "I'm not. It was a good night." She wiggled her eyebrows.

Humor caught Deidre unaware. "Laurel,"

she chided, although her heart lifted. It was good that her daughter had a healthy approach to sex. She should be grateful about that. "For goodness sake."

Laurel took a deep breath. "Mom? We have to talk about this. I thought you were seeing a counsellor?"

"I've seen different counsellors for thirty years," Deidre said. "Anxiety and panic attacks are a manageable part of my life."

The kettle whistled, and Laurel turned to pour two cups of Moon's Gifts. "Your trigger is men and my being alone with them." She turned and brought the cups to the table. "I feel like you haven't really told me where this comes from. Is it because of who my father was? Do you actually remember?"

Deidre's throat closed. She took the mug and drank, even though the tea was still too hot. Her daughter was a profiler, and she was brilliant. Even so, Deidre couldn't help but continue the lie. "Sorry, honey. I don't remember anything from that time after my parents died and I ran away to Seattle. Drugs are bad for you, as you know."

Laurel sighed. "I know, but I do wonder about my eyes and hair. Both red hair and heterochromia tend to be hereditary. Are you sure you don't remember the man?"

Deidre shook her head. "I think I'd remember that, but I don't. It was a terribly rough time, and it's all a blur." She reached over and patted Laurel's hand. "But I wouldn't trade away any of it because I got you." She rubbed her mouth. "Before I forget, Uncle Blake left a farm truck out for you to use while your SUV is getting fixed. My truck needs to be serviced, but I'll take care of that just in case. It's only responsible, even though I don't drive anywhere."

Laurel studied her, no doubt seeing beyond the facade. "All right, but if you ever need to talk about that time before I was born, I'm here. There's nothing you could say that would hurt me."

That's what her daughter thought.

Laurel took a sip of her tea. "Sometimes I wonder who I'd be without you."

Deidre reached over and held her hand. "What do you mean?"

"Without you, I don't know if I'd understand what love feels like. How to find it in other people. What it's like to have family and security, no matter how strange I might seem to others." She flipped her hand around and tangled her fingers with her mom's. "You're all-natural love, and I've been surrounded by it my whole life. Even when I went to college so young, it was you and me. You came with me, and I was never alone."

"Of course you were never alone." Her mom squeezed her hand. "You're my daughter. I wouldn't let you go to college all by yourself." She hesitated. "Where is this coming from?"

Laurel shrugged. "This case and some of the people I've met pursuing it. I know I don't say it much, but I love you. Without you, I'd be a different person. One neither of us would like."

"Oh, sweetie. That's not true. You'd be likable no matter what." Deidre leaned over and gave her a half hug. "I love you, too. You'd be a good person even without me. Don't ever forget that." It really was time to let go of the past and move on to the future. She straightened her shoulders. "I think I'll start driving that truck."

Laurel's eyebrows rose. "Well. Good." Then she tilted her head and studied Deidre again.

Darn it.

CHAPTER TWENTY-SEVEN

Paper snowflakes of all different sizes and shapes had been taped over the nude lady wallpaper leading up the steps to the FBI unit's offices. Laurel held her breath as she opened the door, hoping there would be furniture.

"Hi." Kate sat behind the glass display counter, which now held a Christmas village, complete with sparkling lights. "I brought some decorations from home — I hope that's okay. How are you feeling?"

"I'm well, just have a few contusions that are lovely shades of purple," Laurel said, turning to look at a small Christmas tree decked out with multicolored lights and blue ornaments. "The decorations are nice. Thanks for bringing them."

Kate hopped out of her leather chair. "You're welcome. Since I moved from my house in Seattle to a much smaller one in town, I don't have room for all of my decorations. I'm glad to use them."

Laurel smiled, catching her enthusiasm.

Kate pursed her lips. "You changed out of Butthead Rivers's shirt."

Heat suffused Laurel's face. Was this what friendship felt like? "Yes." She looked down at the cream-colored pants and frilly yellow shirt she was wearing. "I need to get my own clothes so I can stop borrowing from my mother. I don't even feel like myself." She'd had to roll up the pants and tuck the bottoms of them into her boots.

"If you can't get your belongings from DC, you could do some Internet shopping with one-day shipping from Seattle." Kate wore winter-white pants and a blue sweater today, along with high-heeled brown boots. She walked to the door that opened into the rest of the space. "I haven't been able to requisition furniture yet."

Laurel followed. "The supply clog that is the federal government takes time."

"I didn't decorate the rest of the space because I wasn't sure who celebrated what and if anybody would care, but we can go all out if we want." Kate paused by the conference room to the right.

Laurel paused at the sight of Walter Smudgeon on the floor surrounded by scraps of paper. "Morning."

"Morning." Walter looked up. "We need to talk. There's no table yet, but the floor works for me." His eyes gleamed.

Laurel strode inside and dropped to the floor, careful of her mom's light-colored pants. "A team meeting. Okay. What do you have?"

He rubbed his chin, and his jowls shook. His skin still held a tinge of gray, but his breathing seemed even. He pushed a stack of papers toward her, and they caught on splinters in the floor. "So far, we have nothing about the person who shot at you last night. The truck you described could belong to any farmer around here. Most probably wouldn't even notice if one went missing for a while."

That's what Laurel had figured. "My getting shot at illustrates that we're getting somewhere on the Snowblood Peak case." Although she didn't yet know where that might be. "We need to take a closer look at everyone we've already spoken with."

"Agreed." Smudgeon pulled a piece of paper from beneath his coffee cup. "I conducted the research you asked for, and I have computer techs in DC doing deep dives. For now, I found a similar crime in this area that took place about fourteen months ago. A young woman was found strangled, her body dumped near the town square at the edge of the baseball diamond."

Laurel's eyebrows rose. She straightened. "That's quite a distance from Snowblood Peak."

He scanned the papers. "The victim's name was Casey Morgan, she was twenty-four, and she was blond. An arrest was made by Sheriff York, and the defendant is awaiting trial, having been held over without bond after suffering a nervous breakdown and ending up in the county psych ward. He's out of the hospital now, healthy enough for trial, I guess." Smudgeon scratched his head beneath his thinning hair. "The victimology is similar. This is the only case like ours that I've found. So far."

It was a good lead. Smudgeon had skills. "Tell me more," Laurel murmured.

He settled his bulk, warming to the subject. "Casey Morgan was a paralegal for the Bearing Law Firm. They're the best firm in town, and they work in tandem with two of the largest Seattle law firms. From what I could glean from just a couple of phone calls this morning, Casey worked hard, had a lot of friends, and volunteered with high-risk youth in her spare time."

Laurel took note. "High risk? Like in the cities along with the Genesis Community

Church?"

"Yes. My third phone call of the day, with her landlady, confirmed that Casey was a member of the church."

Laurel's heart rate sped up. "If we have an early victim, there's a chance the killer made a mistake. Maybe the quick discovery of Casey's murder taught him to dispose of the bodies over a cliff?" She hummed. "Did Casey have family?"

"Not here. Single mom back in Indiana, and they weren't close. Casey moved out here on a volleyball scholarship from Genesis Valley Community College and graduated with a paralegal degree. She worked in Seattle for a while and got the job with the Bearing Law Firm about two years ago." Walter reached for his coffee mug.

"What about the arrest?" Laurel asked.

"Name is Meyer Jackson. He's the ex-boyfriend, drinker, abusive. That's all I could get from the landlady, and Sheriff York hasn't returned my call, nor has the prosecuting attorney." Walter smiled. "However, I do have friends, and here's the autopsy report. I had it emailed to me, and we printed it out with that crappy printer the kids found and brought in." He handed over yellowed paper.

Laurel hadn't realized they'd acquired a

printer. She read through the autopsy report. "Blunt force trauma, blood at the scene, strangulation as cause of death. No evidence of sexual assault." Facts and patterns morphed together in her mind, creating a blanket of possibilities. "She put up an impressive fight." The defensive wounds were expansive. "No DNA found on her?"

"No. He took her clothing and wiped her down with bleach. Poured it over her entire body and made sure her hands were burned right through," Smudgeon muttered. "The guy was prepared, just in case."

"That might be a great lead." She set her palm on the floor and winced as a sliver cut into her skin. "Call the jail, and let's go see Jackson right now." If the sheriff was going to be a pain about this, she needed to act quickly, before he knew anything. No doubt he'd want to protect his arrest.

"Wait." Walter rolled his shoulders. "There's more, and it's sticky. Before Casey dated Meyer Jackson, she dated Huck Rivers, according to the landlady who was quite a gossip."

Laurel's legs froze, even though she was sitting flat on the floor. "What?"

"Yeah," Smudgeon said. "I haven't had a chance to speak with Huck, so that's all I know."

Well, wasn't that inconvenient, considering Laurel currently had whisker burn across her breasts from the man. She shook her head and tried to concentrate. "You know what's interesting about Casey? She sounds a lot like Lisa Scotford. It's possible . . . ," she murmured.

Smudgeon leaned forward. "Go on."

She looked at him, noting a cut from shaving on his neck. "She's the first victim and things go wrong. He kidnaps her, like the others, and she puts up a fight in his vehicle. Maybe a good enough one that she somehow gets out, gets free, and starts to run."

"There are no security cameras around the sports complex." Smudgeon nodded. "She's running for freedom into the forest, and he catches up to her, they fight, and he kills her right then and there. Maybe that's why he moved to easier targets . . . to perfect his skills."

"That makes sense," Laurel mused.

Smudgeon rubbed his eyes. "Stay with me for a minute. I've been thinking about your profile."

The hair prickled on Laurel's nape. "Okay."

Smudgeon leaned forward. "You said that the killer is methodical and organized."

"Yes," Laurel affirmed.

"Huck Rivers is organized and often takes the lead in search and rescue, which is map oriented. He leads the dive team when they search and recover drowning victims in the river. In addition, you said that the killer is from here and is familiar with the mountains and land." Smudgeon looked deadly serious. "I'm totally just spitballing here, but who knows the land around Genesis Valley better than a Fish and Wildlife officer?"

"That's true," Laurel murmured, trying to keep her expression placid.

"Also, Rivers grew up here before heading to the military," Smudgeon continued. "He was a sniper in the military, and he knows how to hunt humans and take them down." He shifted uneasily. "I'm not sure you knew this, but Monty also grew up in this area. I took him a coffee early this morning and asked a few questions about Huck. It turns out that Huck's mom deserted him, and Monty was fairly certain she was a blonde. Isn't that one of those facts that makes these nutjobs hate women? Then they take out their anger with one woman on surrogate women?"

Laurel fidgeted. That was all true. "Yes, but —"

Smudgeon finished his coffee. "Casey's dumping Huck and dating somebody new could've been the trigger." He flushed. "I've been reading up on serial killers, and they often have triggers."

Laurel took another drink of her coffee, her mind spinning. Her colleague's logic was cutting into her in a new and very uncomfortable way, although she appreciated Walter's attention to detail and his investigative skills.

Smudgeon coughed and then patted his round belly. "I know this is a long shot and crazy, but I wanted to throw it out there. This is fun." He smiled, and long lines extended out from the sides of his hang-dog eyes. "Bouncing ideas off somebody. I'm so used to being the team muscle that theorizing is somewhat new."

The muscle? Seriously?

Laurel swallowed over the lumpy rock now in her throat. "You're good at it." For the first time, she forced herself to forget last night and her interactions with Huck and look at him from an objective perspective. "We'll have to investigate this further." She tapped the papers into order and slid them into the case file. "I'd like to interview Meyer Jackson. Do you think you can get us in to see him before the sheriff finds out?"

Smudgeon smiled. "Definitely."

CHAPTER TWENTY-EIGHT

It no longer had a name.

The wind blew snow against the sides of the cargo container, scattering warning. No other sound remained in the wilderness, especially from the body. Its name had been Yana, a reference to God's Grace.

Now Yana meant nothing.

The smell of blood and death rang through the hold, competing with the bleach slowly spreading across the floor. The blood was thicker this time, mixing with the clear bleach. Red and white, circling each other, not blending without assistance. Time to clean again. Why were bodily functions so putrid?

In the heat, in the moment, all sights and sounds were glorified. Then Yana had died. Too soon and too fast.

This one had been weak. Sadly, pathetically, dangerously weak. Sadness poured through the cargo hold now, along with anger. "How dare you be so useless?" A quick grab at former Yana's ankle pulled the body away from the metal. When she smashed into the icy snow outside, the area smelled much better. Pure. Ready for a new occupant.

Hopefully one who'd be strong and fight. Show a will to live, at least.

Although Yana had been a screamer. The thrill of seeing the soul desert the body, knowing it wanted to be free, had created an orgasm worthy of a climax-inducing sonnet. Lovely.

That final second when life left the body, when the eyes transitioned from sparkling to dull, from occupied to so completely empty, was one most people never saw. Never experienced. Never enjoyed.

To be immersed in that moment was bliss. True, untouched, pure bliss. And Yana had struggled with the inevitability, sounds of denial emerging from her chest, from her lungs, from her soul. Was it possible that even the soul fought death?

The ropes had frayed this time and blood coated the strands. It might be time to buy more ropes, but these had been so helpful. With each blond vision, they'd held tight, allowing plenty of time for play. Blondes truly were more fun, as the saying went. Of course, that was obvious for anybody with a brain.

Hail battered the metal and the body slumped on the cold snow outside the metal container as if even the gods were irritated. What made a god? The ability to bestow life or death — choose between life and death?

Perhaps.

Either way, the next blonde had already been chosen. She was intriguing and different from the rest. A beauty who might be difficult to catch. It would be a challenge to capture her, for sure. She was a worthy prize.

But first, Yana's former shell had one more job to perform, and the timing had to be just right. Laurel was going to love it.

Meyer Jackson looked like a defeated man in his striped, orange jumpsuit. Greasy blond hair hung to his shoulders, red striations permeated the whiteness around his pupils, and his shoulders slumped until his chest appeared concave. "We can talk now," he said wearily.

Laurel sat next to Walter on the other side of a metal table from Meyer Jackson, cataloguing the young man's mannerisms. "You're represented by an attorney. We have to wait," she said.

The door opened and a handsome man in a light beige suit strode in. His blondish hair was swept high on his head and he wore round, black-rimmed metal glasses. His shirt was a starched white, and his tie a deep burgundy with a matching handkerchief in his breast pocket. Fancy. "Sorry I'm late. There was a wreck on Main Street, and I had to stop to make sure everyone was okay." He plunked a leather briefcase on the floor and took the seat next to Jackson, his gaze landing on Laurel. "Oh. Hello." He partially stood and held out a hand, his gaze appreciative.

Laurel shook his hand. His palm was warm and his shake gentle. "I'm Agent Snow."

"Steve Bearing," he said, retaking his seat, his gaze wandering her face. "It really is a pleasure."

Laurel blinked. "From the Bearing Law Firm?"

"Yes." Pleasure flitted across his handsome face. "You've heard of us?"

"I have," Laurel said. Casey Morgan had worked for the Bearing Law Firm and had been kidnapped after leaving work. Laurel would have to interview Bearing separate from his client. Was he a witness? She'd either schedule an interview or just show up at the law firm and see what she could shake out. She shifted her weight on the hard chair, facing the defendant. "Mr. Jackson, tell me about Casey."

Tears instantly filled Meyer's eyes. "Casey was the kindest soul you could ever meet. We started dating a year and a half ago, but it wasn't exclusive, even after Huck Rivers dumped her. She still hooked up with him whenever he bothered to make a booty call. Well, he'd call, and she'd show up with her booty."

Bearing sighed next to Jackson.

Laurel's back tingled and her neck heated. What was that all about? Jealousy? No. That would be ridiculous. "We will be able to obtain a warrant to verify any phone calls made between Ms. Morgan and Captain Rivers, just so you know."

"That won't help." Meyer groused. "He didn't call. No, he was too cool to call. All he had to do was drive by her work. Then she'd call him later when she was off. What a dick."

"She'd contact him from the law firm?" Laurel asked.

"No. Casey had two jobs because she'd gotten herself into some serious debt." Meyer picked a scab on his elbow. "Besides being a paralegal, she was the night manager

337

of the Dairy Dumplin' over on Granite Street. Huck Rivers would go into the drive-through a lot. Casey told me that he just liked their coffee and burgers, but that wasn't it. It was his way of getting her to show up for sex. Bastard probably got free food, too." He stood. "I can't do this. I don't know anything more than that. My trial is coming up, so please remember that I'm not an asshole when I'm not drinking."

Laurel looked up. "The Dairy Dumplin'?" Where Uncle Carl apparently liked to eat? She shuffled the thought to the back of her brain to pick apart later. For now, she needed more from Meyer. "Even if Casey was seeing Huck, why do you think he killed her?"

"She was afraid of him," Meyer said, his head dropping. "Even though she still loved him and thought he could change, she was terrified of him. So when he told her to come over, she did. I don't get it, but it was like her fear and her love were all combined in her head. Hell. Maybe it turned her on."

"Why was she afraid of him?" Laurel asked.

Meyer shrugged. "She said he'd threatened her before, and I know he hit her at least once that she told me about."

Laurel sat back. She hadn't gotten an

338

impression of violence from Huck. "I assume you told the police this once her body was discovered?"

"Sure," Meyer said.

Laurel stored that information away for later. She couldn't imagine Huck hitting a woman. "Were you drinking during the two domestic violence calls that occurred when you were dating Casey?"

Meyer nodded. "Yeah. I've stopped now, and I regret my actions. I was drinking both times and yelled at her. Even hit the wall, but I never touched her. Now I can't show her how much I've changed by giving up booze." A tear slid down his cheek.

Laurel cleared her throat. "You don't have an alibi for her time of death. Care to explain that?"

He shook his head. "If I was gonna kill her, I would've found an alibi. I did not kill her."

"Yet you threatened her and scared her enough that she called the police on you. Twice," Laurel pushed.

He gulped. "Guess I didn't threaten her enough, right? Huck Rivers scared the shit out of her, and she never called the police on him. Of course, he is the police. This ain't fair, and I know I'm screwed. But I did not kill her. Now, I'm out of here." He

339

shuffled to the door, and a guard opened it to lead him back to his cell.

Steve stood. "It was nice to meet you, Agent Snow." Then he looked at Walter. "Meyer is not a killer, and we all know it. There's not enough to convict him on Casey's murder, and I'm assuming the charge of homicide will be dropped soon."

Laurel didn't get a hint that Meyer Jackson was a murderer, but people lied. Sociopaths did it well, and maybe he was one, although she wasn't feeling it. "I believe in facts, Mr. Bearing."

Bearing's smile turned charming. "Honestly. Meyer really has changed now that he's off the booze, and he deeply regrets scaring Casey. He didn't kill her, and now that his case is apparently being connected with the Snowblood Peak murders, I'm thinking I have a decent defense to mount."

Laurel tilted her head. "Since Casey worked for you, I'll need to interview you at your convenience."

His eyes sparkled. "I'd like that, Agent Snow. Call the office, and I'm at your disposal." He leaned over to lift his briefcase and then followed his client out of the dismal room.

Walter's chair croaked beneath his weight. "What a waste of space," he muttered.

340

Laurel turned toward him. "I didn't get a chance to read the rest of the file. Who found Casey Morgan?"

"A couple of moms taking up jogging after work," Walter said. "They both alibied before that time, just happened to find her body. Didn't see anybody else around."

The door burst open, and Sheriff York barreled inside. He was in full uniform, his badge shining brightly from his breast, and his chest puffed out. Fury cascaded off him with enough force that even someone who ignored subtext could feel it.

Walter jumped up, standing at the edge of the table like a bulldog prepared to lunge.

Laurel purposely kept her seat. If the sheriff had intended to startle her, he wasn't going to have the satisfaction of knowing it. "Sheriff York. How are you?"

"I'm pissed off, lady. What the hell are you doing?" Even the sheriff's receding hairline turned a mottled red.

"Investigating." That was her job.

His body shook and spittle gathered at the corner of his mouth. "No. What you're doing is fucking up my case. One that was solid but now looks like jelly. You have just given the defense attorney reasonable doubt. If Bearing can plant enough hints about Casey Morgan being killed by the

Snowblood Peak killer, then a murderer will go free. Is that what you want?" His hand rested on the gun at his waist.

That had to be a rhetorical question.

She stood and slung her laptop bag over her shoulder. "There's a good case to be made that Ms. Morgan was our killer's first victim."

"Bullshit," the sheriff spat, his eyes wild and his pupils dilated. "The body was found nowhere near Snowblood Peak. It was at the opposite side of town near the baseball field, and there were no signs of rape. This was an anger killing, not a planned one."

Laurel watched him, noting his irritation. "I agree that the death and scene weren't planned, but it could've been an initial kidnapping gone bad. She fits the victimology, Sheriff."

"She wasn't a hooker," the sheriff burst out.

Walter hitched up his belt. "Neither was Lisa Scotford."

Laurel's phone buzzed and she pulled it out of her bag to read the screen and see that Huck Rivers would meet her at the office in twenty minutes so they could interview Pastor John Govern again.

She'd have to interview Huck about Casey Morgan at the same time.

CHAPTER TWENTY-NINE

Huck eyed the snowflakes covering the faded wallpaper that featured naked women as he climbed the stairs to the FBI reception area. The waiting room was full of dust and held one glass display case with a sparkling Christmas village inside. He moved toward the only visible door and opened it, staring down a hallway.

"No. To the left." Laurel's voice emerged from a room down to the right.

The sound of her soft tenor shot right to his groin, and he nearly pounded his head into the wall. Last night had been a mistake he would not make again. Clearing his throat, he walked toward the doorway and stopped in the entrance, where Laurel was holding one end of a battered blue door while the blonde he'd seen in the parking lot struggled with the other side. They were trying to center it over a stack of firewood fitted together tighter than any Jenga puzzle.

No doubt Laurel's doing.

He stepped inside and grasped the edge of the wooden door smack in the center. "Need help?" He lifted easily.

"Yes," Laurel grunted, her hair in disarray. "Just a little to the . . . left."

Huck lifted and moved, centering the door. "You need a table."

"This will do until we acquire one." Laurel released her hold and stepped back, dusting off her pale-colored pants. "Thank you for the help. Huck, this is Kate. Kate, Huck."

Kate wiped off dust from her forehead. "Hi." So much clung to her hair that it looked almost gray instead of blond.

"Hi." Huck studied the pictures and arrows on the case board. There were too many blank boxes for victim names as well as suspects. His senses flared awake as Laurel's spicy, strawberry scent wafted over him. He had to get away from her before he did something stupid like ask her out. "I forgot my coffee in my office — I'll meet you by the truck." He took off.

Not only was she gorgeous and smart, but she wasn't high maintenance. The woman had just created a conference table out of firewood and an old door. He did not want to like her, but he couldn't help it.

■ ■ ■ ■

Ten minutes later, travel mug in hand, Huck met Laurel at his truck. She'd apparently dropped into the ice cream store for a latte. The day was clear and bright but cold, and her nose had already turned pink. In the soft, cream-colored pants and feminine blouse beneath her coat, she looked put together and sexy in an understated way. Obviously she still hadn't bought her own clothes.

News vans perched at the end of the parking lot, where Monty had told them they could be. Cameras pointed at him, and his skin itched. A couple of reporters called out questions, but neither he nor Laurel turned toward them.

"Pastor John had better be home this time," she muttered. Her auburn hair was up in a ponytail and pink, natural-stone earrings matched a necklace that nestled beneath her collarbone. An area he'd spent plenty of time exploring and kissing the night before. In the soft light, her blue and green eyes stood out more than ever, making her appear every bit as intriguing as he was discovering her to be. Although that was irrelevant.

Laurel walked around the front of the truck to the passenger side, slipping twice. With any other colleague, he'd get in his truck and wait for them to do the same. But she was different. Different from all the rest. The colleagues, the women, the townspeople. Very different from other women he'd dated, even after just one night. But he had to get over that. They were working together and that had to be all. He forced himself to open his door, letting Aeneas in before getting inside himself, rocking the entire vehicle.

Laurel tossed her laptop bag on the floor, reached for the handle, and pulled herself up and in.

He started the engine, wanting to get the afternoon over as soon as possible.

"The snow finally stopped," she murmured, taking a sip of her latte through a straw.

"For the day," he said, glancing at the weather app on his phone. "In fact, it's going to warm up and drop very nice freezing rain on us before snowing again tomorrow." It was December in the mountains, so that was par for the course. "I called ahead and told Pastor John's secretary that he needs to be there to speak with us this time or I'll put out a BOLO for him. Very publicly."

346

Laurel smiled around her latte cup. "Good move. He'll be there."

"He'd better be." Huck drove out of the parking lot and down Jagged Rock Road, heading toward Main Street and out of town. His tires turned up gravel covering the ice. "I wanted to make sure we were okay." He'd probably been a little too direct with the one-off comment earlier.

She turned toward him, her eyebrows raised. "We're fine."

The woman was being sincere. He shifted uncomfortably in his seat. Okay. That was good, right? He kept silent as he continued to drive.

Laurel turned and watched the world outside, seeming comfortable and relaxed. "Before I forget, I need to make a phone call." She dug her purse out of the bag. "Siri, call the Bearing Law Firm."

Huck glanced her way.

Somebody apparently answered. "Yes, hello. This is FBI Special Agent Laurel Snow, and I'd like to make an appointment with Steve Bearing at his earliest convenience." She waited several moments. "He would? Wonderful. I'll see him then." She clicked off.

"Bearing?" Huck asked.

"Yes. Casey Morgan worked for him, as

I'm sure you know. I just met him while interviewing Meyer Jackson." She sipped more of her drink and kicked her laptop bag to the side with her boot.

The name jolted memories through Huck. "I take it you're aware I dated Casey?"

"Yes," she said. "Jackson told me."

Great. Huck slowed down for a blind corner, his ears ringing. The mention of Meyer Jackson had come out of the blue — nicely done as an interrogation tactic. "What all did Jackson have to say?"

"He's sure you killed Casey Morgan," Laurel said.

Huck snorted. "Yeah, I've heard that. I didn't."

"What happened between you and Casey, anyway?" Laurel asked casually.

The casualness ticked him off. "Is that a personal or a professional question?" he asked.

"Does it matter?" she asked smoothly.

"Yes. We're not personal. I thought I made that clear." Her scent was killing him.

She chuckled. "You did, and I agreed. However, there's a decent chance Casey Morgan was killed by the Snowblood Peak killer. You dated her, and there are people making noises that you should be a suspect. What do you think about that?"

Fire lanced down Huck's arms. "Wait a minute. I insult you this morning, and now you're going after me for murder?" Man, he'd misread her. Like completely.

She turned toward him. "Insult me? How did you insult me?"

It took him two heartbeats to realize that her question was genuine, not sarcastic. His mouth nearly dropped open. "By calling last night a one-off."

"Oh." Her face cleared. "That's a fact and not an insult."

Now *he* felt insulted. Should he feel insulted? This woman was running him in circles . . . without trying to do so. He coughed, took a drink of his coffee, and settled his ass down. "Wait a minute. You think Casey was one of the Snowblood Peak victims?" His brain quickly made the connections. It was possible. "Okay. Let's see. Casey and I met during a search and rescue operation on Tilton Hill, looking for a lost hiker. She was a volunteer from the church, and she ended up in my squad."

"Everything keeps coming back to the Genesis Community Church, doesn't it?" Laurel asked.

"It's a big church." Huck eyed a couple of deer on the side of the road, ready to slow down if one decided to jump across the road. They usually did. "Casey attended services periodically but wasn't immersed in the faith." The deer wisely stayed in place, their gazes frozen on the truck.

Laurel took another drink. "You met her searching for a lost hiker?"

"Yeah. An older guy named Eugene. Don't remember his last name, but Casey was actually the one who found him. Nice guy who just got turned around."

"Okay," she said, yanking on her ponytail hard enough that it had to hurt. "Did you ever threaten her?"

He slowed for another icy curve. "Wait a minute. I'm *really* a suspect in your mind?" Every ounce of amusement fled right out of his body.

"I didn't say that." She also didn't look at him.

He looked right at her. "After last night, you still think I'm a suspect? Do you honestly believe I could've strangled all of those women, including Casey, after raping and torturing them?"

She turned to face him, her green eye lighter than ever. "No. I don't think you're a rapist and a cold-blooded killer, Huck. It'd just be nice to prove it so I can move on to the next suspect."

Well, at least that was something. The heat

350

spiraling through his chest dissipated. "After the search, I asked Casey out for a drink, and we started things from there. We were pretty hot and heavy for about a month, and then she started talking about marriage and babies, and I wasn't there. Wasn't planning to ever go there. She agreed, but apparently she was lying." A hawk flew above the truck, and he admired its wide wingspan. "So I called it quits as nicely as I could."

Laurel stretched her boots toward the heat bursting from the floor. "Meyer Jackson said that you continued to have a sexual relationship and also threatened Casey."

"Nope. Never threatened her, and we didn't have sex again after we broke up. She called quite a bit, but I was done." He eyed the darkening clouds. The rain was coming soon. "She showed up on my doorstep twice, but I sent her away. It was a relief when she started dating somebody else."

"Was there any reason for her to have been afraid of you?" Laurel asked.

"No." Huck turned through the wooden archway to the quaint square owned by the church. "I never threatened her, and I certainly never put hands on her. That was all in Meyer Jackson's head, and don't ask me why. Best guess was that Casey was trying to make him jealous by using me. She liked to play games, a fact I discovered and did not like. It's another reason I broke things off with her sooner rather than later."

"That makes sense," Laurel allowed. "Were those her boots I borrowed?"

He winced. "Yes. Sorry about that."

Laurel made a noncommittal sound.

"I should've thought of her for this case," Huck murmured. "When the bodies were found. But I heard that they'd caught the guy, and the facts of the cases were so different that . . ." He shook his head.

"Until we found Lisa Scotford, another low-risk victim, there was no strong connection to Casey."

Even so, Laurel had put herself in Huck's truck, and they were in the middle of nowhere right now. He shook his head. "What would you do if you thought I was guilty?"

"I don't think you're guilty." She sipped thoughtfully through her straw.

He turned away from the square toward the long fields and groves of trees. The river rushed along next to them, white and chilly. "I know, but what if you did? Would you still be here questioning me? Just the two of us?"

She chewed the inside of her cheek. It was

something he'd seen her do before while thinking things through. "Probably not. That wouldn't be smart, even though I'm armed. You're bigger and you're strong and fast." She pushed a wayward strand of hair out of her eyes. "If I considered you a viable suspect, I would've called you into the office for an official interview."

It was good to know she didn't take unnecessary risks or think she was invincible, even though she was brilliant. He didn't want to like that about her, but he did. "Have you ever been wrong before?"

She looked his way, her dual-colored eyes bright in the truck. "Sure. I'm just human, you know."

CHAPTER THIRTY

Laurel felt much better after speaking with Huck, and she was fine admitting that to herself. Though she hadn't truly considered him a suspect, his easy acceptance of her need to question him went a long way toward reassuring her about his nature. Many men would've gotten angry, especially when they'd been intimate the night before.

Her thighs still tingled, and she was fairly certain he'd left a slight bite mark at the base of her left buttock.

The rain was just starting to fall as he parked at the church.

Her phone buzzed and she answered, "Agent Snow."

"It's Dr. Ortega. I've finished ageing the victims discovered in the avalanche. For the earliest one, I can place time of death at approximately a year ago. I'm sending all the documents to your email address." Something shuffled. "I have to go, Agent. Talk soon." He hung up.

Laurel looked at Huck. "The first murder happened about a year ago."

Huck's eyebrows rose. "About two months after Casey was murdered?"

"Yes." That tracked perfectly. If they had actually even discovered the first body, which they wouldn't know until spring, when they could begin searching again. "Let's go see the pastor," Laurel said.

Aeneas ran ahead, shaking off the rain, as they both pushed their way through the double front doors.

Jasmine Caine was inside the vestibule, tacking a new set of colorful flyers to the bulletin board. She turned and smiled, her brown hair frizzing a little around her head. "Howdy. Oh, shoot. It's started raining already." She took in Laurel's wet hair. "I was hoping it'd hold off until later so I could decorate more outside."

Laurel wiped wetness off her cheeks. "It's a slow pour right now, but the clouds are fairly dark. We're here to see Pastor John."

"I know." Jasmine pointed to the right-hand door, opposite the one which they had gone through last time. "He's in the second meeting room on the left waiting for you. I put coffee and water in there. Is there anything else you'd like?"

"No, thanks." Laurel had enjoyed her latte and was nice and warm. "Thanks, Jasmine."

"Sure. Any time." The woman smiled at Huck. "I didn't mention the other day how much I appreciate your help with the volunteers on search and rescue operations. You probably don't remember me, but I helped out with finding the two teenaged boys who wanted to reenact some movie they'd watched about surviving in the wilderness." She winked at Laurel. "When we finally found them, they were tired and cold and had definitely learned a lesson."

Huck grunted. "That's right. The department made those two do volunteer work for a few weeks to make up for the cost of the search."

Laurel opened the door, peering down the hallway and then moving through. She walked past two classrooms on her right and one meeting room on her left until they reached a room with a conference table and pale yellow chairs. The pastor sat on the far side, next to Steve Bearing.

Laurel moved inside. "You brought your attorney." With a nod to Bearing, she took a seat across from him.

Huck sat next to her, across from the pastor. "Interesting."

Bearing smiled, all teeth and charm. "The

pastor has a brain, and anybody with one would hire an attorney when being questioned by both the FBI and a Washington State police officer. You two both know that, so don't try to start off by putting the pastor on the defensive."

Fair enough. Laurel smiled. "All right. Let's get started, then. Pastor John, how long had you engaged in a sexual relationship with Lisa Scotford?"

Pastor John sputtered. His face looked as if he'd rubbed his eyes repeatedly. "What are you talking about? That's ridiculous. How dare you even imply such a thing? That's slander."

Laurel almost smiled. The guy was the worst liar she'd ever seen. "Pastor? I'm an FBI agent."

"I know."

She gentled her voice. "Lying to a federal agent is a felony. I don't care if you were dating Lisa. She was over the age of consent, so it's not against the law. Lying to me is. Would you like to revise your statement?"

Red colored his face and he looked at his lawyer. "Steve?"

Steve eyed him. "I suggest you tell the truth. We both know you didn't harm Lisa, and we want to know who did. Sure, you might've made a mistake or two, but we're talking about murder here. John? My advice is to tell all, unless it incriminates you. If it does, we'll talk privately first."

Pastor John looked back at Laurel. "Is this confidential?"

"We'll try to keep it confidential, but I can't guarantee it," she said honestly.

The pastor pressed his lips together. "I am not going to discuss it."

Huck scoffed. "Pastor John, give it up. Don't make us interview all of your parishioners and the townspeople about when they saw you together and if they knew you were screwing. Your best move is to talk to us."

Steve reared up. "That's one, Captain. If you threaten my client again, we're ending this interview."

Huck smiled. "That wasn't a threat. This is. Talk to me or I'm going to bulldoze my way through this church community looking for answers."

Pastor John's head dropped. "Fine. Yes. We started seeing each other seven months ago. Obviously we kept it secret, because I'm twelve years older than her and we were engaging in relations outside of marriage, but we were getting serious, and I think we would've gotten married." He sat back and ran a hand over his short hair. "I'm so devastated she was hurt . . . killed in such a brutal way. Who would do this? I can't get my head around it." Lines cut into the sides of his mouth. Pain or stress? Anger or guilt?

"Did you know she was pregnant?" Laurel asked.

Pastor John rocked back so quickly that his chair nearly tipped over. "What? Pregnant? No." He gasped rapidly as if having a seizure. "She didn't say anything. I didn't know. Are you sure?" His pain was palpable.

"No," Laurel said. "She told a friend she might be pregnant, but we haven't received the final autopsy report as of yet." It didn't look as if John had known, but he could be an excellent actor. The guy was smooth, which he probably had to be to run a church. "If so, I am very sorry for this second loss."

Bearing put an arm over John's shoulders. "You didn't have to shock him like that."

Yes, she did. It was the only way to gauge his reaction, as much as was possible. "Do you need a moment to compose yourself?"

He swallowed rapidly. "No. I'm fine. Let's get this over with now."

"What if you had known, *Pastor*?" Huck asked, his voice heavy with sarcasm.

"I would've married her. Right away." John's eyes glistened. "We would've gotten married anyway, I think. I can't believe this happened to her. Why? I don't understand why."

It was a question Laurel could never answer. For anybody. "Tell us about your outreach program in urban areas."

Steve Bearing cocked his head. "Why?"

"Why not?" Huck replied before Laurel could.

Pastor John shrugged. "Sure. We've been administering to the sick and the lost souls on the city streets. We take food and pamphlets, hoping to help them find a better way. Jasmine and Robert Caine have been in charge of the project. They've worked hard and made connections with many of the food banks and shelters in Seattle, Everett, and Tacoma by donating both food and funds. What good is working for God if you don't really get out there and help His children who are so lost?"

Huck leaned back in his yellow chair, and the base creaked. "Does the outreach extend to prostitutes?"

"God's love extends to anybody who needs help," John returned. "Anybody on the streets. There are so many runaways, Captain. Sometimes, I do wonder if Pastor Caine saw too much of the pain and just left. It doesn't make sense, knowing him, but what if? The pain in people can be nerve shattering." His shoulders slumped. "I thought this job might be easier with Lisa by my side, but now she's gone, too. Killed in such a terrible way. How could a just God allow this to happen?"

There definitely was no answer to that question. "Did you know Casey Morgan, Pastor John?"

Steve Bearing stiffened just enough for the movement to be noticeable.

John nodded. "Yes. Casey was a member of the congregation. She attended church periodically and often administered to high-risk youth, but I never worked closely with her. I knew her by face and name, but she never sought my counsel."

"Was she friends with Lisa?" Huck asked.

"Not to my knowledge," John said. "They were both friendly people, but I don't believe they had an association outside of saying 'hi' to each other when Casey did attend services." He looked at Steve. "Casey worked for you, didn't she?"

Steve's sympathetic expression probably worked wonders with a jury. "She worked for my firm, and she was an excellent paralegal. Casey worked closely with two of our associate attorneys, and they've both been devastated by her loss." He scratched

361

his neck. "It's looking more and more like Casey was killed by the Snowblood Peak serial killer." His eyes gleamed as he no doubt plotted the defense for Meyer Jackson.

Laurel would follow up about Casey's personal life with the attorney, and the rest of his firm, during her appointment on Monday. It was the first time the secretary could fit her in, and considering it was already Thursday at noon, she didn't mind. Plus, now she knew exactly why Steve Bearing couldn't meet that afternoon — he was here defending the pastor. "Pastor? I'm going to ask you to look at some pictures, and they're bleak. But do you recognize any of these women?" She brought up the photos on her phone — the victims they'd been able to identify so far.

John took the phone and looked at the pictures of the identified victims, which were mostly mugshots. He flipped through them. "No. I'm sorry." He flipped again to a picture of a decimated body and dropped the phone on the table. It clattered toward Laurel. "God. That's terrible. Who would *do* that?"

"I wish I could answer that question," Laurel said quietly. Honestly. Part of what pushed her every day in this job was her need to answer that impossible-to-fathom question. Who would do that, and more importantly, why would anybody cause such pain and destruction? She looked at Huck to see if he had any more questions.

He shook his head. "I'm done for now." He stood up and pulled Laurel's chair out for her. "We'll be in touch if we have any more questions."

Laurel stood. "Thank you for your time."

Pastor John also stood. "Have you had any leads on finding Pastor Zeke Caine?"

"No," Laurel said. "Not yet, but I'm just getting started on that one. I would like to speak with his daughter soon." Abigail Caine was a mystery on many fronts. "Right now, the Snowblood Peak cases take precedence." She moved into the hallway.

Pastor John followed. "After you were here the other day, I went through some of the records in the basement and found a couple of boxes that belong to the pastor. Most contain journals that look like fairly boring check-off lists." His smile was both fond and sad. "Pastor Zeke loves to-do lists. Just loves them." He walked her into the vestibule and reached for a large box hidden beneath the table holding pamphlets.

Huck intercepted him and accepted the box, which looked fairly heavy.

"Thank you," Laurel said.

Pastor John nodded. "You're welcome. Pastor Zeke resided in a cabin about a mile down the side road from the main parking lot, and you're more than welcome to check it out. There's nothing of his left there, and he lived pretty sparsely before. I was lucky to find that box of his journals and personal effects in the basement."

Laurel looked at Huck. "We'll go there right now, if you don't mind."

"Sure," Huck said.

"Feel free," Pastor John said, waving his hand toward the door. He looked at his attorney. "How about lunch? I can't deal with any more talk about death and crime. The only topic will be the Seahawks and next season. Deal?"

"Deal," Steve Bearing said, his gaze on Laurel's hair. "I look forward to seeing you on Monday, Agent Snow. Perhaps we, too, could grab lunch afterward."

Huck made a sound that could only be interpreted as a growl. Laurel moved toward the door without answering, wondering why that sound had shot straight south of her abdomen in a way she shouldn't appreciate but did.

Life was getting much too peculiar.

CHAPTER THIRTY-ONE

In the conference room of her office, Laurel sat on the rough table and stared at the whiteboard. More snow blanketed the skylight above. Her phone buzzed and she lifted it to her ear. "Snow."

"Hi, Laurel, it's George. I was calling for a status check," the FBI deputy director said.

She should've checked who was calling before answering. "You don't want my status right now. I have more suspects than I'd like, and I'm expecting the killer to make a move soon. In fact, to be honest, I think he probably already has taken another woman." The thought made her want to vomit. "But we don't have any missing persons yet. I have computer techs monitoring for any within this or the surrounding states, and nobody fits the description." Did the guy know the schedules of his victims and exactly when to take them to avoid exposure, or had he just gotten lucky? "I wish I had better news for you," she admitted.

"How's the PR side going?" George asked.

"News vans have been camped out in the parking lot, and reporters keep trying to get inside. So far, we've directed them to the PR arm of the Washington State authorities, and that's working well." She angled her neck to peer out her window at the forest land behind the building. "Last time I checked, I didn't see any vans in the parking lot, and there's nobody climbing trees out back, so maybe they've given up for the night." One could always hope.

George sighed. "All right. Keep me in the loop, and Snow? Make something happen soon. My balls are to the fire on this one."

"I think it's supposed to be your feet to the fire, sir," she said absently, still studying her board.

"Feels like my balls. Talk soon." He clicked off.

Laurel set her phone to the side. She had the oddest urge to call Huck, which was the exact wrong thing to do. He'd made his preferences clear.

Movement sounded in the hallway, and Kate poked her head in.

"What are you still doing here?" Laurel

asked. "I told everyone to head home at five and hope for a weekend with no missing persons."

Kate walked in with two long-necked beers and handed one over. "This has been one long week. My girls are with my ex, and I didn't want to go home to a quiet house. You were still working, so I decided to dust the reception area. You know, my girls are all blond. I'm worried about them." She craned her neck and gingerly pulled a piece of cobweb out of Laurel's hair. "Did you go through a crawlspace?"

"We searched an old cabin formerly occupied by Pastor Zeke Caine." Laurel took a drink of the light brew, letting the liquid cool her throat. "All we found were cobwebs and the accompanying spiders." She shivered. "I understand an ecological need for spiders, but they just creep me out."

"Me, too." Kate hopped up on the end of the table, next to Laurel. "That's not the same whiteboard. You changed it."

Laurel shook her head. "I just flipped it over. The victims and reports are still on the other side." She looked at the boxes she'd drawn with text inside: Casey Morgan, Lisa Scotford, Seattle streets, prostitution, profile, knowledge of surrounding land, and unknown. "I was trying to connect all the facts without looking specifically at one particular suspect. In cases like this, it's easy to get caught up with suspects who knew both Casey and Lisa, but looked at from a different angle, Casey and Lisa had the same appearance as the other victims."

Kate swung her leg. "So the killer might not have known them? They could've been taken opportunistically, just like the blondes from the higher-risk areas?"

"It's possible." Laurel scooted over a little bit and set her feet on a turned-over box to support her back better. "In which case, the question is why did he change hunting grounds? Did somebody recognize him in Seattle or Everett? Were the police getting too close there? And why did he, assuming it was him, shoot at me? What am I getting close to right now?" The unanswered questions battered her brain until her head ached.

"What if it wasn't the killer who shot at you?" Kate asked, catching on to her strategy.

Laurel clicked through the facts available at the moment. "Good question. However, I can't find another explanation. I haven't been home for a couple of years, so I don't have any enemies here. If I have enemies from other cases, they wouldn't have known to find me here in Genesis Valley."

"So the most logical answer is that the serial killer shot at you because you're onto something, even if you don't know what it is," Kate said. "In that case, the murderer is closer to home and isn't afraid of the Seattle cops." The woman was bright and caught on quickly.

"Right. So why did he change his MO? If that line of reasoning is accurate, chances are, he knew either Casey, Lisa, or both of them." Laurel drank more of the beer, her mind spinning. "Sometimes, when I end up at this place in a case, I go for a run until my legs hurt too badly to move. But not in this kind of weather. Is it still raining?"

Kate sipped her beer. "It's more accurate to say 'sleeting,' I think. It's miserable out there."

Laurel sighed.

"What's that?" Kate motioned toward the box in the corner and stood.

"My next project." Laurel jumped off the table, tired of looking at the board.

Kate pushed a clump of dirt out of the way with one foot. "Why don't you save it until tomorrow? I'll come in and work with you. For now, did Huck Rivers realize he was an ass earlier and apologize profusely?"

"We grabbed a late lunch after digging through that creepy cabin, but it was very professional," Laurel said absently, picking up the box and setting it in the middle of the conference table. "He was out all last night on that search and rescue operation and went home early." Her feelings for Huck were unexpected, and she had to tear them apart and figure them out at a distance. That just made sense. Although, not thinking and just feeling his hard body against her again held definite merit as well.

Kate moved closer to the table. "All right. Well, I might as well help you. We can work for a while and then order a pizza."

"Sounds good." Laurel opened the box and drew out several bound journals, handing half to Kate. She opened one and found plans to expand the church from Genesis Valley with satellite churches in Everett and Seattle. "Kate, how old are you?"

"I'm forty-one," Kate said absently, flipping through a journal. "The guy liked lists, didn't he?"

Laurel looked up. "Were you raised in Genesis Valley?"

Kate paused. "Yeah. I graduated from high school here and attended the community college before marrying Vic when he was still in dental school."

Laurel tilted her head. "Vic?"

"I know. Believe me, I know," Kate said. "I should've figured he was an ass when he wanted to name the girls Val, Viv, and Vida. But I liked the names, so whatevs, as the kids would say. Why do you ask?"

Laurel reached into the bottom of the box for a couple of torn and dirty manila file folders. "Are you a member of the Genesis Community Church?"

Kate twisted her mouth, thinking. "No. My family is Catholic, so I've always attended Saint Thomas. As a kid, I did go to parties and dances at the Genesis Valley Church, and I love their offerings at the farmer's markets in the spring and summer and the craft fairs in the fall and winter. If I was looking for a church other than mine, I'd definitely head in that direction. It's a good group of people."

Laurel couldn't remember anything about the church while she'd lived in the Valley before leaving for college at eleven; she hadn't attended any of their events. She flipped open the first file folder to see a stack of handwritten church bulletins. She grinned. "The church adopted a cow for a year. Who adopts a cow?" It was probably fun for the kids.

Kate laughed. "I'm sure it was part of the

4-H club."

Laurel pushed the folder to the side and opened the next one, revealing wrinkled old pictures. "Oh, look. It's the church before they added the two sides and classrooms. It's charming." She slid the photo across the table. There were several other pictures of parishioners picnicking by the river, a couple of wedding pictures, and one of a young Pastor Caine, maybe in his early twenties, with his arm around a woman who looked a lot like Abigail. Her mother? Her sandy blond hair was pulled back in a ponytail and her smile was wide. Both she and the pastor wore eighties-style sunglasses. "Was the pastor always bald?"

"Yeah, even the first time I saw him, when the church sponsored my kindergarten soccer team. I remember thinking that he looked like a pastor, somehow. Serious and old, even though he must've been pretty young at that time." Kate reached for the pictures and looked through, smiling. "Boy, the wedding dresses were puffy back then."

Laurel shifted through more pictures until she found one that set her back on her feet. She looked closer. Her heart rate kicked in, strong and fast.

"What?" Kate asked, leaning to her side. "Oh. That's Pastor Caine with hair. He's just a kid. What? Maybe fourteen?"

Laurel couldn't move. Couldn't even nod. The pastor stared back. He was wearing swim trunks by a riverbank, smiling near a rope swing, his hair to his shoulders. Beautiful auburn hair, red and brown, multicolored. "Look at his eyes," she whispered. Kate squinted and leaned in. "Oh. God." She turned her head to stare into Laurel's eyes. "They're the same as yours. I mean, exactly." She shook her head, leaning back. "I had no idea. Even when he was older and bald, when he'd come into town, he wore either glasses or contacts. I had no clue he had het . . . het . . . I mean . . ."

"Heterochromia," Laurel said quietly. "Pastor Caine had auburn-colored hair and partial heterochromia within full heterochromatic eyes."

Kate's gaze darted around the room and then landed back on Laurel. "Um, is it that rare?"

"Yes." Laurel looked closer at the boy who became a man to lead a church. A man who had disappeared almost a year ago. Her stomach revolted and she tipped back the rest of her beer, forcing the cool liquid into her stomach to keep from throwing up.

"Does that mean . . ."

Laurel finished the beer and set the bottle aside. "Yes. He is my father."

CHAPTER THIRTY-TWO

Rain dripped from Laurel's face as she slammed the door to her mother's home and dropped her laptop bag before throwing her coat on the floor. "Mom?" Her voice shook.

"I'm in the kitchen," Deidre called out.

This was unbelievable. How was it even possible? Laurel stomped into the kitchen, for once not heeding the mess of water she left in her wake. "How could you?" So many feelings bombarded her at once, it was as if somebody else possessed her body.

Deidre turned around from stirring something on the stove, a cheerful pink-checked apron covering her yoga outfit. "What?"

Anger, hot and brutal, washed through Laurel. "Is Zeke Caine my father?"

Deidre dropped the wooden spoon, and a white sauce splashed across the wooden floor. She turned so pale, her lips looked blue. "What did you say?" she croaked.

"I'll take that as a yes," Laurel snapped. "How could you?" She paced to the table and back, her nerves misfiring. "Do you have *any* idea how hard I've looked for him through the years? Every database, every record, everywhere I could search for a male with red hair and heterochromia? Even knowing that it was possible he didn't have either, I kept looking. *Needing* to know." She threw up her hands. "Wondering where I came from. Wondering if I was an anomaly or if I shared this ridiculous way of looking to the world with somebody. With *anybody*. Wondering if I wasn't so totally alone."

"You . . . you aren't alone." Deidre turned and switched off the burner. "Let's sit down and talk about this."

"I don't want to sit," Laurel exploded in a way she never had with her mother. Pain rippled through her like a heated blade. "You *lied* to me. So many times."

Deidre limped over to the table and sank into a chair. "I know. I did."

"Why?" Laurel yelled. "Why would you do that?"

Red bloomed across Deidre's pale skin. "You didn't tell me you were searching for him. I didn't know."

Heat blasted Laurel. "I didn't tell you because what could I say? Hey, Mom. I know you were drugged out and can't remember how many guys you screwed in Seattle, but I still want to find my dad. Maybe I have siblings."

Her mom gasped and looked down at her hands.

Laurel breathed out, her chest hurting. "I'm sorry. I didn't mean that." Her throat felt raw. "I have his eyes."

"And his hair," Deidre said quietly, looking up, tears in her eyes. "I'm sorry. But even knowing how mad you are, I'd do the same thing again. So hate me all you want."

Laurel wasn't ready to sit. Her body felt as if she'd inhaled meth for an hour. "Why? Even if you didn't like him, why couldn't I at least know him? Do you have any idea how difficult it is to grow up having no idea who your father is? Wondering if every older man you see on the street might be him? Wondering if you have such terrible luck with men, with dating, because you lacked having a father?" Uncle Blake and Uncle Carl had done their best, but she'd always felt the absence of a father. Of Zeke Caine. Who was now missing.

"I didn't want you to know him," Deidre said, her chin becoming firm. "When my parents died, I didn't go to Seattle. I camped out and goofed off with friends, and one night, the pastor busted us drinking beer on church property. He made everyone go home. Except me. He offered to give me a ride home." Her voice shook.

Laurel paused and the entire world ground to a stop. She dropped into her chair. "Mom."

"I'm sorry. I never wanted you to know."

She couldn't breathe. "Wh . . . what happened?"

Deidre looked away. "He was older and stronger and a leader in the community. He kissed me and I let him."

Laurel's chest hurt. "In the car?"

Deidre nodded and tears fell onto her chest. "Then I pulled away, and he said I was a tease. He was right — I did kiss him."

"That doesn't make you a tease." Laurel grabbed her mom's hand, pain nearly turning her vision dark. "Mom. You didn't do anything wrong."

Deidre swallowed and her entire neck moved as if it hurt to do so. "He wouldn't stop. I fought him, but he wouldn't stop."

Oh God. Laurel bowed her head. Heat blasted through her chest. She was the result of a rape? "That's why you won't ride in cars? You can't be in a vehicle."

"I know it's dumb," Deidre said. "But the second a car door closes on me, I'm right

378

back there, fighting to make him stop."

"Why didn't you tell me?" Laurel asked, knowing the answer even as she asked the question.

Deidre just shook her head. "Oh, Laurel. It's so confusing. I hate him and what happened, but you're the best thing in my life and have been since the second I first felt you kick inside my belly. You're everything, and I only see good when I look at you."

A fear she hadn't realized she harbored rolled away from Laurel. "Oh, Mom."

Deidre wiped off her face. "There's more. He brought me home, and Carl was outside. Carl saw me and immediately knew what had happened."

Laurel stiffened. "Then what?"

"Carl went after Zeke, and they fought. Zeke had a knife," Deidre whispered.

Laurel's shoulders dropped. "Uncle Carl's injuries are from Zeke Caine?"

Deidre sniffed. "Besides cutting Carl's face, Zeke bashed his head against the car. Carl was in a coma for nearly three months."

Pain seemed to weight the air and Laurel struggled beneath it. "Why?" She tightened her hold. "Why didn't you tell anybody? Go to the authorities?"

Deidre shook her head. "I was seventeen, Laurel. My parents had died. Zeke came to the hospital and told me he'd kill us all if I said anything." She wiped her eyes. "The church owned the farm; my parents had just worked the land. Even if Zeke didn't kill us, and even if anybody would've believed me, where would we go? Blake was farming and just married, and Carl was in a coma. So I kept quiet, and I made Zeke sign the farm over to us."

Laurel blinked. "You did?"

"Yes." Finally, color slid into Deidre's face. "I know it's blackmail, but I didn't want him or the church to have a hold on us. Carl would need a place to recuperate, and as it turned out, I needed a home for a baby."

Laurel gentled her hold. "Did he know? Did he ever find out about me?" It'd be nice for him to know her before she killed him for this.

Deidre shook her head. "I don't know. Our farm is far enough away from the church that I didn't see him again. On purpose. I gave birth to you here and then home-schooled you until you went to college. Until you and I left town. If he did know, he never came looking for you. Thank God."

So much for having missed out on having a father. "I'm so sorry, Mom." Laurel shook her head. "Even so, I have his eyes and hair. How did nobody notice?"

"He was bald by the time he came to Genesis Valley and definitely by the time I met him. As for his eyes, most people never noticed them because he wore contacts or glasses. I only saw his real eyes once, and it was that night. I don't think any of it was planned. I don't know why Zeke hid his heterochromia, but he must've had a reason. Most people, especially in town, have no idea he has different-colored eyes." Deidre shrugged. "Most people in the church didn't know, either. It was a well-kept secret."

"When Abigail Caine was here the other day, you knew who her father was?"

"Yes. I know who she is, but I wasn't ever going to tell you," Deidre whispered.

Laurel stood and leaned over to hug her mother. She kept her hand and pulled her mom along, past the basement stairs, to a square-shaped room with comfortable chairs and multicolored skeins of yarn everywhere. Many assault victims learned to cope by creative means. "You started knitting when we were back east. Was it a counsellor's suggestion?" She gently pushed her mom into a chair with a heaping basket next to it.

"Yes." Deidre automatically reached for round needles and the yarn to make a blanket. "I taught you to deal with stress the same way."

Laurel took the other seat. "It's a good way. I love you, Mom."

The needles started to clack. "I love you, too," Deidre murmured.

Laurel shook her head. "For so many years, you and Carl have stayed out of Zeke Caine's way. Away from his church."

Deidre looked down at her pattern. "Yes. Before you ask, Blake and Betty never knew. Carl and I decided to keep the secret forever, once he was home and recuperating."

The secret was out now. Laurel started knitting, her heart and head at war. This time, her heart was going to win.

Zeke Caine was going to pay. If he was still alive.

After Deidre went to bed, Laurel headed out into the rain, driving across town.

Dr. Abigail Caine lived in an exclusive gated neighborhood separated into five-acre parcels where neighbors wouldn't have to see each other. Laurel waited to the right of the gate, her vehicle pummeled by freezing rain, until a car drove in, and then she fol-

382

lowed, winding through perfectly plowed roads and spectacularly decorated mansions to the farthest house from the gate. One house, surrounded by trees and brush, set away from the road and closer to the dangerous river. The structure rose, tall and stately, with snow-covered trees surrounding it. The house was of a modern design, all angles and hard materials, and the plowed drive seemed to be paved with some type of marble.

Laurel parked in the driveway and took several deep breaths. This was a mistake. She wasn't at top form right now; she should go home and knit some more. Instead, she pushed open her door and stepped into the drizzle, instantly drenched and cold. Her hair stuck to her face, but she lowered her head and strode to the walkway, which was edged with prickly bushes protecting the house.

She climbed three wide stairs and reached toward the massive steel door to ring the doorbell. There were no decorations softening the hard planes of the house. She shivered again, and even her heart chilled.

Abigail opened the door, her eyes widening. "Agent Snow." Her gaze ran over the freezing water drenching Laurel's face.

"Come in. My goodness." She opened the door.

Laurel stepped inside an ultra-modern house built with glass, steel, and sharp angles. A wide wall of windows covered the farthest wall, right up to the pitched ceiling. Snowblood Peak rose in the far distance beyond the rushing river and groves of trees, the snow glowing in the night. Laurel stood in the entryway, cold rain sluicing off her to pool on the massive piece of white tile. She shivered, her mind going numb but her body still firing.

"Stay here." Abigail hurried into what appeared to be a guest bath and returned with a plush white towel. "You're a mess. What is going on?" Without waiting for permission, she unzipped Laurel's jacket and set it on the nearest hook before rubbing the towel in her thick hair. Her eyebrows rose when Laurel allowed her to minister to her. "How did you find me, anyway? I've kept my home address private."

"I'm with the FBI — I found your location with one phone call," Laurel said, her teeth chattering. "Did you know?"

Abigail finished fluffing Laurel's hair. "That's an ambiguous question, isn't it? Come join me for a glass of wine." She strode on bare feet across the chilly-looking tile to the open concept kitchen with its cement backdrop and gleaming pure-white marble countertops. "I just opened a lovely bottle of Chateau Lafite Rothschild Paullac from 2010."

Laurel kicked off her boots and followed Abigail, her body tingling from cold and adrenaline. What was the correct approach? There was too much going on in her head. She ought to return home and prepare for this meeting. Instead, she pulled out a pristine white bar stool with chrome accents and sat at the counter, her body feeling a thousand years old.

Abigail poured two generous glasses of deep red wine. "Are you a wine connoisseur?"

"No." Laurel accepted the glass and watched the light flicker over the red color. "Not at all, but this smells good." Her voice sounded wooden, and her body was numb. So was her brain. This wasn't a smart idea or a safe one. She needed all her faculties in order to deal with Abigail, but she sat frozen in place. Her new reality was too much to absorb right now.

"You really must learn. What is life without enjoying good wine?" Abigail set her nose near her glass and inhaled deeply. "Yes. That's delicious." She wore a thick gray sweater over white yoga pants, and her white-blond hair cascaded over her shoulders. Her deep-blue eyes glowed against her pale face. "Now. Would you care to tell me why you're on my doorstep well into the evening, when the last time we met, you called me crazy and told me to stay away from you?"

She should have followed her own directive. Laurel studied the woman she couldn't read. A woman every bit as intelligent as Laurel, if not more so. Laurel took a drink of the potent wine. She murmured her approval. It was delicious. She set the glass down. "Did you know that Zeke Caine is my father?"

Abigail blinked. Once and then again. She set her glass on the spotless counter. "Excuse me?"

"It's true. Did you know?"

Abigail looked at Laurel, her gaze wandering from one eye to the other. Then she smiled. "Isn't this an unexpected development?" Reaching for her right eye, she pinched out a contact, taking the blue away and revealing a light green iris in its place. She did the same with her other eye, showing a lighter blue than the contact . . . along with a partial heterochromatic spot in the lower corner.

Laurel couldn't breathe. Not at all.

Then Abigail reached beneath her hair, at her nape, bent over, and yanked off the blond hair. It had been a wig? Laurel hadn't had a clue. Thick auburn hair, brown and red, sprang out around Abigail's ears, cut fairly short but still showing a bit of curl at the ends. She looked up at Laurel and her smile showed a slight gap beyond her incisors. "Yes, sister. I knew."

CHAPTER THIRTY-THREE

Laurel could only stare at the face so similar to her own. "Why didn't you say something?" Her voice was hoarse.

Abigail reached for her glass. "What would I say? Hey, sister. I know you're enjoying this blameless life of yours, that you're content and admired in your job and comfortable and enviable in your home life with a mother who'd do anything for you, but hey, you come from bad stock. Really bad stock, and now the father who never would've wanted you in the first place is missing . . . you should go find him?" She took a healthy drink of her extravagant wine. "What kind of sister would that make me?"

Laurel reclaimed her glass for another taste. Her initial analysis of Abigail hadn't changed. It was just as likely as ever that Abigail had enjoyed having the upper hand in their relationship, relishing the fact that she held all pertinent information. "Why the blond wig?" The woman had worn that long before Laurel had appeared in town.

Abigail swirled her wine around in her glass, watching the liquid catch the light. "It's his hair color. His stamp, and I can't get rid of it." Her gaze rose, piercing Laurel. "I've tried. If I dye it any lighter shade, it grows in rapidly, showing the roots. Auburn roots. If I dye it a darker color, the red still shows up, marking me. So wigs are the best idea, and I like to change colors every couple of years. The students think it's eccentric and cool, and I enjoy reinventing myself."

Laurel sipped again.

Abigail looked at Laurel's hair. "Until I met you, I never realized how gorgeous the color really is, when it's not associated with that bastard. Perhaps I'll go natural now."

Laurel would have to tread lightly over the bastard comment. "And your eyes?"

Abigail's eyes remained bright. "He hated his eyes and thus hated mine. His father thought he was possessed, that the eyes were a sign of the devil, and he beat the spirit out of our sperm donor, also known as Zeke. So, he hid his eyes from everyone, and he forced me to do so as well. I've worn sunglasses or contacts ever since I was a child. Plus, our eyes are so identifiable, you know? And going to college so young, entering the work force as a child, I was enough of a freak."

"I understand," Laurel said softly.

Abigail smiled. "Again, meeting you altered my perception. You wear that bizarre combination like it's part of you, and the colors are truly alluring. I'm rethinking my entire look. Wouldn't it be enchanting for our outsides to look as similar as our insides?"

Warning ticked through Laurel. "Our insides?"

"Of course. We're two sides of the same coin, Laurel. Don't you see it? Don't you *feel* it?" Abigail took another drink.

"No," Laurel said honestly. "You play games, some I haven't figured out. I work to save people."

Abigail's chuckle was amused and dark. "Oh, honey. You're smarter than that. With your intelligence and opportunities, you could've done anything. Solved the mysteries of the universe. Cured cancer. Traveled to war-torn countries and created food and medicine supply chains. You didn't."

Laurel shifted on the chair and wiped more rain off her chin.

Abigail lifted her glass in salute. "You dig

into the darkest minds on the planet, the ones filled with real evil, and you hunt them. You're drawn to them in a way you can't understand and don't want to explore, so you appease your soul by chasing them and putting them away. But it's the draw that catches you . . . not the result."

"That's not true," Laurel challenged.

Abigail shrugged. "Tell yourself what you need to in order to navigate this world, sister. But we both know that the darkness calls to you."

Laurel couldn't breathe.

Abigail finished her wine. "Have you ever wondered who you'd be, what you'd do, if you hadn't been raised by your pacifist, tea-loving mother? The one who went to college and grad school with you, so you were never alone?"

Laurel finished her wine, her mind buzzing.

"You'd be me," Abigail whispered. She reached for the bottle and refilled their glasses.

"Did you kill your father, Abigail?" Laurel asked quietly.

"*Our* father." Abigail nudged the now full glass toward Laurel. "Did I hate him? Yes. Did I want to stay away from him for the rest of my life? Yes. Did I kill him? No." She lifted her own glass. "My looks reminded him of his own, and he'd been taught to hate the way he looked. In addition, I was a female, and a king like him deserved a male heir. Finally, the fact that I was so much smarter than he bothered him to the point that he was sure the devil had put me here to mess with him. When the state took me away after my mother died, he smiled. He actually smiled." She took another sip of wine. "That's all you're getting from me about him, Laurel. Don't ask again."

"I'm going to find him." Laurel didn't touch her glass.

"God help you when you do," Abigail murmured. "I'm your blood now, and I'll be here for you if that ever happens. Trust me. You're going to need me."

"All right." Laurel slid off the stool. "Did you hate your mother for dying? For leaving you with him?" Her mother, who was tall and blond and healthy looking.

"No," Abigail whispered. "I loved her. Completely."

Laurel couldn't read her. "Fine. I need to get going." She turned toward the front windows and the door.

Abigail swiftly rounded the marble counter. "It's wet out there. You could stay the night." Her laugh lacked humor. "We could have a sister slumber party. Watch old movies, talk about boys, and share our hopes and dreams." While her voice held sarcasm, when Laurel turned around, she finally spotted a rare vulnerability in Abigail's dual-colored eyes.

"I have to go," Laurel said gently, her legs stiffening with an urgent need to run. She turned back toward the door, and a flash of silver through the window caught her eye. "Duck!" she yelled, pivoting and leaping for Abigail. Gunfire shattered the heavy glass, and pain burst through her left shoulder.

She landed on Abigail, grabbed her, and scrambled behind the metal door.

Shards of deadly sharp glass fell with a loud crash as the window glass scattered across the hard tile. The gunfire continued, exploding dangerously close, hitting the sofa and spitting cotton tufts through the air.

Laurel ducked her head and shoved Abigail even farther behind her, against the wall. Bullet holes dented the metal above their heads. She caught her breath, her ears ringing, and reached for the gun at the back of her waist. "Stay back," she ordered, crouching low, using her healthy hand.

"No." Abigail grabbed her arm and pulled her. "You've been shot."

"I know." Laurel used her still-working

393

arm, leaned slightly past the door, and fired several shots out the now-destroyed window. She angled her head to glimpse the battered farm truck that had chased her the other night, a figure crouched behind it with an automatic weapon balanced on the hood. He fired again, and she pushed back against Abigail, protecting her.

The gunman jumped in the truck and sped away.

"Call 9-1-1," Laurel ordered as the room began to spin around her. How badly had she been hit?

Huck was the first officer through the door, his gun at the ready, his gaze seeking. "Snow?" he bellowed.

"Here." She sat on a white marble hearth in front of a wide, flaming gas fire. "I'm okay." She held a white towel to her left shoulder, the material red from her blood. Her face was pale and her hand shaking. "The threat is gone. One shooter in the same truck that ran me off the road the other night."

Huck paused as emergency vehicles jerked to loud stops. Rain and wind blew into the foyer, where thick glass shards still hung from the top of the window. Glass spread across the white tile, glinting in the night.

His shoulders slowly relaxed and his breath evened out. When he'd received the call, he'd expected the worst.

"I have another towel." A woman hurried out from a hallway near the fireplace, and her accent identified her as Dr. Abigail Caine.

What was Laurel doing at Dr. Caine's home? Huck turned to look at the woman and stopped short. His mind went numb and then flared back to life. "What the hell?" he muttered.

Dr. Caine winked at him and then hurried toward Laurel with a fresh towel. "Good evening, Captain." She appeared cheerful even after having watched her front window burst apart from automatic gunfire. "I suppose my appearance is a surprise. Let me catch you up." She pressed the towel against the bloody one on Laurel's upper shoulder.

Laurel grimaced and planted her hand over the newest towel.

Abigail turned to face him. "We're sisters. Same hair, same now gloriously similar eyes, and same father. It also appears that we're both ambidextrous, considering my talented sister shot from her left hand. We have so much in common. Isn't that just a kick in the proverbial pants?"

Huck froze and craned his neck to look beyond the professor at Laurel.

She closed her eyes and nodded. Then she shook her head. Then she nodded again. Blood dotted her clothing.

Monty burst through the door, followed by paramedics, the sheriff, two state officers, and FBI agent Walter Smudgeon.

"The scene is secure," Huck said quickly.

Monty skidded to a halt next to him, looked at Abigail, at Laurel, and then back at Abigail. "Holy shit."

That about summed it up.

Abigail clapped her hands together. "We're sisters. Isn't that brilliant?" In her excitement, her accent intensified.

The paramedics, one of whom was Bert, strode past her to Laurel, and Huck followed them.

"How bad is it?" he asked, focusing on the most immediate issue.

Laurel shook her head. "Not bad." Then she removed the towels.

Bert leaned forward. "Hmmm. I'm getting accustomed to fixing you up, Agent. You might need to just put me on speed dial." He slipped on rubber gloves and probed the wound. "The bullet didn't hit anything important and went right through, but you're going to need stitches this time."

He gently settled a clean bandage over the wound and then taped it into place. "The ambulance is waiting to take you."

"No." She stood, her hand over the bandage. "I am not going in an ambulance."

"I've got you," Huck said, reaching for her good arm. "Let's go."

Abigail stepped gingerly through the scattered glass shards on the hard tile floor. "You saved my life, Laurel." She smiled. "I'll go to the hospital with you."

Huck sent Monty a quick look.

Monty stepped forward, taking out a notebook. "I'm sorry, ma'am, but I need to interview you and go through the events and the scene. I'm sure Captain Rivers will contact you with any updates."

Abigail faltered. "Laurel?"

Oh, this was just too weird. Huck tightened his grip on Laurel's arm and assisted her around the worst of the glass. He'd like to just pick her up and carry her to the car, but she was the agent in charge, and she wouldn't like that.

"I'm fine, Abigail," Laurel said over her shoulder, her voice low with pain.

"Okay," Abigail chirped, her eyes gleaming. "Call me, sister. We have much to discuss."

Laurel turned even paler. They reached

the blasting rain, and Huck gave in to temptation now that they were outside, sweeping her off the wet ground, careful to keep her healthy shoulder against his chest. It was a tribute to how much pain she was in that she didn't so much as gasp in protest.

In the truck, she put her head back and breathed evenly as she tried to control the pain. Huck had so many questions he wanted to ask, but it appeared she was barely holding it together, so he concentrated on the icy rain and the treacherous driving conditions. When they reached the hospital, the attendee got her right in, stitching her up with seven sutures and giving her a pain pill.

Huck leaned against the doorframe of the examination room, watching as the doctor pressed another wrap in place. "I have two men assigned to your mother's house for the night, and I've already talked to her on the phone to reassure her that you're all right."

Laurel looked at him, her face pale, dark circles beneath her eyes. She'd never appeared so vulnerable before. So fragile and small. "Thank you, but I'm not staying the night in the hospital." She bit her lip.

"I know. Somebody is trying to kill you, so for the night, I'm providing cover." He reached for her and lifted her off the examination table. "You good with this?"

She rested her head against his shoulder. "Pain pills knock me out. I know you want answers, and I wish I had some. For now, same truck, probably the same shooter, but that's all I know. I did return fire, but I don't know if I hit anything." Her voice grew drowsy as she spoke. "Abigail Caine is my sister."

Yeah, that was the shock of the year.

Huck walked out of the hospital with Laurel in his arms, every ounce of protectiveness in him aroused. He had to get rid of that shit, but tonight he had to provide cover for her. For now, she slept quietly against him, not even stirring when he set her in the truck and secured her seatbelt.

Apparently his answers would have to wait until morning.

CHAPTER THIRTY-FOUR

Laurel stretched awake with the smell of pine and male around her and the sound of hail hitting the roof. She turned to see Huck staring at her with heavy-lidded eyes. "Morning."

"Hi. How's the shoulder?" he asked.

She rolled it. "Feels itchy but not bad. The doctor did a good job with the stitches." Thanks to the location of the wound, she wouldn't even need a sling. "Did I hear him say he'd take out the stitches in a week?"

Huck watched her carefully but didn't move closer. "Yeah."

That wasn't so bad. She'd been lucky. "Did I talk in my sleep?"

"Not with that pain pill. You were seriously out."

She ignored the pain from her injuries. Was this awkward? Yep. Even though they'd had sex, been intimate, this felt so weird. If she noticed it, then it was definitely weird.

"I think I did wake up at one point, and you weren't here. It was dark, still raining."

"I had to let Aeneas out," Huck said, his fingers wrapping around the part of the sheet by his cut abs as if maybe he was fighting himself? Fighting to keep from touching her? "I also had to wake up a few times to check you for fever, but I don't think you'll have any ill effects from this wound except maybe a slight scar. You were lucky."

"I know." She took inventory of her hurts. Not bad, but she was close to needing a vacation. "I'm feeling grateful to be alive, although we need to figure out who this guy is and why he keeps trying to kill me. Following me to Abigail's house last night and making it through the security gate took both patience and timing."

Huck frowned. "The serial killer has his ritual, right? And this attack doesn't fit it. From what I know about serial killers, they don't just swap methods or victimology."

"Exactly. This is more focused or personal. He's not trying to kill me because of his compulsion. These attacks are focused and deliberate. He needs me out of the way." Her body heated, so close to Huck's warmth. To his hard and very capable body. "Thank you for bringing me here last night. What time is it?"

"It's just before five," Huck said. "So much for sleeping in."

At least they'd been able to sleep. "That's okay. I promised Kate I'd meet her at six to continue working and organizing the office." Laurel stretched, wincing as bruises made themselves known. She and Kate could work for a few hours and then she'd take breakfast home for her mom.

Huck frowned. "Why so early? It's been a long week. I'd take a half day off, at least."

Laurel instinctively moved closer to his warmth; the morning was chilly. "Kate doesn't want to be home alone because her kids are at their dad's, and I've been working against the clock with this case. The killer either has or will strike again soon. I have to find this guy." She paused. "Thank you for sending officers to my mom's house."

"Glad to help, but I could only get them for one night." His voice was rough and strained.

"That's okay. I'll be home with her tonight, and I'm armed." Right now, Laurel would love to shoot the idiot who kept coming for her.

Huck stretched his neck, and his shoulder popped. "You should get a dog for your mom. They're better than any security system."

That was a decent idea. She stared at him, her mind wandering to the night they'd spent together.

His gaze darkened, as he no doubt remembered the same moments. Regret twisted his lips. "Why don't I make you breakfast?"

Probably a good idea. She began to slide to the other side of the bed before temptation made her do something she'd regret.

His cell phone buzzed. "Early morning calls are never good." He reached for it by his side, and answered. "Rivers, and this had better be good." He paused. "You sure? Okay. I'll be right there."

She stilled. "Bad news?"

"You could say that. Monty said that the Genesis Valley Cemetery early grounds crew just reported a work truck missing. For all they know, it could've been missing for weeks. It fits the description of the one we're looking for — the one with the shooter and the guy who ran you off the road."

The cemetery? Where her uncle worked? "No. Is someone trying to frame my uncle?" So much for breakfast. "Let's go conduct interviews."

Huck planted a hand on her bicep, holding her in place. "Not you. You know you

403

can't be there. Go to work as planned, and I'll call you. I put your clothes in the washer and then dryer last night. If the blood didn't come out of your shirt, borrow one of mine. Trust me."

Her heart sank. Uncle Carl?

A deputy had dropped Uncle Blake's truck off at Huck's house that morning, which had been kind of Huck to arrange, although now there would be gossip.

Laurel kept an eye on the scattered gravel over the ice as she drove toward her office. A sinister mist slithered close to the road and dawn remained concealed by dark clouds. Right now, Huck and additional officers were interrogating her uncle as well as the other cemetery employees. She knew she couldn't be present for the interview, but it hurt to stay on the sidelines. Her uncle wasn't a killer, but he wasn't good with people, either. He would get angry with Huck and probably not respond well. Should she call Steve Bearing? Uncle Carl might need a lawyer.

Huck had said he'd handle it, and he seemed fair. Plus, the man kept carrying her away from danger.

Her abdomen fluttered and she rolled her eyes, reaching for one of the two lattes in the middle cup holders. Neither she nor Huck wanted a relationship, and they didn't fit anyway. She didn't really fit with anybody, but that was all right. Her life was full.

She shook herself back to the moment, appreciating the lack of traffic. That was one thing she'd never liked in DC. Here, the lanes were empty, giving the mist free reign. Nobody was out on this morning at this hour.

Except her. Hopefully Kate would be at the office already, and they could get some work accomplished. It'd be nice to have a full office, but she and Kate would do well enough for now.

The mist caressed Uncle Blake's clean but ancient farm truck as Laurel turned left into the parking area and drove toward the office doorway. Something on the ground caught her eye, and she hit the brakes. It was a body. The latte cup flew out of her hand and broke open against the dash, spilling coffee down the vents, steering wheel, and her legs. She gaped through the windshield, then drew her weapon from the laptop bag, jumping out of the truck.

Her heart battered her ribcage and she sucked in deep breaths, keeping control of her reaction.

Cold assaulted her, and she swung her gun around, clearing the entire area. The building remained dark and silent save for the Christmas lights twinkling merrily from every eave. Apparently, the landlord had put up lights the night before, probably just hours before the victim had been dumped.

Laurel exhaled to keep herself in control and stepped gingerly over the frozen asphalt to study the naked body of a woman, her head positioned toward the building and her feet toward the street. Her hands were palm up and her legs spread obscenely, as if the killer had wanted to pose her for the authorities. There were signs of deep bruising on her thighs. Her eyelids were closed in death, and her skin had turned blue beneath the night's freezing rain.

Laurel swung her gaze around, surrounded by mist, securing the scene. Nothing moved and no sound came through the soft wind.

She shivered.

Keeping on full alert, she edged back to the still-running truck to call in the killing, her voice low and her words clipped. Her breathing shallowed out while she checked the surrounding area again. Just a quiet roadway across from silent trees, their limbs reaching for the sky.

Then she returned to the body, fighting the urge to drape her coat over the woman. The victim was dead and wouldn't feel the cold.

Even so, it was a travesty to leave her like this.

Laurel banished the anger and hurt, the fury and the deep, gut-wrenching determination to find the asshole who'd done this. Instead, she crouched down to study the body, careful not to disturb the scene.

Long blond hair spread out on the icy ground, and bruises marred the woman's neck. There was no doubt they'd find petechiae in the eyes once someone with gloves opened the eyelids. More purple contusions showed on the woman's wrists and ankles, in addition to those across her ribcage. Small cuts were everywhere. Not enough to kill her but to torture. One over the left breast looked deeper than the others.

Laurel spoke to a soul that was no longer present. "I'm so very sorry."

CHAPTER THIRTY-FIVE

From the Fish and Wildlife conference room, Laurel looked through the office across the hall to see the crime tape still in place in the parking lot. News vans were massed across Main Street against the wooded area, but at least they had to stay out of the way. It had been a rough morning for the techs, processing the scene in the freezing mist, but at least the rain had held off until they'd carted the body away.

"All right. Everyone take a seat," Huck said, taking control of his task force. They'd called everyone in. "There's pizza on the credenza if anybody wants some."

Nobody seemed hungry. Laurel turned and took her seat next to Huck's chair with Smudgeon on her right. Monty sat across from her, Sheriff York at his side. Tension rolled through the room, and she twisted her neck to release some of it.

Huck cleared his throat. "We've identified

the victim in our parking lot as Yana Richards, a twenty-five-year-old car salesperson from Woodstone Used Cars. She was last seen Tuesday night and wasn't expected back to work until this morning. He killed her fast rather than keeping her for a week like some of the earlier victims."

Sheriff York reached behind himself for a piece of pepperoni pizza. "So no missing person's report?"

"No," Huck said shortly. "After this meeting, Monty, have somebody dig into her life like never before. Talk to everyone who knew her and trace every second from the time she left work on Tuesday. We're getting warrants to dump her phone and computers now."

Monty nodded. "We photocopied our reports regarding sexual predators in the area as well as records of similar crimes in other states. They're in the blue folders in everyone's stacks," he said.

Huck glanced at the file folders. "Excellent. Thank you. The reports in the red folders are from the state police crime techs regarding the other victims along with possible backgrounds. So far, the connection between all of the victims seems to be the Genesis Valley Church and their physical descriptions — blond and fairly young. That may be all there is to the case." He focused on Sheriff York. "Do you have an update?"

York shrugged. "Not really. I've canvassed the city, and nobody knows anything. I'll keep looking around, though."

"You do that," Huck said grimly. "We just received updated lab results, and there's no viable DNA on or in the victims. This guy is careful. Also, Lisa Scotford was not pregnant, and I notified Pastor John of that fact this morning."

The pastor must've been so relieved. Laurel sat back. "Do we have this guy on video from last night?"

Huck turned toward Laurel. "Yes, and I thought we could create an updated profile after we watch the CCTV from last night as a team. I watched it earlier. It has to show something about his mindset, even if we can't identify him. Right?"

Laurel nodded. "Agreed." Although she'd already updated the profile in her head after finding the body, watching the video couldn't hurt. Would they finally be able to identify the killer? She hadn't even had a chance to ask Huck about his interviews with the cemetery workers and her uncle.

Huck pointed the remote at a flatscreen monitor attached to the wall behind the chair where he usually sat. A grainy video slowly took form. "This was taken around three in the morning, it was raining, and the lighting isn't the best in the parking area."

Laurel twisted her chair to see better.

A truck drove directly across the parking area and turned sideways. "That's the truck apparently stolen from the cemetery," she said quietly. "It's the same one that ran me off the road and was used by the person who shot at me at Dr. Caine's house last night."

Huck paused the video. "Look at the front right panel."

Laurel ducked her head to see better. "Three shots. From me." So she hadn't hit the jerk. Too bad.

Huck started the video again. "Watch this guy. He knew where the cameras were. He's playing with us."

The truck parked crosswise on the parking lot, with the passenger side door toward the camera. The killer opened the driver's side door and then the back door, dropping down and disappearing from sight. The rain poured down, hitting the truck, and nothing happened. Well, nothing they could see. He remained out of sight for about three minutes and then rose, seemingly still crouching, and entered the truck. The

411

windows were blacked out, so it was impossible to see inside or see him. Then he drove away.

Laurel's throat tightened with frustration. "We can't even get an accurate height or weight from this video. There's nothing."

The dead woman lay on the ground, now revealed, just as Laurel had found her only a few hours earlier. She closed her eyes and took a moment to compose herself. She opened them to see Monty watching the video, his face pale. He shook his head.

Huck stopped the video. "Agent Snow?"

Laurel cleared her throat. "This is now a game between him and us. He still has the compulsion to kill, and his victimology is still young blondes, but now we're a part of his ritual. The fact that he left the body in our parking lot, the location of our task force, is a 'fuck you,' I'm smarter than you, and you'll never catch me. He might as well have left a sign saying just that."

Huck took out his chair and sank into it. "Could be a woman. The rape kits all came back with spermicide and condoms, but you don't need a dick to do that kind of damage. Pardon my language."

Laurel eyed the film. "I know, but the profile stands. I think it's a man."

Huck looked at the group. "Monty and

412

my team are still interviewing the cemetery employees, including Carl Snow. Sheriff York, we need you to show a picture of the vehicle to possible witnesses while you keep canvassing the local community." To Huck's credit, he didn't sound a bit sarcastic when addressing the lazy sheriff.

The office phone buzzed from the table beside the screen, and Huck frowned, pushing the speaker button. "Ena? What do you have?"

"It's the ME's office," she said. "You want them?"

"Yes," Huck said. "Put them through."

Laurel sat back. It was doubtful Dr. Ortega had found anything so quickly, especially since the body had been in the elements for hours.

"Hi. It's Dr. Ortega," the man said. "I have something."

The group collectively leaned toward the phone.

"What?" Huck asked.

"Hair caught in the back of the victim's throat," the ME said.

Monty frowned. "Like she bit the guy? Pulled out his hair?"

"No. It's dog hair," Dr. Ortega said. "I'm sending a sample to the lab at Seattle University to determine what kind of dog.

It's white and black. I'll be in touch." He clicked off.

Laurel ran through several scenarios in her brain at once. None of them were good.

Sheriff York pushed his chair away from the table. "Sounds like Karelian Bear Dog hair to me. Let's see. Who has a dog like that around here?"

Huck pinched the bridge of his nose. "Come on."

York crossed his arms. "Tell us, Captain. Where were you last night?"

"Home," Huck growled. "Just like you. I attended the scene at Dr. Caine's house and then went home to get some much-needed sleep. You can't be going down that road again."

"Can't I?" Sheriff York drawled. "Let's see. Both times Agent Snow is attacked, you're close enough by to be the first one on the scene. Then last night, another woman ends up dead in the parking lot, and we all agree the perp knew the placement of the cameras and how to avoid them. Also, for a guy who seems to be so popular, you sure don't have alibis when you need them."

Laurel's temples began to ache. She really had no choice here. "I was with the captain all night. At his house. This morning when I left his house, he was still there, while I came to work and found the body." Her face tingled as she blushed, but her personal life, or lack thereof, was nobody else's business.

York's gaze narrowed. She prepared herself for the blow, but instead, he just shook his head. "No offense, Agent Snow, but you were three sheets to the wind when Rivers took you from the hospital last night."

Laurel turned to look more fully at the sheriff. "You were at the hospital?"

His expression cleared. "See what I mean? I even asked you a few questions last night. You have one of those photographic memories, right?"

"Eidetic memory," she corrected, frowning as flashes of the night before slid through her mind. "I don't recall seeing you."

"I waved at you as the captain took you out of the hospital," Sheriff York said.

Laurel sat back, most of the night a hazy blur after the pain medication she'd taken. "Well."

"Exactly," Sheriff York said, his nostrils flaring. "Forgetting for the moment that you ended up flat on your back for someone on your task force, which has to be against FBI policy, you were drugged at the time and can't provide an alibi."

Huck stood, anger flushing red up his

corded neck. "Apologize to Agent Snow. Now."

Tension rolled through the room.

York's smile was salacious, to say the least. "I do apologize for my characterization, Agent Snow. Chances are you were on top."

Huck lunged.

Monty intercepted him before he could make it across the table, hooking one arm around Huck's waist in a surprisingly fast movement. "Huck, stop. We need you here." He immediately released Huck, who outweighed him by at least thirty pounds of muscle. Maybe more.

Sheriff York jumped to his feet. "Let's go, asshole. I've been waiting for a piece of you ever since you came home to hide in the woods."

Laurel pushed away from the table. "Everyone calm down. We're on the same team here."

"Are we?" the sheriff blurted out, eyeing the other team members, and then staring directly at Huck. "I'm not sure about that. If I wanted a good alibi, a drugged-out FBI special agent, one who's known to dig into criminal minds better than any other, would be the perfect one to have. Do you remember the entire night, Agent Snow? Can you testify, under oath, that Captain Rivers

416

didn't leave his house last night?"

Laurel sank back down in her chair. Not only could she not testify to that fact, she vaguely remembered awakening to find that Huck was not in bed with her. "I'm telling you, I would stake my professional reputation on the fact that Huck Rivers is not the Snowblood Peak killer."

"You're compromised and should be off this case." Sheriff York grinned, moving his mustache, which now had a piece of pepperoni in it. "You know, if I were a serial killer, I'd want you off this case, too, Agent Snow — if you're as good as everyone says, which I kind of doubt. Could it be that the captain played this all perfectly?"

Huck looked as if he was about to tear the room apart. "Would it be humanly possible for you to be any more of a moron, York? Just curious."

The sheriff lost his smile. "I'm not the one fucking an FBI profiler."

"That's it." Monty grabbed the sheriff by the arm and yanked him toward the door. "Everyone needs to cool the hell off. Captain Rivers? I would like to formally interview you again about all of the murders. I can make the request through professional channels, or you can just cooperate. It's up to you."

Huck's chin lifted. "I understand, and I'm happy to speak with you. You're good at your job, Monty."

"Do you want your representative here?" Monty asked, pushing the sheriff out the door and shutting it.

"No," Huck growled.

Laurel swallowed. She should take herself off the case, although she didn't like it. In fact, she wasn't done yet. "Did you get any more information about the cemetery truck?"

Huck shook his head. "No. Got the call about the dead body here and came right away. I do have officers out at the cemetery, and so far, they can't find your uncle or the truck that's missing from the storage building. Doesn't mean he has it. Stay out of this one, Laurel. If he does have that truck, you can't be involved."

"I know, but my uncle would never shoot at me or kill women." Laurel's phone buzzed, and she drew it from her pocket, her mind still reeling. How could dog hair have been found on the latest victim? It was true that Laurel had been out from the pain meds last night and Huck could've gone anywhere. But she knew he hadn't done it. It just didn't track. "Hello?" she said.

"Hello? Is this FBI Agent Snow?" a

woman asked.

"Yes," Laurel said.

"This is Dr. Davis from Genesis Valley Hospital, and you're the emergency contact for Dr. Abigail Caine. Please come right away."

Chapter Thirty-Six

Laurel dashed out of the mist into the hospital emergency entrance, hurrying to the front desk and flipping open her badge. "I'm Agent Snow, and I was called about Dr. Abigail Caine." Was it possible the killer had gone after Abigail when he'd failed to hit Laurel the night before? And why was she Abigail's emergency contact?

A nurse emerged from a closed doorway. "Oh, hello. Please come this way." She appeared to be in her seventies with dark gray hair and spotless white tennis shoes.

Laurel glanced at the receptionist and then followed the nurse by several examination rooms to the one at the end. She walked inside to see Abigail sitting on the edge of a bed while a young doctor wrapped her right wrist. Abigail wore her natural hair and eye colors. "What is going on?" Laurel asked.

Abigail looked up. "Last night, when you

420

tackled me, I hurt my wrist. In all of the excitement, I thought it was just bruised, but the swelling and pain have gotten worse. It's a good thing our family members are ambidextrous." She looked at the young doctor and gifted him with a full smile. The guy was probably in his midthirties with black hair, deep brown skin, and steady hands. "That's my sister. She saved my life, you know."

The doctor looked over his shoulder and smiled. "Hi. Yeah, I definitely see the resemblance."

"Hi," Laurel answered. "Is it broken?"

"Just a bad bruise, but I don't like the swelling," the doctor said. "We're wrapping it, and I want your sister to ice it every other hour or so." He turned back to Abigail. "The pain pill will wear off in a few hours and after that, take ibuprofen for the pain, and you should be okay, Abigail." He finished and stood up. "How's that?"

"Perfect," Abigail said, winking at him. Her auburn hair curled around her ears, and her multicolored eyes sparkled. Apparently she was no longer hiding her true colors. "Are you single?"

The doctor grinned. "I'm engaged. Have a nice day." He turned and strode out of the room.

Laurel leaned against the doorframe, her entire body aching. "Abigail? Why am I your emergency contact?"

Abigail smiled and swung her feet. "You're my sister. Of course, you're my emergency contact. I updated my medical form when I arrived here earlier." She hopped off the table and winced. "Next time you save my life, try to land easier, would you?" Then she reached Laurel. "Although I appreciate it. I really do."

Laurel looked up the four or so inches Abigail had on her. She had to figure out the right way to say what she wasn't sure she even felt. "This doesn't change anything between us."

"Sure it does." Abigail slung her arm through Laurel's and turned her back into the hallway. "We share blood, Laurel. I may not know much or understand a lot about this world, but that means something to me. We look alike, and even though you don't appreciate the fact, deep down, we're *exactly* the same."

"No, we're not," Laurel said, passing through the doorway to the reception area again.

Abigail's laugh was tinkly. "Go ahead and tell yourself that if it helps you to sleep. You know the truth. We both do." She sighed.

"We look exactly alike, and we're ambidextrous. Tell me, do you experience synesthesia?"

"Only if I'm very stressed. Otherwise, I've learned to deal and ignore," Laurel said shortly. People with synesthesia could experience sensations where the brain triggers more than one sense at a time. Sometimes she could smell colors. "I don't want to talk about it, Abigail." She needed space.

Abigail sniffed. "Fine. We'll share our idiosyncrasies later. For now, I have to tell you, watching that hunky Huck Rivers carry you to his truck last night gave me butterflies. I don't suppose you'd be interested in a threesome? A lot of men have fantasies about twins."

Laurel stumbled. "No. I would not be interested in a threesome, and you and I are not twins."

Abigail looked around the vacant reception room. "That's true, although we could pass for twins. I think I'm two years older than you, which makes me your big sister. As your big sister, I should warn you about the good captain. He's not all that you think."

Laurel looked over at her half-sister. "You just asked about a threesome, and now you're telling me to watch out for him?"

Abigail rolled her eyes and nudged Laurel toward a chair. "I was just kidding about the threesome but not kidding about the warning. Lighten up, would you? Life is finally on the right track." She looked toward the reception area. "I have to check out. Have a seat, and then you can drive me home. I took a pain pill, and I shouldn't drive with just one arm." She sauntered over to take a seat in front of a small counter.

Laurel's mind reeled as she moved to the far end of the reception area to call Huck. The call went to voicemail, so she phoned Kate next.

"FBI," Kate answered.

"Hi. Have you heard anything about Huck or Monty?" Laurel whispered.

"No," Kate whispered back. "It's quiet here. Agent Smudgeon is in his office doing some sort of research, so I'm just continuing to tackle the dust. Can I do anything for you?"

Laurel's headache was worsening. Just then, Robert Caine and Pastor John Govern strode inside. "I have to go. I'll call you later." She moved toward the men.

Robert reached her first. "How badly is my sister hurt?" He had dark circles beneath his eyes, and his shoulders slumped.

"Abigail has a bruised wrist but should be

fine," Laurel said, curiosity clamoring through her. "Why are you here? Did she call you?"

Sweat dotted his brow. "A nurse called me and told me to get here."

The pastor put a hand on his shoulder. "I told you I could come, and you weren't needed. You should go back to bed."

Laurel stepped back. "What's going on?"

Robert coughed into his hand. "I caught the flu from Jasmine. She was up all night throwing up, and I held her hair and took care of her, but then I started puking this morning. Pastor John brought over some soup for us and was there when the nurse called."

Laurel discreetly took another step away. "If you're sick, why did you come?"

His bloodshot eyes widened. "Don't you get it? God. You need to understand. When Abigail calls, you come. I thought I explained that to you. You never, and I mean *never*, want to disappoint her."

Abigail strode over from the reception area, tucking her wallet in her purse with her uninjured hand. "Oh, good. I had hoped the nurse got a hold of you, Robert."

Robert gasped and stepped back, hitting the wall. "Oh my God." He looked at Abigail and then Laurel and then back. "What have you done?" He gagged and covered his mouth before coughing wildly. Then he sniffed and shook his shoulders to regain control.

Pastor John's eyebrows lifted high. "Dr. Caine. That's a new look for you. Did you dye your hair?" He looked over at Laurel and then back.

Abigail's smile was dazzling. "No. This is my natural hair color, and these are my real eyes. No contacts."

Pastor John's jaw dropped. "I see." He glanced sideways at Robert. "I think?"

Abigail slapped his arm almost playfully. "This has to be confusing. Here it is — Laurel and I are sisters, though she didn't know it until last night. I did, because of the way we look, but I didn't say anything because your old boss is a fucktard and I thought she was better off not knowing."

Robert sank into the nearest chair, his breath panting out. "Dad is a good guy, Abby. He was just taught some dumb stuff about his eyes, and he used that against you when you were young. Please don't call him names."

Laurel turned to him but stayed feet away. The last thing she needed was to catch the flu. "Why didn't you say something, Robert? You looked so shocked the first time we

426

met, but I thought it was because I was with the FBI and was armed. You had to realize that I looked just like Abigail."

"Just like me," Abigail said happily.

"Like you used to look," Robert said sourly. "You haven't worn your real hair color or showed people your real eyes since you were a young kid. Even way before you left for school."

Abigail slipped her free arm through Laurel's again. "Things are different now. As you can see. I'm all me."

Robert looked up at Laurel. "I hope you know what you're getting into."

Abigail lost the smile. "What does that mean, Robert?"

"Nothing," he said quickly. Wearily. "My wife is sick, and I need to get back home, Abby. Why did you have the nurse call me?"

Pastor John shook his head as if somebody had thrown water into his face. "Agent Snow, Pastor Caine is your father?"

"Apparently," Laurel said. This was all too strange; she needed some time to herself. Strike that. She needed time with her mother.

"Do you know where he is?" Pastor John asked, his eyes lighting. "Has he contacted you? Is he safe? Where is he?"

Laurel sighed. "I have no idea. Sorry. This

is all new to me, and I don't know where he is." Although Abigail was once again staying quiet. "Do you, Abigail?"

"Nope." Abigail drew Laurel toward the outside door. "Laurel is going to drive me home, and Robert, I called for you and Jasmine to come and bring my car home afterward. I am sorry she is sick and hope we can all get together soon, just like the family I always wanted to have." She tossed a smile over her shoulder. "Pastor John? Do you mind helping Robert drive my car to my home? I'd hate to be without it."

Pastor John moved woodenly as if his brain wouldn't catch up with the reality of the day. "I'd be happy to help," he said, assisting Robert up from the chair. "I'll drive your car, Robert can drive mine, and then I'll take him home." He looked down at his friend. "Are you okay to drive?"

Robert gulped down what was probably bile and looked at his sister. "Yes. I can drive, and then I'm going to bed. I hope I don't get you sick, Pastor John."

"See? Family helps family. Maybe the three of us can go on a sibling trip someday." Abigail leaned into Laurel as they walked through the parking lot to Laurel's borrowed truck. "Oh. We're not driving this. We'll take my Escalade." She dug out her keys and handed them to Laurel. "Give your keys to Robert."

Laurel didn't have the energy to argue. Instead she took her keys from her pocket and handed them to Robert. "If you need to throw up, just open the door."

"Thanks," he muttered, not looking at his sister. The guy really was afraid of her, wasn't he?

Laurel shivered in the cold. "Why didn't you say anything, Robert? You knew Zeke was my father, and you knew that Abigail is my sister."

He looked at Abigail and then just shrugged. "I figured you'd be better off not knowing. It's too late for you now." Then he moved toward the old truck.

Abigail led Laurel toward her red Escalade. "We really should talk about everything, don't you think? How about you stay for dinner and I open another bottle of wine? If you let me, I'll teach you everything about wine. It's something we could share with each other. Besides blood and genetics, of course."

Laurel needed to get away from this woman to gain perspective. "I can't tonight but will take a raincheck."

Abigail's mouth pinched. "Is it because of that man? Huck Rivers? I don't want a man to ever get between us, Laurel. They're not worth it. Not a one of them is worth it."

Laurel's eye started to twitch. "No. It's not because of Huck. I'm tired, it's been a long day, and I'm in the middle of a case. I need some rest."

"Oh. Well, I'll make you some dinner, then. It's the least I can do since you're so tired." Abigail drew her closer. "I'd hate for a man to even think about getting between us. In fact, I promise I'll never let that happen. No matter what."

Laurel stumbled and Abigail straightened her.

"You are clumsy, aren't you?" Abigail asked. "It's okay. I'll take care of you."

The statement brought bile from Laurel's stomach, and it was not the flu. "I'll drop you off, and then I have work to do, Abigail. I have a killer to catch."

CHAPTER THIRTY-SEVEN

It was almost time to take her. She was the perfect bird, although older than the others. Smart, sexy, and blond. Oh, she had been evasive for the last few nights, but it wasn't like there had been time to truly watch her. The other bird had to be handled, and leaving that one's body in the parking lot in front of Laurel's office building had been a delight. This one would be another present for sweet Laurel.

After she begged for her life like a bird in a wolf's mouth.

This time the stakes had to be higher. The only way to add more excitement to the match would be to leave her on Laurel's porch. Maybe wearing a Santa hat and nothing else. The idea was hilarious.

It wasn't time to end Laurel yet. There were so many chess moves to play first.

Snow battled the moving vehicle as darkness fell. The newest bird, the one who would soon reside in the nest, would get more time. More attention. Tonight would be the night she learned her new destiny — her new fate. Such a pretty blonde, and she appeared to have spunk. Spunk was a good thing and made the endeavor more enjoyable.

Plus, she seemed smart and would provide a good challenge. The last one had felt like a rushed job because she'd been left alone too long in the container. By the time the end came, she'd been so weak, she'd barely put up a fight.

The drive by the river to the nest took longer than usual because of the conditions. Snowbanks were mounded between the trees that bore silent witness to the triumphs and losses of the birds.

So many but not enough. Would they ever be enough? Doubtful.

The nest was tucked against the rock face across from the river; a lovely white cargo hold that was perfect for winter. It was impossible to see unless one knew it was there. White in the winter and a camo wrap for the summer.

It had been devastating when the resting places of the birds had been discovered over on Snowblood Peak, but perhaps that had been God's will.

Now brilliant Laurel was involved. Such a lovely girl. It was as if she was a gift, and someday she'd be completely unwrapped.

After Laurel would come another challenge.

The container was already prepared for the next bird, with the blanket and lantern with enough fuel to last at least twelve more hours.

Leaving the birds in the dark would be too cruel, and cruelty wasn't the point.

Not really.

Perhaps this time the stun gun would be necessary. Maybe the new bird would be a fighter and require a good stunning.

Life was good. It truly was.

Laurel walked up her mom's steps and opened the front door before kicking off her boots. It had started snowing again, and her hair was wet. Her head hurt, her body ached, and she was just done.

"Hi." Deidre leaned back to look at her through the archway to the kitchen. "Are you okay?"

"No." Laurel dropped her coat and went to her mom, hugging her tightly. "I'm so sorry about everything."

Deidre hugged her back. "Sweetheart, don't worry about it. I was so stressed last night, it made me think of a new tea. I'm calling it 'A Calming Breeze.' Isn't that a great name?"

Tears pricked the back of Laurel's eyes. "I love you, Mom. So much." Who knew who Laurel would be without Deidre as a constant in her life? Even when she'd gone off to college, Deidre had packed up and gone with her, working any job she could get while Laurel studied. "I don't know if I have a right to be upset about your keeping this secret, but if I do, I forgive you."

Deidre's hug tightened, and her ever-present scent of sugar cookies and tea surrounded Laurel with the smell of home. Of love. Of everything. "Come inside, let me make you dinner, and let's talk. I have the feeling that you really need to talk." She kissed the top of Laurel's head and drew her into the warm, already fragrant kitchen.

Laurel sat and within a minute, her mom had placed a cup of tea in front of her.

"It's called 'Soothing the Soul.' Drink it all," Deidre said, returning to the stove. "I'm making a comfy breakfast for dinner. We're doing toast and scrambled eggs with too much cheese. Do you want mild or hot salsa?"

"Mild." Laurel cupped her tea and then took a deep drink. "Oh, that's good. Is that white tea?"

Her mom flashed a smile over her shoulder. "Good catch. Yes. We're offering that one in the December subscription boxes along with a holiday gift list. It's a fantastic package this month." She cracked the eggs and mixed them up in the bowl. "What's going on?"

Laurel sat back and told her mom about the entire situation with Abigail. "I don't know what to do with her, but I need to keep this part of my life safe." Every instinct and brain cell that Laurel had told her that Abigail was about to get as involved as possible in her life. "I don't trust her, and the whole situation is confusing."

Deidre cooked the eggs, adding too much cheese, as promised. "Maybe she's just lonely and needs family. I get that."

"She's a sociopath, Mom. At the very least, she's a narcissist with a personality disorder, lonely or not." Laurel sipped more of the delicious tea, feeling healthier already. "Before I forget, the flu is going around."

Deidre dished up two plates. "I know. I have two workers out right now." She turned and set the plates on the table. "Are you feeling sick?"

"No. Just tired and frustrated because I can't solve this case." Laurel stood and fetched utensils and napkins from the drawer before retaking her seat. "How about you?"

"I don't get sick. There's too much healthy tea in my system." She sat down and unfolded her paper napkin on her lap. "I forgot the salsa." She began to stand.

Laurel waved her down. "I've got it. You deserve to relax." As she moved to the fridge, the stitches in her shoulder pulled, but she hid a wince as she fetched the freshly made salsa. "I wish I'd inherited your talent for cooking and baking." The entire fridge was full of home-cooked food and so many goodies she could just crawl inside and eat for a week. She turned and put the pot of salsa on the table.

"You don't have the patience," Deidre said. "Yet, anyway. I'm sure you'll attack cooking someday like you have everything else, and you'll end up a master chef or baker." She spooned salsa onto her eggs.

Laurel's phone buzzed in her back pocket and she drew it out to read the screen before answering. "Hi, Huck."

"Hi. We can't find your uncle. Where's Carl?" Huck said without preamble.

Laurel ducked her head. "Mom? Do you know where Carl is? Huck wants to talk to him about a missing truck."

436

Her mom shrugged. "It's the weekend, and he often goes fishing up in the mountains, as you know. Weird man loves the cold. He probably has to work on Monday and will be back then." She leaned closer to the phone. "Tell Huck that Carl is eccentric but not dangerous and to leave him alone."

Huck sighed. "All right. If I don't arrest your uncle, or if I don't get arrested myself, we need a refreshed game plan."

"Agreed," Laurel said. "How much trouble is Carl in right now?"

"Not much, but we do need to talk to him about that truck. Anybody could've gotten to it, the way it's kept in that storage unit at the back of the cemetery, and not just cemetery workers. Everyone knows about the truck, and anybody could've borrowed it at any time. The problem is that we can't find it right now, and we also can't find Carl." Huck sounded exhausted; he coughed briefly.

Laurel winced. "I hope you're not getting the flu. It's really going around."

"I don't get sick," he said, sounding like any arrogant man who'd cut off his hand before going to the doctor.

Laurel shook her head. "How did your interview go?"

"Fine. It's just so the department can

cover its butt. Monty doesn't think I killed anybody." Huck snorted. "We'll see what the lab says tomorrow. If the fur found in the newest victim's throat was Aeneas's, then I'm toast. But that's impossible, so I'm not worrying about it right now."

Laurel's head ached again. She was missing something but couldn't quite grasp it. "Have a good night, Huck."

"You, too. I'm going to the office tomorrow morning. Want to meet up and run through the case? There's a clue there we just haven't seen."

"Sure." There was definitely something just out of sight. "I'll see you tomorrow." Laurel hung up.

What was she missing?

CHAPTER THIRTY-EIGHT

It was time for the blond bird to fly.

Or really, to see her new nest.

The chilly air made breathing more difficult than usual. Was there anybody around? No sounds came from the surrounding vicinity. Not even a dog barked.

It had snowed for a couple of hours earlier but now it was just freezing cold.

The knife went smoothly through the screen, which easily tore away from the house. One would think a woman living without a man in her home would have better security — but perhaps she instinctively knew what fate held for her. Maybe she wanted this.

Some things were just destined.

It was easy to use the blade to scrape beneath the thickly painted window and pull it up about an inch so he could slip his fingers inside to open it. The damn thing creaked when lifted, although it was simple to slide inside the basement laundry room. Clothes hung neatly on a rod near an old washer and dryer, and a rug covered the rough cement. Upon a closer look, the shape of a laundry basket stitched into the rug took form.

Cute.

The stairs creaked on the way up, but since it was well after two in the morning, the bird should be asleep. If she got a chance to call for the authorities, everything would go wrong.

The game was going too strong to lose now.

It was surprising how much more enjoyable this hobby was now that Laurel was involved. She could probably create dreams in the dreamless and hope in the hopeless. She'd be able to fight in a way the others couldn't. She was smarter and trained as an agent, and she'd look spectacular as a blonde.

This bird's bedroom was on the second floor, so it was doubtful she'd be able to hear the steps creaking in the basement, as long as she was asleep. Her bedroom light had been extinguished several hours ago, so she should be in dreamland right now.

Did she dream about her fate? It'd be nice to be dreamt about. They both had a destiny to fulfill.

The kitchen was clean though the appliances were not new; the woman had left a light on above the sink. One of those silly habits people had, just in case they needed water in the middle of the night. Actually, the light made a woman alone even more vulnerable.

The staircase leading up had a painted white railing and a runner down the middle, which nicely masked all sound.

Her bedroom was the farthest one down the hall, toward the front of the home. Her breathing was even and deep with a slight snore at the end.

How adorable.

The little bird had a little snore. She slept on her side, turned away from the door, her blond hair light against darker sheets. Oh. This girl liked luxury. The sheets were silk.

She shifted beneath the bedclothes, a defenseless bird somehow knowing a predator was near. Was coming for her.

The challenge had started to wane until Laurel arrived in town to play. Now, the game was exciting again. Strong. Powerful.

The blonde on the bed shifted again, stretching her legs. Her instincts must've awakened her. There was no choice but to bring the tire iron down fast and hard. She cried out and then went limp. Hopefully not dead.

Now it was time to take her to the nest.

Huck found himself underwater, knowing what he'd find if he went just a little deeper. He didn't want to go deeper and find the dead boy. His leg ached from where he'd taken a bullet years ago in the service, but his head remained calm. His body remained cold as he did his job.

He went deeper.

Two years later, his eyes opened to total darkness with the wind blowing hard against his house. The sweet scent of Laurel Snow clung to his pillow, and he buried his face in the soft material until his heart rate slowed down. His neck hurt and his leg ached. It had been a while since he'd had a nightmare.

Knowing he couldn't return to sleep, he pushed the covers out of the way and stood on the cold floor, running through the leg exercises he'd learned after being shot. They helped him enough that he could get through the day without any medication.

Then he went to his home gym in the basement and worked his body hard until it was light outside. He returned to the kitchen, let Aeneas out and then moved to the fridge. Sweat covered his body and he drank about a quart of water.

A sharp rap on the front door had Huck turning. Red and blue lights swirled through the still closed curtains. "What the hell?" He set his cup down and stalked to the door, throwing it open.

Sheriff York slapped a piece of paper against Huck's chest. "Captain Huck Rivers, you're under arrest for the murder of Yana Richards, for a start." He ran through Huck's rights.

Huck tilted his head and spotted two news vans, their logos bright with color, jerk to a stop behind two state police cars. "You have got to be kidding me. You brought backup? Expecting a shootout?"

"No, but it never hurts to be prepared." Sheriff York drew handcuffs out of his back pocket. "Turn around, Captain."

Aeneas barked and bounded back inside, his wet coat wiping across York's pants.

"Kitchen," Huck ordered. "Bed."

The dog obediently ran toward the kitchen, drank water, and dropped into his bed, panting.

"I could've had him eat you," Huck said, not turning around. "I'll give you one chance to stop this right now, or I am going to sue you. Full on, York. I'll go for your job at the very least and a tidy retirement for myself in the process." His jaw was set so hard, his entire head hurt.

Sheriff York rocked back on his heels. "Just so you know, the university lab rushed the results for us, and the dog hair inhaled by Yana Richards was Karelian Bear Dog fur. Black and white, and the lab matched it to your dog, Captain." York showed his teeth. "I served a warrant on the dog bed in your office. Sorry you weren't there to see it."

Another truck slid to a stop and Monty jumped out, running past the reporters and officers to reach the door. His countenance was red beneath his shockingly white hair. "Huck. The news of your arrest just came over the wire." He pivoted and shoved York. "You're a moron, you know that? This will ruin you. I'll make sure of it."

Cameras snapped wildly.

"Monty, stand down," Huck said, his voice calm, his chest filled with warmth. Apparently Monty trusted him and was on his side. He'd forgotten what it was like to work with a team. To trust a team. "I'm fine going in now and suing the shit out of this guy later. In the meantime, you go figure out who killed Yana Richards, and start with anybody who had access to Aeneas's fur. Whoever got ahold of it obviously wanted

444

to frame me."

"That could be anybody," Monty said. "Aeneas has only been in the office a few times, but his fur is everywhere already. If somebody wanted fur, they could get it."

"Good point," Huck allowed. "Monty? You have Aeneas for the day, and I'd like you to coordinate with the FBI until we figure out what's happening. I'm going to step outside, and York and I are going to his car. Sheriff York, if you even think of cuffing me, we're going to get into one newsworthy fight for those reporters, and I promise you won't be standing when we're done." Huck reached for his jacket and pushed York back onto the porch.

"This is a disaster." Monty stepped inside and immediately shut the door.

Early in the morning, Laurel finished another set of booties, this pair in a cute mint color. Her mind wandered through the details of the case, making connections, as she waited to go to work.

Her phone buzzed and she lifted it to her ear. "Agent Snow."

"Hi, Laurel. It's Monty. Huck was just arrested." Monty rattled off the facts.

Laurel hurried to the kitchen and scribbled a quick note for her mom before heading out to her borrowed farm truck. "We have to work fast. You go to the office and create a list of anybody who could've taken Aeneas's fur and put it in the latest victim." She opened the door.

"Wait. Huck wanted us to stick together."

"Huck's in an uncertain situation and he's trying to gain control where there isn't any. I'm not some woman who needs protection, Monty. For a second, Huck forgot that fact." She slid into the cold truck and shivered.

Monty whistled. "What's your plan?"

What was her plan? She needed a plan. Thoughts spun around her brain, forming connections, breaking apart, and forming more. "I can't see it," she said. "It's so close. I think this arrest and throwing suspicion on Huck is the connection I've been looking for." She fumbled for her keys in her bag.

She could hear Aeneas barking over the phone.

"I need to go through my notes and stare at the board in my office." She pushed hair away from her face. "Let's meet in two hours in your conference room and go through everything we have. We'll find the killer in those notes. I'm sure of it."

"Okay. I'll see you at the office." Monty

disengaged the call.

What was she missing? She started the truck and drove slowly down the driveway. Her board. She needed to stare at the board so the pieces could fall into place. Who had access to the fur? According to Monty, that was a wide selection of people.

Her phone buzzed and she lifted it to her ear. "Snow."

"Hey, Laurel. Your mom left a message early last night saying you were looking for me. I was fishin' out at Alley's Creek. What's up?" Uncle Carl asked.

Laurel sped up. "The police were looking for you because of that old truck you use at the cemetery."

"Yeah. I haven't driven it in a while because it's a summer rig. Why?" Carl coughed.

She kept her voice gentle. "Somebody borrowed it, and they shot at me. Think, Uncle Carl. Who could've taken that truck?"

He coughed some more. "No clue. We use it all summer and let the 4-H kids use it as well. Heck. Even some of the farms around here have borrowed it when they needed a rig. You know how folks are with farm trucks. Last year, the senior class of the high school decorated it for a float. Everyone knows it's in the tool shed, and anybody

447

can get in there. If it's stolen, it isn't worth much."

That was true. "Uncle Carl? Have you ever seen Huck's dog?"

"Huh?" Carl asked.

"His dog. The pretty black and white one," Laurel said, her mind working so fast her head hurt.

Carl coughed again. "No. Sorry. Why?"

"No reason." She knew her uncle hadn't done anything wrong.

He coughed again. "I think I got the flu."

Her brain clicked. She was so close to figuring this out. "All right. I have to go."

"Um, let's do dinner soon. I don't like that I'm so weird, I've been a suspect in this," he mumbled.

Her heart ached. "You're not weird and you're not a suspect in anything, Uncle Carl." She cleared her throat. "Mom told me everything. You probably saved her that night."

Carl was silent.

Laurel should've waited to say something in person. "I love you, Carl. Don't worry about this. I've got your back."

"Okay. Be careful, Laurel. You're all we've got." With that, he ended the call.

She rubbed her chest. Poor Carl. He seemed so tough and solitary, but being a suspect had apparently hurt his feelings. She couldn't blame him. She reached over to call her mom, who should be out of bed by now. The call went to voicemail. "Hey, it's Laurel. Call me, would you? Thanks." She ended the call, mildly uneasy. Maybe she should've checked in on her mom that morning, but Laurel hadn't wanted to disturb her sleep.

The parking lot of her office was vacant save for the cars of other staff. The news vans had probably followed the sheriff and Huck to where he'd be booked, or at the very least, interviewed. She jumped out of her car and ran up the stairs to her office, nearly dropping a ball of yarn from her bag.

Her phone dinged and relief filled her. It had to be her mother. "Hi," she answered.

"Um, Agent Snow?" a female voice said.

Laurel paused. "Yes?"

"This, um, this is Vida." Her voice shook so much she didn't even sound like the girl Laurel had met the other day.

"What's going on?" Laurel asked, going cold.

"Um, well, Dad and the bimbo got tired of us, so we decided to come home early. We just got here, and Mom isn't in the house, but her car is here. Her bed isn't made and there's a bunch of blood on her pillow." The girl's voice was pitched high in panic. "There's something wrong, and she told us to call you if we ever needed to. It's weird. What should we do?"

The world crashed down around Laurel's head. "Nothing. I'll be right there. Lock yourselves in a room and wait for me. Stay on the line." She quickly dialed Monty's number. "The killer got Kate last night. Send everyone to her house right now." With that, she ran back down the stairs.

Oh, God.

Kate.

CHAPTER THIRTY-NINE

Kate Vuittron kicked the frozen door again. "You think I'm embarrassed to be naked, you stupid ass? I gave birth three times. Without drugs. Have the episiotomy scars to prove it," she yelled. Oh, this asshole was in for a shock when he opened that door. She'd been in here for hours, and she was freezing.

She didn't remember what had happened. The last thing she recalled was going to bed and then hearing a noise.

Then pain. Splitting, agonizing, desperate pain in her head before darkness came. The bastard had obviously hit her in the back of the head; she now had a lump the size of Texas back there. What wimp hit people in the back of the head? Oh, she wasn't going down easy again.

So she dropped to the blanket that she'd spread on the floor to do more pushups. Not enough to weaken her muscles, but enough to keep her heart pumping and her body warm. The cargo hold smelled like puke and bodily discharges, although the interior had been cleaned out with water and bleach. It stank like bleach. She looked over to a corner that was stained yellow.

A pee corner.

Her bladder felt full. It was probably an animal instinct to create a corner for waste. She walked right up to the door, crouched, and peed. He could wade through it when he came back.

The guy was strong. He'd carried and then tossed her into the container, where she'd landed on her side with the wind knocked out of her. By the time she'd gotten the hood off, the door was closed. The hood was a scratchy pillowcase that she'd used to wrap her freezing feet. Who was he? How had he gotten into her house? Thank God the girls hadn't been there. It was the one small blessing right now.

She purposely didn't look at the four hooks in the floor. Despite the bleach, blood stains showed between those hooks. The lantern flickered weak light from the far corner. She could start a fire with the dirty blanket, but the timing on that would have to be perfect. If she started it now, the smoke would kill her. If she waited until he opened the door, it wouldn't light fast enough.

She sat and hung her head, thinking of her girls. Her three young girls who needed her. Tears pricked the back of her eyes and she batted them away. This guy had killed at least ten, if not twenty women. What had each of them done in here?

Probably tried to make fire. Okay. That was the only weapon she could see. What else? She'd looked the entire place over, up and down, trying to find a piece of steel or metal to use. Nothing. Even the rings set into the floor were smooth and well secured. She'd pulled on one until her skin shredded.

The only weapon in the container was her own body.

She was it.

In the metal prison, she'd lost track of time. From reading the autopsy reports, she knew that the victims were left alone to starve and become weak. Could she eat the blanket? Would that even count as sustenance? So many women had died at the hands of this monster — what made her different? How could she survive when they had not?

How had he subdued all of those women? Sure, they were weak from lack of food and water. But what else? When he opened the door, and he would eventually, her instinct was to rush him. To get out of the prison and into the light, even if it was freezing outside. Was that his expectation? If so, he'd be prepared. With what? A gun? A knife? If he was armed, what was her best chance?

She clutched the blanket to herself. Her only chance was the blanket. If she rushed him with it, she'd go for his head and try to dodge his weapon. Then she'd have to fight.

Her instinct would be to run, but she was barefoot and he was not. She'd have to fight until she overcame him.

She huddled against the wall, trying to stay warm. Yeah.

Fighting was her only chance.

For her girls.

Laurel ran into Kate's house behind several police officers.

Ena Ilemoto emerged from the kitchen. "He broke in through the window down-stairs. I have officers canvassing the neighborhood, but so far, nothing."

Three blond girls sat on the sofa, huddled together. Viv looked up. "Agent Snow."

She hurried toward them and all three tackled her. "Laurel. You know you can call me Laurel."

Vida looked at her, blue eyes full of tears. "Mom says you're the smartest person she's ever met. Is that true? Will you find her?"

Laurel hugged her, just as her phone buzzed. Relief nearly dropped her to her knees when she saw her mother's face on the screen. She stepped back from the girls and answered. "Are you all right?"

"Sure. I was just shopping for fixings for tonight's dinner," Deidre said. "Why? What's wrong?"

Laurel motioned for the girls to follow her. "I'm bringing three friends over. They need to stay with you for a few hours." Hopefully no longer.

"Sure," Deidre said.

"Thanks." Laurel hung up. "Officer Ilemoto? I'm taking the girls. Please call me after you've processed the scene with anything you find." There wasn't going to be a thing. This guy was too good. She stepped outside and ran into Monty. "Hi."

Aeneas barked and lumbered right into the girls, wagging his tail wildly.

They dropped to pet him. The youngest wrapped her arms around his neck and buried her face in his fur.

Monty's eyes were glazed. "Kate?" he whispered.

Laurel tried to keep her emotions in

check. Kate was blond and very pretty, and she worked for Laurel. This guy was going to make a statement with her, and it was going to be ugly. "I need somebody on the girls and my mom until we catch him."

Monty reached for his phone. "Give me the address, and I'll send somebody right now."

She gave him the address and then turned to the girls. "Monty and Aeneas are going to take you to my mom's." She gave Monty a look when he started to object, and he subsided instantly. "Maybe you could leave the dog with them?" It didn't look like Vida was going to let go.

Monty's gaze softened. "I'll take them there and leave an officer as well as the dog."

Laurel paused as an idea hit her. "No. I'll take the dog." She looked at the girls. "Kids? The dog is good at finding people, and I need him to come help me find your mom. Okay?"

The girls released the dog and stepped back. "Okay," Val said, tears on her face.

"Take care of them," she told Monty, whistling for Aeneas, who followed her out to her truck. "Get Huck released, would you? I need his help," she called back, letting the dog inside.

The girls watched the dog go and then

piled into Monty's truck.

"You're good with kids," Laurel said to Aeneas as the dog panted from the passenger seat. She quickly dialed the sheriff and was put through to him after making several threats she probably couldn't back up.

"Now isn't a good time, Agent Snow," the sheriff snapped.

Laurel bit her tongue. "Kate Vuittron was taken last night. Let Captain Rivers free so he can get to work. I need him on this."

"The guy fits your profile to a *T*," the sheriff said. "Now let me do my job."

Laurel slowed down before she wrecked the truck. "I'm a half hour from the station, and I'm picking up the captain. We want him on this, not least because he can use his dog for search and rescue."

"You're not understanding me. We found the dog's fur in the victim's trachea. It's Rivers's dog," York said.

Laurel grunted to keep from yelling at him. "Anybody could've gotten a bit of Aeneas's fur. Give me a break. It's in Huck's vehicle, his home, his office . . ."

"That's just it, Agent," York said. "It wasn't just a piece of fur. It was fully intact hair with the follicle. That only happens when somebody is around the dog a lot, or

457

is very close to the dog. Not just some passerby. Let me do my job and go do yours."

The pieces of the puzzle slammed together. "That's it," she whispered, looking at the dog. "That's it, York," she yelled, turning into the parking area of a gas station and turning around. "Where is Huck right now? Don't mess with me."

"He's right here glaring at me while we wait for his representative," York snarled.

"Good. Put him on speaker. Right now. I want both of you. I know who did this." It was crazy. How had she missed it?

York groaned. "Fine, but be quick. When his rep gets here, I'm hanging up."

Excitement and fear roared through Laurel. "Huck?"

"Yeah, I'm here," Huck said, sounding pissed.

Aeneas barked.

"You've got my dog?" Huck asked.

"Yes. He's a good dog and he likes everyone. Except who?" Laurel pressed on the gas pedal and drove past the entrance to the subdivision. "Who hasn't he liked lately?"

Huck was quiet.

"What does this have to do with anything?" Sheriff York grunted.

458

"Huck? Tell me. Who didn't Aeneas like?" Laurel pushed.

The shifting of a chair echoed over the line. "Dr. Caine. He didn't like her," Huck said.

Through the phone line something slammed on a hard surface like a hand on a table. "You're telling me that Dr. Caine is the killer? She doesn't come close to fitting your profile," York yelled.

"No," Laurel said, speeding up. "Don't you see? It's so clear now. Huck? When Abigail was in your office, if she pulled out a couple of tufts, would Aeneas have bitten her?"

"Probably not," Huck said. "Not in the office where he was technically at work. But he sure wouldn't have been nice to her."

Laurel nodded. "Yes. That's exactly right. I can't believe I missed it before. The blondes and the personal interest in me — it all makes sense. Can you get out of there?"

"I'm on the way," Huck said.

"Hurry, Huck," Laurel said. "Hurry. We have to find Kate. Please hurry." A flash of white caught her eye and then heavy metal slammed into the side of her truck. She screamed, grabbing the wheel, trying to hold on.

Aeneas barked wildly.

Huck yelled her name.

She slid off the road and the truck tipped over, rolling several times before smashing against a tree. Her ears rang as she hung there, upside down, held in place by her seatbelt. Aeneas whined, blood on his nose. Where was she? She couldn't hear anything. What had happened? Pain slid through the numbness in her face.

Her door opened and a man crouched down. He had dark hair, blue eyes, and a beard. It took her a second to recognize him with the blood dripping into her eyes. "Robert Caine," she whispered.

He smiled. "Well, hello there, sister. I've been trying to get your attention for days now. It looks like we're gonna do this my way now."

CHAPTER FORTY

Laurel tried to focus as Robert turned the stolen truck, the one carrying bullet holes from her gun, between two trees off the river road. He'd bound her hands and secured her with the seatbelt, and she kept fading in and out of consciousness. She shook her head and winced at the pain. "You left the dog in the cold."

He chuckled. "You're worried about a dog right now? Aren't you supposed to be some sort of genius?" He pulled onto the shoulder, stopped the truck, cut the engine, and turned to face her, a glittering light in his blue eyes. "I'd take you to my house so we could spend some time together, but I can't be sure who was on that phone call. Plus, my wife is there, although she sleeps like the dead." Regret twisted his lips. "We're not going to have the time I'd hoped for together. I'm sorry about that."

She looked around the quiet area. Snow-covered trees lined the small road that ran by the river. "We're still on your property?"

"No. We're actually on federal land so there's no tie to me." He rubbed his beard. There was a black pistol tucked at his waist, but he didn't seem inclined to grab for it yet. "Sure, it's just a couple of miles from my place, but most people don't even know this road is here. It's more of a trail, really. You can't even see it from my home, which is handy, just in case the authorities show up. I'm at church right now, you know."

She tested the ropes at her wrists as her brain finally caught up. The pain ebbed. The world cleared and she took a deep breath, exhaling her pain. "It's funny. You never gave yourself away. In fact, you were barely on my radar."

"I know." He licked his thumb and reached out to smooth blood away from her cheek. "I never should have listened to my sister. I'm a good guy. I go to church, help the community, and assist my brilliant sister with her marijuana company. My wife is a sweetheart with a heart of gold, and nobody would ever think I have the hobby I do." His grin showed sharp canines. "The women who died, my little birds, were dirty and bad. Every single one of them."

"Like your mother?" Laurel asked, taking

a guess as she twisted to face him. If she could get her feet up between them, she could at least gain some leverage.

His eyes flared. "My mother was a fallen woman. She cheated on my father, who was God's prophet. A truly blessed soul. She deserved to die."

Laurel pulled her right arm back, working the ropes. "Did you kill her?"

Robert shrugged. "God smote her. That's all that matters."

Quiet descended all around them, broken only by the rush of icy water against frozen rocks in the river. "You spoke about your father in past tense. Did you kill him, too?"

Robert's head jerked back. "Of course not. I loved him. Only him. She killed him, and you know it."

"Abigail?" Laurel angled her right elbow beneath the door handle. "You're saying that your sister killed her own father."

"I'm not saying anything," Robert replied wearily. "She did kill him, and you'll never catch her. Or rather, you never would've caught her, if you'd had the chance. You have to go, Laurel. You're in the way." He tapped a finger on her nose. "It's unfortunate that you're not blond."

"Like your mother and the other dirty women?" Laurel asked, her mind focusing.

Could she get inside his brain? "How did you feel when Abigail chose to wear a blond wig? Did she do that to hurt you?"

Robert nodded emphatically. "Of course, she did. She did that to torture me. Sometimes she'd change to a black or brown wig, but then she'd always return to the blond. So cruel." Spittle dropped from his bottom lip and stuck in his beard. "You're lucky you don't have to deal with her any longer. For that, you should thank me."

"You want me to thank you for killing me?" Laurel asked.

He lifted a shoulder. "Sure." He glanced at his watch. "I need to get back to church soon. My time of silent contemplation in the downstairs Zen garden can't last too long."

She gulped, her stomach rolling over. "Where is Kate, Robert? Tell me."

"She's near. I'll bury you together, if you want," he offered as if doing her a great favor.

Laurel closed her eyes. Pain slashed through her chest. Kate was dead? "How many women have there been?" She opened her eyes and tightened her injured shoulder.

"I don't know. Probably around thirty," he said carelessly. "Counting was never my thing." He drew a knife out of the pocket of his door. "I much prefer a blade to a bullet, don't you?"

"Did Casey Morgan prefer a blade?" Laurel asked, her stomach cramping.

He smiled, his eyes glowing. "If you want to know if she was one of mine, just ask."

"Was she?" There had to be a way to get to safety.

"Oh, yeah," he said softly, fondly. "She was a fighter, and man, I wish I could've made her death last longer. Although, she was also a mistake. My first kill."

"So you moved on to prostitutes to perfect your sick game?" Laurel asked, her throat hurting.

He threw back his head and laughed, refocusing quickly. "Yes. That's exactly what I did, and you never would've found those broken birds, those bodies, if the weather hadn't helped you."

Laurel moved fast, kicking her feet toward his face and nailing him in the nose. She jerked her shoulder down and her elbow up, opening the door and falling outside into the snow. She landed hard, performed a somersault, and bounded up on her feet. The world spun around her and she settled her stance, sucking in freezing cold air to center herself.

"You bitch." Robert slammed his door

and stomped through the snow around the front of the truck, blood pouring from his nose.

She glared. "That's going to be hard to explain. Do you often get your nose broken during your silent contemplation at church?" She kept his attention on her face while she slid one leg back, more than ready to use her feet again. Her hands were still tied and she struggled furiously with the ropes. Her injured shoulder and her various bruises all clashed pain through her.

He lifted the knife and snarled. Blood dripped into his teeth, coating them red. He lunged for her, and she kicked him again, hitting him beneath the chin. He roared in anger and lunged, tackling her into the snow. Her butt hit first and then her head. He manacled her around the waist and lifted her to her feet, the knife at her throat.

Panic seized her, and she screamed.

"Hold it right there, Brother." Abigail Caine walked around a tree behind the truck, a Glock 43 with a pink slide in her uninjured hand. Her sprained wrist was still bandaged.

"Abby." Robert turned them both toward her. "What are you doing here?"

Abigail wore tufted snow boots over dark jeans and a long wool coat zipped up tightly.

"I saw you run my sister off the road and I followed you, parking in the hollow on the other side of these trees." The snow was up to her thighs but she continued to push through it, her gun hand steady. "You don't think I'm going to let you hurt my sister, do you? How could you? After everything I've done for you?" She kept moving.

"For me?" Robert spat, throwing his free hand in the air. "Are you kidding me? You killed *my* father. Our father."

Abigail's green and blue eyes darkened. "He wasn't your father, you idiot. He was mine. And hers. Zeke Caine was an evil bastard." Her face cleared. "But I did not kill him. Unlike you, I'm not a killer."

Robert's laugh was grating. Pained. His breath was heated at Laurel's ear. "How can you say that? Do you believe it?" He cocked his head to the side, his beard brushing the top of Laurel's head. "Are you so completely fucked up that you believe your own lies? Or do you just need your new little sister here to believe you?"

Abigail shook her head, her auburn hair flying. "You're sick, Robert. Let us get you help."

"Oh, you've already helped me," Robert said grimly.

Laurel worked one hand out of the rope.

If he would just move the knife a little to the right, she could get her arm between his wrist and her face.

Abigail didn't seem to notice her movement. "I didn't blame Father for trying to help you hide your crimes. You didn't mean to kill those animals, did you?"

"Abby," Robert breathed, the sound full of pain. "That's a *secret.*"

"I know. I obeyed Father and kept your secrets, even when you got caught peeking into women's homes and stealing their panties. You're sick." Her teeth flashed. "The father you want to know, Laurel, he hid these crimes and used his influence as a pastor to protect Robert." Her eyes gleamed. "Even from an accusation of attempted rape when he was fifteen. Dad bought the girl's family off that time."

Robert's body shook behind Laurel. "None of that is true. It wasn't my fault. Father understood."

Abigail's nostrils flared. "But you screwed up here, Brother. You tried to kill Laurel, Robert. You shot at her twice. Why would you do that? Hurt what is *mine*?" Her face contorted, already red from the cold.

Robert gripped Laurel's hip and pressed the blade hard enough against her neck to draw blood. His gun dug into the middle of her back, still stuck in his waistband, but she couldn't get a good angle to grab it. "You hurt what was mine when you killed my father. I knew what would happen. The second I saw her, saw what she looked like, knew who she was, I knew you'd throw me over for her, Abby. Your blood sister. *I knew.* You'd tell on me or make me stop my hobby, and I couldn't do that. I need my birds. I knew what you'd do, and I had to stop you. If she wasn't here, things could go back to the way they were. You and me together. Doing what we do."

Laurel kept her breathing steady. "Why did you take the cemetery truck, Robert?"

He chuckled. "I'm friends with the sheriff, and I knew your uncle was on everyone's radar. It seemed like a smart thing to do, and besides, it's a good truck. It took you off the road twice."

Abigail lowered her chin and pointed the gun over Laurel's shoulder. "Let her go, Robert."

"Why?" He laughed and the sound echoed through the trees silently, bearing witness to the painful drama. "You think she could love somebody like you? That she'll be your real sister? Oh, Abby. If she only had an idea of what you've done. She knows about the dog's fur. She knows that you took it and

469

gave it to me to frame her lover. The guy who rejected you, right? Oh, you couldn't have a mere man between you. Laurel has no idea what you'll do to family."

Abigail's mouth twitched. "Why, Robert. I think you're batshit crazy. You're a serial killer, Brother. You lie to everyone and pretend to be normal."

"You should know," Robert said, his fingers digging into Laurel's hip. "You lie more than I do but you don't know you're lying. At least I know exactly what I am."

Laurel stiffened, just waiting for a chance. An opening. If Abigail could keep him talking, keep getting him angry, she might get that chance. "What is Abigail, Robert?" Laurel whispered. "Tell me. I want to know."

Robert tightened his hold. "She's a monster. You think I don't have feelings? She doesn't feel *anything* except pleasure in using people like puppets to get what she wants in life. You're her special new project, and that's why you have to die. It's better than what she'll do to you. She'll take everything you want, everything you love, until there's only her."

Abigail shook her head, her mouth turned down. "I had no idea you were this far gone. How could you kill all those women? I still can't believe it."

"Ha," Robert said. "You lying —" He moved just enough.

Laurel shot her arm up and twisted, digging her hip into his thigh. She grabbed his arm, yanking him to the ground. The knife flashed across her lower neck, and she ducked back, even as it cut across her clavicle. She punched him in his broken nose and rolled away, catching her sweater on a rock.

He howled in pain and lunged for her, stabbing wildly with the knife.

She scrambled back across the snow, kicking, trying to avoid the blade.

Abigail fired three times, smoothly hitting Robert in the upper chest. His eyes widened and blood dribbled out of his mouth. Then he dropped to his knees, paused, and pitched forward, his face planting in the snow and his legs kicking out. Blood poured from beneath him to stain the white a bleak red.

Abigail paled and tilted her head, watching the blood. "Are you okay, Laurel?"

Laurel slowly stood, her gaze on the pink and black gun. "Yes."

Abigail looked at her with eyes the exact same as the ones Laurel saw in the mirror every morning. "I killed him for you. My brother for my little sister. For you, Laurel."

Laurel's chest compressed. "Did you take the dog's fur to help him implicate Huck?"

"Of course not," Abigail said, her accent slight.

Laurel steadied herself. "Put down the gun, Abigail."

Sirens sounded and emergency vehicles careened down the road.

Abigail slipped her gun into her jacket pocket. "I called the authorities on my way here, just in case I didn't win this. Anything for you, Laurel." She smiled sadly. "He lied about everything, you know. I had no idea he was a killer, and whatever that was about dog fur makes no sense. Do you think dogs spoke to him? That he took orders from animals or something like that?"

Laurel couldn't think of a thing to say. There was no evidence against Abigail, and there wouldn't be. The woman was too smart. Plus, Aeneas had been in Robert's house, so the man would've had access to the fur. Maybe Abigail was innocent? Laurel's gut said otherwise, but that could be emotion talking.

The vehicles lurched to a stop, and Huck bounded out of the nearest one with Aeneas right behind him. Huck reached them, his gaze scouting the entire area for threats.

"Are you okay?"

"Yes," Laurel said, relief flooding through her. A glimmer through the trees caught her eye. A piece of metal. "What's that?"

Huck turned. He ducked his head. "I don't know. There's a trail, though." He pivoted and walked between two tall pines, his long strides quickening as he grew closer to the rock face. "It's a cargo container. Get a bolt cutter," he bellowed.

An officer quickly ran up to them with a bolt cutter, and Huck took it.

Laurel ran through the snow, leaving a trail of blood from her neck. Her legs shook as she reached the white container. "Robert indicated she was dead," she warned Huck.

His jaw tightened and he lifted the cutters to slice through the bolt. "Stand back." He grabbed the door and pulled it open.

A gray blur burst out, covering his head as a naked Kate Vuittron kicked and punched him wildly.

"Whoa," Huck yelled, wrapping both hands around her to stop the attack.

"Kate!" Laurel rushed to her. "You're alive. You're okay." She immediately yanked off her coat.

Kate looked at her, eyes wild, hair flying. "Laurel?"

"Yes." Laurel wrapped the coat around

Kate. "Here you go. You're safe." She hugged her. "You're safe."

Kate hugged her back. "Oh, God."

Huck yanked the blanket off his head. "You good?"

Kate smiled through tears. "Yeah. Sorry about that."

"Great tackle," Laurel said, wrapping an arm around her shoulders. "Let's get you to the hospital."

"I'm just hungry," Kate said wearily. "He didn't have time to hurt me, but I'd love a burger. Or ice cream."

They walked back through the trees, and Laurel looked up to find Abigail watching them, her unreadable gaze on Laurel's arm over Kate's shoulders. Laurel shivered.

Huck jogged up to their side. "An ambulance is just down the way."

Movement scraped across icy rock. Laurel stumbled and lifted her head to see Robert Caine turn on the ground, gun in his hand, and fire at her.

Huck pivoted and threw himself in front of her, knocking both Laurel and Kate to the snowy ground. Blood burst from his body.

Robert groaned, blood dripped from his mouth, and his head dropped to the red snow in death.

Abigail slowly smiled.

"Huck!" Laurel yelled.

CHAPTER FORTY-ONE

Laurel sat in the waiting area of the emergency room with Monty on one side of her and Walter on the other. Aeneas rested at her feet. The receptionist gave them the stink eye a couple of times, but she didn't tell them to take the dog outside, so they pretended they didn't see her.

Snowflakes and snowmen decorated the walls while somebody had expertly painted the windows with peaceful snow scenes. Christmas music played quietly through invisible speakers.

"Are you sure you shouldn't be in a bed?" Walter asked Laurel.

She nodded. "Yes. The doctor already checked me out, and my head is okay. Slight concussion and several contusions down my ribs and sternum from the impact of my vehicle with the tree. Plus seventeen stitches from a knife wound, but I'm happy to be alive. I just require some rest. But thank

476

you for asking." Her entire body hurt and she needed time off to heal, but right now, she was grateful to be coherent.

She patted his shoulder and looked again at the closed door to the right that led to the operating rooms. Was Huck okay? She hadn't been able to see how badly he'd been hurt. "He saved my life," she murmured.

"That's what he does," Monty said, lines by the sides of his eyes. "Huck's always the first to jump into any danger. I'm just getting used to having him around — he'd better be okay."

Laurel forced a smile. Apparently whatever distance had once existed between the officers had now narrowed.

The sliding door to the exit opened and snow billowed inside. Three girls ran in with Deidre on their heels.

Laurel stood and hugged her mom. She turned to the girls. "Your mom is fine. I'll take you to her."

All three of them leaped for her, careful of her many bandages and bruises. She gingerly held them tight. "Mom? I'll be right back. Sit with Monty, would you?"

Monty stood and then waited for Deidre to claim Laurel's seat before sitting back down. Two of the girls grabbed Laurel's hands, and she looked down, startled. They were so open and friendly.

Catching herself, she drew them to the doorway and flashed her badge at the receptionist. "We need to see Kate Vuittron. The doctor said she'd be in a room soon. Which room?"

The receptionist typed onto a keyboard and read the screen. "She's in room one-twelve but can only have two visitors at a time."

Laurel tucked her badge away. "Sorry. This is official FBI business. We all work for the agency." Without waiting for a reply, she pushed open the door to the left and ushered the girls through. They went down a long hallway and past various rooms until reaching the correct one. The girls released her and ran inside before she could stop them.

Kate laughed and hugged all three of them as they barreled onto the bed with her. She was sitting up with an IV in her arm, watching television. "I'm fine, gang. Seriously. You didn't think one little serial killer could get me, did you?" She winked at Laurel.

Viv sat up and sniffed. "We were so scared."

Val nodded and hugged her mom. "I'm never sleeping in the dark again."

Vida rolled her eyes. "Oh, man. Are we

going to therapy again? Come on. I thought we figured everything out when Dad left us."

Kate kissed the top of Vida's head. "Therapy never hurt anybody, and I have a feeling we might end up there again for a bit. It's okay. I like talking with the three of you." She smiled at Laurel over the girls' heads. "Thank you for taking care of them and for finding me. You're a good friend."

Laurel rocked back. Friend? They were friends? She smiled, her heart warming. "You're welcome. Anytime. They're strong girls, and you're amazing." She chuckled. "You three should've seen her jump out and attack poor Huck Rivers. The guy is huge, and even he didn't know what to do." Then she sobered.

Kate caught her expression. "Any news on Huck?"

"No." Laurel looked over her shoulder at the empty hallway. "What did the doctor say about you?"

"I have to stay the night here, but I can go home tomorrow. I'm fine, really. Just dehydrated with a small bump on my head." Kate looked at her girls, her brow furrowing.

"Well then, I guess it's slumber party time at our place," Laurel said. "I'm sure my mom would love to try out a couple of new cookie recipes on the girls, if they're game."

Kate smiled, her eyes glowing. "Like I said, you're a good friend. Go find out how Huck is doing. We'll be here waiting for you."

Laurel nodded and turned, hurrying back down the hallway. As she emerged into the waiting area, she nearly ran Abigail over. "Oh. Hi."

Abigail grasped her arm to keep her from falling back. "Hi. I wanted to check on you. Are you all right?"

"Yes. Just waiting to hear about Huck." Laurel stared at the woman who looked so much like her. "I don't know what to say about Robert. No matter what else he was or did, he grew up as your brother, and I'm sorry for your loss. I'm sorry you had to shoot him to save me."

"Thank you for saying that." Abigail pulled her in for a quick hug and then stepped back. "I need to go stay with Jasmine and help her with the arrangements after the police are finished tearing apart her house. It's the least I can do." Her dual-colored eyes focused intently on Laurel. "I'll be in touch, Sister." She turned on her heel and strode out the side door.

Laurel watched her go, took a deep breath,

and then continued across the waiting area, where the doctor was emerging from the other side of the hospital, still in scrubs.

Monty jumped to his feet. "Huck?"

The young doctor nodded. "Captain Rivers is going to be fine. He was shot in the upper shoulder, and I had to remove the bullet. He's in recovery now, and you should be able to see him in about an hour."

Laurel's legs gave out, and she sank into the nearest chair.

Huck was all right.

Laurel's knees finally regained strength after sitting for a while, and then she helped her mother load the three girls and the dog into her SUV to head back home. Viv was driving. Her phone buzzed just as she shook the snow off inside again. "Agent Snow."

"Hey there, Laurel. Nice job with this one," George said. "You caught the guy."

"I had a lot of help," Laurel admitted, sitting again. Monty had disappeared, so hopefully he'd gotten back to see Huck.

George cleared his throat. "Speaking of which, we have some juice, and I'd like to create the FBI Pacific Northwest Violent Crimes Unit right now. It could be located in Genesis Valley but would still be subordinate to the chief of the Seattle office. What do you think? We have a lot of cases in the area, and aren't you ready for a home base? Isn't it time?"

She swallowed. Huck was hurt because of her. Her uncle needed help being around people, and her mother was lonely. In addition, she now had a sister who was probably a sociopath and should be watched, as well as a missing biological father who should pay for his crimes. "Yes, it's time. I'm needed here." She wanted to be home for a lot of reasons. "I'd like to stay."

"Good. You're hired. We'll talk logistics next week. Great job, again." George clicked off.

The door opened and Monty strode through. His smile was wide. "Huck is in room twenty, and you'd better get back there so he knows taking that bullet was worth it and you're fine."

She chuckled. "I'm fine and would be here for any colleague." Even so, she had to school herself not to run through the doorway and down the hallway. Finally, she sedately made it to room twenty, where Huck sat up in his bed, a cup of green Jell-O in his hand.

His broad torso was bare, with a bandage over his left shoulder. "Hi."

She sat in the chair next to the bed.

"Don't you ever do that again."

He licked green Jell-O off his spoon. "Save your life? I can't promise that. However, now that I have, don't you have to be my personal servant for a month or something?"

"No." She took his empty Jell-O cup and set it on the table. "Huck? Seriously. Jumping in front of bullets is a bad habit, although I appreciate it. It's just . . . I don't want you hurt, either."

He sat back, his gaze inscrutable. The moment stretched on as he studied her, tension spiraling all around them and heating the atmosphere. Finally, he sighed. "Is it just the pain meds they're pumping inside me, or is this the beginning of a beautiful friendship?"

"It's the pain meds." She patted his good shoulder, wondering the same thing but not willing to define anything right now. "I'll check on you tomorrow."

She walked out of the room and smiled. A beautiful friendship? Something told her that wasn't going to be their story, if they had a story. The jury was out on that one right now. Her heart lighter than it had been in a while and her brain finally calming, she strode out to the waiting room, where Walter Smudgeon waited, flirting with the receptionist. Or trying to, anyway.

He straightened when she approached. "Hey, boss. Just checked on Kate and wanted to do the same with you. You good?" She paused, noting he had spilled coffee on his shirt. She was home with her mom, there was time to help Uncle Carl, and she was developing a good team in her hometown. One that had gotten the job done and found the bad guy. It was a good path for both her career and her personal life. She smiled, finally *feeling* that she was home. "Yes. I'm good."

ABOUT THE AUTHOR

Rebecca Zanetti is the *New York Times* and *USA Today* bestselling author of over fifty romantic suspense, dark paranormal, and contemporary romances, many of which have also appeared on the Amazon, Barnes and Noble, and iBooks bestseller lists. She is a two-time *RT* Reviewers Choice Award-winner, the recipient of the RWA Daphne du Maurier Award, a five-time Daphne du Maurier Award-finalist, a PRISM Award-winner, and a two-time PRISM Award-finalist. Nearly a dozen of her novels have been selected as Amazon Best Romances of the Month, including *Lethal Lies, Mercury Striking* and *Fallen,* which were also Amazon Best Books of the Year. Zanetti has worked as an art curator, Senate aide, lawyer, college professor, and a hearing examiner — only to culminate it all in stories about alpha males and the women who claim them. Please visit her online at Rebecca Zanetti.com.

486